Graham's Wicked Kiss

Bad Boys Book Seven

Christine Young

Chapter One

November 1826
North of Edinburgh

Graham Chamberlin pulled Draco to a halt just as the large drive to the Chamberlin estate began. He'd spent too many weeks in Edinburgh. With luck on his side, he made it to his ancestral estate, gifted to him by his grandmother, just before the first snows of winter would start. What he discovered in the city was that the life of leisure and balls he was invited to didn't suit. Neither did any of the debutants he met there.

Leaning on the saddle horn, he looked over his soon to be home, Runningmeade Manner. Over the years there had been little change on the outside. Now, he wondered about the interior. His brother, Donal Chamberlin, had been sending coin to keep the home well appointed. Yet he'd also heard rumors the home had fallen into disrepair at the hands of the current manager.

His brother's holdings stretched to the states. He had little time for this home or the surrounding lands. When Graham volunteered to check out the manor as well as the grounds and perhaps live here, Donal agreed whole-heartedly. This suited Graham just fine.

As he studied the lane and the row of trees leading to the front steps, he noticed three different heads poking out from three trees along with spindly arms and legs waving at him. He laughed outright remembering days long past. Times when he and Donal played in the same trees, usually not in the dead of winter though.

After watching for a few minutes, he nudged Draco forward

keeping his attention on the lads while wondering just how old the boys were as well as to whom they belonged. Clearly, they appeared to be at home in his trees. He pulled up beneath the first tree.

"Come down, lads. All of you present yourselves. Front and center," he called out in his sternest voice, hoping they would obey but not having any illusions.

They seemed to take his order to heart, all three dropping to the ground in almost perfect unison. Urchins to be sure landed sure-footed on the grass beside the lane. They all needed to be scrubbed from head to toe, possibly twice, but they would clean up well. He needed to laugh although he didn't want the laughter to come at their expense. So, he held the laughter he felt behind his teeth.

The threesome lined up in front of him, straight faced and stiff as boards.

The tallest and he assumed the oldest of the trio spoke. "We were told to watch out for you and welcome you home. Heard you were coming just last month." He inhaled a deep breath obviously meaning to say more but was interrupted.

"No one told us we'd have to be here on the lane for two weeks. Did you know it's cold out here?"

"I was never informed I had a deadline." Graham's laughter was unchecked this time.

"Well, someone should have done just that or you could have sent a message," the tallest said indignantly. "Not like it's summer, ya know."

He'd just been properly chastised by the boy and meant to proceed with further introductions lest they think it okay to reprimand an elder. "Do the lot of you have names? I'm Graham Chamberlin." He waited for acknowledgement and perhaps some information if they were agreeable.

"I'm Dodge," the tallest said as he cleared his throat. "Been called that for a long time now."

Graham reckoned he must be nearing eleven or twelve years. He directed his attention to the next in line.

"I'm Ollie." The lad nodded, his hair falling in front of his face before he looked up and pushed it away with his hands. It was hard to tell

Ollie's age while he was pretty sure the boy was younger than Dodge, perhaps eight or nine. He had no way of proving the fact.

"And you?" This lad was small and seemed to need at least three good meals in his belly. The others must have helped him into the tree because he wasn't tall enough to reach the lowest limbs.

"Midget," the lad grinned, "Please to meet you, sir. We're supposed to make sure you have everything you need and show you to the house."

"Who sent you?"

From what Graham heard about the estate, he didn't think anyone here would care if he was greeted or not.

The boys looked at each other sharing glances several times before they seemed to come to a silent agreement.

"Ria sent us."

Graham found himself nodding his head and rolling all the names around in the cobwebs that made up his brains right now and could not come up with one person on his list of employees who was named Ria.

He dismounted, intending to walk with the boys to the stables and while there discover a little bit more about their truths along with how much more they would be willing to tell him. "Who is Ria?"

As he walked past them, he wondered if they intended to stay on the lane. Looking over his shoulder, Ollie was drawing circles in the dirt with one foot and Dodge was tugging on Midget's hand.

Once again, seeming to reach some form of silent agreement all three started walking.

"Ria's no concern of yours," Dodge said, his voice gruff and taking on a prickly edge. "We protect her so you don't have to worry about her or go near her."

Protect her? Bloody hell who or why would she need protection from. For a moment he thought to ask them for more information. By the slant of their lips, he didn't think any more material about this mysterious Ria would be forthcoming. Instead, he decided to let them lead the way to the stables and give them time to become accustomed to him. Clearly, they had trust issues.

A few minutes later, Graham stopped in front of the stable doors.

"Do you know how to take care of a horse? Draco needs a brushing down then food and water. Any of you want to do that?"

"Don't know nothing about horses," Dodge said, looking at him as if he had mush for brains. "Don't know how to ride neither."

"I'm afraid of the huge beasts," Ollie said, once again his gaze directed to the ground below and what he was doing with his foot.

"I'm not afraid," Midget volunteered. "Don't think I'm big enough to brush him."

"Perhaps at least one of you should learn. What do the three of you do around the house besides wallow in the dirt?"

The words were uttered harsher than he'd intended. Nonetheless he meant what he said. Everyone would have to do something in his household if they expected to be fed and clothed.

Once again Dodge, the apparent spokesperson for the trio, said, "I'd like to learn how to take care of your horse. It's the only one in the stable now but don't have the time. The others are in the pasture along with the highland cattle. Have to protect Ria and right now she could be in trouble. We've been away too long watching for you."

His words were said defensively and to make a point of telling him he was at fault if anything happened to the mystery lady.

The boys looked at each other for a few seconds. Once again it seemed the silent conversation between them was understood. They took off at a fast clip. Graham watched them speed around the back of the house where the servant's staircase would be found emptying into the scullery.

If there were no horses in the stable, would it figure there was no stable boy? Graham led his horse around the house, resigned to the care of Draco. Entering the outbuilding, he searched for anyone who could help him.

"What can I do?" A man strode from a room at the far end of the building.

"Draco needs to be brushed down then fed and given water. Is that your job?" Graham asked, handing the reins over to the man, impatient now to discover what was going on in the main house and establish himself as the owner.

Apparently, there were things that needed tending.

"I'll take care of anything you ask, sir. Nice to have you back in residence, sir. You staying this time?" the man asked.

Graham stared hard, his eyes narrowing. "Shamus, is that you?"

He held out his hand in greeting. As lads Shamus played with him as well as his brother.

"It is and you're a sight for sore eyes, I tell you. It's about time someone arrived here to right the wrongs going on in this place."

Graham clapped his old friend on the back, thinking he might have to take a few minutes more to find out a bit more information. "Got some questions if you're up to answering them."

Shamus looked over his shoulder as he rid Draco of his saddle and blanket. He took a few seconds to start brushing the stallion. "What do you want to know?"

Graham positioned himself against the stall, crossing his arms in front of him. "Let's start with the lads. Who are they and why are they here?"

Shamus grinned as he stroked the horse several times. "The lads, so you met them. Not surprised that Ria sent them to greet you. What did they tell you?"

"Not much, just that there job is to protect this woman, Ria." He waited then, studying the man.

Shamus hauled out a bucket of water and once Draco had his fill gave him his food.

"Dodge do the talking?" Shamus laughed.

Graham nodded, his brows drawing together as he waited impatiently for Shamus to be a bit more forthcoming.

"He's the oldest. If you were looking closely without assuming anything, Ollie is a little girl and Midget of course is the youngest. They came with Ria one day. They've stayed although Ria keeps herself scarce with good reason. Not really sure why they stayed but the house is shelter for them."

"Where did they come from?"

"If Dodge can be trusted to speak the truth, the worst streets in Edinburgh. Had to do things, if you get my drift, just to eat. I'm surprised they let on that Ria is a woman."

"I'm beginning to understand a few things. Why does Ria have reason to keep herself scarce?"

He didn't like the direction of his thoughts, although there were a myriad of reasons why the lady might not want to be found.

"Around these parts the main reason is well known. I'd be hopin' that your first order of business would be to get rid of Leod, your manager of the estate. Don't recall his last name, whether or not I was ever told I can't be remembering. Think the lady is hiding from something that happened to her in the city but that's just my gut telling me things. There's no evidence I could be right or wrong."

"And why would I want to get rid of this man?"

He didn't like the fact the questioning and answers began with Ria and ended with Leod. Again, his mind travelled in a direction Graham didn't appreciate nor would he allow.

"He's turned Runningmead Manor into a whorehouse. Pretty simple. Don't think it's what you would want for your home. Now, is there anything else I can do for you?"

"Answer more questions when I have them."

"Whatever you like."

"Millie still here?" he asked as he pushed away from his position, meaning to see for himself at the main house.

"Only because she keeps praying either you or your brother will show up and set this mess to rights. Suppose her prayers have been answered."

"Suppose they have."

Determined, Graham strode to the manor, walking up the broad front porch steps. When he stepped inside, a man stumbled drunkenly down the stairway from above. His pants were unfastened and his shirt hung loosely from his shoulders.

This must be the man Shamus was alluding to a few minutes before. He spread his legs, his hand at his side. "Who are you?"

"Leod is the name. I took up residency here when it seemed no one was going to claim the land and the crumbling home. Didn't ken why it should go to waste. So many in these parts are homeless."

"Graham Chamberlin, owner of this crumbling home is now in residence."

"You own this?" he asked as he quickly tried to put his clothing to rights.

"I do and, well, you'll have to move out. You're no longer welcome here in any capacity."

"How do I know you're tellin' the truth and you are who you say you are?" He stumbled a bit then hanging on to the back of the chair the man glared at him, his eyes narrowing in seeming concentration.

"You don't, except for my word as a Chamberlin." Graham couldn't imagine anyone living here unless they were desperate. Everything was in disrepair and needed hard work as well as a sizeable amount of groats to make it livable. "You haven't seen fit to make improvements? Have you been taking the money that has been sent your way?"

The man shrugged, his body seeming to relax. "No funds. If you'd sent money, I would have done something."

"My brother has been sending funds for the last five years. Most likely you drank the coin away or spent it on yourself," Graham mumbled as he studied the shabby entryway to his home.

A woman ran down the steps naked but holding a dress in front of her. Graham watched her leave the house. His breath nearly stopped as did his heart as he processed the scene. "You use my home as a whorehouse. I heard that from my employee in the stable." Anger began to simmer inside as he perused the rapid flight as well as the woman's backside.

"She wanted it. I was just obliging her wishes. She came to me beggin' for me to take her." The man grinned as he too watched the woman.

"That's why she was naked and racing away. Because she was asking for it? Get out!" With a shaking hand, he pointed to the door. "Don't ever want to see you again."

"My things..." the man started up the steps.

"I'll have whatever is in your room put on the front lawn. You can have them picked up when you please. Don't ever want to see you

7

again."

Arms crossed in front of him both impatient and angry, he waited for the man to leave. As far as he was concerned Leod's departure couldn't be soon enough. The puzzle that was Ria was still before him. He meant to get to the bottom of that riddle as soon as he possibly could.

When Leod finally exited the house, Graham let out a long sigh of relief rumbling from his lungs. Striding through his new home, he examined every part of it, every nook and cranny. He was just about finished on the third and last stage when he noticed a movement, a tiny shadow push back against the wall coupled with the softest whimper.

He reached the spot in two quick strides then crouching down he peered behind a lose wallboard. What he saw surprised him. Two huge blue eyes peered at him from behind a set of knees drawn to her chest. Her hair was matted and tangled against her scalp, shortly cropped and greased with black boot grease.

"Who are you?"

He hunkered down beside her, wishing he could draw her out from her hiding place. There wasn't one doubt in his mind she was ensconced in this tiny corner because of the man he just sent packing.

She pushed back farther, her breaths almost nil as she was attempting to hold the air inside her lungs. From beneath her ragged skirts two sets of dirty, bare toes caught his attention. She pushed her grimy and disheveled hair from her face, but the terror he saw in her eyes was real. While he watched and studied her, the apprehension seemed to linger.

"Cat got your tongue? He almost laughed but held the chortle back not believing for a second she was seeing anything humorous in this situation. In truth neither did he.

She was shaking her head, clearly terrified of him. In all his life he couldn't recall any woman every being frightened let alone terrified when he was present. His thoughts travelled back to the man, Leod.

"Did Leod hurt you?" He would have the man tarred and feathered if he harmed this tiny delicate woman in any way.

She was shaking her head no. To his surprise and pleasure, she seemed to be relaxing. Her chest was no longer pressed tightly against her legs, nor were eyes blazing with fear or anger. He wasn't sure.

"Good then. Come on out and tell me your name." He held out a hand to her in hopes she would accept his peace offering. Was not surprised when she declined the invitation.

She pushed back farther. Her hands remained tight around her legs, which were still pushed up against her chest.

"I promise I won't hurt you," he paused realizing he wasn't getting anywhere with her. "At least tell me your name."

Her lashes fluttered for a second then she focused on him, appearing to come to some conclusion. "Ria."

"That's a fine name, Ria. Now tell me why you are hiding here on the third floor?"

"Leod."

He expected to see tears but there were none, only determination in the set of her jaw. "Blessed hell," he muttered. One look at the man and he knew trouble surrounded him. "You told me he didn't hurt you."

"Aye, but he wanted to rape me. The lads were able to keep me safe and hidden these last weeks that we've been here."

"I understand." Yet he didn't. He figured getting to the bottom of this would be easier with the children in hand than with her. They were more likely to let something slip that would give him a better comprehension of her circumstances. "Are you going to stay there or come out?"

She looked at her feet then back to him seeming to consider. However, a few seconds later it didn't appear she was willing to leave her hiding place any time soon. "Suppose Leod didn't like to exert himself to come to the third floor."

"He got winded and had to stop every so often to drag in air," she said, her voice to soft for him to hear clearly but he understood the gist of it.

"A bit overweight you're saying?" He laughed hoping to reassure her enough so she would leave the place.

She nodded, her fingers winding through the fabric of her gown, her eyes focused there. "Yes, he rarely searched for me here. The lads always found a way to make it harder for him to walk to the third floor."

"The lads are protecting you from Leod then? They understand what he intends?" His speculation was true but would she admit it? He was watching her closely and realized the dirt was an affect also. Where her gown slipped a little, he saw clean white skin.

"They shouldn't but they do. We've dealt with this for a couple of years now." She lifted her shoulders slightly, looking resigned to the fact she was addressing but unwilling to put before him.

"You know," she picked up the fabric of her gown then let it fall softly around her, "that I'm a fake."

"A fake?" he queried. "What on earth can you mean by that."

"I'm not innocent or naïve as you probably believe I am," she told him, her voice soft as she spoke the words.

He had to wonder what exactly was behind her admission now.

"As long as you don't lie to me, I don't care. I'll wager though that the lads bring you dirt so you can paint your face and hands with it. Quite a clever disguise if you ask me, but then you didn't. Does it discourage Leod from taking liberties you aren't willing to give?"

"I don't know. It was Dodge's idea. I refused at first but wondered about the possibilities to give into his wishes. Well, he told me the dirt on my face wouldn't hurt when they weren't there for me. I agreed."

"You mean they don't stay by your side night and day?" He wanted to laugh but wisely refrained after seeing the expression on her face.

She was shaking her head. Her eyes wide once more, "They do some work for Millie when she asks. You aren't going to put us out, are you?"

"I don't know. What kind of work can you do?"

He smiled, watching her closely for a reaction to his question. Where her mind went would tell him a lot about this woman who intrigued him more than he thought she should.

She visibly bristled at his unspoken suggestion. "I won't be warming your bed if that's what you're getting at, sir." Instead of pushing back and cowering she rose. Her hands were fisted at her sides, eyes blazing.

He was quite pleased with her reaction. He showed her with a half-smile. Standing beside her, he wanted to show her he would control the situation but also that despite what would happen to her now was up to him, he would help her. "Do relax, Miss Ria. I'm not going to make you pay for your residency here in my bed. I'm not Leod, nothing like him at all. I appreciate a willing woman as much as any man. However, since you are obviously unwilling, we won't pursue this."

The sigh of relief was visible as well as the tentative smile she graced him with. "I can work in the kitchen with Millie if she'll have me. If not that, I'm quite capable of cleaning. Everything here needs attention from the floors to the stairs to the walls. At the convent I did a lot of cleaning."

At the convent?

"It's true. I believe it would take a small army to put everything to right by the New Year. Even then it might not happen." He wanted her to be a part of this and he wondered what skills she had that might give her at least a bit of a recommendation for something more than cleaning.

"I'd be happy to help." She turned to him then, smoothing the folds of her gown. "I don't have a place to sleep."

He waved his hand a bit, wishing to pursue the other line of his questioning a little more thoroughly. "Miss Ria..." he paused hoping she would provide a last name.

"Ashton."

"Miss Ashton, can you read and write? Calculate numbers?"

She nodded her head, seeming to wait for him to disclose the reason for his questions. "Yes. I've had schooling."

"At the convent."

"Yes."

Miss Ashton was inadvertently adding to the puzzle surrounding her. She was well spoken, could read and write as well as calculate numbers yet here she was under the protection of three little urchins. He needed to get to the bottom of this if for no other reason save, he was curious.

"Then I'd like to put you in charge of the staff. I will give you permission to go into the village with me tomorrow. You may help me decide who we need to hire. Also," he held up his hand when it appeared she might protest, "you will be my second in command here. It will be up to you to make sure everyone is doing their job properly."

"What about the lads?" she asked, once again finding the folds in her gown with her fingers.

"You are aware that one of the lads is a lassie." He was tired of secrecy and would accept nothing but the truth from Miss Ashton.

Her face paled and for a second she looked away from him. He thought she might lie.

"Ah, I see that you are aware. Is Ollie in need of protection also?" he asked. "Does she have the same needs as you?"

He watched the line of her neck as she swallowed then looked at her bare toes. "If you don't mind my feet are cold. I'd like to know where we will be sleeping. If it's not too much trouble the children, well the... I'd like them close by."

Accepting the diversion for the moment, "Do the children have other clothing to wear besides the ones they managed to soil today?"

"No, I wash them out every night and hang them up to dry."

"They sleep with nothing on? That must be embarrassing for the lass."

He didn't wait for an answer but poked his head around the corner to motion for the children to show themselves. "I've an idea if all of you will follow me. We'll see to some used clothing for the children then I'll show you where you all can sleep."

"Thank you," she moistened her lips. "The children do need something else to wear."

"You shouldn't have to wash their clothing every night. In any case that will be up to the new scullery maid we'll hire tomorrow. Follow me."

~ * ~

Ria wasn't at all sure following this man was prudent or safe, but she had no other options. He told her he wasn't like Leod. Of course, she understood all too well that only the passage of time would tell her the truth of the matter. The larger question was if he was like the other men who had been in her life.

"It seems I've remembered that my mother used to fold up our outgrown clothing before putting them in storage up here in the attic." He pushed open a door at the end of the hallway.

She and the children stood at the opening all unwilling to enter into the darkness. He marched to the window at the far end, drawing up the window and opening the shutters. Light slanted across the floor as well as the myriad of trunks sitting in the room while collecting dust. Still in the doorway, she watched as he sifted through various trunks opening lids then closing them until he discovered the ones he wanted.

Finally, she stepped forward, standing beside him and peering into the trunk. "Just what are you doing?"

He held up several items, britches and shirts both small and large. "These should fit Dodge and these Midget. Don't have any dresses for Olivia though."

"Ollie," she persisted.

One perfectly arched brow rose a fraction as he studied her for a moment. "I will purchase a few garments in town for her tomorrow."

"She would prefer to wear boys clothing," Ria said through gritted teeth, wishing she didn't need to accept charity even if it was for Ollie's sake and not hers. Otherwise, she would refuse it. "We do not need or want, nor will we accept your offer until I've the funds to pay for her clothing myself. Until then, maybe we could find some boys clothing that would fit her."

A tentative smile formed across his lips before he pressed them tightly together. "These clothes are used. They were my brothers and mine. There is no charity involved. They will earn these through the work they will start doing. As for Olivia..."

"What about the dress for Ollie? I don't have money. Besides she is safer for the time being if people think of her as a boy."

"Olivia need not hide behind britches any longer."

"Ollie."

Graham let out a long slow breath of air, his features rigid with what she assumed was anger. "In any case, she needs to be a girl now. I will make sure she is treated as she should be. You no longer have to worry about her or yourself. Other than perhaps what you would prefer to do during the day."

He strode to another trunk before pulling out a couple of dresses. "These were my mother's. Feel free to look through them. Pick out anything you'd like. There is something of everything a woman might want or need. Can't make any promises about the fit. I believe at least in height the two of you are of a similar size."

She was breathing hard. She knew despite his good intentions he couldn't promise anything of the sort. She put aside his offer of his mother's clothing intent on finishing the previous conversation first. "As long as he's alive, she'll be in danger as will I. You cannot think to gainsay me in this. As they think to protect me, I do my best to keep them safe as well."

Frozen and without a word in his defense, he watched her then went on as if nothing had been said to him to negate what he thought. Giving in to her wishes, he brought out a pair of britches and a shirt he thought might fit Ollie. He held them up, "Until I can purchase a few dresses for her."

He was of a mindset she couldn't fight so she chose to say nothing. Over his shoulder, she peered into the trunk, seeing a few pieces that might fit her. The door had not been locked. She decided she would make a trip up here some time when he wasn't home. In the second trunk she picked out a gown and a few other things for herself.

"Very well." With submissiveness she didn't feel, she clasped her hands in front of her. "We will proceed as you dictate."

He laughed, his gaze focused on her as he crossed his arms. "Why do I get the feeling you don't mean to comply to any of my wishes?"

She lowered her lashes before looking at him, "As long as she has a choice, I won't gainsay you. If there comes a time when I feel Ollie is in danger, we'll leave."

"You're free to leave here anytime you like." His voice was calm but she heard the underlying irritation coupled with anger.

It didn't make sense. He didn't know her. "Good, then we understand each other." She collected the clothing, handing the items to the children as they left.

"We don't, Ria. That's the problem here, but you'll discover the truth soon enough. Now, I'll show you to your rooms. I'm putting the lot of you in the south wing. My residence is in the north. You will have free access to anything you need."

Without another word, he stepped in front of them, striding down the steps to the second floor and turning when he reached the landing. She still wasn't at all sure about his intentions, unwilling to test his words. There was no reason she could see that he should put them in some of the best rooms in the manor unless it was for his own purposes.

He stopped then, opening a door for her. "This will be yours, Ria. There is a sitting room as well as the usual bathing and sleeping rooms. I'll send enough hot water for all of you to bathe sufficiently."

"Thank you," she said but by the look in his eyes, he noticed her reservations to his good deeds.

"I suggest you let me bathe the boys. You can take care of Olivia... She will have a room for herself"

"Ollie," she said, understanding he was growing impatient with her insistence. "Even with a room all to herself, we'll probably find her curled up with the boys in the morning. In my recollection, she has never willingly left their sides.

He cleared his throat several times before continuing his speech. "I don't trust the boys to get themselves clean without aide. Since Dodge is far too old for you to be in the bathing room with him, I'll attend to the lads."

"I've a feeling you've jumped over some details. Are you going to force them into the tub when they bathe?" She nodded toward the room he'd pointed out was for the baths. "You will find them quite unwilling participants."

"If I recall as a lad, I wasn't willing either. Seemed I liked the dirt better than soap and water. Also didn't see what was wrong with a few well-earned smudges, badges of honor."

"Would you like us to take a bath there?" She pointed to the room in her suite. "Us? By that you mean Ollie and me. You and the boys will go somewhere else." Again, she was left in the dark as to what he was saying as well as his intentions.

"Yes, after my journey I'm also in need of a soak in nice hot water."

"You will not get a nice hot soak if the boys are involved in any of this. If you wish for peace and calm, your bath should be taken in your sleeping quarters, not here."

With what looked like disappointment, changing to a strange smile, "I suppose you are right but only after I see to Dodge and Midget."

Millie appeared suddenly as if she'd been summoned. Ria was sure she had been in some way listening at the door. She was grinning at the lord and waiting expectantly for the orders that were sure to come.

"We need hot water, lots of it. The first water should come here for Olivia and Miss Ashton."

This time she refrained from correcting him, nearly biting her tongue to do so. He slanted her an amused grin before continuing his orders to Millie who curtsied and left. She understood he'd won this round. He would continue to address Ollie with her female name for as long as he chose.

He made himself comfortable in a wing chair in the sitting room. She wanted to know what he was thinking as well as expecting from them. The control was absolute. She cringed at the thought. A few weeks ago, she'd been under the power of another man. She'd vowed when she escaped that servitude it would never happen again. If the children were not involved, she would leave as soon as he retired for the night. With the children came intense responsibility she could never flee.

She chose to stand. In any case, sitting was an impossible task for her. Even when she was hiding, she kept herself off the floor. He motioned to the wing chair facing toward his.

"She can't sit," Dodge spoke out. "Don't expect her to do so."

"Or?" he queried with proper politeness that left Ria cringing.

"She'll leave tonight. I know it. She won't take us with her this time seein' we've got a respectable home to live in until we mess it up. She'll sneak out when no one is the wiser."

"You're not going..." Both Ria and Graham spoke at the same time.

Ria, however was directing her command to the children,

specifically Dodge who was the leader of the little troupe. She understood all too clearly if she left, he would try to find a way to follow.

"Just like Graham can't hold you here, you can't keep us from going with you. We're family. I'm not going to let you be out there, alone," Dodge's voice rose with surprising fury.

"Enough," Graham slashed his hand in the air, obviously frustrated with all of them. "Baths first then we'll talk about dinner. Perhaps after that someone will explain to me why Ria cannot sit."

Dodge let out a soft whistle. He fastened his gaze on the window and something outside while Olivia shifted from one foot to the other her view of them doing the same shifting while Midget stood his ground his lip tucked beneath his teeth as if that was keeping him from spilling the information.

Millie led the way with the hot water. Two men followed her with buckets, left then returned to finish filling the tub. Ria nodded at Graham, telling him without so many words that it was time for him to leave with the boys.

"I will see you at seven when dinner is served." He led the two boys from the room, a hand on each of their backs.

"Do we have to take a bath?" Dodge asked as the door closed behind them. "Not really feelin' the need."

Ria couldn't understand Graham's response though she could guess at what he would say. In any case she would see Ollie to the dinner table. However, she didn't plan on joining them and undergoing another bout of humiliating questions. Why she couldn't sit was none of his blessed business, and she was pretty sure the boys would stay quiet. When the question was posed, she shot Dodge the sternest expression she could summon.

"Come, Ollie, let's get you cleaned up."

"I would like that. Why don't the boys want to take a bath?" she asked as she stripped the filthy clothes from her body. "I hate being dirty."

Ria tested the water with her hand. "It's not too hot. You can get in." Then, "Don't know why. Boys are just like that."

Ollie lowered herself in the tub, playing with the soap and the sponge. Between her hands she squirted the bar into the air and giggled. "Watch." She repeated the process and they both laughed.

"Do you want some help?" Ria handed her the sponge.

"You can do my hair. It's so filthy and tangled I don't think it will ever be clean again."

"We'll get it clean. I promise you."

Ria smiled at the little girl who'd become so precious to her. The thought of Ollie's life in Edinburgh brought tears to her eyes. She hoped this manor with Mr. Chamberlin at its helm would be somewhere they could stay. Ria understood she would have been unable to maintain the little girl's disguise much longer. When the men understood what she could do for them, she would have been pimped out. Ollie was beautiful so she wouldn't have been left on the streets or placed in a bordello. No, she would have gone to one of the expensive bordellos where only the finest politicians and lords convened. Not that a situation like that was tenable.

"Are you going to get clean water?"

"This will do." Ria grimaced at the water that was growing a darker brown with every washing. "There now, let's rinse your hair and get you dried off. Then it will be my turn."

Ollie was sitting on the hearth dressed now in her clean britches and shirt while Ria was humming and finger combing her hair in an attempt to rid the little girl of all the snarls.

"Knock, knock, everybody decent in there?" Millie didn't wait for an answer but pushed the door open for a peek. "Good, here's some more hot water for you, Miss Ria. Under the circumstances, thought you'd appreciate clean water for yourself."

The tub was emptied and filled again, just waiting for Ria and the hot soak Graham had spoken of earlier, but this one was for her. "Oh my, thank you. I thought I'd be using Ollie's water."

"You think I'd let you do that? Never. Now, I'll bring a comb up as well as few other things I can find. Besides the boys' mother, you're the first woman to live here. Most of my life, it's been a house of males. They could have put a sign on the doorstep, no women allowed."

Ria waited until Millie appeared and disappeared again before disrobing and stepping into the hot water. She sucked in a swift breath of air as the water hit her back. Millie brought her valise with her second dress in it a few minutes later and set it near the tub. Ollie combed her hair, tugging at the tangles until Ria saw tears in her eyes.

"You going to wash your hair?" Ollie stood over her. "You should you know. This black grease is ugly."

"I'd like to but I don't want to be recognized. You know that." She ran the cloth over her body. The soap smelled of lavender. She closed her eyes for a moment, wishing she dared wash the filthy stuff away.

"Who would recognize you? There is no one here except Sir Graham."

Ollie was right. If she didn't wash her hair, it would not surprise her if Graham didn't insist she do so in some overbearing way of his she was beginning to recognize. He wasn't like any other man she'd known, but she hadn't known many. Her life in the nunnery near Edinburgh certainly didn't prepare her for the life afterward.

Ria ducked under the water for a moment to get all of her short hair dripping wet. When she rose, she soaped and rinsed. With Ollie's encouragement, she washed her hair three times before it was finally devoid of the black stuff she'd rubbed into it.

Feeling clean and better than she had in a very long time, she rose and wrapped the towel around her. Standing by the fire she combed her hair until all the tangles were gone.

"Now we are both ready for dinner."

Ollie's stomach rumbled hungrily, the sound generating laughter between the both of them.

"I cannot go as well you ken. Sitting in the tub was all I can manage for one day. Do you think you remember where the dining room is?" Ria inhaled a deep breath. "Perhaps you can bring me a little something to eat after the meal is finished."

"I can but you really think he will let me without investigating for himself?" Ollie asked, her hands on her hips.

"You are much too wise for a ten-year-old. However, we will deal with the repercussions when they are here. Not a minute sooner."

"I'm nearer to eleven."

"Nearer to the age where concealing you would be all that much harder. I'm glad we left when we did."

"You did it. No one knew you were a girl," Ollie pointed out, a slight smile on her tiny face.

"We left because we were found out. Blue discovered the truth one night when I was careless. Staying in the city was out of the question. I would have lost you and the boys."

Ria was determined to never go back to that life. Thinking about it sent a shiver down her spine.

"Is that when he beat you?" Tears slid down her cheeks and Ria brushed them away.

"Yes, yes it was. He was very angry. While I made a mistake, he made one too. That's when I took advantage. He didn't think I would be able to move because of the pain. So, he left me untied, unguarded too."

"If he wanted to pimp you out, why did he beat you?"

"He knew I would heal. He wanted to make me hurt as well as understand that I couldn't deceive him and get away with it. I know he had big plans for me. If he ever finds us..." She couldn't bear to think about that scenario. Ria made herself believe the man would never discover their whereabouts.

"I ken it." Ollie wrapped her arms around her, hugging her tight. "He won't find out because of me. If he finds you, he'll find the rest of us and I think I like it here."

"Now, I want you to go on downstairs and eat with them. Don't let on how I'm feeling. If Graham asks just tell him I wasn't hungry."

"The boys are going to insist they see you. They always need to make sure you have not been hurt."

"You have a question or comment for everything. Of course they will, but they can wait until after dinner. The important thing now is that no one tells him about my back."

She slipped into the cotton shift she pulled out of the small valise she brought with them. One of Blue's ladies gave her two dresses she'd outgrown and could no longer wear otherwise she would have still been wearing pants and a shirt. She had one pair of pants along with one shirt with her. Blue lashed her while she was still wearing her clothing emphasizing with each stroke that she was never to ape a man again. If she did, this would be her punishment until she understood the orders. By the time he finished, her clothing was in shreds around her and useless.

"I'll go now," Ollie said, "as soon as you lie down. I'll cover you up so you'll be all warm and toasty."

"I'd like that. Thank you. Now enjoy your dinner. You can tell me all about it tomorrow or tonight if I'm still awake."

She turned then to walk to the bed. The gasp behind her startled her. "You're bleeding."

Ria pulled at the shift as it stuck to her back. Unable to help herself, she groaned. "Help me. I need to get this off."

Ria knelt down and held up her arms. Slowly the shift fluttered over her head. Ollie let it drop to the floor, tears in her eyes.

"You're back is all red. It's not just the blood." Ollie's voice was shaking. "It's your skin too. I have to tell Sir Graham."

"No!"

The last thing Ria wanted was for Graham to see her back. If he was told, she didn't have any doubts that he would force her to show him her injuries.

"Then..."

"Go, I'll be just fine. You know I will." Ria slanted her a shaky smile. "I always land on my feet. I'll sleep on my stomach."

Slowly, Ollie backed out of the room. Ria tried to get comfortable, struggling with the pillow until she had it where she wanted it. She managed to bring the sheet to her waist. The tiny effort proved to taxing to continue. She closed her eyes trying not to relive the events of her life.

She'd suffered far worse than this lashing by the hands of another man after he took her from the nunnery. Going back to that was not tenable. If it happened, she would once again find a way to leave. That day was bleak. She recalled every moment. Mary Margret tried to save her, gave her money and the means to flee to London. The sister even booked passage on a ship for her.

Unfortunately, she never made it on board. The man who wanted her intercepted her and hauled her back to his home near the city. Ria groaned softly, her back aching now that she had no obligations to take her mind off the pain. The lashes had been burning for the last three hours. Now the pain was nearly unbearable.

Ria didn't know how long she'd been lying on the bed in the dark. A soft breeze from a slightly open window attempted to cool her back but was fairly useless. She supposed the air rippling across her was better than nothing. Her head pounded as she passed in and out of consciousness. The clock in the hallway chimed eight times. Truly she didn't know if Ollie would keep quiet about her condition. She hoped she would. She was proud of the little girl and her efforts. Now, it just remained for her to return to the room and go to sleep. The boys would show up. She'd have to make them vow their silence.

She groaned again and it seemed the sound came from outside herself. The heat she was feeling touched all of her from the inside out. Moving her arms and legs was impossible now. Her eyes were closed. She thought perhaps she heard voices but that would mean Ollie told. She was sure the little girl would do as asked.

"Bloody eyes!"

No mistaking Graham's voice or his anger. Fighting from the black fog swirling in her head, she tried to sit up then remembered she wore nothing.

"Don't move a muscle," he said as he kneeled beside the bed. The back of his hand touched her forehead then he swore again.

"Dodge, go get a bucket of water from Millie and bring her here. Tell her it's urgent."

"You don't need to be here," she whispered, her voice barely a croak.

"Water?" he asked pouring her a glass.

"If I'm going to drink that you'll have to leave the room." Her head was turned sideways. She saw the stern expression on his face and the crease line between his brows.

"Not a chance. If you can push up a little ways, I'll get the rim to your lips and you can sip."

"I'm naked."

"True. Do you want some water or not?"

To her, his voice sounded patient yet despite the earlier sternness she heard a touch of amusement.

"I'd tell you I won't look, but if I don't all the water will probably end up on you as well as the bed instead of where we want it to go."

She pushed up and sipped then a few seconds later they repeated the process.

"Thank you," she mouthed and fell back to the bed, closing her eyes, understanding he wasn't the first man to see her unclothed.

"Now that you've been refreshed, who did this to you?"

If she closed her eyes and pretended to sleep, maybe he would go away or at least forget the question she didn't want to answer.

"Ria." His voice was stern and held the insistence that he wasn't going to let this go without an answer.

"Blue did it to her," Dodge spoke up from behind, his voice taking on a tone Ria had never heard before from the young boy.

"Who is Blue?" Graham spoke the words slowly.

"The man who was going to pimp her out," Ollie said, her tiny voice filled with anger. "He would have done the same to me, but Ria was disguising me as a boy."

Graham didn't respond to Ollie. Instead, he lightly touched the slash marks then pulled the cover all the way off almost as if he remembered that she couldn't sit.

She gasped when she felt the air across her backside.

"Bloody hell," he said again but this time the whisper held a touch of venom in his anger.

All the way to the tips of her toes, she felt the emotion emanating from him but didn't understand what it was. She'd never felt as if any man in her life cared one way or the other for her. Fending for her survival one day at a time since she left the abbey had been her predominate goal.

"Should I send for the doctor?" Millie asked.

"No, I'm going to tend to her. What I need you to do is get my saddlebags for me. Bring them here. It's in my room on one of the wing chairs facing the fireplace."

"Do you think it's proper?" she asked.

"No, no," he said. "I'm sure there is nothing proper about any of this. Nor was there anything about Ria's beating."

Ria heard the sound of Millie's steps as she left the room. When she returned. "Here it is, sir."

He rumbled around in the packs, pulling out things before letting them drop to the floor. Then, "Go brew some tea with this. It's willow bark. It will help with the pain. Do it as quickly as you can."

"Pain?" she groaned softly and wondered if anyone heard her.

She felt his breath across her cheek. "I'm sorry but your back is infected. I'm going to have to cut you in places so the pus will drain."

"No, no there is no need for that."

He wasn't a doctor. What did he know?

"There is. I'm sorry but if I don't take care of you now, there is a good chance you'll die. Drink this."

He handed her the bottle of whiskey he retrieved. Once more he held the bottle to her lips until she downed a few tablespoons of the liquid. From the corner of her eye, she watched him pour the whiskey on his knife. Her gut clenched as her entire body tightened.

He was gone for a few seconds then, "Put this in your mouth. Clamp down hard."

"Sh-sh-shouldn't you wait for the tea?"

"The whiskey should be enough for now." He told her as he began to wipe her back with a cool cloth. "I'm going to pull the remaining vestiges of cloth from the lashes. That's what's infecting you. Have to get rid of them or none of this will do you any good."

Chapter Two

"Bring the lantern closer, Olivia," he said as he bent closer to Ria. There were a lot of lashes to look at. He wondered how Ria had survived this beating. It must have been the children. From what he knew of her, the children's survival would have been her soul purpose for putting one step in front of the other. "Now all three of you need to go to your rooms. Tonight, Olivia, if that's what you would like, go with the boys."

He watched and waited until they left knowing that at least Dodge would return when the others fell asleep to check on her. He appreciated that loyalty they all shared for each other.

Each time he touched her, pulled fabric strands from her wounds, she flinched. She didn't yell at him or complain. She was very stoic and brave. Her courage was undeniable. This procedure was probably a bit like gnats taking tiny bites. By the time he was satisfied with his work, Millie returned with the tea. The worst part was yet to come though.

"Ria," he began, "I need to have you drink the tea. It will be a little bitter, however it will take some of the pain away. Not instantly but this combined with the whiskey you drank will help."

"Some?"

"Not all of it. I'm not going to lie. You'll wish you didn't know me but a doctor would do the same if he's any good. Do you understand?"

She nodded then, "How do you know what to do?"

He chuckled softly, his memories some good some bad, filling his head. "Learned from an Indian shaman in western Virginia.

"An Indian?"

"Yes, no more questions. Millie, you need to stay in the room. If the blood is going to bother you sit in one of those chairs. No, on second thought, bring me a warm saltwater solution."

He helped her again until Ria drank the entire contents, no longer concerned that he would see her breasts. Other matters at this time were more important. He waited until Millie left the room.

With the first cut, Ria screamed then whimpered. Thank God he didn't have to drain all of the lashes, only about half of them. He gritted his jaw, determined to finish this as soon as he possibly could. Hurting her, seeing her body quiver with the pain, nearly did him in. He knew the second she passed out and thanked the good lord above.

Dodge stood beside him. He expected the boy to appear with the first scream.

Sweat dripped from his forehead. He tried to brush it off with the back of his sleeve. "Dodge."

"Yes, sir."

"Can you get one those cloths and wipe the sweat from my forehead?"

Dodge was beside him before Millie. "Here, sir." The boy stood by his side then. "It's terrible bad isn't it?"

"Pretty much so." He didn't want to paint a solemn picture, but the boy deserved the truth as he saw it.

"Is Ria going to die?"

"Not if I can help it."

He meant every word. When he turned to look at the boy, he saw the fear in his eyes.

"What can I do?" Dodge asked straightening his shoulders. "I can't let her die."

"Hand me that bandage. I'm going to need help, but Millie will have to do it. I have to get Ria in a sitting position."

Here it is," Millie set the solution on the side table.

He soaked several cloths in the solution then set each one on the wounds. "We're going to leave these on for a while then do it again until there is no more pus and scabs."

"That's not going to get rid of all the red," Dodge stared at Ria's back moisture pooling in his eyes. He wiped the tears away and straightened his back, his brows drawing together.

"No, but we'll make a poultice to do that as soon as these marks are cleaned up. You'll help me?"

"Yes."

Finally, after two more applications of saltwater solution, Graham was satisfied. While Dodge applied new cloths every half hour or so, Millie helped him make a poultice of charcoal powder and water.

He spread the paste on Ria's back. She was still unconscious. He was glad of that. She was going to have to stay on her stomach most of the night even with the bandages he meant to wrap around her body.

"How long you going to keep that on?" Dodge asked. His worried appearance didn't go unnoticed.

"About ten minutes then we're going to wrap those bandages around. If she moves wrong in the middle of the night, they will give her some protection. In the morning we're going to do it again."

She moaned softly, moving and pushing herself up from the mattress. "Dodge?"

"Yes." He was beside her, running his hand on her head in a soothing gesture.

"Tell me what is happening."

"Graham, sir, is fixing you up. You're going to be just fine in a couple of days. You'll see. You're going to have to behave yourself."

He wasn't sure, thought he heard her laugh for a second. Could have been his imagination.

"I always behave myself, Dodge," she murmured.

Graham bent down close to her, moving her silver-blond hair away so he could see her face to judge the pain. He was amazed at the unusual color. Fascinated by the length she went to disguise herself. "I'm going to wash the poultice off your back then bandage you up. The poultice is there to remove the infection." He dipped the cloth in warm water, slowly erasing all the evidence of the paste he applied, repeating the process until her back was clean. "We'll have to do it again in the morning, until all the redness goes away."

She nodded her understanding before closing her eyes.

"Don't go to sleep just yet. Need to wrap the bandage around you. Then we'll leave you alone to sleep. I'll need your help to do that."

She pushed up again, "I don't want you to leave me." Her voice was thready and thin. He felt a strange draw to her. He felt a need to stay and make sure she didn't have any nightmares.

"I'll stay the night," he assured her. "Now let's get those bandages on so you can rest."

"If it's doesn't matter to you, I'd like to do that. I've seen her with nothing on, dressed her after the beating when she couldn't stand and her clothing hung in tatters around her feet. I doubt if she'll mind," Dodge spoke softly. "Don't think she'll want a man seeing her though."

Graham paused in thought considering everything the boy told him then looked to Millie who didn't seem up to the task. This would take two. "Very well. You can help but this process will need me as well. Come here."

Graham lifted her so she was sitting, her legs over the side of the bed. The boy waited for directions.

"Get on the bed behind her. I'm going to have to wrap the cloth around her. You just hold her up."

Dodge nodded then did what he asked. Graham wanted to smile thinking he'd make a good soldier. The boy took orders quite well. Wrapping the bandage and tying it off didn't take as long as the other things he'd done to her.

"What now?" Dodge hopped off the bed and waited.

"You're going to find the others and sleep." Graham held up his hands to stop the boy's protest. "I'll come get you in a few hours. We both are going to need sleep. I'm assuming you don't want to be too far away if she wakes up. The others need you too. Can I count on your cooperation?"

Dodge nodded. "Yes, sir."

"Good then, help me get Ria on her stomach and you go to your room."

He moved back one step, looking hesitant then turned and left.

Graham ran his hands through his dark red hair, closing his eyes and trying not to think about what Ria endured. He guessed this was only part of the story of her life at the hands of men. Knowing what little he learned this evening, he was surprised she'd trusted him at all. After seeing the unusual color of her hair, he understood why she blacked it.

He pulled one of the wing chairs close to the bed. Exhausted, he fell back, closing his eyes, trying to chase his demons from behind his eyes. He'd wanted to get here early so he rose at the crack of dawn and pushed Draco to the animal's limit. Finding a woman and three children taking refuge in Runningmead Manor was unexpected.

After dinner, he thought to retire to his suite of rooms, relax with a brandy then fall asleep. The ensuing scream jolted him awake. Ria thrashed in the covers, flailing her arms as if she was trying to ward off an attacker.

Quickly he sat down beside her, holding her shoulders. "Hush now, no one is going to hurt you. It's me, Graham. You're going to be fine now. There is nothing to fear."

"No!" she screamed again, this time managing to whip a hand across his face. "Get away from me. No!"

He didn't want to restrain her but she needed to stay on her stomach. "Wake up, Ria. Everything is fine. Hush now. No one is going to hurt you," he repeated. "The children are all asleep. You don't want to wake them."

She moaned softly, excepting his help to turn back to her stomach. "Graham? Is that you?"

"Yes, I'm here now. Dodge stayed with you through most of the night. He's asleep at this hour as well as the other children. I'm assuming they're altogether."

"Good, what did you do to me?" She pushed away then realized she was practically naked and let herself fall back to the mattress. "I see some of what you did."

"Do you want to know all the details or suffice it to say I tried to get rid of all the infection? How are you feeling?"

"Do I want to know everything you did? My head aches as well as my back, so no, I don't actually feel much better."

"I can get more tea for you. I have to go to the kitchen so it will be a few minutes. I'm hoping Millie left the water with the bark in on the stove so it will be warm and well steeped. Should I go get it?"

He meant for his smile to be reassuring but he knew she couldn't see it. He wanted this to be finished. What he really wanted was to throttle the man who did this to her.

"If it will help ease the throbbing, please. I feel as if I'm going to jump out of my skin."

"I'll be back in a minute or two. Don't be surprised if at least Dodge comes in to see you. Your scream was pretty loud."

She groaned again, "I didn't mean to wake them."

"So far it doesn't seem you have. Just relax now. When I get back, you can tell me about the nightmare."

He left. In the kitchen he found the brewed tea. The liquid was still warm. He hoped the children were not in the room when he returned. As long as Ria was awake, he wanted to find out a little more about what happened to her. At the moment everything he'd learned was veiled in shadows and innuendos. He wanted to know what brought her to the bowls of the city.

When he stepped into the room, the children were absent. He splashed a little of the whiskey into the tea hoping the alcohol would help her sleep. She turned slightly when she heard him.

He sat down beside her and assisted her with the liquid. She didn't shy away from him, obviously getting used to the situation she found herself in now. When she finished and was lying on her stomach again, he decided to proceed with a few more questions hoping she would answer.

"I suppose you want to know what I did to deserve the whipping." Her head was to the side, one arm beneath it propping herself up slightly.

It seemed she beat him to the conversation. "No one deserves a thrashing like this. That would be nice to understand. Who is this Blue?"

"Suffice it to say, the man discovered I wasn't a he. It seems he took exception to that notion as well as the fact I deceived him." She closed her eyes then, seeming to relax. The whiskey shouldn't take affect yet.

"You were pretending to be a boy. That's why your hair is short. Now that I've seen your hair, I understand why you covered it with boot grease to make it black."

"Yes, and the latter is an entirely different story. Nothing to do with Blue, I didn't want to be recognized. My hair is like a beacon in case you haven't noticed."

"What do you say? For now, let's just stick with Blue." With her breasts the size they were, masquerading as a boy would be difficult at best. Letting his gaze roam across her slim back and seeing how her body sweetly flared at her hips, he didn't see how she could have been successful for very long.

"I bound my breasts. Dodge helped me when Ollie couldn't and before you say anything, there was no other way. I didn't like what he had to do but..."

"He was a boy about to become a man and things would be expected of him sooner where you were living than if he were brought up in a normal household."

"You ken it then."

"No, but if it happened that way, I'll believe you. Why would Olivia not be able to help?"

"We were all accountable to Blue. If she was sent somewhere to pick pockets, she had to go. There were times I could barely breathe because of the bindings and times when the sores from keeping them on would be rubbed raw. If I could get rid of them for a night, I was always grateful. It was a risk though."

He couldn't help but recoil at her words even though he'd seen things just as bad in Indian Territory. That was part of why he thought to return to a more civilized country. Now, he was faced with this. For a few seconds he held his breath, praying for the strength needed to shelter these children and Ria. He understood with very little thought that he would protect them with his life.

"How did you come to Blue?" He strode to the window then, gazing over his land, soaking up the sight, which was slightly lit by the moon. He saw the horses, the large, shaggy highland cattle all in shadows. She was speaking. He heard the movement of the covers against her skin. Knew then she was trying to sit up.

"Could you bring me the robe over there?"

When he turned the covers were pulled to her neck. He smiled. They both knew he'd seen her several times. Had even told her he wouldn't look. Impossible task though.

"Of course," he said, knowing his smile was wider with each second. "Would you like help putting it on?"

"If you turn your back, I'm sure I can manage by myself." She let a long breath of air rush from her lungs. "Now I ken what you're about. It's not the same thing, not the same thing at all."

The chuckle he was about to let free, he held in check. "You're right of course. What I saw was not the same thing. Your breasts haven't changed in the last hour or so since you been asleep. I gather you are more comfortable this way." He paused then, as he turned before he spoke once more. "If I don't look at you right now while you put on your robe, you will feel as if I haven't seen you. What are you going to do tomorrow morning when I unwrap your bandages?"

"I will do it myself. You can turn now." Her voice was prim so very proper he was once more, harder pressed not to chuckle.

When he did see her again, she was propped gingerly against the headboard, a pillow behind her back. Graham knew her back pressed against even something as soft as a pillow had to hurt. He flashed her a broad smile, striding to the wing chair. "What about Blue? Everything you know."

She blanched. There was no other word for the sudden whitening of her face. She fiddled with the collar of her robe until it nearly hung from her shoulder. Then, "I really don't know much other than he's the man everyone reports to. He gathers the booty and gives the thief what he thinks is deserved. The rest he takes on to someone else."

"Dodge, Olivia and Midget are thieves." *She will get used to me calling the lass Olivia* he thought again as he watched creases between her eyebrows deepen. He didn't mean to annoy. It was just the way he saw things.

"What were you?" He leaned forward, his arms resting on his thighs. "At least before he discovered you were female."

She pushed back golden blond hair that was very nearly white from her eyes, her breasts moving slightly beneath the robe catching his attention. Lifting her shoulders, enhancing the curves she thought to conceal, "nothing to him. I was able to stay in the shadows and take care of the children for several weeks before he realized there was someone in his territory who didn't belong."

"I gather he was angry but you said your breasts were bound for good reason. I'm sure he expected you to carry through with some job. Did he expect you to join the children in their thievery?" She would have been caught the first time she tried to lift some valuable.

"No, he wanted me to rob houses. He set me up with two other men. It was actually one of them who eventually discovered my ruse." She pulled the slipping fabric back over her shoulder. Then she smiled. "They were punished also for not realizing sooner. They weren't flogged though. Each one received naught but a slap on the palm with the lash."

"So, you took the brunt of the punishment."

Ria nodded. "I did."

"Did you ever think he might have violated you instead?"

He was taken by surprise when she turned inward and didn't answer for several seconds. With his question, he touched on something that made her uncomfortable. The quivering of her shoulders was unmistakable.

"That would have been something I could have endured more easily than what he did. I would have just gone to another place in my..." She stopped suddenly, her eyes wide and her hand on her lips.

"You would have gone to another place?" he queried his mind reaching into venues best left alone.

Once more he understood with this woman there was more left unsaid than what she willingly told him.

"It's just a phrase I learned from the children." Her hand still against her lips she yawned. "I'm really tired. Perhaps we should both go to sleep."

"Liar."

He could wait for more answers. After all she'd told him enough for one night. What was left to be said couldn't nearly be as degrading as what she already unfolded for him.

"You doubt my word?" She blinked a few times, staring out the window clearly telling him she was through talking.

"Just this time. It's just that I understand it is something you don't wish to speak of. "Do the children know?"

She was shaking her head. "No, they don't know the truth of it all. Just that I was running away and they found me. They don't know what I was running from or where I came from."

"They found you?"

"Yes, I collapsed in an alley. They discovered me. Dodge gave me his last meat pie, thinking I hadn't eaten in days."

"Had you? Not eaten? I don't think you would have eaten his food if you hadn't been starving. He's a bright lad. I'm sure he guessed or knew just by looking at you that you needed his meat pie more than he did."

"It was like that, just as you said. Dodge, I think, had a family at one time. He's closed mouth about them."

"As you had a family at one time and not just the sisters at the abbey."

"My parents are dead. I've no one. No siblings or aunts and uncles. No one. No family ever."

"That you know of." He needed to hear her admit there might be someone he could contact, someone who might care if she lived or died.

"No one."

~ * ~

The children were sitting quietly on the floor, eating fresh baked bread with sweet butter and drinking the warm highland cattle milk Millie brought them when Graham walked into her room, his hair still damp from his bath. Sunlight slipped between the curtains to brighten her day, at least until the clouds would open up and drench them. She could sit today without too much pain. Little things, she laughed softly while she watched the children.

Graham told her they would go into the village today to find laborers to work on the manor house. She didn't think that was going to happen for her. He would have to go by himself. Getting outdoors would have been nice although the day was chilly. When she opened the window first thing this morning and leaned out, a crisp breeze stirred against her cheek.

"Good morning, how are you feeling?" Graham sauntered through the room stopping momentarily to pat Ollie and Midget on the head.

Ria was sitting as she did last evening, her back to the headboard and a pillow behind her. She smiled at him and greeted, "Good as new. You fixed me up quite splendidly last night."

"Yes, I did but I doubt those crease lines between your eyes as well as the lines radiating out from them speak of as good as new. Don't lie to me, Ria. How are you?"

Whining about how she felt wasn't something she was going to do, not on this beautiful day. She had a good idea she would be in pain for several days. Still, she meant to be blunt. "Millie brought me more willow bark tea this morning. It has eased some of the agony radiating from my back but not all. I found I can sit today without too much pain. Is that better, sir?"

His grin changed his entire demeanor. He should smile more often. The change of expression made him even more handsome than without. It was like Dodge. If the boy ever smiled, his features would soften and he would look more like a mischievous little boy. In his short life, Dodge had very little to smile about. At his tender age he was indeed a man. In protecting Ria he'd taken on a man's role.

Graham sat down on the wing chair he left near the bed last night, stretching his legs out in front of him appearing relaxed, at ease. His fingers were formed into a steeple beneath his chin, one finger lightly tapping.

"I don't want you to be afraid. This Blue person won't find you or the children here. In any case if he did, I wouldn't let him hurt any of you." He looked to the children who, except for Dodge, were chatting easily unconcerned about her.

She did appreciate his efforts as well as the way his eyes shimmered when he looked at the children. Yes, Blue was formidable. She sensed Graham was more so. He held himself aloof in most things, saying little of what he was thinking. The hard edge he carried himself could not be concealed.

"You might not be able to hold him off. He has resources at his disposal, despicable men who would go to hell with him if he asked it of them." She smoothed the blanket lying on top of her legs before she looked at him again. He was staring at her, his eyes narrowed. She was sure he saw into her mind and was even now reading what she meant to keep from him.

While Ollie and Midget still seemed intent on breakfast at the mention of Blue's name, Dodge came to stand by the chair. His small hand rested on the top, Dodge's back stiff.

"Sir Graham has friends too. They might be more formidable than Blue. I saw them this morning talking to him. They are outside. They told me they just arrived late last night. Followed Graham here."

Graham chuckled. "So, you saw my men this morning, did you? What did you think?"

Dodge nodded his head, his eyes wide with knowledge of some sort Ria didn't understand. "Indians. They had feathers in their hair, each a bow and arrow, a pistol and a knife on their belt. Do you think they'd teach me to shoot?"

"Yes, Cherokee." He smiled, his gaze focused on the window and what couldn't be seen. "If you ask them, they wouldn't say no. However, they taught me everything I know about survival."

"Aren't they dangerous?" She leaned toward the window, trying to see the men. "Indians? You say Cherokee? Is there a difference?"

"Only dangerous to their enemies. Every tribe is different in some way." His gaze returned to her, his brows drawn together. "Cherokee people live near my brother's plantation. As the white man moves in, they move west."

"We are friends?" she asked, unsure of anything. In a moment, she could take the children and flee. Perhaps she'd do just that.

It seemed he read her mind. "In your condition you wouldn't get very far. The men are not dangerous to you or the children. For a while I lived with the Cherokee in one of their villages. These men decided they wanted to see what was on the other side of the ocean. They are both part Cherokee and part black."

Her heart thundered in her chest. This man was nothing like she thought him to be. When she lifted her hand slightly, it was trembling. Air didn't want to find its way into her body.

"I read stories," she said quietly, her voice changing to a whisper.

"Most likely none of them are true." His voice was solemn, gruff with impatience.

He didn't seem to like her fear of these men. She couldn't accept them as friends just yet but she was willing to give them a chance. "You care about those men as I do for the children." At the tightening of his jaw, she understood she hit upon the truth, perhaps a nerve as well. "What are they to you besides friends?"

He stood walking away from her. She understood he didn't want to share anything further. The subject was closed for now. Well, they both harbored secrets. Somehow, she would discover the truth. For now, the subject needed to be changed to the necessities for the trip into town.

"We need to talk about today and what you are not going to do. Obviously, you cannot go into the village with me. Therefore, you will have to trust me to pick out the workers."

She nodded they were his workers after all. "You should do an excellent job. Much better than I would most likely. I'll rely on your decisions since I've no experience."

His grin was slow and smooth, one eyebrow rising above the normal line. "I've no experience either. I suspect if we were both trying to decide we would lead each other a merry chase."

"Suppose so, I do read people rather well. It's from all my years..." she cut herself off not wanting to divulge anything more to Graham. He heard enough of her sob story yesterday and didn't need to listen to anything else. Her best way to change her life around was to make the best of this miracle that fell into her life quite by accident.

He tilted his head sideways seeming to contemplate what she was going to say next then thought better of pursuing the conversation. He agreed. "Reading people is an admirable character trait. What else are you good at?"

She ignored that, again not wishing to burden him with her previous life. "What is it you've planned?"

She suspected he would ask to take Dodge with him. The little boy would prove good company. She wasn't sure why else he would want the lad to travel to the village other than to maybe let him get to know some of the neighbors.

He cleared his throat, a pained expression forming around his mouth. "First, I need to see to your back. Hopefully the infection will be nearly gone, however, I'm of the notion it will take at least two more poultices to draw out all of the poison from the deeper wounds."

She grimaced at the notion of spending most of the morning on her stomach again. "Is it really necessary? I'm sure it will get better given time," she asked, even though she understood he would think it was.

"If you want to live." His smile didn't reach his eyes. He turned to Dodge who still hovered next to him. "Will you go downstairs? Ask Millie for more of the poultice she made last night and bring it here, please."

Dodge was off, moving past the other children so quickly they stopped what they were doing to stare open mouthed at him. Graham chuckled softly as he watched him leave.

"Now, we should talk about what you will need." He sat back again, appearing more relaxed than ever. His eyes focused on her once more. "It won't take Dodge long to return. When I lay out what is expected here, I don't want any argument. Disputing what I'm about to tell you is a waste of time. I've made up my mind."

She nodded, winding the sheet between her hands. "I don't need anything."

Graham spoke in a perfectly pleasant voice. "Thought you would say as much. I won't have you running around in men's clothing."

Her startled gasp didn't surprise him. "How did you know?"

"As I was going to say, you need at least three decent dresses. My mother's dresses are far too big in the bosom to fit you. The ones you borrowed from your friends in Edinburgh border on decent. They did fine for you in a pinch but you are no longer in desperate need of something to wear," he paused, stroking his beard. "In a pinch. You will be directing people here in this household. You will need to be respected and appear respectable as well. While I don't care what you wear, rather appreciate the britches, other people will have differing opinions."

"You will use my wages for managing your workers to pay for the dresses." If he wouldn't abide by her wishes, it was the first step in becoming his whore or his mistress depending what he wanted to call her. She wouldn't have it.

"Even though I would like to give them as a gift with nothing expected from you, I understand your reluctance. I will dock your wages to pay for the purchases."

He was of a like mind. She let out a long sigh of relief, erasing the dread she felt for the seconds it took him to answer. "Thank you. I trust you will not spend too much of my soon to be hard earned money."

"Ah, there is Dodge with the poultice. If you don't' mind." He took the bowl from Dodge. "Would you take the children to your rooms. You can play there and I'll let you know when it is time to leave. Ollie and Midget can return here. In the process keep Ria company and out of trouble."

Dodge held back for a few seconds, his body tense. She understood he didn't want to leave her for the same reasons she wouldn't accept the dresses as gifts. "How long will you be gone?"

He waited for them to exit and the door to shut behind them. "A few hours. The village isn't far from here. I've several childhood friends I'll visit for information. The tavern is also a likely source of people who might be in need of honest work."

She rubbed her neck before pulling up the shoulder of the over large robe. Seconds seemed to pass by while he watched her. It seemed he wanted to give her time to adjust to the circumstances. This had been different in the dark while she was in so much pain she couldn't see straight. Now it was the light of day. He would see the ugly gashes again, would be reminded of the horrible things she did, the terrible things that had been expected of her.

"Any time you're ready, but it would be nice if we didn't reach the lunch hour first. I'd like to be on my way home by then." His words were uttered with such calm patience. If she were standing, her knees would have crumbled.

He was turned away from her, staring out the window, giving her the privacy she needed to take the robe off and turn onto her stomach.

She didn't know how he was going to take the bandages off without seeing her. He saw just about every inch of her last night. She drew in a deep ragged breath before untying the rode and slipping it off.

With that done, she turned on to her stomach, hoping she would not have to bare herself again. "I'm ready."

His steps were soft, nearly nonexistent to her hearing as he walked from the window to the bed. "Lie still. I'm going to cut these off. You'll feel the steel on your back. I won't hurt you."

She closed her eyes and mumbled some of the prayers she learned in the Abbey when she was there. The steel was cold against her flesh. When he was done and nothing covered her back, she shivered. His fingers lightly touched her, traced a few of the deeper welts. The gentleness surprised her. Last night his ministrations where tender also.

He sat back then, "The infection is better. Two more times should do the trick as long as you don't do anything foolish and break open some of the deeper wounds."

"What possible foolish thing could I do?" She knew her sarcasm didn't go unnoticed by him when she heard the low masculine chuckle.

"I hope nothing but where the female mind is concerned, one never knows. You are not to leave the room unless for some strange reason your life is in danger. My two friends will remain outside the house. They prefer the outdoors. You need not worry about an attack on your person. I assure you the Cherokee can be quite civilized as well as peace loving."

"Never thought different," she mumbled, her head resting on the backs of her hands, thinking of some of the things she wanted to do while he was gone. All of them involved searching the trunks in the attic.

"The paste will feel cool, not so much as last night when your back was burning up." He began to spread the paste on her wounded flesh, starting at her shoulders where the cuts were the deepest and slowly working his way down. "I'm going to have to push the sheet down but I promise I won't look too closely."

"I'm resigned." She closed her eyes as he did what he told her.

She had been through far worse than this. Another man's eyes on her buttocks could not possibly be as bad.

"Ten minutes or so we have to leave this on." He stood covering her lightly with the sheet as the paste began to dry.

"Millie could have done this."

"She would have fainted. Known her since I was a boy. She wilts whenever she sees a wound of any sort, even a sliver. No, Millie would not have done well with this task."

"You need to be careful with Dodge when you go into the village. I want to talk with him before you leave. If Blue is looking for us, he will recognize him and drag him back then he would look for the children and me." She didn't want to say anything more. They represented a monetary as well as a public loss for Blue even touching upon his pride. If others thought to escape him, he would have to constantly be on the lookout.

"You don't think I can protect the boy from him?" His question sounded strangely angry.

"It's not that and you ken it. Blue doesn't want to lose face with his cohorts. He lost a female as well as three children. If he discovers Ollie is a girl, he will make sure he doubles his efforts to get us back."

She found herself shaking with the frustration and anger swamping her.

"What do you want to say to the boy?" He began to clean the paste from her back, stroking her. The warm water felt heavenly. She'd never been cherished before that she could remember. The gentle care he was giving her unnerved her, sent her brain spinning. Feeling anything for a man was inconceivable.

"If he sees Blue, he needs to hide. Whatever happens he cannot ride back with you. That would lead the man to your doorstep and us. He wouldn't think anything of killing you to get what he wants."

"So soon, you forget my friends." He stopped for a moment, his hand resting on the small of her back. "So soon you forget. They have ways the English cannot even imagine to torture their enemies."

"For all the things he's done, Blue deserves torture and more. I wouldn't want them to hang for murder though. Stopping Blue from getting what he wants is enough."

"They would not be caught." He pulled the sheet lower and finished washing the paste from her buttocks. He sat back on the chair, looking smugly pleased. "Much better. You should be as good as new tomorrow. Unfortunately, you will have scars."

She sucked in her breath when she felt his knuckles graze her body, feelings like that didn't exist at least not in her experience. Men weren't tender or gentle. They took what they wanted. Another person's feelings be damned.

"Are you going to wrap me up again?"

"Like a Christmas package? No. If you only wear the robe, you should be fine until this evening.

"As I said, one more time should do it. You sleep now. Allow your body to heal. I will talk to Dodge and explain that if he sees this man he's to tell me post-haste then hightail it out of town. I will meet up with him on the road if it takes me longer to finish my business. Does that work for you?"

"I suppose it has to." She tried to reach for the robe with little success. His hands brushed her arms as he brought the covering to her, holding the sleeves so she fit into them. "Thank you." The best she could, she wrapped the robe across her front as she changed to a sitting position.

When she looked up, he was standing in front of her, his feet braced apart, an expression on his face she recognized all too well although he wasn't acting on it. The following seconds were eerily quiet as she held her breath. Thinking this was it. She would have to make excuses to the children and leave tonight.

He didn't act on his thoughts. Instead, he held his hands behind his back and began speaking.

"I will send Dodge to check on you as soon as we return home. Millie has the directive not to let anyone inside. My friends will be asked to guard the front and back doors as a just in case the worst happens."

She pulled the sides of the robe closer, looking down, unable to meet his gaze until she was composed, telling herself he was nothing like the other men in her life. Graham was different. Thank god. How different could he be? He was a man.

"Thank you," she murmured. "Don't let anything happen to him."

"Dodge no longer needs your protection. He has mine." The reminder was gruff, his irritation unmistakable.

Once again, she wasn't going to argue over something that would not reach his ears. He would never give in. Neither would she agree with what the other was saying.

"I see." She didn't want to relinquish control of the children to a man. He wasn't any man, she told herself in an attempt to justify this. In any case, she didn't want to understand even while determining the man saved her life and perhaps the children's as well. Blessed hell, he'd only been in her life for a little over a day.

"Not sure you do. You and the other children are under my protection also."

With a shallow breath and fear drawn from years of servitude under a man's thumb she asked, "What do you want from me?"

He smiled while his eyes darkened to a deep striking color, "Only what you want to give."

"Was that meant to be provocative or are you being purposely obtuse?" Her frustration and anger with him seemed to grow the more innuendos he spouted. "Be candid with me. Surprises are not appreciated."

"No, just the truth between us, Ria. You are going to be the manager and director in this cleanup project, one that I am happily embarking on. Don't think I could do this without a woman's touch. If you ever want to quit, all you need do is say the word."

After hearing his words, she turned inward, wishing she didn't always believe the worst of a person. "May I tutor the children?" She asked knowing she needed his permission; sure she spotted some readers when they were in the attic looking for clothing for the children.

A few seconds before she asked, he was half way to the door. Hearing her question, he stopped, froze for a moment then turned to her. She waited for his answer as she watched him stroke his chin. When he looked up and spoke, "I can't think of a better idea. You are an anomaly to me. How can you be so learned and end up in the gutters of Edinburgh subservient to a man like Blue?" he asked blandly.

She waited, hoped he would continue to exit the room. He didn't. Instead, he crossed his arms over his chest, his gaze pointed directly at her and her fumbling fingers.

"Thank you." She looked down, smoothing the folds of her robe, hoping he would vacate the room.

"Tomorrow we can look for the primers. I believe they are upstairs in the musty old attic where we found the clothing for the children."

"You have primers?" Her unrestrained smile seemed to give him pause.

"Don't even think about looking for them today. With my help we can find their whereabouts much easier tomorrow and you won't risk hurting yourself. If I hear of you rummaging through those trunks, you will..." He rubbed his chin seeming to have no idea what to say to her. "I will not be pleased. There is not one single reason I can think of for you to rush any of this and risk your health."

She listened as he strode away from her door before heading down the steps. When she was sure he was outside her room, she walked to the window. She saw Dodge settle beside him on the wagon, talking animatedly to him, waving his hands. The boy was happy here. In this home, he could grow up to be a good and honest man. He wouldn't have to fear ending up on a prison ship to God knew where.

Graham must have sensed her at the window or noticed a movement, turning to wave at her. She brought her hand up just as he bent close to Dodge's ear, saying something and the boy turned around to wave.

Her breath caught in her throat as she watched the wagon trundle around the corner, leaving her view. Her hand at her chest to ease her ragged breathing, she heard the tiny footsteps approaching. The pair seemed to be just as curious as she was.

"That took long enough." Midget stood beside her, tugging at the robe. "Thought he would never leave."

"Why ever would you think that?" She looked at the two children, loving them more each day.

"Because we have things to do, important things," Ollie said grinning.

"Things we need to keep secret," Midget added, lifting his arms to her.

Despite the pain, she picked the boy up and cuddled him close for a few seconds. At least he was still young enough to crave affection. She set him down.

"We are fortunate, you understand. Graham is a good man. If we're careful today, he won't know we were doing something he asked me not to do." She prayed she wasn't making another grave mistake. Not that she'd been given a choice in her other missteps.

"He didn't hurt you," Ollie said, her voice soft and filled with more knowledge of matters like this than a ten-year-old should have.

"Only when he cleaned the lashes Blue gave me. He had no choice if he was going to save my life."

Ollie leaned into her. Midget tugged on her robe again. He wanted to still be in her arms. Once more, she picked him up, holding him close. They were her children. She would protect them with her life and understood she should be thankful Graham was willing to protect them from the men who wished them harm.

"Would the two of you like to go on an adventure today?"

"The one you talked about yesterday?

"Yes."

~ * ~

Blue paced the dirty room where he expected Ria and the boys to be. He left them locked in for two days. How the devil did they get away? His frustration and anger rose to a fever pitch as he searched the place. He kicked at a stool, sending it flying across the room. It thudded against the wall.

When he came to get them, he expected to hear them begging for food, for his kindness. Needed to hear they would do anything for him. He had plans for the little bitch, big plans. They couldn't be very far. He beat her to an inch of her life. She had no clothing.

He was shaking his head, confused and furious, his mind reeling with different scenarios. Someone must have heard her screams. Someone must have picked the lock, letting them out before helping them. They couldn't be very far. He ran his hands through his hair, swearing, cursing everyone he could think of. He tried to remember who rented the rooms next door. Unable to think, he cursed again.

Blue walked to the stool, placed it right side up. He sat down. She would be his. He would get her back. She would grovel at his feet, begging for the mercy he would never give her. Not after this little trick of hers. Where Ria was concerned there would be no more games.

Evan joined him a grim, determined look on his face. "Well, the little mite got away. What do you plan to do about it?"

Blue studied the man who'd been loyal to him for countless years, remained at his side over the years as their tiny empire grew and flourished. Their band of pickpockets, thieves and whores brought in a tasty living. One that left them both more than satisfied. Now, this was a vendetta. No one escaped his hold. Evan was broad of shoulder with a barrel of chest. His black hair curled around his collar. The eyes he turned on him now were dark, brooding. He too wanted revenge for this injustice done to them coupled with the loss of revenue.

"Go after her. She couldn't have gotten very far away." His heavy thoughts did nothing to alleviate his fury. "She must have had help. We will punish all who gave them aide."

"I'll start by asking the ladies. Some of them have kind hearts. They might have lent assistance. What do you plan when you get her back?" Evan's calm voice held a deep fury.

"Haven't decided. When I first saw her, thought she'd be perfect for the little whorehouse down the block. Now I think I can sell her to the highest bidder. She has a haughty air about her that needs to be broken. I know just the man who can do that."

"Like to do the breakin' myself." Evan chuckled in the back of his throat. "Wouldn't mind puttin' the lady through the paces before you sell her. See what she's made of."

"Maybe I'll let you do that very thing. After I've tried her out."

Chapter Three

The day was slowly growing colder, dark clouds lending the threat of snow to the chill developed in the west. Dodge wrapped his arms around himself, trying unsuccessfully to hide his shivering. Graham cursed softly, taking off his jacket before settling it over the boy's shoulders. He should have foreseen this. Hell, he wasn't used to taking care of children, something he would have to learn quickly if they were all to survive the winter.

"Soon as we get to town, I'm buying you a warm coat, you, Olivia and Midget. Can't live in these times without a warm coat. Boots too, think all of you will need something warm for the feet"

"Thank you, sir. Think we'll see Blue in town?"

"No, no I don't," Graham said thoughtfully. "He's going to look for the four of you in the city first. He'll go to every possible hiding place he can think of, ask everyone who knew you. How long ago did the beating take place?" he asked, trying to refresh his mind and get Dodge to talk to him.

"Nearly two weeks now," then with a slight lift to his shoulders, "Maybe more."

"He wouldn't think to look anywhere but the city. Why did the four of you leave? Wouldn't you have been more comfortable staying where you had your usual haunts?" Graham kept his gaze on the clouds along with the road, thinking about the woman who rescued these children. She didn't have to take them with her. She could have left them with Blue.

"It was Ria's idea. She said we'd be safer. She knew just the place to go, place where we could lie low until Blue got tired of looking for us.

When we got to the old church, she remembered nobody was there. She stopped and said, 'Well hell'.'" Dodge grinned then, looking up at him his large brown eyes shimmering with a tiny bit of laughter. "She curses funny, almost as if she feels guilty about saying the words."

"I'm assuming my home is not the place she directed you to," he said, laughing at Dodge's expression as well as what he told him about her swearing.

"It was an old crumbling church. No one had been there for a long time. Ria said she remembered the minister from when she was living in the abbey. She didn't realize it would be empty."

Graham nodded, his head also recalling the place from his younger days, the man too. "It's just down the road. How long did you stay there?" He pulled a blanket from behind him, wrapping the warmth around Dodge.

"Two nights, until our stomachs seemed to be touching our backbones. Ria said we had to risk leaving. Had to find some other place to hide. This wasn't any place we could stay. Thing is, we would have never gone hungry if we'd remained in the city."

"Blue would have you now."

Graham urged the horses to a faster pace, wishing he could get this errand done and return to the house before the storm hit full force. An uneasy feeling that Ria wasn't resting came to mind. She would do what she pleased. He sensed from the other day, she wanted to go to the attic, to the trunks. If she tried to move any of them, she would open up her back again. Blessed hell.

"Probably," Dodge spoke, clearing his throat.

"Would you have been punished?"

"When he found out I was hiding Ollie from him. He wouldn't have liked that any more than when he discovered Ria was a lady. So yes, Blue would exact most of the punishment on Ria and Ollie though. I would most likely get a stern reprimand."

"Do you have any family, Dodge?" When Graham turned his attention to Dodge, he looked surprised and sheepish, very much a little boy now.

He squinted his eyes together for a moment. "Not that I want to remember. Midget, Ollie and Ria are my family. The only ones I ever want."

He stared hard at Graham for a few seconds, his gaze penetrating all Graham's defenses.

"What about me, Dodge? Since I'm protecting you now, would you want me to be your family too?"

Damn, but he never thought he'd find children in his home and a woman when he set his sights to renovate his inheritance. Seemed he acquired a family overnight.

"Suppose so, sir. By my mind though, you've got to prove yourself. You did fix up Ria. That was a good start. Don't trust anyone. That way I might stay alive."

Graham was nodding, his thoughts turning inward. While he lived with the Cherokee, those words had been his silent mantra as well. He pointed down the road, "Looks like we're almost to the village."

A few minutes later, he pulled up in front of the general store selling the clothing and supplies he needed to buy. Down the street was the tavern, across was a bakery. He wanted to pick up some sweet pastries for the children and Ria as well. He doubted if they had anything like that living in the poverty they spent most if not all of their lives in. Mentally, he ticked off the list of items trying not to forget anything.

He stepped into the store, Dodge by his side. When Mrs. O'Brian, the proprietress, saw him, she rushed over to give him a huge hug. She put her hands on his shoulders before looking him up and down. Graham chuckled at the ardent perusal.

"You're the spittin' image of your da. Would've recognized you anywhere. You back for good?" She stood with her hands on her hips, still surveying him.

"Back for good. Going to fix up the manor. This is Dodge. He's going to need a warm coat. There are two other children living at Runningmeade. Guess one can say they adopted the place a few days ago before I came home. Decided they can stay."

"Don't forget Ria," Dodge piped up.

"Ria," he said her name softly, a touch of awe in his voice he wasn't quite sure where the emotion came from. "Yes, Ria is with the children. She will need three dresses. Don't know her size but we can try to guess. One of the children is a little girl. She will need a couple of dresses also." He was ticking off the list in his mind.

Mrs. O'Brian set about collecting items as Graham read them to her, holding the dresses up for inspection and sizes. They settled on two for Olivia and three for Ria. He didn't want Ria to wear any pants she might haul down from the attic, suspecting she would disobey him and go up there today. He hoped she wouldn't start pushing the heavy trunks around the rooms.

When they finished with the clothing, they moved on to the cleaning supplies; the oils and soaps as well as the cloths that would be needed to make the grand place sparkle. He bought several brooms along with various items for the stable then put in an order for staples since Millie handed him a list before he left. One of Mrs. O'Brian clerks helped load everything in the wagon.

"There ye be. You come back to the village soon." She stood back dusting her hands together, a satisfied expression on her face. "It's only an hour past noon. What else can I do for you? You going to be needing people to clean? A few servants? I'll spread the word. There is a family just outside of town needing work. Good folks. I can vouch for them. Sure both of them will show up tomorrow mornin' if that's what you'll be wantin'."

"Tomorrow morning is perfect. Tell everyone who comes into your store I'm in need of workers if anyone wants a job. Thanks." He tipped his hat and taking Dodge by the hand, they strolled to the tavern where he left the same message with the bartender. They would have to sort out the people when they showed up, if anyone came to work.

"You ready to go home and show off the purchases to the ladies and Midget? Think they'll like the things we bought?"

Dodge was nodding his head. "The dresses for Ollie are nicer than anything she's had before, at least to my recollection. Don't know if she's going to want to wear a dress though. Seems she prefers pants."

"It's because she doesn't know anything different. Once she wears a gown for a few days, she'll like it better than the pants."

Chuckling, Graham tried to reassure himself as much as Dodge.

He wanted Olivia to look like a girl.

"Don't know why you'd say something like that," Dodge muttered. "Who would rather wear a dress than pants? You can't run as fast in a dress. The skirt will trip you up."

"Olivia's a girl. Of course, she'll like a dress better," he said with all the confidence he could muster.

There was an element of truth in Dodge's words he couldn't deny.

They made it halfway before snow began to fall, a howling wind deciding to follow a few minutes later. Graham pulled his coat around his neck, hunkering down while he urged the horse to a faster pace. By the time they pulled the wagon into the stables, they were frozen through to the bone.

He jumped from the wagon before he helped Dodge. "Go on into the house and get warm. Millie will run you a hot bath."

"What about you?" He stood stubbornly beside him not appearing eager to follow his orders. "I'm no colder than you. Been just as cold before and never got a hot bath."

"You want to help unload the wagon?"

Graham was suddenly proud of the boy. He would do well.

"It won't take long with all of us working. That's what we did back in Edinburgh. We all worked and shared so when we got enough between all of us, we could quit for the night."

"Gray Hawk?"

Graham tuned, smiling at the men who approached.

"Red Deer and Runs With The Wind, anything I should know about? Any unwanted intruders?"

Red Deer laughed. The sound was low and deep, reminding him of what he lost. It seemed so long ago now, distant and unreal.

"Your woman didn't stay in the bedroom. She spent quite a bit of time in the attic searching for something." Red Deer looked out the stable doors as if he expected to see her striding through them. "Shamus milked the highland cattle, those huge hairy beasts. They seem friendly enough though."

"Yes, the cattle are docile. I take it you didn't spend all of your time at the back door," he said dryly.

"I did, just heard her opening the window. She leaned on the sill for a few minutes, looking around the yard. Leaned so far, thought she was going to fall out."

"Must have been looking for you," Running With The Wind said with a chuckle that matched Red Deer's. "You never were good at keeping your woman in line. Always let her do exactly what she pleased. Falling out of third floor window would not have been good. You should have locked her in her room to make sure she obeyed."

No, he wasn't, simply because he could never carry out his threats. He didn't threaten Ria. Told her the truth of what would happen if she did anything too strenuous. Perhaps she didn't. He could always hope.

"Ria is not my woman," he said, turning toward the house with the sudden hope of seeing her. "Let's get the wagon unloaded so we can warm up. I've rooms in the house for the two of you if you want."

"For now, the barn will be fine. If we get too cold, we'll come inside."

"I'll bring dinner for you when Millie has it ready." He wished they would take a room in the house. There were more than enough for ten more people. As it was the extra rooms were all sitting empty.

"She fed us lunch," Red Deer said with a smile, rubbing his stomach with gratefulness. "I can appreciate that woman."

"If it gets any colder, you'll need more blankets. I'll leave them in the scullery. You can get the coverings when it's convenient for you."

A half hour later the wagon was unloaded. He and Dodge stepped into the back room, stamping off the snow from their boots. Dodge's were newly purchased in town today. The scent of venison stew wafted through to the scullery. Graham's stomach rumbled. It had not been his intention to forego lunch. He should have taken the time to eat while in the village but he'd been in a hurry to get back, in a hurry to see if Ria did as he strongly suggested.

Millie waltzed into the back room where they were hanging their coats. All the boxes were stacked, taking up most of the space.

"I see you've brought a lot of things back with you. Is anyone going to come tomorrow to start cleaning the house?" she asked grinning before she looked at the boxes. "Where do we start?"

Graham laughed, "With hot baths along with a hearty meal. We didn't eat anything at the noon hour so as soon as that stew we're smelling is done, we need to have two big plates filled along with some of that freshly baked bread I see sitting on the counter."

"I've hot water on the stove. You two go up to your rooms. I'll have the water brought to you. Stew should be finished by the time you warm up."

"Bless you," Graham said thinking of soaking for as long as the water stayed hot.

He had not expected the weather to turn nasty as quickly as it did.

No more than a few minutes passed before his tub was being filled. He stripped. Just as expected when he slipped into the water, it was hot and soothing. He closed his eyes. Reflections of the children along with everything they'd been through rushed through his brain. He tried to keep from thinking about Ria. There was so much she wasn't telling him. Finally, he felt warmed all the way through to his core. He stood, water sluicing from him and picked up the large towel Millie sent up. Dressing quickly, he headed downstairs.

Red Deer said he'd seen Ria on the third floor. He hoped she didn't undo the progress made with her back. Tonight should be the last time she would need the poultice. If any of the wounds broke open, he would have to start from the beginning with the warm salted water.

Smiling to himself, she did have a beautiful back minus the lashes. Perhaps his opinions where they concerned her should be reined in to something more acceptable. She wasn't someone who would fill his nights with pleasure. He needed to consider her, needed to look at her with something different than the way Blue treated her.

"Here, I prepared a tray for you and Ria. The children will probably join you. They've all been fed except for Dodge. I'm going to have him eat down here with your friends. Red Deer told me to call him Charles and Running With The Wind thought Harold would be a fine name."

"Red—Charles likes your cooking." He watched as her face warmed to a nice red hue.

"Lordy? He said that?" Her hands were on her cheeks as she looked out the door in an effort to see the man.

"Aye, also said that he could get used to it." Graham laughed, picking up the tray and heading upstairs. He was eager to see Ria, impatient to talk over his purchases then he wanted to know what she'd done while he and Dodge were gone.

"Send Dodge down when you see him. You and Ria need a few minutes of privacy I would think."

Millie must know what Ria did this morning. Everyone knew. He wondered if she meant to keep it a secret. When he reached the top of the steps, he poked his head into Dodge's room telling him where he'd find his dinner when he was ready.

"We want to eat with you," Midget and Ollie chimed in.

"Millie tells me the two of you have eaten. If you're looking for company, join Dodge downstairs.

They took off, legs flying. He hoped neither would trip on their way down the stairs. A few seconds later, he stepped into Ria's room. Her back was turned away from him. She was gazing out the window. Thoughts of her on the third floor leaning far enough out Charles thought she might fall sent a small wave of anger to his gut. Surely a gown woman would understand how far she could test gravity.

Graham set the tray on the round table in the bedroom. She turned, her hand on her chest, eyes wide. She drew in a shaky breath.

"If I frightened you, I didn't mean to." He pulled up a second chair and gestured for her to sit. "Hungry?"

"Not so much." She graced him with a small smile.

"You need to eat something," he told her, lifting the lids and smelling the delicious aroma. "It's a long time until breakfast. Look, Millie gave us some of her lemon seed cakes."

She nodded her agreement. He pulled out a chair for her. She sat down, placing a napkin on her lap. She poured two cups of tea, adding sugar to hers as well as a bit of milk. He sat down across from her, his fingers winding into the handle of the teacup while he worried over what to say.

"Are you going to yell at me?" She peered at him over the rim of her cup as it was poised at eye level.

"Do you think I should?"

"No." Her voice sounded cautious. "However, I wouldn't be surprised if you did.

"You should drink the tea. I'm going to my room for brandy."

He rose, walking away. He wished she wouldn't look at him as she did. With the glint in her eyes, she accused him of being a monster. It didn't matter to him what she did this morning, other than he would have liked her to take better care of herself.

It took him a few minutes to find the brandy and return to the room. He held the bottle up, "Would you like some."

Declining, she shook her head, "No."

"I bought three dresses for you. When the weather improves, you will have to come with me. At that time, I can purchase you shoes. You will need winter boots. I've a receipt here for the price of the dresses. As you asked, I will take the money from your wages." He pulled paper from his pocket, sliding it across the table to her. "Look it over."

He didn't think he'd ever seen her eyes so blue or so wide. She was hiding behind her teacup, he realized, finding the thought amusing.

"Thank you."

"You will want to see if they fit."

She was looking around the room. "Where are they? I will pay for the children's things too. When I brought them here and Millie let us hide, I never intended for you to pay for new clothing. I was thankful for a roof over our heads and food to eat."

"Of course not. You won't pay for the children's things. I wasn't here at the time. No one had any idea that I would be arriving. The purchases are still downstairs. My friends are helping Millie unpack the supplies. Someone will be along with the items when they find them. We did purchase a wagon full of things. It will take a bit of time."

He placed a bowl of stew in front of her then one for him. Before he said anything to her, he needed to eat. With the spoon she held, she pushed the food around in the bowl, staring at it before turning her attention to him. "I'd really like to talk about what's on your mind."

"At the moment, this delicious bowl of stew is on my mind." He grinned at her before tearing off a chunk of bread. "I suppose we can talk as well as eat. How was your day?"

Her eyes widened even farther. She left the spoon in the bowl, settling her hands in her lap. "How was yours?"

"Mine? Uneventful, cold, at the same time gratifying to discover how much Dodge is taking to me, to this new home for him. Blue was never spotted. However, I'm sure we will see him eventually. When he does show his face, we need to have it figured out how best to keep him from taking the children as well as you." He paused. "Really, Ria, you should eat before it gets cold."

It seemed she tried to. It seemed to Graham more of the food was pushed around than made it through her lips. "I went upstairs with Midget and Ollie." She set the spoon beside the bowl, her eyes wide with apprehension.

He pointed to her. After swallowing, "You hurt yourself. That was not very smart of you." He didn't know how to ease this unwarranted fear she had of him.

"Not much," she sighed softly.

He was sure she knew she was lying to him. "Your robe has stuck to your back with the dried blood. That wasn't well done of you. How many trunks did you push out of the way so you could find more treasure?"

~ * ~

"I would not have done it if I'd known this would happen." She told him with a note of defiance in her voice. "The children were curious as was I. None of us has ever seen an attic full of things that were once cherished."

"You are not used to orders."

Ria kept her hesitant smile behind her lips. Until recently, obeying orders had been her life. "If I recall, you suggested. Midget and Ollie wanted to explore. I was bored nearly to tears, could think of nothing worse than sitting for hours on end in this room."

"You could have visited with Millie."

"I wouldn't have known what to say."

One perfectly shaped eyebrow arched upward. "More poultice. More lying on your stomach naked in front of me? You like that choice better?"

His questions set her on edge, her nerves stretched dangerously close to the breaking point. "For most of my life I have only known orders, first in the abbey then..." She swallowed looking away, unwilling to illustrate that horrible part of her life.

"Then? Someday I would appreciate your explaining what comes after then. I've lost track of how many times you stopped there."

"What comes after then is shame and embarrassment, humiliation as well as a deep loathing for that part of my life. I did not choose it or accept it. It was thrust upon me."

He finished the last bite of food before wiping the bowl clean with a chunk of Millie's fresh baked bread.

Graham sat back; his eyes narrowed at her. "I see."

He didn't. Could not possibly understand her life after the abbey. He wanted her to tell him, trust him. Clarifying that part of her past was not something she could do. At least not right now. "Ah there are the packages."

Dodge appearing in the doorway was a nice diversion, a respite from his simple questions that she needed desperately.

"Good, shall we go through them? It was nice of Mrs. O'Brian to label everything. Let's look at the children's new clothing first. The boys did not need much so warm boots and coats were the extent of what I bought them for now. They cannot live on hand-me-downs for the rest of their lives. These will do until there is more time to shop. Can you sew?"

"No, sewing was never a duty I was ordered to perform."

"Very well, perhaps if you are here long enough, Millie can teach you."

Ria grimaced at what he implied before she unwrapped both of Ollie's dresses. "These are nice. Do you like them?" She turned to the little girl, who eyes seemed to be crossing.

"Don't want to wear dresses. I like the pants we found this morning in the attic." She twirled around showing them off. "Do you like them, Sir Graham?"

"Why don't the two of us go into the other room and try one of the gowns on and see what you think. You should keep an open mind where the gowns are concerned. Graham went to a great deal of trouble to pick these out just for you. We should show our appreciation," Ria said softly, understanding that putting Ollie in a dress was not going to be an easy task.

With her hand on Ollie's shoulder, they brought the two packages into Ollie's room. One was a dark blue that would bring out the color of the little girl's eyes and the other a soft pink, a color most little girls loved. Each had lace edging and a ruffle along the bottom. The garments were similar in design, simple and serviceable.

"I like the pink one." Ollie did smile then. It seemed she was beginning to change her opinion.

"It's much like Christmas today," Ria said, helping her into the dress along with the fasteners.

She moved back, remembering the stark Christmases at the abbey while wishing she could have ones like the parish children's. "You're very pretty. When your hair grows, I can fix it. You'll be the prettiest girl in this part of Scotland. Go, see for yourself," she pointed to a mirror.

"It is nice." She looked at herself from different angels. "Should I show Sir Graham and Dodge? Do you think Dodge will like it?"

"Yes, and from what Graham has told me, Dodge was an integral part in selecting both dresses, the boots as well."

"You'll come with me."

"Of course, sweetheart."

When they walked into the room, Ollie ran to Dodge then Graham giving them each a big hug. "Thank you."

"You're pleased," Graham said, watching with a hint of amusement in his expression. When he looked at her it was as if to say see, I was right. What little girl doesn't love a new dress?

Ria turned to Midget, "These are new boots and this is your coat."

Midget nodded seeming to be at a loss for words. "He likes them," Dodge said. He thanked Master Graham for them. "We're all going to work, do chores to help pay for them."

"I agreed to that," Graham said, his voice gruff, filled with emotion, surprising Ria.

"It will give them a sense of accomplishment. They've never worked just stolen," she said. "It is good of you to give them honest tasks."

"Back to you." His fingers formed a steeple as the tips touched his chin. He appeared to be thinking, trying to make a decision about her. "Why did you do it?"

"Do what?"

She blinked a few times understanding exactly what he was asking her. He wanted her to answer. She wanted to put it off as long as she could. The punishment would be the same as all the other times. She didn't know if she could bear it, the pain, humiliation.

"You know what I'm talking about. Why?"

"I thought I told you."

She hadn't been exact. Boredom wasn't a good reason for disobeying. Neither was curiosity. She inhaled a deep ragged breath, closing her eyes, tensing as she realized he stood over her, his large hand on her arm.

This is what came after the then...

"You should have just looked. Should have opened the lids and peeked inside. There was no reason, not even curiosity to push yourself this far. How many trunks did you move so you could get to the next one then the next?"

He led her to the bed. She could not cease the shaking taking over her body. If it was going to be anyone, she supposed he was better than the last man.

"I know." She didn't know what she knew. Her brain filled with cobwebs along with stark terror. She prayed this morning her life here would not come to this.

"You broke open some of the wounds. The blood has dried. Your robe is stuck to your flesh. I had not thought to do this again."

"Here you are, sir." Dodge's voice was loud and clear in the fog of her brain. Groping her way from the self-inflicted daze, she was beginning to understand she was wrong about what he wanted.

"As you did last night, Dodge, I need you to set the warm water on the table. I don't want to try and pull the fabric from her back. We'll soak it off. Now, Ria, would you please lie down on your stomach so I can undo the damage you did to yourself."

She was nodding, in any case not understanding the tenor of his words. In a stupor she did as he bade, incapable of resisting, in any case knowing defiance would lead to a beating.

Ria felt the warm cloth he set on her back. She was semi aware what he did was not what she expected. He set another cloth on her back, his hands falling at his sides.

He leaned back in the wing chair, stretching out his legs, his eyes closed.

"W-what are you doing?"

She tried to turn so she could see his face. Needed to understand what he expected from her so she could comply do all his wishes.

"Same as last night. I have to soak the gown off before I can spread the poultice on your back." He sat up, leaned closer, "Remember, we spoke of one last paste tonight and the infection, while it wouldn't be gone, it would not require more attention from me. I can't promise that now. Not after all the fun you had with the children this morning."

She was beside herself, realizing this was not happening the way she expected. Her breath exhaled with a small quiver.

"Dodge, go downstairs and have Millie make up the potion for her."

"Yes, sir." She heard Dodge's footsteps leave the room then down the stairs. He must have jumped the last few steps. She heard the silence before the thud of him landing.

"Now, I don't know why you were shaking a few minutes ago. What did you think I was going to do? No, I'm not sure I want to know. I'll bet you don't want to tell me."

He leaned close to her. She felt the whisper of his words across her cheek. "I believe it must have something to do with..." he paused. She heard his roughly drawn breath, "Then..."

He guessed far too much about her. Privacy was something she needed but in time she would make a mistake, misunderstand what he asked of her. She would give herself away. Her instincts needed to be finely tuned. She didn't want to make a blunder.

Thankfully Ollie had grown restless. "Sir Graham, do you like this other dress on me?"

Ria smiled, seeing the precious little girl twirling in circles in her imagination. She heard her sit on the floor.

"It's almost as beautiful as you, Olivia," he said softly. "Now you need to go back to your room and play with Midget. I'm going to have to put more of the poultice on Ria."

"Why can't I watch?" she asked walking closer.

"Because watching is not for little girls."

"You let Dodge help."

"He will join you and Midget as soon as he brings me the paste. You can wait here until he comes up from the kitchen."

"Ria was afraid you'd be angry with her. She doesn't want men to be mad at her. We found some toys, boats and horses. There weren't any dolls though." Ollie blinked a few times. She spied the lemon cakes. Without asking she grabbed one then darted out of the room

"What did she do?" Ria's voice was a soft murmur. "You laughed."

"She stole a lemon seed cake from the tray. It might be harder than I expected to break the children of that habit."

"Given time, she will learn to ask for things. She doesn't know what it's like to have food whenever she wants it. Is that Dodge?"

"Yes." He took the bowl from the boy. Then, "You may go now. Keep them from the room. The three of you should go to bed soon. Olivia needs to try and sleep in her room."

"Yes, sir."

Quickly, his footsteps faded away. The door to a room down the hall closed. There it was, they were alone again. She made a fool out of herself a few minutes ago. He noticed but it didn't seem he was going to pursue the conversation. Graham wasn't like her first keeper.

"Ria..."

She felt him remove the cloth. He slowly lifted the fabric of the robe from her back. She gasped suddenly when he tugged too hard.

"I'm sorry," he told her. "I'd say this hurts me more than it does you but I know I'd be wrong."

"I'm fine."

"There." He sat back for a second before lowering the robe once more.

She felt him touch her back in a few places. Nothing hurt. She supposed that was a good thing.

"What is it?" She tried not to laugh. He was making strange noises as he examined her.

"Tonight will be the last time. The infection is getting better. It won't be too many more days before it is gone all together. Just to make sure, I'm going to put the paste on you one more time. This evening, you should be able to lie in any position you'd like. It still might be best if you try to sleep on your stomach."

"I'm really tired of this," she told him on a ragged breath as he smoothed the paste across her back.

"What did you find upstairs?"

Ria closed her eyes. "Besides toys for the children? Clothes for Ollie, pants and shirts. She does like the dresses so we'll see. If she's doing chores, she's going to want to do the same ones as the boys. The pants might come in handy."

"Olivia will be given chores suitable for a little girl. There are things she will need to learn. I've talked to Millie. She is more than happy to give her lessons."

She stiffened, feeling suddenly inadequate even though she knew she was. Her education at the abbey had been based solely on book learning. "What kind of lessons?"

He stopped for a few seconds. She supposed he was thinking. That brought a smile to her lips as she tried to relax and enjoy the conversation.

"Sewing and cooking I would guess. What else should a woman need to know how to do?"

She did laugh then. "How would I know? Ollie can pick a pocket. Have you checked for your handkerchiefs lately? A coin purse rarely gives her any trouble. She is so small she can weave in and out of the crowds. She will be gone way before the gent notices anything has left his possession. The only thing I know..." Once more she caught herself on the verge of telling him.

He ignored her near slip of the tongue. "Would you like a bath after I wash this off? I'll bring you another one of my dressing gowns. This one is too wet to wear this evening. I never thought to buy you a nightdress."

"That's fine. A bath would be nice. We got dusty in the attic. I'll sleep in the robe just as I did last night."

He finished wiping the paste off then sat back. "I'll order you a bath. After that I'll find another robe you can wear. You will freeze if you try to wear this one."

After she heard him leave the room, she pulled the damp robe on, slipping it over her arms. At this rate, he wouldn't have a clean robe to wear. She didn't know whether to laugh or cry. Men in her life had never been nice or the least bit gentlemanly. He was so fine, handsome, caring. She might be willing to do those things with him if he asked, even if he didn't. Men always liked what was forced on her. It might not be too bad. He might not even hurt her.

"Ria, you've a muddled head for brains. You almost made a fool of yourself a few minutes ago. He didn't want anything to do with you," she murmured, talking to herself.

She was sitting on the bed, staring at the door when the bath water was brought in. From her vantage point, she could see the steam rising from the tub. It would feel good. She was surprised he didn't want to talk afterward. He still needed to bring her the dry robe.

Once in the tub, she closed her eyes, soaking up the warmth and wondering what tomorrow would bring. She'd not had a chance to open the packages he brought her yet. Had not tried on the dresses to see if they would fit. He did give her the bill for the clothing. Tomorrow would be a busy day.

Ria knew the instant when he walked through the door. Understood he would do what he wanted, go where he pleased. She sunk lower into the soapy water, waiting for him to appear.

It was Millie who stood in front of her with a huge bath sheet and

Graham's robe. "Here you are, dear. Graham is in the sitting room. He wanted me to tell you the two of you need to speak."

With a heavy sigh, "I expected as much." Just didn't expect him to be so gracious. Courteousness was not something she was used to experiencing.

Ria slipped the robe over shoulders before tying the sash. The fabric hung around her body. At least the dressing gown covered her to her toes. Tonight, with Graham, she felt more vulnerable than before. Last night she experienced so much pain she wanted to scream. She didn't have time to think of anything except herself even though she tried to also think of the children. Last night she had to trust him explicitly. Tonight, she needed to be wary.

He was a man after all.

When she stepped into the room, he sat in one of the wing chairs. He pulled the one by the bed next to the other one, facing the fire, which crackled and popped. He handed her a glass of wine, the rest of the bottle sitting on the table.

"Wine?" she asked, sitting down before arranging the dressing gown, making sure she was covered. She rarely had wine, only when the gentleman she serviced insisted.

"What did you expect?"

Silence stretched between them as he watched her closely. "I don't know," she answered truthfully.

His hair was disheveled. She thought possibly from running his bronzed hands through it. His legs were long and heavily muscled, his chest broad. He had long slim fingers, which were now in a steeple beneath his chin.

"You are thinking, milord." She was looking at him closely. He didn't give any of his thoughts away, his expression bland.

"I'm trying to decide how to proceed tomorrow morning. We must be up at the crack of dawn. So as soon as we are finished here, you need to go to bed. I will check on the children just to make sure Ollie is in her proper room. She is ten you say, almost eleven. Dodge will be a young man soon with needs. We cannot let them continue in this vein of sleeping together."

"We could let them get settled and feeling secure before we deprive them of what they've known for many years. I thought we agreed on that earlier. Did I misunderstand?"

"You didn't misconstrue anything. I do agree with you. Now, as for the morning do you have a plan?"

"Me?" She nearly choked on her wine sputtering then trying to wipe the extra drops around her lips with her hand.

"You said you would direct them in the cleaning." He pointed out her earlier words to her.

"Yes, yes, I did. I suppose I will have to do that. Do you think there will be anyone here tomorrow to clean? Otherwise, we will have to do it all ourselves." The chores were sure to keep them busy for at least two months.

"We should be ready by six o'clock to speak with anyone who stops by. Mrs. O'Brian told me there was a nice couple who were down on their luck who might show up."

"Do you think you should hire some of these hoards of people to work here?" She laughed, realizing they would probably only have this nice couple. If they were lucky, a handful of villagers would come seeking employment. Hoards was just too funny a word.

"More wine?" he asked, holding up the bottle. "Perhaps I should put up a notice in some of the nearby villages as well.

"NO, I would not like to be sick in the morning when we initiate the cleaning of the place."

~ * ~

Blue stood in the library, waiting an audience with the earl of Rushaven. He supplied women to this one for a very sizable finder's fee. The plan when he first saw the woman, he thought, was to hand her over to the earl. Since then, he discovered her name was Ria. Several of the whores on the street knew her to be a woman, declining to inform him. He immediately had them soundly beaten. Now, Ria disappeared. He would have to find the female soon.

The room was bright, windows at the far end stretched from

ceiling to near the floor with a dark red Aubusson carpet. In front of the fireplace were two brocaded wing chairs. Dark red drapes were open on either side of the windows. Volumes of books lined one wall. The room was impressive.

He didn't like to be kept waiting. When the clock chimed two hours past his appointment, Blue thought to leave. While the finder's fee for this woman was impressive, he wasn't about to wait around just because this man bore a title. Other than the title, the earl was no different from any other man who kept women to sell.

"Thank you for waiting," William walked in, hand extended in greeting. "I hope it has not been too tedious for you. My apologies, I was involved in a meeting with several of my colleagues. The talks drew on forever even though I made numerous pleas to excuse myself."

"Not a problem."

Not as if I don't have pressing engagements myself. Blue prided himself in his ability to deal with noblemen even though he detested them for what they had and he did not.

Two servants followed the earl, now waiting for directions.

"Set the tray on the table. Brandy?" he asked Blue as he held up the bottle for inspection.

"Wouldn't mind a glass," Blue said, sitting down in one of the chairs at William's direction.

They sat in silence for several seconds. Blue heard each ticking of the clock. He decided to enjoy the brandy before he spoke of the girl. When he did speak, the meeting was sure to take a nasty turn.

"You say you have a young lady perfect for me." William sat back, his attention on the fireplace.

"Had, she ran away but I'll find her."

Blue would beat her again when he found her. She needed to understand she would be better off if she did as he wished. He had no time for disobedience.

"You lost her. Why are you here?"

Blue recognized the anger in the man's voice. He didn't care. Anger wouldn't hurt him. "I'll find the chit."

He would too. No one got away from him, at least not for very long. Problem was he was going to have to get more creative. She wasn't in any of the normal haunts, even some that weren't so normal. He knew he would eventually have to expand the search to outlying areas.

"You can come back when you do. I've not found a suitable woman since Maria left me. Don't know how she got away. Had the doors bolted closed since the first time she ran." The earl downed his drink then poured himself another.

"Not many places in Edinburgh a lassie can hide without any coin. She can steal or whore, that's about it," Blue mused blandly.

"Did you think to look outside the city? Check out some of the villages?"

"Evan's doing that as we speak. Going to join him as soon as I'm done here." Blue finished off the brandy, rising to go. "Startin' south of Edinburgh."

"Wait." William held out a hand to stop him from leaving. "Do you have anyone else in the interim? I do need another girl. A red-head would be nice."

Blue stroked his chin, thinking, not wanting to give up on income. One of the ladies who harbored Ria's secret would do just fine. She was young, probably not more than sixteen or seventeen, pretty.

"I do but she's not well trained. Speaks her mind and thinks she's the queen. You might have to enforce some rules before you can enjoy her. Her hair is blondish-red. Might do for you."

"Just the way I like my ladies. Send her. Go home. Make sure I have her tonight. I've the perfect gentleman for her."

Chapter Four

Graham waited in the breakfast room for Ria. Millie had a full platter of eggs and bacon waiting for them along with a tray of fried potatoes as well as bread baked fresh just this morning. She brewed a pot of tea. He noticed a jug of milk was set on the table ready for the children. When he passed by Ria's room on the way downstairs, he peeked in to make sure she was up. He heard her humming in the dressing room.

"Good morning."

Ria walked in with a smile on her face, sitting across from him. He heaped a plate full of food for her before pouring her a cup of tea. "Are any of the hoards of people here yet?"

"Not even one hoard," he said watching her.

Her hair was pulled back pinned tightly away from her face, her eyes glimmering a beautiful blue green. She wore one of the dresses he bought for her, the bodice a bit large for her. Otherwise, the gown fit fine. Perhaps Millie could fix the gowns to her proportions.

"It's still early. As soon as we're finished with breakfast, we can get out the cleaning supplies. My this looks good." She picked up a piece of bacon and took a bite.

"Where do you plan to begin?" he asked leaning back, relaxing. She was smiling. He found he liked the way the grin looked on her face, made her eyes sparkle.

"The marble I noticed needs a good scrubbing as well as the bannisters; scouring and waxing until they shine. All the floors except for the kitchen need a decent cleaning. Do you think we can keep any of these people on as servants? If you plan on staying here, you are going to need help." Animatedly, she waved her fork in the air.

He thought for a while. "We'll see how it goes. Don't want to hire someone just because they showed up."

"What can I do?" Dodge surprised them bounding into the room, full of more energy than anyone ought to have especially at this time in the morning.

"Sit down and eat," Ria said. "When you've finished your breakfast, you can start sweeping. Where are the others?"

"They'll be down in a minute. Ollie couldn't decide what dress to wear. She's never had anything to choose from," Dodge said a devilish grin on his little-boy's face.

"I see that Graham bought two brooms. You and Ollie can sweep all the rooms. See if you can do them all today."

"Isn't that women's work?" Dodge asked grudgingly. "Don't want to do women's work."

Graham couldn't help the chuckle. "Today there is no such thing as men's or women's work. Our mission is to get the manor house ready to live in. You're right though. In normal times a woman would probably do most of the sweeping. Don't complain too much. Ria could have asked you to get down on your hands and knees to scrub the marble."

Dodge looked to Ria seeing if he spoke the truth. She nodded agreeing with Graham. "What about Charles and Harry? Are they going to help?"

"Millie sent them hunting. Doubt if they would sweep or scrub. Not a chore they've ever had presented to them."

"Why can't I go with them? They can teach me how to hunt. Rather do a man's work."

"Today you are going to sweep as Ria asked. If you do a good job, I'll ask my friends to teach you everything they know about hunting. They might even teach you how to shoot with a bow and arrow." A shadow passed across the window. He looked up. "Ah, it seems we might have a worker or two."

Graham stood, quickly striding to the servants' entrance to greet the man and the woman.

The man helped his wife from the wagon before walking to Graham with an outstretched hand. "Good morning. We came to work if you'll have us. I'm Bernard and this is my wife, Annie."

"Come in. We've lots to do here to get the manor up and running. If you do a good job, we'll hire you permanently."

Graham made the introductions naming Ria as a cousin, the children as hers. Ria put them to work, the children as well, sweeping up dust until he sneezed. Told them he would bring in wood for the fire. Hell, he should have told Ria he needed to see to the horses and gone for a ride.

Three more women showed up around ten thirty. Ria put them to work, polishing the banisters along with the table in the dining room. The manor was humming with activity. He wanted to escape. Charles with Harry beside him walked into the yard with a deer slung over his shoulder.

He joined them, helping them hang the deer from a rafter in the barn.

"Your woman behave herself last night?" Charles laughed. "You didn't need to give her a lecture about overexerting herself, did you?"

"Ria is not my woman."

She could be though. When he left the house this morning, she wore an endearing smudge of dirt on her cheeks. Her fingers had turned a dull grey from all the dust and grime. She smiled at him. He wanted her then. Thought a kiss right at that moment would have been nice. When he left the house for the stables, she laughed calling him a coward. She knew he didn't want to be in the house until it was finished.

"She will be," Harry said, sitting down on the floor. He'd picked up a piece of wood, carving it as they talked.

"What makes you think that?" Graham wasn't sure what to think. The two of them had barely seen him with her.

Charles shrugged, placing his foot on a stool. "The way you talk about her. Not hard to guess you care more than you're willing to admit. The way you keep looking toward the house so you can get a glimpse of her. Those are only two of the things I've noticed."

"She was hurt. In my place, you would have acted the same." He found he didn't like having to defend himself quite this much. He wondered where Ria was now.

"Think I'll go see what's happening in the house."

He'd been gone all morning, as well as most of the afternoon. In the kitchen, he found a plate warming for him. Cornbread and chicken dumplings were piled high on his plate. Millie left a pot of tea, which was still warm.

He had finished half the plate when Ria waltzed into the room, covered it seemed from head to toes in dirt and filth. She flashed him a smile. "Thought you were directing the cleaning."

"That's what I thought too. Guess I got carried away when we lowered a chandelier to clean the glass pieces. I spent the entire day working on it. Now it sparkles when the sun hits it casting prisms on the ground. Unfortunately, most of the dirt from fixture ended up on me."

"The chandelier is clean. How is the rest of the house?"

"Coming along nicely. We should hire Annie and Bernard. They work hard and they live down the road about a mile. After I talked to them, they were amenable to working but they want to stay at their home."

"Don't have a problem with that as long as they get to work on time."

"They are committed and grateful for the chance to put food on the table. Two older children, a boy and a girl are at home, old enough to be left alone all day but not old enough to work. I was wondering if along with the children, I could school them. The parents would have to be agreeable."

"They could bring them to work each day, a wonderful solution to their problem. The children will have to be well behaved though." He thought about his newly found three children running around, creating havoc then smiled. He thought about two more or possibly more than that joining his. He cringed. While he always wanted children someday, a ready-made family would certainly tax his patience along with his limited experience.

Ria tossed him a suspicious look, her eyes narrowing as if she read his mind. "It will not be all that bad. You will see."

"I plan on making myself useful outside until I can gain the scope of the goings on here. I can take Dodge with me. Did they say if their children were boys or girls?"

She was laughing at him, "You wipe that sour expression off your face. It might freeze there permanently. You weren't listening. Don't suppose I should repeat myself until you are."

"That sounds distinctly like something a mother would say." He stopped with the rest of his thoughts when he saw a look of dismay cross her face. "I'm sorry." He set a hand on hers.

"Don't be. I think I can remember my mother telling me something like that. She was always spouting things, little sayings so I would learn how to behave. I don't remember much about her. What I remember most is that I thought of her as the most beautiful woman I'd ever seen."

"Did you tell the family they were hired?"

"No, I didn't feel I had the authority. It's something you should address since this is your house. If you recall, I work for you."

He had not thought of it that way. She was only paying for the dresses he purchased for her, nothing more. When he looked at her now, her lips were pressed together in a thin line. He wanted to change that, knew the fastest way. His forthcoming sigh was long and deep.

"I'll talk to them. We'll see what can be worked out."

"Thank you. I'm exhausted and would like to retire. Can I assume we'll start again at the crack of dawn?"

"Crack of dawn? Bite your tongue. Guess we'll have to be up." he murmured, wondering where his bachelor life disappeared. "You going to bed?

"I'm going to take a long hot bath. Washing all this muck from my person is first and foremost in the front of my mind."

"How is your back?"

"It doesn't hurt at all." She smiled at him with a quick tilt to her head. "I'm not lying. If you look at my back you will see there is no blood. All I did was wrestle with the chandelier."

"You are sure? You cannot see your back."

She blanched, turning her back to him. "You can look if you like."

"I believe I will." He did run his hand across her back, feeling a sudden urge to stroke other parts of her. Before he did something he'd regret, he dropped his hand. "Appears you are mending nicely. Are you going to bed afterwards?"

"No, I'm going to see to the children then I'd like to read. I found a book in your library that seems interesting."

"I will be up later with a bottle of wine. I do want to take a closer look at the wounds. Perhaps we can talk further about today."

He watched her leave the room, heard her steps as she made her way up the steps then to the children's rooms. She would give them each a hug before putting them to bed. He wanted to get to the bottom of her lies by omission. Needed to find out what came after that single word 'then'. Eventually, she would tell him. He wouldn't push for the knowledge. It was enough she understood she could tell him when she wanted.

He selected a bottle of wine before heading up the steps to his room. Flames crackled merrily in the fireplace. Sitting in the chair by the fire, he closed his eyes. He remembered his wife, her long black hair caught by a breeze, Red Deer's, Charles' little sister. For months they'd been inseparable. He didn't know if he ever loved her. Hell, he didn't know if there was such a thing as love. He cared about her, mourned for her and his child when they died even though she ran off taking his son with her. He earned the tribes trust and admiration when he successfully ran the gauntlet. If not, he'd probably still be a slave of the Cherokee.

When she died along with his son, there was nothing for him with the Cherokee. He left with the promise to Red Deer to come find him if he wanted to go to Scotland. Red Deer showed up two weeks later with Runs With The Wind beside him, saying they wanted to see what was on the other side of the great ocean. That pleased him. For the time he lived in the Cherokee camp they all became close friends.

The water for his bath arrived. He bathed quickly, eager to see Ria, to get a new prospective on the day's accomplishments. Bloody eyes, he just wanted to see her. Dressing causally in a clean pair of doeskins and a white shirt he strode down the hallway to her room.

As she told him, she was reading by the fireplace. "You're going to strain your eyes. It's too dark."

She looked up with a smile on her face, pushing a few wayward strands of silver hair from her face. "I really didn't expect you to come."

"I said I would." He opened the bottle of wine then poured them both a glass. "I wanted to see to your back one last time."

"I told you I'm fine." Her voice was soft, silky, seductive. She tilted her head slightly, "So, I'm your cousin. What is my last name?"

It seemed she was settling in, making herself at home. "Do you remember your last name or anything else about your life before the abbey? Did you make up the name Ashton?" He sat down across from her, handing her the wine.

She looked at the dark liquid for a moment, swirling the contents, seeming mesmerized by the movement. Her eyes closed. She was nodding, rocking her upper body. "I remember."

He didn't say anything, concentrating on her movements. For some reason he was sure she didn't want to remember. She would tell him in time. As for now she seemed to be immersed in dark memories. He thought of the children and wondered if they had any idea about their names. Dodge and Olivia perhaps but he doubted if Midget had any idea. Maybe none of them had last names.

They both stared into the fire as time seemed to pass slowly. Shadows danced on the hearth, lights flickering from the dancing flames. When he looked at her again, sadness seemed to encompass her. She'd set the wine glass down. Her arms were wrapped around her now.

"I didn't mean to bring back bad memories better left in the past."

It hurt him to watch her, to understand the sorrow swamping her. He wanted to know so he could ease the pain.

A single tear slipped down her cheek. She ignored it, letting the drop fall onto her shoulder before looking away for a moment. "My mother had the most beautiful hair. In the sunlight the strands were different colors of blond, sometimes it almost looked white." She ran her fingers through her short-cropped hair. "Ashton. I made up the last name of Ashton for lack of anything better."

"Ashton," he repeated, thinking of all the people he knew in this part of Scotland and trying to come up with a family. In any case, if she made it up, there would be no reason to search. "You ken none of them are left alive."

"That's what they told me at the abbey. She was sweet. She loved to play with me. When I was little, my father would toss me in the air and tickle me." She fell silent again, her lashes lowered.

"You should drink your wine."

He had no idea what to say to her, had never meant to dredge up memories that would make her cry, mourn for a lost life she barely recalled. If her parents lived, she would not be here with him, would have never met the children. She would not have been beaten to an inch of her life.

"They died the same day," she went on to say, looking at him with a blank expression on her pale face. "My mother first, my father a few hours later. They were murdered, or so I was told."

Her words caught in the back of his throat. "Murdered?"

She was nodding her head then shaking it. "The magistrate was there, investigated. At least he said he did. Could find nothing. I was taken to the abbey since there was no other family who would care for me."

"How old were you?" He was having a damn difficult time listening to her story. Moisture pooled in his eyes. His gut churned. He drew in a shaky breath hoping to stop the liquid tears hovering in his eyes.

"I was six, younger than Ollie is now, younger than I should have been. The abbey was not a good place. It was stark, cold to the very marrow of a person's bones. The nuns were mostly silent, disapproving of me. I was always afraid, more so as I grew older. I always displeased them."

He tried to piece together the information he gave her. "How old are you now?"

A soft sigh escaped her lips. She tilted her face upward. "I'm twenty now. How old are you?"

He kept his laughter behind his teeth, reminding himself age was insignificant. "Twenty-six. Does it matter?"

"No, no, not at all. I was just curious since you asked me."

"Curiosity can be a good thing." He refilled her glass before putting the cork into the bottle. Once again, they gazed into the flames.

He wanted her to finish her glass. The alcohol would help her sleep. Conjuring bad memories would keep her awake without the added benefit of the wine. He watched and waited.

She finished, setting the glass on the table. "You wanted to look at my back. What are you going to do if it's worse?"

"Start over again."

Seemingly resigned she walked to the bed undoing the sash on her way. The robe slipped to her waist as she dutifully climbed onto the bed, positioning herself on her stomach.

He thought those seconds were strangely disconcerting. To Graham it seemed she walked in a trance, obeying his command as if she had no choice. It wasn't the first time he'd felt the blind obedience, the resignation to something she couldn't control. The realization brought his breath to a sudden abrupt halt.

This time he didn't pull the chair beside the bed. He wasn't going to be here very long. One look told him she was right in her assessment. Her back was healing nicely. The redness, while it was still apparent was slowly fading. He reached out his hand before pulling it quickly back to his side. If he touched her, she would assume all the wrong things. She might run. He didn't think she would take the children with her.

His breath was ragged. He inhaled long and deep, closed his eyes trying not to remember his or her past. They were both starting again in a place far different for each of them. This would be a new beginning for both of them. What it meant for the two of them, he wasn't sure.

"You are fine, well on the way to mending." He pulled her robe up her back, careful not to touch her; helped her put her arms through the sleeves. "I'll go now."

She sat up and retied it, running her tongue across her lips. "No, not just yet."

She reached her hand to him, caught him by the wrist. Her lips were parted but she didn't say anything else.

Graham stopped, turning to her, surprised by her request. "What? Can I get you something? Would you like more wine?"

She touched a finger to her lips, her gaze focused on his mouth, her lower lip caught between her teeth. Her eyes were wide luminous pools. He thought they would be possible to drown in. He saw a moment of fear then another moment of hesitation that turned to desire.

"Yes, no." She brought her gaze from the floor to look at him again.

He waited with no idea where her mind was revolving. "Ria?"

Her eyes closed. He watched her drag in a deep breath as if to summon courage before she opened them again. "Would you kiss me?"

She closed her eyes a second time. When she opened them, he saw the desire in their vivid blue depths still but also something a kin to terror.

Stunned, he held his breath a few seconds. He'd wanted to kiss her since the first time he saw her cleaned up. He grinned, thinking she was joking and the fear he saw was his imagination. "That's not exactly what I had in mind when I asked you if I could do something for you."

Color flooded her cheeks, her hands pressed against them as if she could cool them off. "I'm sorry. Forget I asked that. It was totally wrong of me. You don't want to. It's dastardly inappropriate."

He pulled her to her feet, removing her hands from her face. "I would be honored. However, I'm a wee bit surprised by the request. Why?"

"I'm not a whore, Graham."

Once again, she surprised him. "I never thought you were. It still doesn't tell me why you would want me to kiss you."

"I'm not a virgin either."

He had nothing to say to that. He needed to delve further into the question. He wondered if this had something to do with what came after the word then. "I had no idea one way or the other, nor do I care. So, why do you want me to kiss you?"

For a few seconds she lowered her lashes, seeming to study her toes. When she looked at him again, her blue-green eyes were focused on him. "I've never been kissed before. Not a real kiss anyway."

After what she told him, he did find her words hard to believe. She had no reason to lie. "I'd like to kiss you."

"No tongues," she said.

He wondered how she would know such a thing if she'd never

been kissed.

He paused, his hands on her shoulders. She lightly touched his chest. "No tongues? I can do that." He would discover more later.

The situation was beyond anything he ever experienced This woman who was not a whore but not a virgin wanted him to kiss her. She'd been used and misused in countless ways he was sure. Now she wanted him to kiss her. No tongues. He kept his laughter behind his teeth.

She swept her small pink tongue across her lips. He wondered if this was learned or instinctive. He traced the line of her jaw, her eyebrows, watching her for a sign that she would tell him no. Her eyes were a dark blue green now changing color as he watched. They held a hint of desperation something he needed to understand. He wanted to know what she was feeling inside, deep inside where all her emotions were held in check.

Slowly, he touched her lips with his, sipping and nibbling along the lower lip, pulling at the softness with his teeth. He kissed the corners of her mouth, deliberately teasing her lips with his. She wrapped her arms around his neck, pulling him closer then ran her hands along his back.

He kissed her again and again, soaking in the warmth of Ria, the depth of her passion. She would undo him any moment now. Control was of the essence. The kiss continued though as she found his lips with hers, nibbled and teased just as he'd done to her. Her fingers wound into his hair. He needed to end this now but the good lord knew he didn't want to. A tiny ripple of pleasure caught in the back of her throat.

Reluctantly, he pulled away, gazing at her kiss swollen lips. "Was that of your liking?"

She nodded, her finger on her lips, her eyes dark and shimmering with passion, raw and deep. "Thank you."

~ * ~

Once more the snow was falling hard and fast. She wondered if it would let up anytime soon. The weather didn't seem to bother the children or Gray for that matter. A few days ago, she started calling Graham Gray at his request. All three were frolicking in the snow, rolling the white stuff into large balls and small ones, tossing the small ones at each other. The laughter was infections, her smile growing wider as she watched the antics. This would be so hard to give up if she had to leave, if either man discovered her whereabouts.

The manor was finally finished, at least for what they intended on the first round of the remodeling. They worked for three weeks. Annie and Bernard were wonderful. Millie liked them so that was nice. Their children played and learned with her children. She thought of them as hers now.

Gray came to her room every night with a bottle of wine. Some nights they talked about her life, sometimes his. He rarely left the room without kissing her. He still didn't understand why she told him she'd never been kissed and asked that he not use his tongue. What she couldn't tell him yet was the only kisses she knew were savage, brutal and painful. Her breath caught in the back of her throat. The memories were best left unthought-of as well as unspoken.

One night about a week ago, he told her he had adopted the children. They were his now and protected. She wasn't though. She had more than one enemy, one he knew about, one he did not. Perhaps it was time to tell him more. Yet in the telling she would feel the humiliation and terror all over again. It was the "then" he was looking for, the what happened to her that she didn't want to talk about.

He rose, dusting the snow from his greatcoat before motioning for her to come. He was mouthing some words she couldn't understand. She wasn't too sure about finding herself in the falling snow and the cold. The children were inside the stable, warmer at least having given up on the rough and tumble games they played with Gray.

She grabbed her cape, pulling the hood over her head before starting out the back door to see what he wanted. Snow crunched under feet. White flakes settled on her coat as well as her hair. Sometime when she wasn't looking, he disappeared. She peeked around the corner of the stable.

A snowball hit her in the chest. She gasped surprised. When she looked up, he was grinning, another missile formed in his hands. "Graham Chamberlin!" She didn't know how to feel. Bending down she picked up a batch of snow, pushing it together into a ball. She heaved at him. He ducked before tossing the one he held at her then another. She darted but couldn't get away from the hail of snow.

"Stop!" she cried out, tossing more at him until he was beside her, his arms wrapped snuggly around her. "Why did you...?" His lips met hers cutting off her words. He kissed her, tumbled to the ground with her laughing and rolling in the snow.

She'd never seen him this carefree before. He acted as a little boy. When they stopped rolling, she lay on top of him. Her body tensed as she told herself over and over this was Gray, only Gray, not William or the countless other men he allowed into her room. She inhaled a shaky breath. His hands held her face as she felt the gentleness, the slow intoxication as he stared at her, his eyes darkening as he watched her.

"Kiss me," he whispered, still grinning up at her.

She could leave at any time. His hold upon her was easy. "Gray," she said his name as she kissed him. He tasted as he always did, minus the sweet wine. She ran her tongue across his bottom lip.

He stopped, his brilliant green eyes shining. "Tongues are alright now?"

She laughed nodding, "I believe so. Should we try and see?"

"You first," he said, his voice soft as she leaned toward him.

Tentatively, she touched his bottom lip with her tongue then slipped it inside his slightly parted lips. He groaned as she ran it beneath his upper lip then along his teeth. He met hers with his. She felt his smile as they continued, tasting and exploring each other. He rolled her over, his hard body above her as he controlled the kisses now. Hungrily, she responded to him.

She was cupping his cheeks, staring into his eyes; piercing eyes, hot green, mesmerizing green. It happened then, lips to lips, his to hers, covering opening, flaming hot. She was sucked into the vortex, sinking, whirlpools of sensations taking her deeper and deeper.

"Storms picking up. Probably should take this inside unless the two of you want to freeze to death." Charles spoke with a touch of humor in his voice as he stood behind them.

"Don't ken why the two of you are rolling around in the snow,"

Dodge said with a touch of disgust in his voice.

Graham laughed, easily bringing Ria to her feet as he stood brushing off the bits of snow covering her. "Someday you won't ask that question. Should we go inside and get warmed up. Perhaps Millie has dinner almost finished."

He hoisted Midget in his arms, Ollie and Dodge walked in front of them. When he looked at her, he mouthed the words. "Are you alright?"

Feeling the embarrassment from getting caught by the children, she looked down for a moment then, "I'm fine."

She was too. She was fine with the kiss, also fine with the way it felt. He kissed her with raw passion and desire, not brutally. She didn't think he would ever hurt her. He would want his pleasure though. She wasn't sure she could do it again. Perhaps she asked for too much. In her experience, men always wanted and needed.

So far Gray only gave what she asked for, nothing more. She would tell him tonight. Explain things, no, perhaps she should have to show him. She didn't have the words to tell him all she went through after finding herself forced from the abbey. She trusted him though.

They stomped into the scullery, ridding their shoes of snow before setting them to the side and trying to miss all the wet spots as they walked into the kitchen in just their socks. Millie left the food to warm in the warming oven; hearty fare, nothing fancy. Chicken with dumplings, a couple of loaves of bread with stewed turnips left in the cellar after harvesting.

Her stomach rumbled. It seemed to have been morning since she'd eaten last. She knew Millie fed the children approximately at noon. They all gathered around the big dining room table which Millie set with the more serviceable dishes since the children would be there this evening. On weekdays they ate in the kitchen with Annie and Bernard's children. Gray and Ria ate later.

She and Ollie brought the food from the kitchen. Grace was said. The dishes were passed around the table. For a few minutes, silence was the only conversation. She would miss this if she ever had to leave, sure that at least one of the men hunting for her would find her eventually.

Graham would not be able to protect her from the earl if he found her.

She sipped at the tea, pushing her food to different sections on her plate. Thoughts of the earl always left her uncomfortable even though Gray told her over and over again nothing bad could touch her here. He would protect her from any demons haunting her. She didn't think he could. William was a powerful man.

He didn't know, couldn't comprehend the evil possessing that man.

"You're not hungry?" Gray leaned toward her asking, concern in his eyes.

He knew whenever she drifted away from him, her mind was on the past. He caught her numerous times.

"Not so much," she lied.

Only a few minutes earlier her stomach rumbled with hunger. She should eat, otherwise she would be hungry later on tonight. Well, she could always come downstairs for a late-night snack.

"Alright then." He passed the bread around the table.

The children finished their meals, wanting to leave and play with the new toys Gray bought for them last week when he visited the village. Asking to be excused and gaining a positive answer, they raced from the dining room.

Annie's girl brought Ollie a couple of her cast off dolls, which Ollie loved more than anything. Ria found her one day sitting and hugging the toy, humming to the doll. The sight brought tears to her eyes. Midget was happy playing with the toys from the attic. Dodge didn't want to play at all. His only interest was learning how to shoot a bow and arrow. Charles and Harry were more than happy to oblige. Gray didn't say no. Under the circumstances, she didn't dare.

She understood all too well the skills he was learning were meant for hunting not murder. In another year or so if he'd stayed in Edinburgh, he'd learn to wield a knife with deadly skill. Blue would give him a pistol. There was no reason for him to learn any of that except to defend himself or to commit murder. She heard so many stories of people who crossed Blue that were found dead. Blue didn't do it though. He always had one of his minions commit the crime.

"I heard Millie baked a pumpkin pie." Gray was leaning toward her again, speaking to her.

"What?" She smiled realizing she'd been caught in her musings. "What did you say?"

"Pumpkin pie?" he asked one dark brow arching skyward.

"Yes, I'll get it."

She slipped from the dining room to the kitchen, hearing the laughter and conversation behind her. Finding a serving tray, she piled it with plates along with the pie before backing through the door into the dining room.

To Charles and Harry many of the foods they served were new and different. She didn't think they had pie before although she knew various squashes were probably part of their natural diet.

In the dining room, she cut pieces for everyone as well as ones for the children, which she meant to take to them as soon as the men retired for a brandy. Admittedly, she was nervous about tonight and her intentions to help Gray understand her. She wasn't at all sure why she wanted him to comprehend something that was so private, something she never shared with anyone, not that she had anyone except Gray to share it with.

When they finished the pie, the men retired to the library. She placed the children's dessert on the tray along with forks and a small glass of milk for each of them. As usual they were all in the boys' room. She set the tray on the table.

"You brought us pie." Dodge stood by the table looking at it. "I'm not used to this, not being hungry."

"Are you happy here? Pleased that Graham adopted all of you?"

A moment of concern tilted her thoughts. What if Dodge wanted to go back?

"I never thought I would get out of thieving and murdering. It's not what I ever wanted to do." Dodge looked to Ollie and Midget. "I'm glad they are safe too. I ken what you're thinking, Ria. I would never willingly go back there."

Dodge was older than he should be, understanding things no twelve-year-old should know. Yet there it was. Now at least he had a chance for a normal life.

"I'm glad all of you are safe too."

"But you're not," Dodge said. "I can tell when all of a sudden you seem to be miles away. You have to be protected. Lord Graham can keep you away from Blue if you let him. I know you. You'll get frightened by something and leave. You'll run. That's what you always do."

"You're right of course, but running has kept me alive."

"It won't now. You never had anyone you could rely on, no one to defend you. Graham will do that. Charles and Harry will help. Shamus as well."

Dodge might be right. She didn't know if she could ever take that chance if pressed. "When you finish the pie, get ready for bed. I'll be up in about an hour to tuck you in then give you a good night kiss."

When she went downstairs, the men were still talking. She cleaned up the dishes, stacking them on the counter for the morning chores. Pouring herself a cup of tea, she sat down at the kitchen table. All the while she argued with herself about tonight. Another kiss would be nice and appropriate, not showing Gray...

If she was honest with herself, she didn't know what Gray wanted from her. He let her stay in his home, in a room on the second floor, not a servant's room. People in the village were most assuredly talking about the impropriety of the living arrangement. Her reputation be damned. She didn't want to ruin his.

"You are woolgathering?"

Ria's head shot up. He was standing in the doorway watching her. His hard unreadable gaze fastened on her. As usual, he showed no emotion. He looked as if he might have done so for a while now. She found that her hands were shaking "It's not well done of you to surprise me."

'I'm sorry. You're skittish tonight. Is that because of the..."

"Because of the different kiss. No, Gray. I'm learning about things, things that are different from my perceptions and experiences. I'm ignorant about love and sex, normal sex anyway. I don't know what it is, how to go about it. You're teaching me but I have to move slowly."

This was also something she wasn't comfortable speaking about.

For a few seconds, she studied the painting on the wall while he walked around her sitting beside her.

"Normal sex? Does it have to do with the 'then'...?"

She nodded afraid to speak of it, knowing she would need to because it wasn't fair to him. He should know who she was and why... He would kick her out when he discovered all the lies of omission.

We can talk about it anytime." He held her hand in his. Whenever you feel comfortable. The gentleness always surprised her.

The warmth of this touch felt right. She wished her past was far different. She needed the courage to show him simply because she could never tell him, never be able to form the words that would help him understand.

"I need to tuck the children in then we can talk some more if you want." She rose with her teacup in hand, leaving the dish in the sink before she left.

When she reached Ollie's room, she wasn't there. Ria knew she'd find the little girl in bed with the boys. She sighed knowing it was going to be devilishly hard to keep her from sleeping with them. The little girl still craved the support and confidence only they could give her. After a kiss to each forehead, she brought the tray downstairs, setting it on the counter.

Gray was gone. She supposed he'd retired and wondered if he would bring wine to her room or just go to bed. She had not been very talkative. He wanted to talk. Her stomach was filled with butterflies at her thoughts of confronting Graham with her truth. He might kick her out, but the children were fine.

At least the children would be sheltered. He had adopted them.

Reluctantly, she walked up the steps to her room. He was there, sitting in front of the fire as usual, a bottle of wine along with two glasses on the table. When he heard her, he turned, his brows drawn together in question.

After she sat down in the second chair, he handed her a glass of wine. One brow arched. "Normal sex...?"

It was not a question but a subtle demand to know, an indirect ultimatum for her to tell him more than she felt comfortable explaining to him even though she thought he would be patient with her, perhaps understanding as well. She sipped, staring at the fire, wondering if she put the explanation off longer, he would give up and retire for the night.

She let out a heavy ragged sigh, her entire body weak from worry as well as the viscous burden that was her life. "I don't know what normal sex is. I assume it is not what happened to me."

He was leaning on the back of the chair, long legs stretched out in front of him, his glass of wine he held in both hands rested on his flat belly. His eyes darkened while his brows drew together in absolute concentration. "You care to enlighten me?"

His voice was soft and low yet she heard the anger residing deep within. She looked away for a moment in a feeble attempt to swallow her pride. The act didn't work. She hesitated for several more seconds unable to look at him. "I was made to do things I'm ashamed of."

He leaned forward as if he wasn't able to hear everything. He asked again. "Care to enlighten me?"

"No, not really."

"That's what I thought. When you do, you know where to find me." He downed the rest of his wine before leaving.

She watched his back as he disappeared. "Well, that went well," she sighed, still sipping the wine remaining in her glass.

There was only one way to remedy this. She couldn't say the words. She would have to show him. When she set the glass on the table beside her, her hand was shaking so hard the crystal shattered to the floor.

When he discovered what she did for five years, he would tell her she could have said no. A man would believe that. A woman would understand she had no choice. There had been no way to refuse. The consequences of saying no were too dreadful.

She slipped out of her clothes before wrapping a silk robe around her then she took all the pins from her hair, letting the strands fall delicately to the top of her shoulders. Looking into the mirror, she wiped the tears from her eyes with the backs of her hands. As she had been ordered so many times before because men liked a red mouth, she bit her lips until they were swollen and red. Her heart beat fast, too fast but that was always as it had been. Her terror showed in her eyes as it was supposed to be.

This was it then.

Tomorrow she would have to find a new home for herself. She would run again. So be it. At least then he would know the truth about her.

All of it.

Her mind in a foggy daze she started for his room before she lost her courage and turned around. The floor was cold on her bare feet, the silence echoing around her. All she heard was the pounding inside her head along with her rapid breaths. She wrapped her arms around her body, chilled through to the bone. The feelings were the same, exactly as she felt those five long years when she was directed to a man's room to give him pleasure. There had been so many, too many to count or keep track of. At first, she tried to do just that before finally giving up, no longer caring in any case. One day was much like the other.

Most nights it was William, the man who took her from the abbey who she came to see. He was the worst. She learned right away if she didn't do everything he demanded, she was punished. He would beat her but only where the bruising wouldn't show. When that was the case, he wouldn't give her to the men who came mostly on the weekends.

He had other girls too. She didn't know how he found them but he did, probably in the seamier streets of Edinburgh giving them false promises. Gray's door was in front of her. Hesitantly, she reached out to turn the knob, wondering if he would still be awake and what she would do if he wasn't.

He was sitting on his bed reading, a robe wrapped around him. She bit her lip even as her breath stopped. When he looked at her, his smile of greeting changed to a dark scowl. She almost fled.

"You wanted to know what I did for five years? Have you changed your mind?" She stepped forward then closer as she watched him, not ever removing her gaze. His focus never wavered from hers, his eyes darkening. While she knew he could see her through the thin material covering her, it seemed he didn't look.

"I did." There was no hint of amusement in his voice, no suggestion of tolerance or that he even cared. "Is that what you're doing now? Showing me what you did?"

She nodded, standing in front of his bed. "A man needs his pleasure. This afternoon I felt you against me. I ken you were aroused. I know what a man feels like."

Slowly, just as she'd been taught, she untied her robe, letting the fabric slip down her shoulders to pool on the floor. For the longest time she made no movement, just let him look at her.

~ * ~

William St. Bride, Earl of Rushaven stomped around the room of his home in Edinburgh. He had searched everywhere for the girl, everywhere. It was fun, a game of his, to let them escape, allow them to believe they would get away from him. The terror in their eyes when he cornered them gave him thrills he craved. Until now no one had ever made it farther than the end of the dark lane.

Maria did, however. Now, he had no clue as to where she was hiding. She could not have gotten far without money. He searched every brothel in the city to no avail, looked in the seamiest parts of town. No one saw her. If they had, they weren't talking about it.

He needed a new girl. Blue, who supplied most of his girls, told him he had the perfect lady for him. He couldn't get over the fact the woman found her way out of a locked room. Damned clever of her but once in his possession, he wouldn't make the same mistake with her as he did with Maria. For a few seconds he thought it might be his Maria, however Blue told him her name was Ria. In any case, the lady Blue promised had dirty black hair not silver-blond. Had promised she would clean up nice. He hoped she would be a challenge to him. Where his women were concerned, he didn't like being bored.

Blue promised he would find her, assured him she would be his for a small sum. Exorbitant sum, William snickered seeing he would still have to train the gel. He grinned seeing his current woman sprawled on her back, her arms tied while he beat her. When Maria first came to him, he'd not mastered the training to the perfection he honed it to now. Figuring out just what he liked had taken him several months to impress the rules on her. She was a stubborn feisty little thing. This time when he found her, he might spend more time with her so she would clearly understand her place in his home. Overstepping her bounds would not happen again.

"Sir."

"What is it Henley?"

Blue was supposed to arrive thirty minutes ago. He was a busy man, too busy to waste time waiting around for a thief and pimp. He didn't like dirtying his hands with the sniveling weasel, but there were times he had to do it for his own pleasure.

"It's Blue, sir. He's here and is requesting an audience," Henley said. "Do you want me to let him in? Or would you prefer he waited."

"Let him in. I do need to speak with him. I'd rather not delay this any longer."

"As you wish."

Blue stood just inside the door, the big man Evan beside him. He didn't need protection from him, not if he accomplished what he promised. If he didn't, there would be repercussions to his business that he might never recover from.

"I brought two of the ladies with me I promised. Haven't found Ria yet. I ken she traveled north. Couldn't have gotten very far with three kids in tow and the beating I gave her. I'll find her."

"Are the two young women sufficiently cowed for me to start their training?" William was rubbing his hands together, just thinking about this was affecting him.

Blue grinned, seeming to be thinking about what had transpired the last few days. "Did just what you told me. I set the fear of God into them but I didn't lay a hand on either one. That was hard though. All that pretty white flesh just laying open for me."

"Good restraint is always a blessing in these matters. I want them bent to my will not yours. They can have pleasures of their own when they show me they've learned their lessons and have become obedient."

"When you find Ria though, punish her a little longer than the other two. Do whatever you think reasonable for her betrayal of you. If she steps out of line, you may beat her again not, however, within an inch of her life as you did last time. She needs to be useful and making top dollar for me as soon as possible. If you happen to discover my Maria, I'll pay double for her."

"I beat her because I was angry about her lies. Won't do that again. This time I'll be overjoyed. I'll find Ria for sure. Rumor has it she hid up in an old church not too far from Edinburgh. Heard she was with the three young'uns. Had to be Ria. Couldn't be nobody else."

"I'll count on it then. Perhaps in the next week or two?" He turned then, silently dismissing the man. He heard Blue leave the room, his footsteps as he strode down the long hallway. Ah, he would see to the girls in the morning. They should worry a little longer.

Chapter Four

"Christ, Ria..." He ran his hands through his hair, shocked at what he was seeing. He never gave any indication he wanted her this way, yet he wasn't going to refuse an open invitation like this. "You don't have to do this, this whatever it is that you're doing?"

He watched her lift her shoulders ever so slightly, her breasts swaying with the slight movement, the tips hard from the chill in the air. The embers from the fire behind her backlit her hair and made it glow. Her features were set as if she didn't mean to give him any reason to guess as to what she was feeling. She was clearly one of the loveliest women he'd ever seen. He was drawn to her in a way that was outside his experience. He'd known that before but now his breath caught in his throat his heart ardently pounding in anticipation.

"You're a man. You want to be satisfied, crave it more than anything. This is what I was taught to do when I was fifteen. I like you, Gray, so this shouldn't be too hard."

Too hard?

His heart thundered inside his chest. Warning thoughts flashed through his head. There was something terribly wrong. Part of him wanted to find out what she was about to do, the other part understood this was not a choice for her. He had pushed her today for explanations. Perchance he pushed her too far. Now, guilt swamped him. By all the powers of heaven he could not remove his gaze from her lovely soft white flesh, from her breasts, from the very feminine curve of her hips and the long slender legs guiding him to a hard awakening.

She was now on the bed straddling him, pushing his dressing gown to the side. He was aroused, hard, aching for her. Unsure of anything at this point in time, he kept his hands at his sides afraid if he touched her, he would lose what little control he had. The need to caress her, flip her onto her back and kiss her everywhere flooded every thought he possessed.

Her fingers stroked his sex, slowly, lightly. Her gentleness overwhelmed. He thought he would jump from his skin when her lips caressed, sipped at him, her tongue sliding down his length. "Ria."

When she looked up, her eyes were glazed over as if she was somewhere else. A groan rumbled upward from the back of his throat. Unable to help himself, his hands were on the swell of her hips just below her waist. She settled on top of him, not taking him inside, just resting there for a moment where the tip of his rod touched her folds. He felt her then, realizing this was not something she should be doing.

She was dry and cold. This act she initiated was nothing to her, no arousal whatsoever. Blessed hell! There were no emotions involved, not even lust. It was just an act she had to perform. Pushing herself upward, she held his rod in her hands, guiding him inside her unwilling body. Her lips thinned as her brows creased together anticipating the pain. Christ, but she was trying to put him inside her when she clearly knew doing so would hurt her.

"Ria, no. No!" He lifted her from him, rolling her to her side. "Christ, you will hurt yourself. I will hurt you if you do that. I won't be a party to this. To whatever it is you think to do."

His anger consumed him. In this instant, the fury wasn't directed toward Ria but to the man who did this to her.

"You have to let me," she said, her eyes still foggy, her voice soft, beguiling yet he recognized the sheer terror. "If you don't, he'll beat me for not pleasing you. I have to satisfy you so you'll come back."

Bloody hell, what to do now?

His arm was around her, holding her close, afraid now to let her go in case she would try to impale herself on him again. Her mind was somewhere else, her words taken from a time not so long ago. She was not rational or coherent.

"No one is going to beat you." He smoothed the tangled hair from her face. "Look at me, Ria."

She did look at him. What he saw angered him more.

"You don't like me?" she queried, "You have to like me."

"Have you been biting your lips?" He touched her red swollen mouth with his fingertip, cursing the man once more, vowing to find him and hand him a just punishment.

"I have to. It's what they, the men, he wants. When I come to them, I'm supposed to appear kiss swollen. I have to bite my lips."

It seemed she recognized him now, her eyes startling blue and clear. She flushed then, pushing slightly from him. He didn't allow her to leave. His voice took on a harder edge. "Who is he?"

"I can't say." She was shaking her head, a flush covering her face, embarrassed now.

He expected tears from her. Tears were not going to fall. Her eyes were dry, filled with resignation. "You wanted to know what the 'then' meant."

"How often?" He couldn't help himself from asking. He ran his hand through her hair, traced her eyebrows with his finger. His emotions so ragged he had trouble controlling them.

"Almost every night," her whisper was thin and filled with the remembered pain. "I ran away three times. He found me all but the last time," she said, a tiny smile forming on her red swollen lips. "Dodge found me then."

"He fed you his meat pie. What happened when you ran and were caught?" He wasn't sure he wanted to know yet he had to ask.

"He would beat me then he left me in a room for a week without food. I would get water after the first two days. Why did you stop me? I did want to give you your man's pleasure. You were aroused, craving me. You would have enjoyed the sex. I know it."

"As you said when we spoke earlier, what you were doing is not normal sex. If I let you continue, it would have been rape. I would not have enjoyed it. Look at me, Ria." He touched her chin with a fingertip, slowly lifted until she looked at him. "Know I will never hurt you nor will I allow you to hurt yourself."

She nodded, biting her lower lip again. He settled her head on his chest, enjoying the feel of her soft curves lying next to him, the sensations her hair created while it flowed gently across his flesh. The need to kill this man who did this to her swelled shockingly inside him. Maybe that was why she wouldn't tell him his name.

What did she know about him?

The man was powerful so he had to be a lord. He would most likely live near to Edinburgh, perhaps own more than one home. Gray wagered in the opposite direction from him, so south. It was possible the man owned a second home, one that wasn't close to a village or another manor in a secluded untraveled place. In time he would discover the missing identity and deal with the man. He could always call in a favor or two if necessary. The Duke of Southcliff, Leslie Stewart, owned a manor near his, a summer retreat. Perhaps he'd like to visit and bring his new wife.

Graham felt her breath whisper across his chest, heeded the sensations when her finger ran across a nipple. Her lashes fluttered softly on his skin. "What are you thinking, Gray? I hope it's not what I'm afraid it is."

"What would that be, lassie?"

"That you mean to kill the man. He is too powerful for you to take on. Leave it be. I survived."

"Why would I do that?" He ran his hand along her arm, realizing she was still absolutely naked and completely at ease lying next to him.

"If you failed, I would have to go back to him."

She rose up on her elbows, her breasts touching his ribs, teasing him. He didn't think she had any idea what that simple gesture did to his already aroused body parts. She only knew one thing about men and women and the way sex was shared between them. To Ria this had nothing to do with what she understood happened between a man and a woman.

He kept the groan of desire climbing inside him behind his teeth. "But if I was successful, you would have no more fears. Thoughts of seeing him again would not terrify you."

"True enough but I dinna want to take that risk." She settled back down, lying beside him, still tantalizing him with the long, slow strokes of her hand.

At this point, Graham wasn't sure if she knew what she was doing to him. The movements were not practiced as was the initial contact with her. She was just frivolously stroking him as if there was nothing else she wanted to do, as if she had no control of her fingers.

He set his hand on top of hers. "You dinna ken what you are doing to me. I certainly won't chance telling you, but you need to stop," he gritted out, his voice gruffer than he would have liked. "I might not feel responsible for what happens next if you keep up this torture."

She snatched her hand away. "I'm sorry. I didn't mean to cause you pain."

He sighed long and deep realizing completely now that although she was no longer a virgin, she was an innocent in every way. Making love to her tonight was not an option as he thought it would be when she first appeared in his room. Holding her through the night to keep her fears at bay certainly was. Falling asleep however, might be damn near impossible.

"You didn't hurt me, Ria."

"You equated what I was doing as torture."

"Dinna fash yourself. Someday I might find the time to explain it to you. Showing you would be more enjoyable. What you did was not torture in the true sense of the word."

Her sigh was barely perceptible, her lashes fluttering against him again. "Good."

"How did you get away from him?"

He thought that a perfectly innocuous question. Perhaps in her telling of the story, he would learn something more about the disreputable lord. He wondered how much he sold her for, along with the identity of the men who would buy the time with her. Again, the buyers would have to be men, depraved men who had the coin to spare.

More nobility.

Merchants possibly. There were a lot of wealthy men who were not lords. He didn't have many ties in Edinburgh. The Duke of Southcliff might have some idea as to the depravity going on. In the morning, he would write Leslie Stewart in order to see if he could shed any light on the situation.

"Do you really want to know?" She sighed sleepily.

He was afraid she would fall asleep before he had a chance to talk to her more. Sleep might be what she needed now.

"I do. I'm glad you did..." he paused, "get away. It's difficult for me to think of you doing things, forced to do things... I don't want to believe you were required against your will to do that on a daily basis."

"Then you don't judge me?"

"Of course I don't lass. You've no motive to lie about this. So, how did you escape the house?"

"I'm not really sure. This last time I was lucky. When I looked into the drawing room, I believe he was foxed. When I left by the back staircase, no one was there. The guard who caught me the other two times wasn't around. I began to think he wanted me to try to get away so he could beat me again. That it might be just a game for him."

"He sounds like a man who would like to play games with his prey, a game of cat and mouse."

"But that never happened, the playing, at least not the first two times. Don't know about the third attempt. He could have just wanted me to leave. I might have been too old. Several times he did mention he wanted a younger girl." She shrugged against him, her shoulders making a delightful contact against his arm.

"How did you know where to go, the direction?"

Lazily, he played with her hair. When his fingers traveled softly against her skin, he felt her shiver in response. He needed to keep her relaxed and talking to him now that her fear of him vanished.

"I didn't. Suppose I got lucky when I decided to travel north. I was blindfolded in the carriage when we left the abbey, so I had no idea which direction to head. Once I got into Edinburgh, I had no ideas."

"Was it then you stumbled onto Dodge and his friends?"

"No, I kept walking. I knew I needed to get as far away as I could. At one time I was sure I was moving in circles. Two days later I stumbled over Dodge who was sitting, his back against a wall, eating his meat pie."

His finger beneath her chin, he tenderly lifted her so he could see into her eyes. Slowly, his lips descended to meet hers, touch and explore. He ran his tongue across the fullness of her lower lip, enjoying the soft texture. She opened for him. He decided that tonight, if she was willing, he would give her a woman's pleasure. Pulling back, he traced her eyebrows, her chin, her neck, lower and with a feather light caress on the hard buds of her breasts.

"I like the way that feels," she whispered, bringing her hand to his cheek. "Your mouth makes me shiver and gives me strange flutters in my stomach. Almost as if there are butterflies there."

"You would be liking me to do this some more?"

He held her gaze, a single brow arching upward. His mouth came within a hair's breath of hers before his teeth and lips followed the path his finger traveled a few moments before. She ran her fingers through his hair, pushing him closer, silently giving her consent.

"I would," she said with a soft surrendering moan.

His lips closed over hers again, taking in all that she knew how to give before giving more in return. She held on with her arms, sliding them over his shoulders and around his neck. His hands secured her, pulling her closer so she nearly rested on top of him. Against him, her body shuddered with a need he generated inside her.

The kiss was long and deep searing every part of her. He was smoothly taking his time. It had now become a series of kisses, each one a staccato burst of passion that consumed his frenzy until he drew back fearing he might frighten her with the hunger she so easily fed him.

He flipped her then, placing her beneath him. Her mouth parted as if she was trying to catch her breath. Her eyes had a vaguely slumberous appeal, yet there was such a question in the way she looked at him that he could not doubt she was beginning to understand what might be coming.

His hand rested on her belly, felt the query in her movements as she arched her back, seeking something she had no idea about. Tiny sounds rippled in the back of her throat. He moved lower touching the light-colored nest of hair at the apex of her thighs. When he touched her more intimately running his finger along her sleek, hot, feminine petals, her eyes widened in surprise.

"Hush now, don't be embarrassed this will only give you pleasure. I promise you." He smiled at her, hoping to give encouragement as his fingers parted and delved in the soft, moist folds. When he pushed one finger inside her then the second, he felt the tightening of her sheathe and the clenching of her muscles, heard the gasp of pleasure as he moved slowly within her. With his thumb he rubbed lightly on the small satin nub within the dewy folds that would grant her more ecstasy than she had ever known before.

He kissed her again as he continued his onslaught, his need to let her know she was cherished.

"I canna help but be embarrassed. Never kenned that such a thing was possible."

Her eyes were wide with wonder when she looked at him, her back arched, hips moving in the gentle rhythm he set.

He felt the ripples of her pleasure as they began to spread within her and grow. Realized the tremors as her body pulsed, seeking the essence of what he was gifting her with. She cried out his name as he absorbed the sounds into his mouth. When she was finished, he raised himself on his forearms, pushing sweaty tangled hair from her face. She looked well loved.

He grinned at her pleased with himself. "Did you like that, lass?" he asked, tracing his finger over her eyebrows, staring into her eyes.

She nodded, moistening her lips with her sweet pink tongue. Behind them the fire crackled and popped, hissing as an ember jumped from a log. "Yes. What about you?"

"I'm a man well satisfied," he laughed, realizing the utter and absolute truth of his words even though he was still fully aroused.

"I didn't understand," she murmured, running her hands along his back, caressing his buttocks.

"Of course, you didn't. Now is the time to go to sleep." He didn't plan to make love to her even though he felt an incredible amount of lust so strong he trembled with the need. Something he'd never felt before with a woman. He would wait until she came to him with a different reason than she did tonight. She approached him tonight to show him her reality. He appreciated that but this evening was not the time to take her though he knew could.

He tucked her against his side again before he kissed her. "Go to sleep, Ria."

"But... but Gray..."

"We'll talk about it tomorrow."

He didn't know when he fell asleep. He knew when he woke up. She was running her hands along his chest, moving lower until she cupped him in one hand. He groaned in the back of his throat realizing that once more he was hard and aroused to such an extent if he were to stand it would send him to his knees. He ached for her.

She rose above him, removing her slight weight from his arm, an arm that was soundly numb, his fingers now starting to tingle as the blood swamped the length. She kissed him, grazing her teeth along his flesh, stopping at strategic spots to tease and arouse. The lust returned more intense and startling than it had been last night when he watched the beautiful play of emotions across her face while she experienced her first woman's pleasure.

He ran his hands along her back, stopping to cup her buttocks, pulling her between his legs. His thoughts were set. He kissed her soft mouth. Kissed her again, nearly jumping when she caught his lip between her teeth. A groan rumbled up from his chest, surrounding him. Her nimble fingers seemed to be everywhere. He closed his eyes, willing his body to calm. They could not do this now. The children would be awake, looking for them. Sunlight fell in ribbons across the bed, across her naked back, the picture so erotic he didn't want it to end.

"Ria," he held her hands in his. "We cannot... we cannot do this right now as much as I would like to continue these moments, bring them to their proper conclusion." He stole a ragged breath from the air. "The children."

It was at that moment the door swung open and the footsteps could be heard.

"What are you doing in Sir Graham's room, Ria?" Dodge asked with a protective tone. "Naked."

Graham pulled the covers up, concealing her as he felt her duck beneath them. "The three of you should go downstairs now and see what Millie has made for breakfast."

"You told me I couldn't sleep in the same bed as Midget and

Dodge. Why is it different for you?" Ollie asked, her little hands on her hips and an indignant glint in her eyes. "Are you just as lonely as I am?"

Ria buried her face in his shoulder, whispering. "Can you get them to leave now? Please?"

"That's what I'm trying to do." By the narrowest margin, he kept his laughter from booming out, understanding Ria's discomfort was something she didn't need to be feeling.

"Go on, Dodge, you lead the way. We'll talk about this later." He tried for harshness but failed miserably. His body tense with his arousal was making it difficult to convey any feelings at all.

With seeming reluctance, Dodge herded Midget and Ollie from the room. The fact he was obeying didn't stop him from turning before he left and scowling at Graham.

Gray closed his eyes, running his hands along her back. "I'm sorry, lass. Are you embarrassed more?"

Her nose was still buried in his chest but she pushed away from him. "Mortified. I don't want to talk to them."

"You're going to have to figure out something to tell Olivia. I'll speak with Dodge."

"Midget?"

"Midget, too, but I doubt if he's going to pose any problems." He kissed her mouth again before he stood. Naked, he enjoyed the way she stared at him, her gaze seemingly mesmerized.

"I like the way you look," she told him thoughtfully, tilting her head a bit as if she tried to take in all of him at once. "Nothing like the other men I've known."

With those words he felt as if he'd just been punched in the gut.

~ *~

Ria studied the man who gave her a pleasure she never realized was possible. He didn't take anything from her, never asked for his pleasure in return. Even now he was grinning at her, his eyes darkening as she slipped from the bed to wrap her robe around herself. She backed from the room until she was outside his door. Needing to flee, craving a moment of privacy before she had to speak with Ollie, she fled to her room. Her thoughts in a jumbled mess, she searched for words unable to think of anything suitable for a little girl.

Once inside, she closed the door leaning against the wood, her hand on her chest trying to ease the frantic breathing. Dodge would comprehend exactly what they had been doing. Midget wouldn't nor would he care. She didn't have any idea if Ollie would know but she'd been around prostitutes almost her entire life until she'd been set on the streets to cover her identity. Ollie would also know.

Would they judge her?

She found a bath had been sent up for her. Slipping from the single garment, she allowed herself the luxury of the hot water along with the rose scented soap that had been placed nearby for her convenience. This talk would have to take place today before she lost her nerve. Leaning back, she closed her eyes, remembering his touch, the way he made her feel. She was in awe of the magic and fire he created in her. Heat filled her now thinking about the places his fingers had been.

The amazing pleasure...

"When are you going to get out of the bath and eat breakfast? Sir Graham said you were going to talk to me after you ate. Are you?" Ollie stood beside the tub, glaring down at her, her childlike demeanor having disappeared when she first looked at the two of them in bed together.

"Yes, I am." She rose, wrapping a bath sheet around her before she walked to her armoire, looking for something to wear. "Why don't you go on downstairs and wait for me?"

"Because Dodge and Midget are waiting there while I was told to leave. I shouldn't have to leave because I'm a girl. What's sir going to tell the boys that I can't hear?"

Ria sighed softly. "Probably nothing. The truth is, we're both girls. If you want to ask Dodge later what Gray told him, please do. I agree with you. You are entitled to any and all knowledge."

She had never thought to be speaking with a ten-year-old girl about what she was doing in bed with a man, about sex. But then she'd never thought to be responsible for children. There were no words that came to her mind that would be appropriate. She started getting sweaty just thinking about the dilemma in front of her.

"I'll meet you in the kitchen or your room. Your choice," Ria told her, wishing the little girl would choose not to ask any questions.

"Don't want to wait." Ollie acted stubborn even while she knew she had to behave. "Want to know now what you and Sir Graham were doing. Seems to me it's what whores do. You've told me so many times that it's not right."

The breath she tried to inhale was ragged, nearly nonexistent. She grimaced. "Alright then, go to your room. As soon as I'm dressed, I'll talk to you. To the best of my ability, I'll try to answer all your questions."

Only minutes later Ria knocked on the door before pushing it open. Ollie sat on the bed playing with her doll. She looked up. Her pulse racing, Ria pulled up a chair in order to sit down. She set her hands in her lap. They were folded as she continued to strive for the necessary words to explain. Yet she wondered why she was explaining anything to a little girl.

"What do you want to know?"

Ollie was finger combing the dolls hair, arranging it then rearranging. She was sitting cross-legged, her shoulders slumped. Her lashes lowered covering any expression Ria might have seen in her eyes.

"What were you doing?"

Her nerves stretched thin, ready to snap at a moment's notice. "What was I doing?" That was a good question.

"Yes. You weren't wearing anything. You were in his arms, his bed, beneath him." It didn't seem Ollie was going to give up any time soon.

"Adult things," she sighed, her words whispering into the stilted air inside the room. "If you must know he was making me feel very good. I hoped I was doing the same to him. We were both willing participants."

"Is that what the prostitutes do to their—"

"Fire!" The call came from outside.

Forgetting why she was speaking with the little girl, Ria raced to the window, Ollie behind her. She looked over the property, seeing nothing. A slight scent of smoke hung on the air, making her cough as it filled her lungs. She renewed her efforts to find anything that might be on fire.

"Fire!" The shout came again and again.

Heart in her throat, Ria raced down the steps, Ollie behind her. She headed to the front door where she was brought up short behind Gray. One man pulled his horse to an abrupt stop in front of the porch, his horse's legs pawing the air until the rider got the animal under control.

"The church near the village is on fire. We need all hands before it spreads to other places."

Graham turned to her, raking his hands through his hair, frown lines on his face. "I'm going. You stay here with the children. This might have been set on purpose."

"As am I. If you take all the men with you, we won't be safe here."

She knew he didn't want to take the time to argue. She also knew Charles, Shamus, and Harry would also leave to help with the fire. They were safer with the men. If Blue was behind this, he would take the opportunity to grab them and run.

"The children are going too." For all she knew Blue started the fire to distract him, to get to her along with the children. Blue would have been patient. Would know she could not have traveled far in her condition. She wouldn't be surprised if he did something like this every small village around Edinburgh with the intention of ferreting them from their hiding place.

Gray shot out orders to everyone. He and Harry left within the next few minutes. Except for Millie everyone else piled into the wagon about five minutes later. Charles drove with Shamus riding next to him.

"Was that the church we hid in?" Dodge asked seeming to be thinking along similar lines. "You think Blue guessed we'd hide there? We would have run right out and into him if we had."

She nodded, understanding the complexities of this situation along with the luck they had in finding this home as well as being received versus a kick in the rear on the way out the door. "Yes, it is. You don't have to blurt anything out. I ken what you're thinking. Remember, we haven't seen the man. We dinna ken if Blue or Evan had anything to do with the fire."

"He's not going to go away, is he? You know." Dodge was quick to say. "He wants you back really bad, Ria. There has got to be some reason he would go to this much trouble. I've never seen him obsessed over anyone as he is you. Nor have I seen him nearly kill a person who brings in money for him. I just don't get what is driving him."

Lord, but she didn't understand either. "Well, I'm not going to fret over it. Gray will make sure none of what you just said happens. You, Ollie and Midget are all safe from him since Gray adopted all of you."

"Blue doesn't know that," Dodge added, speaking in a clear voice as if beginning to understand better. "Blue doesn't know anything except you humiliated him in front of all his people by getting away and bringing us with you. You shamed him mightily. He won't stand to lose control. He's a man who needs that. People are supposed to obey him."

"He'll find out about the adoptions soon enough." Ria tried to concentrate on anything except Blue and the threat he offered. Her mind kept returning to the beating as well as all the things he said when he laid into her back. She kept silent, watching the road.

"What did Graham tell you this morning when he had that talk with you, Dodge," Ollie asked. "I think I deserve to know. Ria didn't tell me anything."

That brought Ria out of her musings. While she knew Ollie was going to ask, she didn't expect it to be in front of her or Midget. "That should wait until a better time. Dodge can hardly make any comments here."

"What time would that be? When I'm old and gray?" Ollie asked belligerently. "Seems there is never a right time when something important is supposed to be told to me."

The little girl had never reacted quite this way to anything before. Ria was at a loss for words. She reminded herself she'd only known Ollie for a month or so before this all started and they ran.

"It's not what it looked like," Dodge told Ollie. "You wouldn't understand anyway. Best you do what Ria says. Best for you to wait for another time. I'll talk to you tonight when I get the chance."

Ollie leaned against the sideboard, pursing her lip, pouting dramatically with her little arms crossed over her chest. She didn't say anything. Once again, the conversation was stilted, silence prevailing. When they reached the old church, a bucket brigade was set up. Men and women were passing buckets of water from the nearby river to be dumped on the burning timbers. Backs strained as the nearly continuous line moved with precision. Smoke filled the tiny glen, flames reaching upward toward the heavens. Ria didn't think the church could be saved. She hoped no one had been caught inside.

When she searched for Gray, she couldn't see him. She held a hand over her eyes to keep the glare from blinding her. Then she did see him. The sight stole the breath from her. He was running from the burning building, carrying someone, his big body covered with soot and ashes. He slowed his stride now that he was no longer in danger. People called out questions, some he answered, some he didn't.

All three men, Charles, Shamus and Harry left to help with the buckets, falling into line. Gray brought the person to a place that seemed to be set up for injuries, setting him on the grass before covering him with his coat. His white teeth flashed behind the blackness of his face.

"We need to see if we can help. Dodge, relieve someone who is passing the water to the fire. People are going to need breaks. Go on. See what you can do. I'll be with you in a minute."

Ria walked to Gray, staring at the man he set on the grass. Possible implications of all this crept into her head. "Is he alive?"

Gray shook his head as he looked at her. "No. When you were hiding here was anyone living in the church? Was there a pastor perhaps?"

"There was a man who came sometimes just to pray. I don't know if he was a minister. Could have been, I guess. We hid when he was there. Didn't want anyone to tell tales." Shivering, she stared at the fire for several seconds. "You had no reason to go in there, Graham. You shouldnae have risked your life like that." She couldn't tell him how much she needed him, resented his fearless courage.

"He didn't die because of the fire. There's a bullet wound in his chest. Someone shot him," Gray said as he looked around the scene ignoring her comment.

She reached out to touch Gray who was covered in soot and ashes, his face black. He smelled of smoke and the fire. The grim lines of his face told Ria more than she wanted to know. This was arson.

Ria retrieved an old blanket from the wagon and covered the dead man. Stepping back, she said a silent prayer for him, crossing herself. Gray saw that he was removed to a place farther away. The minister arrived as a burial would be planned later.

Mrs. O'Brian from the village store with help from a few other women brought a table and food to the small area where Ria stood. She arranged the food and drink on the platform, waiting for the people who had been relieved to get nourishment as well as a moments rest.

Flames shot into the air, sparks flying into the sky. Ria rubbed her arms, suddenly chilled as if someone was staring at her. She looked for the cause. Ollie tugged on her arm, then again. "Ria. Ria, he's over there. It's Blue." Fear bit down hard, creating unwanted tremors.

Ollie pointed to a spot away from them, shaded by trees. Her breath caught in the back of her throat with a sudden gasp. *Blue.* She started coughing, unable to breathe for the longest time. Her hands clasped at her throat panic beginning to consume her.

"I see him."

Ollie's arms wrapped around her while Ria settled her hand on the little girl's shoulder in an attempt to reassure her. Blue could not get his hands on her or the boys. "Where's midget?"

"Midget!" Panicked, she called out, the boy running to her side. "Midget, stay here. Blue is out there. I'm going to get Gray."

When she looked up the man was gone as was Evan. The damage was done. Blue knew where they were. Time was all that stood between her now and becoming Blue's possession once more.

After several hours, the old church crashed in on itself. The noise thundering, Ria held her breath as she watched with avid fascination the structure of the church dissolve, turning to nothing but charred remains. Nothing else burned that day. The fire was contained, Gray returned to her side, hugging her despite the ashes. She didn't see Blue again. She knew with a few questions it was only a matter of days before Blue reappeared, most likely at her doorstep.

She inhaled a deep ragged breath. Then to the children in a voice harsher than she intended, "Stay close."

Gray returned to the fire, moving from place to place, searching the debris. She gathered the children around her. It wasn't long before Dodge stood beside her, learning about Blue's presence.

"I'm getting Gray."

"No, Blue won't do anything here with all these people. He'll wait until we're alone. If he doesn't know where were living now, he will find out. Until he knows the three of you are adopted, he will try to bring you back with him. You mustn't let him. Yes, the men need to be apprised of the situation. We will tell them on the way home."

Ria found she was shaking, her fear all too real. It didn't matter how many times she told herself Gray would protect her, she was still terrified, knew nothing was for certain if Blue was determined to get her back. There was also a chance Blue could take her without Gray's knowledge. He often hunted with Harry and Charles. So, there were days he was away from the manor for hours at a time.

When Gray finished, he strode to her, a slight smile on his face, his teeth appearing so very white behind the blackness of his face. Even his ginger-colored beard was black now. He pulled her into his arms, kissing her hard.

"You are black all over. It becomes you." She touched his face with a finger, laughing, trying to hide the fear the presence of Blue created.

"Now you share some of the ashes and soot." He laughed, closing his eyes for a moment. He wrapped an arm around her shoulder. "Let's go home."

She sat next to him on the wagon. He slipped his arm around her waist, drawing her close to him. "You reek of smoke."

"I know. Is it so terrible?"

"No," she said, leaning into him, absorbing his strength into her. She wanted all her fears to be vanquished.

"It seems I've been up for twenty-four hours now or more as have you. I've lost count."

"You can go to bed when we get home."

She needed to tell him about Blue. The telling would wait. He looked so exhausted she couldn't burden him with the news until he was feeling better.

"Need to eat first, a bath second. I want you, Ria," he whispered to her. "Will you let me make love to you tonight?"

His words sent her stomach fluttering again, her body quivering with need to feel the ecstasy he gave her last night. She placed a finger on her lips, remembering the caress of his mouth on hers, the softness of his beard. Ria couldn't think of anything to say other than *I want you too.* "I would like that."

He urged the horses forward. "Think..." He turned to look at her. "Before we eat, Millie won't let me in the kitchen like this anyway, not until I'm clean. I'll order a bath."

"We saw Blue," Ollie blurted at that moment. "He was standing over there then he wasn't."

"You sure?" Gray asked, thoughtfully rubbing his chin.

"She saw him as did I," Ria said, her voice shaking.

She hoped to never see him again, or Evan. She hoped the telling would have waited until after dinner or sometime tomorrow.

"When were you going to tell me?" he asked, anger and hurt in his voice.

"Ria said he wouldn't hurt us if we stayed all together so we did," Dodge said, suddenly becoming the voice of reason. "Don't take it out on Ria. You know you've been busy with the fire. There's been no time to tell you anything."

She smiled at that. Even now Dodge defended her. He always tried to protect her as well as Ollie and Midget. If Gray could keep him away from Blue, he'd grow up to be a fine man.

They were approaching the house. She couldn't help from periodically turning to see if anyone followed. Charles rode Gray's horse. He made several loops to check behind them. With the sparse landscape there were relatively few places for anyone to conceal himself. One could hide behind hills perhaps. If a person was small, perhaps one could hide underneath the heather. Still, she knew Blue would only have to ask a few pointed questions in the village to discover the location of the manor.

They all understood it was just a matter of time before Blue would come for her.

When they pulled up to the house, Gray helped her and the children except Dodge down from the wagon. Harry drove it around to the barn. She wiped her sweaty hands down her dress, her nerves stretched thin. It was a matter of time, just a matter of time. Waiting for something to happen seemed impossible.

"Stay here," Gray told the children when they stepped into the kitchen. "Millie has dinner cooking. You can eat as soon as it's ready. Ria and I have things to talk about upstairs. We don't want to be disturbed," he told them with a pointed look to each child, only if it is a matter of life or death.

She felt the grip of his hand on hers as he tugged her upstairs, seemingly eager to reach his chamber. Her breath caught in her throat as she remembered this morning and how it felt to have Gray's muscular arms around her. "The children are going to know," she whispered, holding back somewhat reluctant to appear so obvious. "They will have more questions I don't know how to answer."

"Of course they are but we're not going to hide from them or lie about what we are doing in bed. I want you, Ria. Do you want me?" He tugged on her hand, moving quickly up the steps to his room. Once inside, he locked the door before pulling her into his arms. He kissed her mouth, unable to draw away, the grin of his deepening. Frantically, his hands pushed at her clothing. He groaned when the tiny pearl buttons of her dress would not compromise by letting go of the holes they were encased within.

She felt his craving, understood the power of lust along with the urgency of his need simply because she felt it too. He kissed her, nibbling at her lips, tugging on the bottom one, tracing his way along her cheek to the sensitive underside of her ear, worrying the lobe while his fingers continued their quest to disrobe her. She undid his cravat, dropping it on the floor. His pull was strong and incessant. This was how they began the morning but were interrupted.

"The children...?" The knock on the door came at that same instant. Her gut tightened with the knowledge they would ask more questions that she had no answers for.

"Who is it?"

"Your bath water, sir."

Gray opened the door, pushing Ria behind him, waiting for the buckets to be dumped into the tub. When they were gone, he strode back to her, his eyes so deep and dark, becoming the color of the darkest part of a forest.

When the man left, she stepped back, looking to the tub then to him.

"You've got becoming smudges on your cheeks." His lazy grin sent ragged heat to simmer inside, her stomach fluttering, butterflies seeming to dance inside her. He touched her where the soot was then kissed her again. She knew the pleasure he could bring her, understood what they did together was not about pain as she had known from other men.

"Is all that soot rubbing off on me?" she asked, backing away from him with a partial smile, her hands still resting on his chest. He reached out holding on to her waist, bringing her against him again.

"You're not going to get away so easily," he murmured, pushing strands of hair away from her neck where he sipped, his teeth grazing on her sensitive skin. His fingers once more focused on the tiny buttons to her gown. When he finished, he pushed the sleeves from her shoulders, staring at her white breasts, holding them in his hands, tracing lazily across the taut buds.

She was still so unused to anything like this, this sweetness from a man and gentleness as well. The feelings that centered and heated in the pit of her stomach before they travelled lower surprised and delighted her. The hard planes and angles of his body as she molded herself against him gave her good reason to accept all he wanted to bless her with, her body quivering with the need he managed to create. This was so much more than she could have ever expected from a man. While she knew it was sinful, what did it matter? She been so used and abused by men...

She kissed him as if her life would have no significance if she did not, uncaring if she became just as painted in soot and grime as he was. For a moment she became the aggressor in this lovemaking. Her mouth slanted across his, parting his lips with the pressure of hers. Her arms slid forward. She cupped his face lightly in her palms as she moved her mouth to the corner of his then to his cheek to his temple and finally along the line of his jaw. She caught him again, deeply this time, her tongue pushing against his. She felt her breasts swell even before his arms circled her back to press her closer. His woolen frock coat was slightly abrasive against her bared breasts while the buttons scraped delightfully against her. The air between them was warm but threatened to become charged with heat. She delighted in his masculine groan of pleasure, realizing she could do that to him.

His fingers wound through her hair, dislodging all the pins until the strands settled just above her shoulders. He paused, slowly running his fingers through her hair, his eyes focusing on her eyes. He moistened his lips, tenderness the only emotion that sprang from him. She heard the long indrawn breath as he set his cheek against her forehead for a moment.

Sensing that something had changed, Ria broke off the kiss and buried her face in the smoky folds of Grays neckcloth. She held him tightly a second longer while her uneven breathing quieted then she raised her face. "I hope I am doing it right this time. Except for this morning, I've never felt tenderness from a man. I don't want to do this wrong."

It seemed he still had the wherewithal to chuckle. "Ah but you could not do this wrong even if you tried. However, you will need more water to clean your face and your breasts when we are finished here. You might be as soot covered as I am."

Ria touched her face and regarded her smudged fingers before she grinned at him. She hoped he understood her feelings for him. He saved her soul and probably didn't know.

"Here too," he said, placing an index finger against her lips then showing her the evidence. "You are as soot smeared as any chimney sweep."

She arched a brow reminding him how she had come to be so. Her disgruntlement did not last long. She held out her hand to him. "Come, I ken what is needed now."

Ria held his hand, leading him to the bed. Without a word she helped him out of his frock coat and his shirt then bade him sit down on the bed before grappling with his boots. The more she touched him the sootier she became and she didn't care at all. This was Gray, her Gray. She would love him for as long as he would have her.

She realized his need without him saying the words. She wanted to give him everything she could. Gray lay on the bed naked save for his drawers and watched her strip from her clothing before she climbed into bed with him. Her pale breasts were tipped in pink. She brushed them invitingly against his chest as she moved closer. He looked at his hands before he showed them to her as if she wouldn't know how filthy they were. "I will mark your skin if I touch you with them."

She couldn't speak. Didn't want to in any case. She caught his hands and brought them to her breasts. She allowed his fingertips to graze her skin and his thumbs to pass across her nipples. The trail of his hands left the faint smudge he predicted. Ria raised her earnest gaze to his. "I will be made beautiful by them," she whispered softly. "Everywhere you touch me I will remember with happiness."

The compassionate look in his eyes stunned her. It was as if he was trying to tell her she was already beautiful. "I will show you how beautiful you are," he murmured his voice gruff with the desire she hoped he felt for her.

He rolled onto his side, pressing her back then placing his mark on her, first with his hands then with his mouth.

He swept back the silver-blond hair at her temples, sifting the silky strands with his fingertips. His lips found the soft hollow where her pulse beat so rapidly and he kissed her there, sipped. Her skin was warm. He kissed her forehead, the corner of her eyes. His head dipped. He caught her earlobe with his teeth, tugging before his lips touched that spot. He flicked it with the tip of his tongue before he heard her breath catch.

His smile imprinted itself on the skin of her throat. He nuzzled the curve of her neck, sipping lightly on her flesh. His mouth left a mark that was different from his fingerprints on her breasts, but no less proof of his intimate possession. He kissed the impression he left on her skin then made another.

She moved restlessly against him, urging him without words. He sensed her impatience but would not be hurried. In this at least, it seemed to her he would have his way.

"You're amused. Why?" The words came from deep in Ria's throat, a husky, heavy whisper that was foreign to her.

"Mmm." Gray lifted his head and nudged his mouth against hers, parting her lips. His breath was warm against her. "Always," he said. He kissed her for a long time, holding her still with nothing but the pressure of his mouth on hers. He made that kiss an end in its own right, sucking on her full lower lip, her tongue, tracing the ridge of her teeth, licking at the sensitive velvet underside of her lips, making them wet, making the whole of her mouth humid and hot.

She seized his neck when he would have drawn back, would have held her to him if he had permitted it. What he did was remove her hands and place a kiss in the heart of each palm. Then he let them fall away and find purchase in the sheets as he bent to her again.

This time his mouth settled at the hollow of her throat. He made a damp trail to her breasts, loving each separately. Her heart beat a steady tattoo. He kissed her there then again at the curve of her breast. He took the puckered aureole into his mouth and suckled her. Her nipple was taut and equally tender; he rolled it between his lips, flicked it with his tongue.

His hand fell on her hip, steadying her as she rose off the bed in an arch. "Shhh," he said, not to quiet her but to calm her. "I have you. I shall always have you. There is nothing to fret about, but you must have patience."

She didn't know why she needed to be patient. Her mouth parted as she tried to speak then she merely shook her head. She breathed in deeply wondering at all he did and the sensations coursing within. Wondered if it would end the same as last evening when he gave her so much pleasure. "When you come to the precipice again," he told her, "I will let you fall. Then I will catch you." She nodded, not because she understood but because she trusted him. He saved her from all past injustices. She had no doubt of it as her fingers wound in his hair and gently tugged.

Before, she had only survived. Now, she was beginning to live.

That intuitive sense of hers, the one that linked her to him and allowed her to not only to see his soul but to be unafraid of it had divined his faltering resolve. It was not that he did not desire her still but that he did not want to desire her. He wondered if she could distinguish the difference when he could barely do the same.

He felt her tug again. Noticed the corners of her mouth lift in a shy smile. No siren's tasty curve this time. No coy, flirty beckoning. She made herself vulnerable with her honesty, in doing so made him want to be her equal. "Witch," he said as he bent his head then sipped her other breast into his mouth.

Gray was glad for the slim bars of moonlight that touched the bed and laid their transparent brilliance across Ria's body. He slid his hand under one soft breast, stroking her hip, letting his fingers trail lightly along the curve of her bottom. She stirred again, softly sighing her pleasure. His hand moved upward to her waist, his thumb passing over her soft belly, dipping slightly when her skin retracted in response.

She fit perfectly as if every curve was made to fill his hand. He made a slow study of her, learning the shape of her shoulder, her arm, the delicate depression at the inside of her elbow. Her breasts spilled over his palms, firm and taut; her skin had the blush of a ripening peach.

His hands slid along the length of her thighs, the back of her knees. The pressure of his fingertips, light but insistent, made her part her legs for him. He slid down her body, no longer making a trail with his hands but with his mouth.

Gray stripped off his drawers before tossing them over the side of the bed. He urged Ria's knees upward as he bent between them. That she found a way to hook her legs over his shoulders was her own doing. It meant the intimate kiss he pressed to her feminine parts began as a smile.

He felt her give a start at the first touch of his lips, again when he applied his tongue. This was all new to her, new sensations, new pleasures. She was warm, humid, sultry in the midst of her feminine petals. Desire made her damp. Now he used his mouth to make her wet.

All around them were the sounds of wind stinging the windowpane. The frigid temperature outside drowned by the warmth they created inside. Gray was aware of it only superficially. The sharpest focus of his attention was Ria and giving her uncompromised memories.

Gray lifted his head to see into her eyes. From the quick sips of air, the tension in her frame, the way her back curved, and her soft lips parted, he judged that she was ready for him. He raised himself up, dipping one shoulder to let Ria's leg fall, cupped her bottom. She helped him lift her hips but her gaze remained on his face, his eyes.

Her body was prepared to receive him. Gray found her hand guided it to his erection. "Watch," he told her. "Watch what we shall do together."

Ria did exactly as he instructed her. She watched his first thrust then the lift of her hips taking him deeply inside her body. She closed her eyes. Her hands went to his forearms as she gripped him tightly.

"Ria?" He spoke her name as a question. "Look at me."

Her lashes fluttered upward. He was in her as deeply as was possible for a man to be inside a woman. To the hilt and it was exactly as it should be.

"I can stop now," he told her. "Only now."

His words were uttered from the back of his throat, both smooth and rough. He saw the shivers raised on her arms, felt the trembling beneath him, her body clenching him tightly. "I know what I want," she said on a thread of sound. "It's not for you to stop. I need you more than I've ever needed anything."

His hips jerked in response, withdrawing and plunging again. He leaned over her, resting his weight on his forearms. Slowly this time, exercising a degree of restraint he did not know he possessed, he taught her the rhythm that would pleasure them both drive them to the ecstasy they both desired.

She was small, so very tight around him, but she fit him here as she did everywhere else. When she rose and fell, her breath quivered. He prepared her to take him deeply and hard. When he kissed her, every invasion of his tongue was a foreshadowing of what he was doing to her at this moment. He had thrust and withdrawn, thrust again. He made her reach for him, not just welcome his touch but demand it. Nothing had changed.

Ria did reach for him, looping her arms around his back, splaying her fingers across his shoulders. The tapered tips of her nails scored a light crease on either side of his spine from the small of his back to his nape, then down again to his buttocks. The shiver that slipped under his skin became hers as well. When he edged her toward all that was unfamiliar about this pleasure, he was as good as his word, pushing her to experience the lightness of falling from a very great height then sweeping her safely into his arms at the very moment she would have shattered.

He moved between her open thighs a minute longer, his strokes becoming short and quick, rocking them both hard. The last test of what remained of his strength and resolve happened as he felt his release. He jerked away from her, withdrawing then collapsing beside her, giving up his seed to her naked hip and flat belly and finally to the sheets.

"So there will be no bastard," he said quietly.

~ * ~

Dodge stood inside the stables, staring at Charles. The man fascinated him like nothing else ever had. He was Cherokee and Dodge wanted to know all about the tribe as well as how they lived. So much about Red Deer and Runs With The Wind captivated Dodge. Gray lived with them for several years in America before returning home to Scotland. Gray traveled with them, ate with them, married a Cherokee woman. She had his baby even though the child died. Now he was home again, a Scottish Highlander.

Charles' head was shaved except for a strip of hair down the middle of his head. Three black tipped eagle feathers poked from the top and three thongs holding beads dangled down his back. He seldom went anywhere without a knife sheathed at his waist, a pistol stuck in the back of his waistband and a bow over his shoulder with arrows in a quiver on his back. Mostly he rode bareback wildly through the rolling hills.

Dodge wanted to be just like the man. He sought to learn how to ride and shoot.

The man wore English clothing, a greatcoat, his breeches were made from doeskin along with a white shirt tucked in at the waist and boots reaching nearly to his knees. Harry looked much the same as Charles. They spoke rarely, many times in their native language. Dodge wanted to learn everything about them and upon first meeting them decided he wanted someday to live in Maryland.

Dodge stood just behind Charles who was shooting arrows into a target made from hay. One more thing he needed to learn so he could explore the frontier. "Can I learn to do that? Shoot?" He'd asked several times before and received mostly grunts for his efforts. His persistence, he hoped, would eventually pay off.

"Has Graham given you permission? You know you need that before I can teach you." Charles asked as he shot another arrow that nearly split the first one in the very center of the target.

"He said you can teach me to hunt, but you and Harry go out early in the morning. You can wake me up, you know. I want to go with you. I'll even sleep in the barn so it will be easier."

Dodge was eager to learn to hunt. Now that he had seen Blue and Evan he was more interested in learning how to use a weapon to kill. If Blue ever got close to Ria, he would murder him on the spot. Gray would never let him use a pistol yet but perhaps a bow and arrow. He'd received a bit of an education on the use of a knife. Both Charles and Harry were more proficient than anyone he'd seen in the slums of Edinburgh.

Charles grunted handing him the bow and one arrow. The instructions were succinct and to the point. Charles notched the arrow. Despite his best efforts as well as a few grunts he was unable to draw the string back.

"I'll have to make you a lighter bow to use until you are stronger." Charles stared at him, seeming to look from his head to his toes. Uncomfortable with the way he was observing him, Dodge shifted from one foot to the other before straightening to his full height.

"I can do it. I'm not a little boy, bigger than most my age. I'm strong." Dodge insisted, giving it several more tries before he had to admit to the fact he couldn't pull the string back. Dodge wanted desperately to leave his life in the city behind him and become more like Gray and these two men. Still, he had a lot to learn.

Charles laughed softly, ruffling Dodge's hair, "You will grow into it so why are you so eager to learn? Is it because of Miss Ria? Is she in trouble?"

"No more than usual. It's because she is so beautiful."

"Is that so. Gray Hawk seems to think so too."

Dodge tensed, knowing he needed to protect Ria from everyone including Gray. No one else understood just how evil Blue was. Blue would take more than his vengeance out on all of them if he caught up with them. This time Ria would pay more than with just a quick beating.

"Yes, as is Ollie in more danger than either Midget or me. We will only have to steal for Blue. Ria and Ollie will be sold to whorehouses. Ollie will never survive. She is small and fragile."

Dodge knew enough about Ollie's life to understand that if it wasn't for Miss Ria she would already live in a whorehouse. Her life done before it barely began. Of course, she would have been sold to a rich man for her virginity before she was put into her new home when the rich cove tired of her.

"Come, let's make you a bow. There are some nice oak trees on the property we can use. Once that is done, I can teach you how to use it properly."

Chapter Five

Over the last few weeks, the weather gradually warmed. Instead of snow falling from the sky, most days rain sluiced in heavy torrents. Gray wished from time to time to see sunshine for more than a few minutes a week, but until spring arrived that wasn't going to happen. He set about formulating lists in his mind of the things that needed to be done as the warmer weather increased and the days grew longer.

Ria spent the nights in his bed, the children beginning to accept their tenuous relationship with no more nagging and embarrassing questions for Ria who didn't seem to have any answers. She had no experience with children and was at a loss where they were concerned.

He didn't understand what drove him to keep her in his bed every night not wishing to make any commitments. His thoughts always returned to his Cherokee wife, White Dove, and the pain he inflicted on her by carelessly getting her with child. His gut churned thinking about her and their life although he understood now that he really hadn't loved her. He'd wanted her though, wanted the child too, mourning the loss for months until he decided to leave the Cherokee and return to Scotland.

Slipping on his greatcoat and pulling the hood over his head, he walked around the house to the stables looking for Ria. She wasn't in the house and now he saw she wasn't here either. He strode around the outside of the stables making his way to the barn. Charles and Dodge were in the back shooting at the makeshift target. Watching for a while, he noticed most of Dodge's arrows landed outside the preferred area. The boy had perseverance though. There wasn't a doubt in Gray's mind that he'd gain proficiency sooner than expected.

Forgetting for a moment about Ria, enjoying this moment, he

grinned lazily as he walked to meet them and oversee their shooting. Dodge jumped for joy when he was given actual permission and didn't have to pretend in front of Charles that he had it.

"Anyone seen Ria?"

He didn't remember her asking to go into the village. It was such a bloody cursed day she would have looked at the skies and changed her mind. No one man or beast should be out in the torrential rains that blanketed the sky.

"Not lately, why?" Dodge asked, a frown forming on his face. "She's not in any trouble, is she? You haven't seen Blue or Evan?"

"No, don't think she's in trouble. Can't find her anywhere. Just wondering if anyone has seen her. Would like to speak with her about tonight."

The chill shuddering through his body caught him off guard, all thoughts leveled at Blue and Evan. They all understood it was just a matter of time before the two men appeared. It would have been hard for them to take her away from the house. She would have to leave the grounds for them to get close enough to snatch her away.

"Did you try the attic?" Dodge asked. "She likes to sift through those old trunks you have up there, treasures to find you ken. Sometimes she likes to sit on the window seat and read."

"Yes, there are a lot of things in those old trunks, mice too. Don't know why she likes to spend time in the attic. I'll try up there. We might have just passed each other by using different staircases."

He thought he should get a cat. Maybe someone in town had kittens they might like to give away, one for the stables and one for the attic. Ollie and Midget would love to have one too.

Gray headed back to the house trying to not think about the fact she might have been taken right under his nose, telling himself only a fool would be out and about on a day such as this one. He stepped quickly up the back steps entering the scullery. His heart in his throat, he was relieved to hear her laughter coming from the kitchen. When he stepped inside, Ria was enjoying a cup of tea and a scone while Millie bustled about the stove.

He needed to take the offense in this instead of playing this waiting game with Blue and Evan. He was afraid to leave her alone at the house. At the moment he didn't have enough men at his disposal to pursue Blue. "I found you.'

"I didn't think I was lost," Ria answered.

A sultry smile formed on her mouth which reminded him of this morning's activities as well as all the past nights as well as the way she gave herself to him. In bed together, she was open and honest, giving as well as receiving her pleasures. Still, she held information about herself in check, closely guarding things that he assumed were too embarrassing and humiliating for her to speak of even to him.

One look at her shining eyes and beguiling soft lips he wanted to pull her into his arms and kiss her soundly. Still, he didn't want to embarrass Millie who was working madly on tonight's meal. He was having company this evening, an old friend. William St. Bride, the earl of Rushaven was going to join them. Gray had more than one reservation about entertaining this specific old friend. More than once he was tempted to call it off or at least postpone.

The man wrote to him a few months after he arrived in Scotland. Over the following weeks they arranged a day and time for dinner. Gray wasn't eager to bring him into his home. Renewing their tentative friendship was not something he intended. If he recalled, in their younger days the man had a mean streak that manifested itself in the demise of small animals. Things he thought funny often turned Gray's stomach into knots. Something in his gut rebelled, an instinct that renewing this old relationship would not be good for himself or Ria, for some reason especially Ria.

"You remember the earl is coming to dinner?" he asked, wrapping his arm around her, holding her close.

He recognized the grin on Millie's face while she watched them cuddle. He wanted to do more than just place a chaste kiss on the back of Ria's neck. Unfortunately, now was not the time to be amorous.

"You two should run along and take care of what's on your minds now if you want to be on time for dinner. I've got the little ones fixing to eat in another few minutes then everything will be cleaned up and ready for your guest."

"The earl, yes. He's a friend of yours?" she asked, turning in his arms, her eyes wide with fear or was it just concentration.

"Not really but he wanted to officially welcome me back to Scotland. I would have preferred to meet him at his home. Instead of agreeing with my request, he relentlessly manipulated the invitation to come here. He has a manor house south of Edinburgh. Not really that far away when young men have horses and a penchant for exploration. We used to meet half way, my brother and I. He was older."

"You don't like him," she said, touching his shoulder. "Why on earth is he coming to dinner then?"

"Now what makes you think that?" He wrapped an arm around her waist, heading for the stairs. She leaned into him, her soft curves pressing against him shamefully enticing him. He nearly groaned giving into the temptation of making love to her right now and forgetting the upcoming dinner.

"I've a bath drawn for both of you," Millie called out as they left the kitchen behind them. "In separate rooms, mind you."

Gray flashed Ria a lazy grin, thinking once more that perhaps there would be enough time to make love to her before dinner as well as take a nice hot bath. Memories of their nights together sent a surge of desire to his groin that was difficult to ignore.

"Thank you, Millie."

He kissed Ria on the forehead while his hands travelled upward to cup one of her breasts, his thumb moving lazily over one hardened tip. He felt the swift shiver of her response, heard the indrawn breath sucked through her mouth.

"Now don't think you can have your way with me before dinner. I need all the time that is left to get myself ready. I want to look nice." She giggled before slipping away from him and into her own room.

"I dinna suppose you are going to let me, now are you?"

He sighed heavily watching her back and the saucy flair of her hips disappear into the room, his thoughts of an enjoyable interlude before dinner vanishing. It was just as well. He needed to get his thoughts together concerning William. When all this transpired over a month ago, he sent a letter to a judge he knew in Edinburgh seeking information. So far everything he received from the man was disturbing even though there was no definitive proof. Most of the accusations were subtle innuendos of wrong doing, things heard via gossip.

Before she closed the door, she peeked out and with a flirtatious smile, "You'll have to wait until afterward." Then the door closed with a soft swish behind her.

Her transformation from the shy hesitant young woman he met in November to a flirtatious uninhibited woman in the bedroom never ceased to surprise him. She never ceased to intrigue him with her honest giving nature. Walking into his own room, thoughts of the boring evening ahead of them, he undressed then slipped into the hot water. For a few minutes he closed his eyes, seeing only Ria and her sensual body as she walked to him naked that first evening when she was bent on giving him his pleasure.

Gray stayed in the liquid heat longer than he intended. Finally, when the water began to grow cold, he finished with the bath. Hastily dressing, he left his room, knocking on Ria's door. "Are you ready?"

"No, I'll be down later."

He heard the laughter in her voice as well as a bit of hesitancy. If she wasn't down in another hour, he would come get her. Entertaining the earl by himself wasn't part of his plans. He could always introduce William to Charles and Harry in order to see what the earl thought about them. Not a smart idea since he was the last person to put the men on display. He also wanted to create a bit of fear in the earl's mind. Graham wanted to give warning but he wasn't yet sure what it was he was warning the man about.

"Make sure you are. I dinna ken to do this without you by my side, sweetheart." Lord but he'd grown more accustomed to her than he ever thought he would. In such a short time she had become an integral part of his life, changing the despair that had been centered deep in his heart to smiles. She delighted him in every way. He yearned to find a means to put her fears at rest. Short of leaving her unprotected there was no way he could vacate the manor house even for a short stay in the city. If he took her with him, that act might also put her life in danger.

Gray wandered into the kitchen, sampling some of the foods

Millie prepared only to get his hand slapped away. "Keep your fingers out of the food. My goodness but you're worse than the children," she admonished him, laughing happily.

"But your heart loves it doesn't it, Millie?"

"You know it does. I've missed the lot of you all these years and would give just about anything to see your brother, Donal, again."

Charles appeared from the scullery. "You've got a message just came in from town." Charles stole a taste of the chicken curry Millie prepared.

"You've had your dinner," she admonished him, "It was exactly the same food. Do you mean you didn't get your fill?" she demanded, her hands resting on her ample hips. "I'll have to start sending more, or are you feeding it to the animals?"

"Can always eat more and I would never feed these delicious meals to animals," Charles laughed, giving Millie a quick kiss to her forehead.

"Good or bad news?"

Grays brows drew together as he read the letter. Unsure of his feelings, he didn't want to give up his nights with Ria. Well, he supposed he could leave where she slept up to her. He didn't think his brother or Leslie would comment on where Ria spent her nights. "We're going to have visitors in less than a week, sooner if the weather changes."

"Anyone I know?" Charles asked, a lazy grin on his face. "If you don't like them, Harry and I could hog-tie them and take them so far north it would take them months to find their way home."

"Lands, I'm going to have to get Annie to prepare rooms. How many?" Millie asked, interrupting while drying her hands on the dishtowel near the skink. "Perhaps Annie's oldest can help with some of the cleaning. We haven't even started work in the other wing of the house; content I guess to keep the part you're living in up to standards."

"My brother and his wife, the duke also," Gray began, running his hands through his hair, leaving it disheveled and standing on end. A month ago, he sent a message requesting assistance with discovering the truth about Ria's past. This was exactly what he needed, yet the invasion of his home and the tranquil existence he was living in was not

Christine Young

accommodating to the idyllic life he was becoming accustomed to. "Also, a friend, the Duke of Southcliff and his wife."

"Does the duke have a name?" Millie asked, her curiosity seeming to get the better of her. "Would I happen to know this duke?"

"Leslie and Lacie Stewart. You ken my brother's name. His wife is Daryl." They were just wed. Suppose this is a wedding trip of sorts for both of them. Leslie and Daryl have been best friends since they first met in school. I requested Leslie's help. He was a spy, you understand, worked for the government for several years. Leslie knows people no one else of his rank would even consider speaking to."

"Well, we'll welcome them all with open arms. I'm sure this old house will be as lively as it used to be not so long ago. Perhaps you can hire another maid. I'm sure Annie and Bernard could do everything that needs to be done but we don't need to have them run ragged. As I said there is a lot to do in the other wing."

"Your right of course. Even if the weather is abysmal, I'll ride into the village tomorrow morning and see if Mrs. O'Brian knows anyone who can use a few more coins."

"Seems your dinner company is here." She nodded to the carriage as Shamus drove the vehicle into the stables. A huge black coach with the earl's emblem on the side lumbered past the back door.

"So it is." Gray glanced up the staircase looking for Ria. He started up the steps only to stop.

She stood at the top, her soft lips forming a smile, "I'll be down in about ten minutes. I want to check on the children."

He nodded, grinning at her and appreciating the care she took in dressing. Her hair was pulled up and back fastened with two combs leaving tendrils curling intricately around her small face. She wore a dark blue satin dress with blond Belgium lace around the neck. The sleeves were tight on her arms. A large ruffle decorated the bottom of the gown. She was stunning. Still, all he could think of at the moment was how he would slowly take it off her, kissing and sipping each tender part as he unveiled her silken skin.

Gray greeted William before leading him into the library, which was quickly becoming his favorite room. He'd made love to Ria in here

125

one blistery day when he was sure the children were all occupied on the third floor with their newly found toys. The trunks turned a wealth of idle time into exploration and discovery. When one trunk was emptied the children used the empty box to play inside with the dire warning never to lock anyone inside. Needless to say, if any of the children went missing the adults raced to the attic to make sure no one was locked in a trunk.

Millie entered behind the men with a tray of various cheeses and breads, thinly sliced ham and roast beef to top it off. She didn't plan on serving dinner for another hour, so a brief repast beforehand would be appreciated. There was also a bottle of wine for Ria or the men if they so choose.

"Brandy or port?" Graham asked, sliding his gaze over the elegantly dressed earl. He wasn't flamboyant in his dress as many of the lords these days were. His fawn-colored breeches fit snugly to his legs. His frock coat a dark blue color nearly black was impeccably tailored to his body. His hessians were shined to perfection. The only sign of decadence was the slight pouch to his belly, which spoke of overindulgence. Otherwise, he appeared in mint condition for a man of forty-two years.

William leaned back in one of the wing chairs pointed at the fire, his legs stretched out in front of him. The snifter of brandy held in one hand he swirled the contents for a moment before taking a sip and placing the glass on an end table.

His brows drawn slightly together, his eyes narrowed, he asked. "So, what have you been doing since we were young lads? Anything interesting?"

Graham was sure the look on the man's face was a sneer. William had not been young even then. "I've been in the states, Maryland to be exact." Telling William of his life with the Cherokee would shock the man, explaining two of the native Americans he met and befriended there travelled with him might cause a bout of apoplexy, or enlightening his past acquaintance that he just adopted three children having saved them from the slums of Edinburgh along with a seamier life style might send him packing.

His eyes brightened as if curiosity drove the next questions, but

Gray felt sure it was more from profound boredom. He wasn't at all sure why the man insisted on meeting with him especially over a dinner at his manor house. The quest for answers might have prompted him, but Gray had no idea what answers he sought.

"What were you doing there? In the wilds of America? I've heard it is very primitive and the natives are barbaric."

Getting abducted by the Cherokee to become a slave then running the gauntlet successfully to become a member of the tribe and marrying one of their own, having a baby who died along with its mother. "My family as well as Leslie Stewart's have plantations there. It was my mission to oversee the daily workings."

Gray watched the man's eyes narrow in thought before he downed the entire glass of brandy in one gulp. "The blacks? Did you have many working for you?"

Disgusted by the question and wondering where that would lead, "We have some." Enlightening him about their working relationships with the black people on the tobacco farm was not part of his intended conversation. The less this man knew about the Chamberlin's business dealings the better.

"Were the black women willing or did you have to force them?" he asked, his eyes shining with what Gray could only guess was lust not curiosity. "They were slaves after all. Yours to do with as you pleased."

"I beg your pardon?"

Bile churned in his stomach tuning it sour as he realized the man had not changed as he became an adult. If he could he'd like to take him by his collar and the seat of his pants and violently show him the door.

"The women, you owned them. You could do as you pleased with them." He poured another glass for himself, sipped his brandy leaning negligently back in the chair as if he owned the world or at least his little part of it. "I certainly can think of a few pleasing things to do with those women."

"More brandy?" Even though he could see William's glass was nearly full.

He stood breaching the distance between them. Filling his glass and topping off the earl's, "The running of the plantation did not leave much time for dallying with the help. Besides, most of the men we purchased had families, the men, wives and children. What have you been doing?" he asked hoping to divert the subject of the conversation from him to the man who invited himself into Gray's home.

"Enjoying myself mostly. The running of the estate takes time. I've crofters I need to see to, taxes to collect. I much prefer my house in the city though. You're not married."

"Are you?" Gray asked. Out of the corner of his eye he noticed Ria at the door. She was on the verge of entering before she suddenly shook her head, lifting her skirts, she fled.

What the devil?

The depths of Ria's blue-green eyes held a terror he'd never seen before, not even when she saw Blue at the fire had he seen such naked fear and anxiety. He wanted to go after her; see what was wrong but sensed this was not the right time to confront her. Giving anything away to this man he distrusted was a repugnant notion he wasn't about to cave into.

"No, as of yet, I haven't found the right woman," he said, turning his attention to the glass windows stretching from floor to ceiling, watching the downpour.

Gray realized something was terribly wrong with Ria. He stood, eager to finish the meal and the conversation with the earl so he could speak with her. "I believe dinner is ready."

"I thought your friend, mistress, would join us," William said, unmoving. "Where is she?"

"Oh my," Millie waltzed unbidden into the room. "She has taken sick in the most horrible way. Her head is aching. I'm afraid she won't be joining the two of you. She sends her apologies and hopes that maybe another time she will have the splendid opportunity to meet you. After I've served the two of you, I will take her some of that willow bark tea you brought from America."

"Should I check on her?" Gray asked, but he was sure her sudden disappearance had something to do with the present company.

"No, she said she would be just fine with a wee bit of rest. I'll take a tray to her." Millie exited without further comment.

"Shall we go eat?" he asked standing, looking to the stairs and wishing he could run after Ria to discover what was wrong as well as what he could do to ease the problem.

"Your mistress?" William asked seeking more information. "Has a fragile constitution?"

"She will be fine, I'm sure. I'll see her later tonight." His fists clenched at the tone William used when he sneered the word mistress. Schooling his features, he smiled.

They followed Millie into the dining room. Gray needed to talk with Ria, infuriated he could not take the time now. This was unlike her yet he knew she had a good reason or she wouldn't have run off the moment she saw the earl. Perhaps she just didn't want to meet this man.

But why?

Through the next two hours his thoughts were centered on Ria and what the presence of this man had to do with her sudden departure. Before she saw William, she'd been looking forward to the evening. Without discovering any more clues about Ria's sudden departure, the next few hours drug by with excruciatingly slowness. When the earl finally said his goodbyes and gave an invitation to visit with him in a week or so at his manor house, Gray raced upstairs.

It took some minutes of diligent searching to finally locate Ria on the third floor nestled back behind all of the trunks in the attic storage closet. When he held the candelabra up, she blinked a few times from the sudden light. Her face was pale as death, her eyes dazed with fear. He was reminded of the first time she came to him and tried to give him pleasure at her expense. Obvious to him she was in some faraway place, where no could reach her or hurt her, his mind raced with concern. She would survive.

He set the light on one of the closed trunks before sitting down next to her. Staring straight ahead and for several very long seconds, he didn't say a word, listening to her breathing and the pounding of his heart. His thoughts were in turmoil, recognizing the fear but there were underlying currents of emotions he couldn't see or recognize.

"William is gone. He will never return here. I promise you that." Christ, but he found it necessary to know what caused this reversal into herself in order to help her. "What can I do for you?"

His shoulder was pressed against her hoping his warmth would fill her with much needed confidence to break out of the shell she encompassed herself inside. Silence continued but he felt her lean against him accepting his strength into her. In time, she would give herself to his strength and acknowledge his protection once again.

"The children are safe as are you. No one will get to you as long as you stay within the boundaries of this property. Don't go anywhere by yourself. If I'm not close by, seek out Charles and Harry. They are more than capable of protecting you."

Lord but he knew if anyone harmed or threatened any of them, that person might very well find themselves scalped alive.

Allowing Red Deer and Running With The Wind to follow him to Scotland might well have been the best decision of his life. He smiled, memories of his time with the Cherokee assailing him.

"Would you like to retire to our bedroom or would you prefer to stay in your room tonight? I'm sure Millie has set a bottle of wine on the table near the fire and some food on the tray nearby. You must be hungry."

Wrapping an arm around her, he pulled her close, drawing in a ragged breath, telling himself more patience was necessary. He knew the trauma she dealt with was very real and wouldn't dissipate with his wishes.

She tilted her head just the tiniest bit, the movement barely perceptible. He turned, gently touching her chin and turning her face so he could see her eyes. He closed his, taking a moment to say a silent prayer.

Slowly she nodded yes. "I am hungry. Thank you for being so tolerant."

~ * ~

Ria tried valiantly to put that night behind her. Several days passed. While she told Gray nothing about the earl and how he pertained to her she was afraid for his life if he knew the truth. She regretted she didn't dare say anything, but he was so noble and brave. He had no idea he couldn't fight the earl. The man was too powerful, had too many resources. If she understood one thing about Gray, he would try to fight the man.

For the last few days, she had busied herself on the third floor teaching the children. She knew she was hiding. She didn't care. Dodge was not learning as quickly as Ollie. He was much more interested in discovering how to shoot a bow and arrow, how to wield a knife with deadly accuracy among other things he considered manly. Midget on the other hand tolerated everything as a young child would. He liked to play so all his lessons needed to be directed toward what the young child would consider to be a game.

It seemed she waited for the world to crash down around her head. She could only hope the children would be saved because they were Graham's children now. Finding she cared more for Gray than she ever wanted to admit, she gave as much of herself as she was capable each night when she slept next to him, wishing this would be for a lifetime, knowing it would only last until the earl discovered who Gray was keeping in his home.

She waved to Charles before she stepped inside the house, thinking a walk would be nice but not having the courage to leave the confines of the manor house. Charles, Harry and even Dodge rode across the land. She wondered where they were off to this early in the morning, too late in the day to be going hunting. The two men only hunted at the crack of dawn. While this was early, it was long past the usual time.

Dodge was becoming a man under their influence. She smiled wondering if this was the same way the Cherokee treated all the children in their care. To Ria it seemed they were all part of one large family. From her limited experience, children were only for adult's pleasures. It had certainly been so in her case. She shivered suddenly trying to put those thoughts into the back of her head where they belonged.

"My family along with the duke and his wife should be here soon. Are you prepared to deal with them?" Gray asked, standing beside her, watching the scene enfold in front of them. Wrapping a protective arm around her, it seemed he studied her carefully for any lasting impressions from that horrible night when she was beaten nearly to death. She realized of course that he would always have his say.

"Your family, yes. What will you tell them about us? I'm not ready to spend the nights alone in my bed. If you think it's necessary, I will." She looked up at him. "Begrudgingly."

She had grown way too used to his big hard body next to her along with his gentle lovemaking that left her breathless and in need of more.

"I've no reason to think either man will judge us. Neither do we owe them an explanation. We are adults, Ria. They simply have no say in what I, we, choose to do."

He couldn't help touching her as they stood on the porch. Running his strong hand along her back, Ria sighed with the sheer enjoyment of the simple touch. When she had to leave, gestures like this, the simple things, were what she would miss nearly as much as making love.

"That's nice but it will be me they are judging not you," she reminded him, setting her head against his chest trying to absorb the heat from his big body. "I suppose I should..."

She didn't really know what she should be doing. Move from the house is what came to mind, but she had the strongest notion Gray would strongly object. Despite her thoughts that leaving would be for the best at least for Gray, she had no money to do anything of the sort. Until he set her out, she would stay.

"I promise you they won't stand in judgment of you. They will respect my wishes as this is my home." His voice was strong, tender as well.

"They will believe I'm your mistress which is actually what I am. Suppose I've known that fact for months now," her head bowed, "have just chosen to ignore the fact. The name never made a difference to me simply because without you I would truly have become a whore with no options but to continue in that vein in order to survive." She paused thoughtfully for a few seconds, "Or I would be dead. There are no alternatives for me."

Long ago she learned never to cry over a fact she had no control over. Her fate in life had been stolen from her when the earl took her out of the abbey for his personal uses. She closed her eyes, wishing she could forget but forgetting was never going to happen. In the darkest part of the night, his image would always be in front of her, his needs forced upon her.

Perhaps in another lifetime if she believed such nonsense.

His hand travelled idly over her shoulder and down here arm, possessively stroking, gently supportive. She knew he was trying to think of something reassuring to say to her. There was nothing. Her body shuddered at his touch reliving other moments and wishing she could hold them all close to her heart for the rest of her life. While she didn't know how long she would be Gray's mistress, she knew the children would never want for anything. They would stay here with him forever or at least until they moved on with their lives.

"My brother just wed. I can tell you Daryl led him a merry dance. She refused to marry him because she didn't want him to control her. I've heard there were many nights he slept upstairs over her bakery just so he would be there when she finished work. He bought her a bed big enough for him so he could sleep without his feet hanging over the end and had it installed in her bedroom." His laughter was deep and rough.

She liked the way it sounded as well as the way it made her feel. He didn't laugh enough.

"You never talk about your brother," she said, touching his face gently with the palm of her hand. He spoke even less of his time in America. There was deep pain he'd experienced during that time. She could try to imagine the agony of losing a wife and a child all in the same day. When they made love, he still withdrew from her refusing to leave his seed inside her even though she told him she was barren. He didn't want a bastard, he told her but did he not want any children at all? Of course, he wouldn't want hers. That didn't bother her too much. She didn't know what she would do with a baby, another burden to contend with in her dark world.

His heavy sigh stole the lightness of a few moments past. She regretted the change, had no idea speaking of his brother would create the new distance between them.

"Except for a few days before I moved to this manor house five years passed without seeing Donal. I was on the planation in Maryland since I was nineteen years old, expected to oversee everything. Thought I would remain there, put down roots for the rest of my life. Life there was enjoyable, exciting and truly never boring." He was staring into the distance as if he was seeing things only he could see, remembering. "Don't get me wrong, I loved it there. Life was so different and in ways carefree even though that was deceptive too. It was only carefree to me because the rules were different. Being a second son, I did not have to adhere as strictly as my brother but the assumptions were in place."

They watched the antics of Midget and Dodge for a few minutes. The pair were wrestling. While Dodge was bigger and stronger, he let Midget have his way more than not. Ollie stood by them, her little hands clasped beneath her chin, studying the unruly boys. They would all grow up to be fine young people with the world in front of them. That single thought kept her going every day when her life seemed so fragile, ready to fall apart with her discovery in his home and Graham kept her nights free of the nightmares that used to claim her sleep.

She pointed down the tree-lined road leading to the manor. "Do you think those carriages are bringing your brother and his friends?"

She was suddenly afraid of meeting these new lords and ladies. Her body shuddering, she wrapped her arms around herself, warding off the chill.

He slowly lifted his shoulders, touching her chin so she would look at him. "Most likely. Don't know who else it would be. Are you afraid?"

"A little. Never known a duke before. I trust you though. I'm trying to believe what you've told me about them. They are nice and they are genuine. Still..." She was staring at the two carriages as well as the men accompanying them. There had to be at least five men on horseback with each carriage. "The girls are sisters?"

"Yes, two of the four MacTavish ladies. Seems they all set their sights on the man they wanted before they could have them, except the oldest, Bliss." His mouth curved in a warm lazy smile. "Donal warned me away from Daryl."

"You stayed away, I gather."

For some reason he found this amusing and the thought puzzled her.

"I was on my way here and I had no intention of settling down in Glasgow. While I did want to find someone special, I needed to be away from the familial ties. Grandmother left this estate to me. I headed here a few days after our conversation about Daryl."

She stiffened at his words before her gaze drifted back to the vehicles trundling down the long drive, growing ever closer. The words he spoke terrified her even though she understood from the beginning he would not desire her as his special woman. He deserved better. She wasn't the kind of a woman a man would want to share his life with, only his bed until he found someone suitable. Her suitability had never been in question because she would not suit anyone of good breeding.

"Do we have enough rooms prepared?" She counted the men in his entourage. "Guess a Duke has to have his protection."

"Millie made sure the outbuildings were ready. They will stay warm and dry, as well as nearby for his personal use."

"Good then."

The carriages came to a stop while she held her breath, wishing her feet would move and take her upstairs to the attic where she could hide. His hand went over hers, lifting her fingers from the railing before enclosing her hand within both of his.

"Relax."

She drew in a ragged breath praying the blessed air would reach her lungs. It seemed that for a few seconds her heart forgot how to beat. "That is much easier for you to say than for me to do."

With her hand still held in his, he strode forward, stopping at the foot of the steps. He embraced Donal then acknowledged the duke and the ladies. Stepping back, "This is Miss Ria Ashton. She is a guest in my home." He finished with the introductions of Lacie and Daryl.

"Nice to meet all of you," she said, her voice softer, sounding less confident than she wanted, a bit awed by meeting a real duke and duchess. "Millie will show you to your rooms. If you would like baths, please let her know. Gray, Graham has arranged for some midafternoon snacks in the library. When you are ready, please come down."

"Thank you so much," Daryl stepped forward, taking her hand in hers, Lacie following suit.

"Graham is such a handsome man. When are the two you getting married?" Daryl asked while Donal ran a finger around his neckcloth and Leslie coughed behind a hand.

Ria felt the heat rise to her face as she looked away, her heart in her throat. She spoke before Graham could answer. "We don't plan on marrying any time soon if ever."

Gray watched her with hooded eyes, his lips thinned. She so wanted to know what he was thinking. This wasn't the time or the place. She knew he wouldn't divulge anything different though he might have wanted the words held back a little longer. In any case, what she said was the truth and nothing would change that.

At her words there was no comment from anyone. She watched Millie lead them up the steps and to the opposite wing from their rooms.

Gray bent close, "Why did you say that? It was presumptive of you and made everyone uncomfortable."

"What?" She felt stunned by his comment as she swayed into him.

"Say we weren't going to be married."

His blue eyes shimmered with an angry intensity she rarely saw. With her heart in her throat, "Because it's the truth."

"Your truth maybe? One eyebrow arched speculatively. "I see."

He never told her what exactly it was that he saw and she was too afraid to ask. Instead, she strode into the library. Sunlight filtered in through the large window after she pushed the heavy draperies back. The scene felt cheery and bright after the long rainy days of winter. Millie brought in a tray, holding thin slices of roast beef and ham as well as cheeses. There were scones and butter along with strawberry jam. Her stomach rumbled a bit having missed lunch in the preparations for their guest's arrival.

"Our truth," she told him after Millie left the room. "Even if you wanted to do so, you couldn't wed me. The very thought would create such a scandal. I don't want to hurt your family any more than I already have by being here. As soon as we can find evidence that will convict the earl, I'll leave."

If possible, his eyes grew even darker than before. "Where will you go? You don't have any money, besides the children will miss you."

Yes, the children would miss her but not as much as she would miss them. "Perhaps Daryl will let me stay in the room over her bakery in Glasgow. I could work for her, earn an honest wage and support myself." Her money would not come from lying on her back every night.

Gray sat down in a brocade-backed chair, crossing his arms and stretching his long well-muscled legs in front of him. "You don't know the first thing about cooking or baking. You would burn Daryl's profits."

"I'm a fast learner." She paused for a moment, her finger resting on her lip. "I could clean. I'm very adept at cleaning."

"Well, you did do a remarkable job with the manor house as well as the outbuildings. Even put a few feminine touches on the walls and the new furniture. If you like, I'll speak to Donal."

"No, I'm sure it's not up to Donal. I'll ask Daryl. It's my future after all. I would begin now. I don't need a man's help."

She didn't like the direction of this discussion or the tone of her voice while Gray was trying to help her. Didn't enjoy the thought of leaving Gray in this remote spot where he came to find someone with whom to fall in love. She certainly didn't know what she was doing planning something so loathsome for her.

"Ask me what?" Daryl waltzed into the library Donal behind her. Her smile seemed to lighten the day even more than the sunshine beaming through the window.

Once again her cheeks flamed with heat. "It's nothing really. It's premature. Gray and I were just discussing what I should do once the earl is convicted of his misdeeds and I can safely leave here."

"Why would you want to leave?" Daryl asked, helping herself to a cup of tea. "This is such a nice place to live." She looked between her and Graham as if she sought answers.

Donal chose to pour a snifter of brandy, swirling it around in the glass as he watched over the top, his expression failing to reveal any of his thoughts.

Ria had somehow put herself out on a limb. She wasn't used to others listening to her conversations with Gray.

"Ria thinks she's a burden to me, don't you?" Gray asked, once more his heavy-lidded gaze watching while absorbing all her strength. "What she doesn't realize is that if I thought she was a burden, I would have let her go months ago."

"You kept me here because of the children." She turned then glancing up to see Leslie and Lacie step inside the room. "The children and I came with the house. He was kindhearted and allowed us to stay." She couldn't possibly tell them he enjoyed her company in bed and that might have had something to do with the tenor of their relationship as well as her place in the household. "I should see to the children."

"No," Gray held out his hand stopping her. "I'll do it. You should get to know our guests." He strode purposefully from the room.

He knew her too well, understood if she left, she would not have returned. He would have found her in the attic behind all the trunks. While everyone here was related somehow, except her, she was more than uncomfortable. She fiddled with the cups and saucers on the tray before pouring Lacie a cup of tea and herself as well. The delay did not help her gain any equilibrium.

"Would you like to retire to Gray's office? Leave the ladies here. I believe we can get more accomplished there. We can let the ladies discuss whatever it is that pleases them without our constant perusal," Leslie said.

She watched as Donal and Leslie left, drinks in hand. Now it was only her and two sisters who were watching her with narrowed eyes of disapproval. She tried to swallow the huge lump in her throat.

"What do you mean you came with the house?" Daryl asked, setting her cup on the table then leaning forward expectantly. "And why would Gray want you to stay if he didn't..." she picked up the cup and sipped her tea, "If he didn't want you to stay. If he's anything like his brother, which I heartily suspect he is, he doesn't do anything that doesn't suit him."

"Leslie is the same," Lacie put in with a smile. "Unless it concerns me, he does exactly what pleases him."

These two ladies suddenly overwhelmed her. With no experience speaking or dealing with females, she was left with nothing to say. "I..."

Daryl leaned forward again, "We won't bite you know. I like you already, simply because Gray adores you. He never stopped looking at you."

"Yes, it is absolutely obvious to anyone with eyes in their heads that Graham is in love with you. So, let's start with what do you mean you came with the house?"

Nervously Ria stared at her hands in her lap crunching the fabric of her gown between her fingers. When she looked up both Daryl and Lacie were wearing warm encouraging smiles. "The day he arrived I was already here." She paused for what seemed as if hours had gone by. "He didn't send me away."

"Well, that says a lot. Not that he would have sent a woman out into the cold. He must have had a good reason to keep you and adopt your children. There is much more to this story than you're telling us."

"They aren't my children. They just came with me. It seems he fell in love with them. That's all." She blurted more things about Blue and his wish to put Ollie in a whorehouse.

Both looked bewildered. Yet Daryl encouraged her seeming interested in the tale. "Tell us more. Who is this Blue person and why would they want to put a sweet little girl in a whorehouse?"

"Perhaps I should begin at the beginning," Ria stood, walking around the room, agitated and wishing she could somehow blend into the walls. She began with the death of her parents then her installation into the abbey. By the time she finished with the beating she took at the hands of Blue because she dared lie to him about her sex, both ladies were in tears.

"I believe we have a job to do here," Daryl said, avidly regarding her sister. "These two obviously need help ferreting out how they feel about each other. We are just the people to do the job."

"Yes, we were sent here to right two wrongs. Since Graham can't seem to do it, then it will be left up to us. Can you shoot?" Lacie asked.

Ria was shaking her head wishing with all her heart the answer was yes, realizing also these women were more than a little overwhelming. With her words whispered, "What do you mean right two wrongs?"

They immediately explained how they found the man who slashed open their brother, Flynt's leg and took the capture and punishment into their hands.

"We marched those men naked to the sultan's ship, Arie's ship. Arie is a friend of Flynt's wife, Hope. No, he is a friend of all of us. They were sold into slavery," Daryl said. "The men didn't think we could do it. All five of us were there. We held pistols on them, made them strip. Told them they could either go naked or they could die right there on the spot."

"We can do the same for you. Don't have to wait until there is evidence. Men take too long in these things. Probably can find a ship sailing off to Botany Bay in port where no one will ever hear from him again."

"Charles and Harry threatened to scalp him if they ever caught up with him. They also said they would need proof," Ria said with a hesitant smile thinking about the men being led through town naked. It was, after all what the earl deserved. "Or catch them in the act."

"You just can't wait for men to protect you," Daryl said with a hint of sternness. "You have to do it yourself if you want justice. We are here to help you. We didn't know it at the time we left but now that you've explained your circumstances, we will do it."

"We have to take matters into our more than capable hands," Lacie added with a slight tilt to her head when she saw her husband, the duke stride into the room, his features grim.

"You are not taking anything into your capable hands, Lacie. You will cease and desist with this plan of yours. I will not allow you to put yourself in harm's way."

"Or what? What if I can do it with no harm at all to my person or anyone else." She blatantly stared at the man's mouth, obviously and seeming very eagerly baiting him.

He growled low in his throat, striding to her chair and possessively placing his hands on her shoulders. "We'll talk about it later in private, my love. As you well know, this is not the time or the place." Then he smiled what Ria could only assume was an all-knowing confident duke smile, proclaiming I'm the Duke of Southcliff. She will obey me. How could she not?

Lacie reached up and touched his hand with hers as if conceding to his wishes even though her eyes flashed with barely concealed amusement. Ria was shocked at the change coming over the duke's expression when Lacie touched him, his eyes shimmering with what she could only assume was tenderness and love. Ria wondered what it would feel like to be loved like that, so completely so thoroughly.

"From experience we ken they will do what they please," Donal said showing a lazy grin yet a finely arched brow spoke of something different, something unleashed. "We just have to make sure we don't let them out of our sight long enough for the two of them to act irrationally." He kissed Daryl on the mouth then drew away an interesting smirk on his handsome face. "That won't be hard. I intend to keep my wife in my bed."

"I trust everyone is enjoying themselves." Gray didn't wait for an answer but turned his attention to Ria. "The children are fine now. Millie will put them to bed in an hour. After dinner you should go upstairs and kiss them goodnight if you like."

She found the couples were grinning shamelessly at each other and seemed to have found something humorous about the situation. Ria, however, didn't see anything amusing at the moment, her fears for her future escalating with each inhaled breath of the fragile air surrounding her. Everyone knew she shared Gray's bed, was essentially his mistress. Among his friends and sibling, she was terribly embarrassed.

Dinner and drinks afterward passed without further ado, the couples saying goodnight and leaving for their rooms. Gray tugged on her hand, nodding in the direction of the steps, seemingly eager to be alone with her. As was their habit they sat in front of the fireplace in Gray's suite of rooms drinking a glass of wine.

The time was usually spent talking about the children along with anything important that might have occurred during the day. Truly, she didn't want to speak of their company as well as how she felt right now. He would try to assuage her emotions along with her fears but it would do little good.

She was an imposter. Realized the truth of that word more vividly while they talked. He seemed to put today's events to the back of his mind. Once she thought perhaps she would find a home here, with Graham. Now she understood she would never fit in with his family or even his friends. The expression on their faces was enough to realize she was just too different from any woman Gray could love. What she had been through in her short life was far too much to overcome for her to fit in with these people Gray called family.

"What is it? Something is bothering you beyond the fact that we have guests." Gray reached out to touch her hand, a different countenance on his handsome chiseled features, his eyes growing darker as he seemed to study her. She reached out to touch his jaw, feeling the soft beard on his chin. "What's bothering you?" he repeated. He placed her hand in his, kissing the palm before setting it on his thigh his hand above hers holding her still.

She didn't want to talk about her feelings, just needed to love him for as long as time would permit. Complaisant the last few weeks, she'd begun to assume things she had no right to assume. There had been times she saw a place in his heart and his home.

Lifting her shoulders slightly she gazed at him, "Let's talk about this later. I'm tired."

"That's not an answer."

"I know but is it that hard to wait for a few more hours?" she asked, watching him as he pulled her onto his lap, his mouth slanting hungrily across hers. He kissed her hard and deep until he pulled a tiny moan of desire from her throat. Desperately she clung to him, needing his comfort and strength. She understood now what she must do.

"I want to know now before we go to bed and make love. Need to understand what has changed your beautiful smile to a frown, not even a frown but a look of despair," he told her while his hand cupped her breast as his tongue delved even deeper into her mouth, giving her those memories she wanted hold onto for the rest of her life.

She didn't want him to stop, not now, not ever but she reluctantly decided she would enjoy every second as if each moment with him was her last one. He pulled back then staring at her, touched her lip with his fingertip. He aroused her. Now he waited for her to answer his question.

"That was not well done of you," she murmured, sliding her fingers through his soft hair.

"What? Kissing you?" His brows arched in speculation. "What has happened? What is wrong? Did someone say something?"

~ * ~

Shivering in the cold dark corner of the stable, Blue slanted Evan a black look. "Did you know they would have company? These gents appear to be staying for a while, all the trunks and extra men."

This situation with Ria was a matter of pride for him as well as the money the earl offered for the girl. He wanted to set things to right and show the gel she couldn't get away from him. Ria was skittish barely ever leaving the confines of the house. Possibly as the weather warmed, she would be more inclined.

"Of course not. We wouldn't be here if I had known. Perhaps we should wait until they are gone."

"We should get ourselves back to the city to wait this out. Our luck is bound to change," Blue muttered with a disgusted look toward the house. This was not at all what he'd imagined.

"I say we get it done with today. Even if we don't get the wench, we can grab the children. The little ones are always out and about. The little girl, well..." he paused. "The earl was interested in her as well. She will fetch a handsome sum for the both of us."

"The children would be perfect. Ollie and Midget will be easy, not so sure about the older one though," Blue muttered, whistling between his teeth as he watched amazed then delighted as Ria walked toward the stable with one of her guests. They could nab two without lifting a finger. The carriage they rented was down the road about a half-mile just waiting for them along with their soon to be captive prey.

Evan caught sight of the two women, nodding toward them. "Well, look at that bosom. Wouldn't mind if I got a feel for that one before we turn her over. We'll just wait until they get inside. You ready?"

Blue nodded then hunkered farther back into the shadows, his breath held tightly in check. He held his gun ready to knock Ria in the head with the handle. His luck had changed for the better. The earl would pay more than handsomely for the ladies. He grinned wickedly thinking about the truth of Evan's words and the lady who walked beside Ria.

His breath caught inside his lungs, tension radiating through his body as he tried to keep the elation from overpowering common sense and street smarts. They needed to be careful here. The risks they were taking enormous. If they were caught, Gray would not go easy on them.

The ladies were chatting, not paying much attention to anything but themselves and whatever conversation they were pursuing. None of their men were in view. Blue hoped everyone else was preoccupied with other business and would not see them. They needed time to put their plan in action and get away, losing themselves with the ladies in the bowels of Edinburgh.

"Look at him," one of the ladies said as she stroked the nose of one of the huge stallions that arrived with the party. "Isn't he just so gorgeous you can't believe. Do you ride?"

Ria was shaking her head, seeming hesitant to get anywhere near the stallion. "No, no, never had the chance to learn. Don't think I'd like to either." She backed away as the horse sidestepped, pushing his nose curiously toward her.

"He won't hurt you." Lacie held out a flattened palm letting the big horse nibble at the apple slice she brought him. "Would you like to feed him?" Her eyes widened when she saw him. Opening her mouth to scream, Evan quickly hit her on the side of the head, hauling her back against him, one big arm beneath her breasts.

Blue managed the same with Ria. Quickly rolling each into a blanket, they carried the ladies from the stable slung over their shoulders. The two men reached the carriage seemingly unseen by anyone at the manor house. Tossing the ladies into the carriage and onto the floor, Blue sat inside while Evan took the reins, heading toward the city of Edinburgh.

A smile grew on his face as the carriage slowly gained speed. This had not been so hard nor had Graham Chamberlin been as vigilant as he should have been. While he sat back, Blue counted the money in his mind when he turned over the two women to the earl. He didn't have the little girl yet but he had time. These two ladies were priceless, worth far more than he could have ever expected when he thought of the huge bubbies of the one lady. Every gentleman who visited the earl's little playhouse would ask for her.

Only a few more minutes passed before a startling cry roused him from his musings sending a wave of sheer terror down his spine. His heart sped, landing in his throat while his breath caught in his lungs, absolute horror catapulting through his body.

"Ayiee, ayiee..." The cry went on and on sending dread into his bloodstream.

When he peered out the window, he saw the two Cherokee men Chamberlin brought with him from America. They were riding bareback, their bodies in perfect harmony with the horse, a bow held in one hand. An arrow whizzed by and Evan's startled scream of pain gave Blue good reason to believe he'd been hit. The carriage slowed. While he reached into his pocket for the gun he always carried, the door was thrown open and he found himself yanked from the interior.

He lay on the ground looking up into the harsh face of Red Deer. Before he could defend himself, he was tied, bound hand and foot then thrown over the horse, his arms and legs dangling uselessly on either side of the steed. Taking his time, the Cherokee mounted, heading back to the manor house.

Blue didn't know what happened to Evan, knew he was either dead or was being treated in the same manner as he was. Another chill swept through him. While he understood the vengeance Chamberlin and the other lady's husband might seek, he had no idea what these Indians would do to him. As any other Scotsman, he'd heard stories about the Indians in America, the tortures they committed to white folk who dared invade their land.

Red Deer dumped him in front of the barn. Slipping off his horse, the man slung him over his shoulder, striding purposefully into the building. With only a few minutes passing he found that he'd been retied, his arms stretched over his head, his feet dangling, his toes barely touching the floor. Evan was beside him, trussed in the same manner, blood dripping from his arm.

No words were exchanged. The men left. Blue could only assume they were going to get the husbands and bring them out here.

Chapter Six

Gray heard the war cry that would strike terror into anyone, even someone who lived with the Cherokee for several years. With the cry in his head, his heart nearly stuck in his throat. He raced to the front porch to see both Charles and Harry speeding toward the village, their cries shattering the air around them.

"What the devil is that all about?" Leslie asked as he stepped next to Graham, one hand shielding his eyes from the sun. "Never heard anything like that."

"Don't know."

Gray had the sinking feeling something had happened to Ria. With a radiating tension the likes of which he'd never known before, he asked, "Have you seen the ladies?"

"Daryl was with me in the library. However, I haven't seen Ria or Lacey," Donal said, having followed the other two men to the front porch Daryl beside him, her hand clutching his arm.

Gray raced down the steps heading for the stables. Without saddling his horse, he swung himself over and tore down the road. Leslie and Donal followed. By the time he reached the stopped carriage, Blue and Evan were subdued captives of Red Deer and Runs With The Wind.

"They took your women," Charles said his voice clear and vibrantly filled with anger. "No time to get you."

"Lacie too?" He was slowly opening the door to find the ladies lying on the floor unmoving. His body shuddered at the thought Ria might be harmed. Slowly, he unwrapped her, her face pale, her short hair sliding across his fingers as he touched her pulse point on her neck. His heart quickened as he felt the slow steady pulse.

Leslie stood on the other side of the carriage doing the same for Lacie. "She is breathing but unconscious."

"As is Ria."

"I'll drive back," Donal tied the horses to the back of the carriage then easily leaping onto the seat, he waited for the men to climb inside before urging the horses forward.

"We will meet you in the stable," Charles said and he and Harry took the captives back to the barn.

Graham held Ria in his arms while they traveled to the house, smoothing her forehead, willing her to open her eyes. He'd never been so frightened. While he'd known Blue would try something, he had not expected it to be when the house was full of guests. When Ria told them, they were going to see the horses, he'd been engrossed in business and just nodded as if her idea was excellent. What had he done? Let down his guard, he admonished himself.

Now, because of his relaxed vigilance Ria was unconscious and in his arms. He consoled himself with the realization that his men had come through for him, saving her when he was oblivious to her trauma. Blue would have had her and Lacie if not for his trusted friends. On the other side of the carriage, Leslie was rocking his wife, gently stroking her cheek with his fingers.

Short of killing Blue and Evan, he would have to make sure they were sufficiently frightened of the slow painful death they would endure if they ever tried anything like this again. He would, he decided with fierce determination, scalp them alive.

After making sure Ria was comfortable on his bed and that Millie had been appraised of both Lacie's as well as Ria's condition, he strode to the barn. The sight in front of him put a smile to his face.

"So, the two of you got caught. I'm pleased. This should put an end to Ria's daily terrors." He looked to his friends, nodding his approval. He would like to lash them as they had Ria then make sure they would understand true fear. He didn't doubt for a second a simple lashing would convince them to never set foot near her again. It would make him feel better in addition get rid of some of the unleashed anger surging through his body. Blue was his. He would leave Evan for Leslie to deal with.

Pulling the knife he always kept hidden in his boot, he strode to the men. In a quick move he slit Blue's shirt from his back. Handing the weapon to Leslie, the duke did the same to Evan.

"Would you like to go first? How many?" Leslie asked, grinning solidly as he ran the knifepoint down Evan's back. The man tried to cringe away from the point with little success.

Remembering all the brutal marks that festered on Ria's back form the beating Blue inflicted on her, any thoughts of letting this go with only a few lashes vanished from Gray's mind. "Thirty might do to begin with. We'll have to see."

Leslie slanted him a glance, his eyes narrowed. "You know something I don't?"

Nodding his head, a grim determination etched between his eyes, he spoke slowly. "These two beat Ria within an inch of her life. If I hadn't arrived at the manor house when I did, there is no doubt in my mind she would have died."

"Thirty it is then," Leslie said, laying into Evan's back until the man started screaming on the second stroke. Once Leslie finished, Gray did his job, reveling in the pathetic whimpering made by Blue. By the time they were finished both men hung unconscious, their head lolling to the side, arms stretched high.

During the punishment, Charles escorted Daryl back to the house. Graham could hear her protests, but the man-made sure Daryl didn't see anything before he escorted her inside. This was not something a sheltered woman should see. He told her she should check on Lacie and Ria. See how they were doing.

"Can't have them avoiding the pain," Gray said, eyeing the men with such fury and distaste he could barely inhale a breath. "Want them to suffer."

Charles and Harry seeming to have read his mind stood beside him each with a bucket of startling cold water. Handing each a pail, Leslie and Gray tossed the contents into Blue's and Evan's faces. They woke almost instantly, sputtering and moaning. They were pathetic little bullies who took advantage of the weak.

The haunted fearful look in Blue's eyes pleased Gray to no end. "Now we know a simple lashing will not keep you away so..." Gray pulled out his knife, stepping toward Blue. "By the time I'm finished you'll comprehend the facts here," turning with a sweeping gesture of his arm. "If anything happens to me or anyone I hold dear there will be someone here to finish what I'm going to start."

"And what would that be?" Blue asked, a mocking smile on his face and holding too much disdain in his voice to suit Gray.

Gray looked to Charles for a moment. It seemed they understood what the other was thinking, "Hold his head still and Leslie, keep a bucket of water handy. Don't want him passing out. If there is any justice, he needs to feel this from the moment I start to long after I'm finished."

Blues eyes widened as he drew closer, the shining steel of the knife clear to anyone that Gray meant to inflict pain. "If you come back for any reason, I will scalp you alive. If you touch a finger to Ria, Lacie or Daryl I will scalp you alive. What I'm going to do today is to define the line where I will begin."

Slowly and meticulously Gray cut Blue around the outlines of his face, slowly pushing at the skin to remove it a fraction from bone and muscle. Once done and after several buckets of ice water tossed in Blue's face to keep him aware of what was happening to him blood dripped to the floor as Gray deepened the line ignoring Blue's cries of pain and reveling in them. He turned to Leslie, holding up the knife, "Do you want to do the honors with Evan?"

Leslie's contemptuous smile told Gray all he needed to know. Handing him the knife, he moved back, arms crossed in front of him while Leslie repeated the process.

When Leslie finished, he stepped back, handing the knife to Gray. "Now what?"

"We allow them to hang for a day or two before we send them on their way. Need some time to think about what will happen if they do anything I dislike."

Blood dripped down their faces, sliding into their eyes as well as finding its way between their lips. They tasted their own blood and it would dry on them before Gray would cut them down. For now, they could stay unconscious. They would wake soon enough with the satisfactory understanding they would never repeat their actions.

"Keep an eye on them," he told Charles and Harry. "I'm going to see Ria. Hopefully she is awake and willing to talk about today's events."

Striding toward the house, he realized he didn't care if they talked. All he wanted, craved, was to hold her and reassure her these men would never come after her again since they had an inkling as to what it would feel like to lose their hair. It was a horrible death he admitted. If anyone deserved something like that, these two did.

He wasn't surprised to finally find her sleeping on his bed, tucked into the covers by either Daryl or Millie, he couldn't be sure. All he knew right now was that she belonged in his bed, not in the other room where she was supposed to sleep. Olivia, Midget and Dodge sat cross-legged on the floor beside the bed, peering up at him as he strode into the room.

"You kept a vigil? Good for you," he said roughing Midget's hair. "She will appreciate your loyalty when she wakes up."

"It's what she would have done for us." Dodge's stoic answer gave Gray more reasons to reconsider his options. "Don't ken why you don't do something to protect her. After all you love her, don't you?"

The truth of Dodge's words hit his heart with a vengeance. The only way he could protect her more thoroughly than he already did was to marry her. Not too long ago he'd sworn to himself that he would never marry or sire any more children. The pain of losing his family had overwhelmed him with grief. Finding his wife as well as her lover dead and his child as well through no fault of the baby's spiraled him into a deep despair.

"I've done everything I can do," he told Dodge as he sat down on the bed, picking up Ria's hand. "Don't have any other means to keep her safe. As you well know, she should have stayed in the house. If she doesn't act prudently and with some reserve, there is nothing I can do for her."

"You could marry her, give her your name just as you gave us your name. That would keep Blue and Evan away from her," Olivia said bitterly, her young voice a fountain of emotions. She continued in the same hostile vein, "Now all you're doing is making her into your whore."

He admitted, he had done just that, but he preferred the title of mistress or lover to whore. In any case, he would never let her go nor would he grow tired of her. He just couldn't marry her. That was not going to happen.

In a gruff voice, feeling the urge to be alone with Ria and his thoughts, he told the children, "You should go see what Millie has cooking for dinner. Maybe you could help out and set the table," he told the three of them, needing to find solace with his thoughts. He pulled up the wing chair that was in front of the fireplace, sitting down by the bed.

"Lacie is still asleep," Daryl said walking into the room after the children left, standing and watching with her hands clasped in front of her. Her gaze focused on Ria she said, "They should be coming out of the stupor soon. You can find out what happened."

"With blinding headaches," Gray agreed, thinking he wished Daryl would leave and trying to find a subtle way to make it happen.

He couldn't think of anything short of just asking her outright. He smoothly sent the children away. Now he didn't know what to do about his sister-in-law.

"What happened to you over the years?" She stood beside him, regarding him closely. When she spoke again her voice was soft yet filled with curiosity, "Donal says you are very different. Not at all like your old self. The only time you aren't watching Ria is when she's not in the same room with you. You never laugh."

"Nothing I care to talk about." No, life happened to him. True enough he wasn't like his nineteen-year-old self who left with eager steps for Maryland. Who was? "In a lot of ways Donal has changed too. I suppose you are part of the reason for the changes. When I left for the plantation, he vowed not to marry until he was thirty-five. Believe it was one of the pacts the bad boys made with themselves."

"None of them kept any of those pacts, at least not the ones I've heard about," Daryl said her voice a whisper of concern, reaching out to him in a way he had every intention of ignoring. She started to turn, "Now that Leslie is with his wife, I'm going downstairs. Ring the bell if you need anything. I won't bother you and Ria any longer."

He didn't say anything as he heard Daryl's footsteps leaving the room then heading to the first floor. Killing Blue and Evan was too kind. While he felt sure they would never risk the punishment he laid out, he could never be positive, afraid he might have made a gruesome mistake with these two. His gut twisted sourly with the knowledge of Blue's plans for Ria and Lacie.

Watching the steady rise and fall of Ria breasts gave him confidence that she was unhurt this afternoon. He did want her to wake though, needed to hold her close, see her eyes lighten with trust. Letting her go anytime soon, if ever, was not an option for him. He needed her by his side just so he could breathe.

When she did begin to stir, he smiled, brushing her hair away from her pale face. Remembering how her arms would go around him in the night and her heady unabashed responses to him created a deep hunger only she could quench.

She moaned softly, her hand rising to her forehead as she opened her startling blue eyes and looked at him with avid interest. "What happened? I was with Lacie. She was showing me the stallion, wanted me to feed him." She closed her eyes, her dark lashes fanning across her pale cheekbones. He needed to see her face filled with more color. The violet-blue circles beneath her eyes frightened him. Blue put her through too much. At the moment he was likely to leave him hanging in his barn to rot.

"Blue happened but Red Deer and Running With The Wind rescued you." He turned away not wanting to show Ria his palpable fear his heart desperately pounding in his chest.

Her smile faint as she reached up to touch his face, her fingertip caressing his lip, "I would have thought you would do the rescuing."

Trapping her hand gently in his, "I believe Leslie and I doled out the punishment. I'm forever grateful you were rescued before anything terrible happened."

"Punishment? You didn't kill them, did you?"

"No, while," he paused thoughtfully, "where those two weasels are concerned, I am bloodthirsty. However, I don't want to hang no matter how much they deserve to die." The thought of them hanging by their wrists in the stable, a grim smile touched his mouth.

"What did you do?" She tried to sit but fell back with a soft groan, her lashes fluttering across her cheeks for a moment. When she opened her eyes and looked at him again, "I would really appreciate a new head."

As if Millie heard her or thought she might be waking she appeared in the room with a tray. She set the tray on the table. While pouring her a cup she asked, "A little willow bark tea for you to ease the pain? Are you feeling as if you can eat anything yet?"

"Yes, I would like the tea but no food right now," she said as Gray helped her to sit, plopping several pillows behind her back. She sipped the tea Millie handed her, staring at him over the rim as Millie fussed for a few minutes then left.

For the longest time, he didn't say anything, content to watch her and give thanks Blue did not get away with her in the process vanish into the slums. There wasn't a doubt in his mind if that had happened, he would have had to tear Edinburgh apart to find her. It was becoming more apparent than ever to him this nonsense with the earl now needed to come to an end.

Her head seeming to feel better she asked again, "What did you do to them?"

He felt the laziness of his smile create one on Ria. Her lips were slightly parted, moist, giving him an urgent need to kiss her, "I horse whipped Bleu and Leslie did the honors on Evan. Thirty lashes, no small thing. My arm was tired when I finished."

"Thirty lashes, hmm... we both know that won't keep them away. More than anything they want me, and Ollie would be an added bonus. They are greedy men."

"There was one more thing which I believe will do the trick. I think you will like this although the lashes were appropriate given what Blue did to you."

"What was that? I can't imagine anything that would frighten them so much they wouldn't keep trying to bring us back into Blue's fold. He's voracious. The thought of money is all-powerful with him. Then there is his pride. You trampled it into the ground again today."

He shrugged thinking about the two men, "They are bullies but they are also cowards."

"So, what did you do?"

"I told him that if he ever touched anyone, I cared about I would scalp him alive and if for some reason I couldn't do the honors either Red Deer or Running With The Wind would make sure the scalping happened."

He sat back then, his arms crossed in front of him well pleased with the knowledge he imparted to Ria.

She inhaled softly. It seemed she understood the current of his words. "That would deter even the most courageous of men."

"Thank you. I do believe our stoic duke is chomping at the bit to learn how it is done. Now, I think it would be nice if you came downstairs with me for a casual dinner. Does your head feel any better? It has been a while since breakfast. I will carry you and cater to your every need."

Her hand fluttered in the air a moment, the smile on her face fading. "I really don't want to talk to anyone but you. I'm horribly aware of my position here and while everyone has been very nice..."

"You need not concern yourself about your so-called position. I won't have it. You are here under my protection. No one need know anything different." He found he was furious with himself for not making it clearer to her that his family didn't care what they did or did not do in the privacy of his bedchamber. No tales would be told.

She looked at her hands for several seconds, "I don't know what to say to you now or to your family downstairs. I look in their eyes and I only see the disapproval."

He swore savagely, his thoughts too violent to repeat. "Their disapproval is for me, not you besides I think you are reading something that isn't there. If anything, they firmly believe I should marry you and in the process put all the gossip to rest. What they don't understand is that I cannot marry you or anyone."

Moisture filled her eyes, her soft lips quivering slightly at his harsh words. "I never asked you to marry me nor did I come to your bed in hopes of such a commitment. I'm not deserving of you and your status but I will always cherish the moments we've spent with each other."

A wave of anger coupled with frustration swept through him at her softly spoken words. She was more than worthy to become his wife.

It was just that he didn't want to make a promise to another woman and risk another betrayal. Love was wasted on him, having tried it once only to find unbearable disappointment.

"Do not talk about yourself that way. It is me who is not deserving of you and all the kindness you've shown me." Yet he knew by keeping her in his bed there was gossip that could well develop into nasty rumors.

He sat back, raking his hands through his hair until a lock fell over his eyes. "Humor me. If you come with me downstairs for just a short time, I would be pleased. Perhaps you would like to visit Blue and spit in his face."

She giggled softly at his words. "I would do both for you even though I'm not really up for visiting. If you don't expect me to talk..."

"Thank you." He swept her into his arms. In a few minutes they were sitting in the library with all his guests surrounding them.

When they entered, the lively chatter stopped for a few seconds then, "I trust you are feeling better. Just as Lacie is," the duke said as he ran his hand up and down Lacie's arm as if to reassure himself of her recovery. She was leaning into him, totally absorbed in what he was saying and doing.

Ria slowly nodded as she looked around the room. "My head almost feels normal thanks to Gray's amazing tea."

"Willow bark tea, something the Cherokee use," Gray said. "I believe Lacie was given a cup also."

Millie bustled about, pouring her a glass of wine now then handing her a plate of finger foods. She sipped a moment then setting the glass on the table with the plate she picked out a few morsels.

He didn't want to let her go. He had the sinking feeling that when his brother left to go back to Glasgow, Ria would ask to go along with them. Everything she was saying to him indicated she didn't want to remain in his home.

"This has been an eventful first day," Daryl said looking outside.

"Too much so," Lacie whispered, her voice thin as if remembering the events of the afternoon.

"We will find this earl for you and deal with him," Leslie promised.

The evening passed with small talk and not much said as to what they were going to do about the earl. It seemed everyone wanted to dwell on more pleasant topics of conversation. All that was confirmed was that they should drive to Edinburgh and stay a few days. They were all welcome to reside at the duke's residence there. They all agreed that in three day's time they should make the trip, a day after sending Evan and Blue on their way home. He was pleased that Ria remained in the room occasionally joining the conversations. She decided to wait until the following day to see Blue and Evan and as Gray encouraged her, to maybe spit in their faces. When they left for bed, he was sure she was going to ask to sleep in her room. She didn't. Instead, she told him she would be leaving soon, not even waiting until his brother left for home.

"I can't put you and the children in any more danger. The events of today are a tragic example of what men can do. Lacie had no part in any of this intrigue yet she fell victim just because she was close to me."

He raised one eyebrow in speculation. "So, where will you go? You've no funds available, no way except by foot to go anywhere. This is obviously not a well thought out plan."

Gray didn't understand the careless shrug she presented him with. Did she have no care for her own safety?

"I will try to find a way to get to Glasgow. Daryl told me already I could stay above her bakery. She said she would write a note to Justine, one of her employees. She will give me the key. I don't suppose you could lend me the money I might need. I will pay you back as soon as I can."

Even with her foolishness, Gray tried to see this situation from her point of view but found he was failing miserably. If she just up and left, she would put herself in more danger than ever before.

He didn't want her to leave him, but was forced with the painful reality his wife left him too. So how was she any different?

"I have come to the conclusion despite all your efforts and now your family's efforts, he will find me. It's only a matter of time. Truly I've no idea how you can protect me from him."

"You believe you will be far enough away if you flee to Glasgow. You have this nasty habit of running away from your problems rather than facing them."

He didn't mean to hurt. By the look in her eyes, he'd done that very thing.

"Fine, and it has worked every time. I am safe."

She was fuming now, her temper escalating. He found he liked that side of her. He would rather see her anger rather than complaisance.

"Only because you are in my arms and my bed. If you leave now..."

He wasn't at all sure where he wanted this conversation to go at the moment. He certainly didn't want to make her so furious she would storm from the room in the middle of the night.

Ria spun on her heels. Her eyes were luminous with a mixture of hurt linked with indignation. "Do you think I am leaving to punish you? You know why I have to leave. He was here in this house only a few days ago, as a dinner guest. Since Blue and Evan found me, I ken he will too. If you believe you can protect me or even the duke of Southcliff can keep that man from possessing me again then you are sorely mistaken. You've no idea what the earl is capable of, just how evil he is. I have no choice save to run." She blinked back the tears threatening to fall and inhaled a long steadying breath.

"Did I miss something?" He was clearly taken aback by her words. His heated curses echoed in the room. "The earl is the man who held you?"

She lowered her lashes, "Yes."

"It might not be easy. If you remain with me, no harm will come to you. I promise you that." His voice filled with uncontrolled emotion. Christ the earl was the man who caused her worst fears.

"Remaining here at your house makes me vulnerable. You make me vulnerable. He will exploit my affection for all of you the children included and force my hand. By threats to you, he will find a way to see that I come to him in return for your safety."

Gray leaned forward in his chair, regarding her intently. "Is that what he did before? Threaten you? I'm perfectly capable of protecting myself as well as the children, you know."

"Not me but with his own children, yes. He never threatened to harm them physically. He had subtle ways of destroying them, of putting doubt in their precious young minds."

Gray tried to push Ria's words aside. "He doesn't have that power over my children. He couldn't manipulate them in such a way. Because of their street life they understand their lives have never been filled with love and joy until now," Gray said, trying to reassure but realizing he wasn't gaining any ground.

"No, of course not. He would have a vested interest in whether they lived or died. There are always more boys who can be plucked for his uses. There would be no reason for subtlety there. He would see them with broken bones or broken necks first. All except Ollie, she would suffer the same fate I did, perhaps worse because she is younger." She waved a hand in front of her face. "The first year I was with him, still defiant and disobedient, he brought a young street girl home. She had been ill used many times in her short life and thought she knew what to expect from her encounter with the earl. What she failed to comprehend was that he meant her to be naught but a lesson to me. Her sole purpose was to serve as an example so he could break me down, to serve him as he pleased. If Glasgow is not far enough away, I'll find some way to book passage to America. Perhaps someone at your plantation will take me in if you're willing to write a letter for me. I can work."

"Ria, you don't have—"

"No, before we go any farther in this conversation, I have to tell you more of the truth than you've heard from me before," she told him, her voice soft yet filled with venom. "The girl who was meant to be my example was unrecognizable when he was finished with her. Her face was blackened from the blows and the blood was everywhere. He flayed the skin from her back as well as her thighs. That is what he can do to someone whom he regards with the same compassion he has for a cockroach." Her voice shook with raw savage emotion. "I can bear whatever he does to me, Gray, but I cannot bear what he will do to you because of me."

Gray rose to his feet. He stood in front of her a moment, hands at his sides, palms out. He was unused to hesitation, even less to the numbing fear that kept him rooted to the spot where he stood. He needed to approach her, wanted to hold her and anticipating, dreading that because of all she just revealed, she would flinch from him, kept him standing in place.

It was then Gray understood how different his feelings were for Ria than he previously thought. How he could still not accept the fact that he might care for her more than he was willing to admit even to himself. What he did know was that her leaving him for whatever reason was not tenable. Did she think he could not protect her? As long as she remained by his side, he could do just that. If she left, there would be no way.

"You're not going to leave, Ria." His words were said with such brutal ferocity, his voice so low and dark, her face lost every vestige of color. "You must realize I won't allow it."

Ria pressed her lips together shaking her head as she stepped back, moving away from him. "No, I can leave in the middle of the night when you are asleep."

"It's true, you can refuse to accept my mandate. You can try your best," he said. "Indeed, you can be angry that I commanded anything from you which until now I've asked nothing in return you weren't willing to give. Know that if you leave, I will find you and bring you home. It matters not to me that people believe you are my mistress. You are not. You are my light in the darkest part of the night. Without you near me, I doubt if I could breathe. I ken my heart would forget to beat."

Ria's knees went out from under her. She might have dropped to the floor but Gray moved quickly to scoop her into his arms. Far from flinching away from him she anchored herself to him, held on as if he was her lifeline. He didn't move. He barely breathed as he regarded her more closely than ever before. Security was what he offered and what she should gratefully accept.

He saw no moisture in her eyes yet he was sure in any other circumstance she would have allowed tears to fall. She pressed her cheek against his frock coat with a long drawn-out sigh.

"How is it possible that one heart can make room for both despair and joy?" she whispered, her words broken and ragged. "Can you feel how desperately mine pounds?"

Gray turned his head and lowered his chin just enough to place a kiss on her forehead then hiding his smile, "Are you speaking of my heart or yours?"

She raised her face before touching his cheek gently with a fingertip. "Is it the same for you?"

"Perhaps that is how it is supposed to be done," he told her his voice soft, resonating beyond anything he'd know or understood before. "Not with one heart, but two beating as one." He took her hand from where it now rested at his side and brought it to his chest. "Does it seem as if it might be so?"

Ria touched the corner of his mouth where a slight smile formed. "Are you teasing me? That cannot be mistaken for a scientific sentiment simply because it is too terribly romantic."

"Perhaps it is both." He held her gaze, her eyes shimmering with what he hoped was passion as well as desire for him. His smile faded as his mouth came within a hairsbreadth of hers. "Shall we find out?"

Ria's reply was a soft, surrendering moan of acknowledgment. His mouth accepted hers. She held on again, this time with her arms sliding over his shoulders to find purchase around his neck. His hands secured her at the small of her back, her pliant slim body shuddering against his.

Eagerness sent them to their knees. Urgency made them careless. They could not rid themselves of their clothing quick enough to suit either one. She helped him out of his frock coat. He unfastened the buttons down the back of her dress. A pearl button rolled under the bed clattering before it came to a halt against the far wall. The delicate lace circling the hem of her dress was rent where it was caught under his boot. The pile of clothes beside them grew then was scattered as they lowered themselves the rest of the way to the floor.

While they were still on their feet his kiss had been long and drugging. The moist hot caress had now become a staccato burst of passion that fed their frenzy to become a part of each other. In a bid for dominance, they rolled on the floor tangling their arms and legs. Ria's fingers caught in his hair. She tugged pulling him back with enough insistence so for a moment he yielded her the high ground. She straddled his hips just long enough for him to surge powerfully beneath her then she was turned, mouth parted, still trying to catch her breath and pulled under him once more. She simply wanted him more deeply inside her. It was not surrender now but the expression of his raging desire.

Supporting himself on his forearms, Gray held himself still and looked down at Ria's flushed face. Her eyes had a vaguely slumberous appeal, yet there was such purpose in the way she looked at him that he did not doubt she knew the sirens' song. He moved then only a little but it was enough to make her contract around him and pull a harsh groan from his throat.

"Witch," he murmured, nudging her mouth just once with his.

~ * ~

"Only because you make me so." She felt his quiet chuckle against her breast. Her fingers lightly trailed along his shoulders, coming to rest on his upper arms. His skin was smooth and warm. Beneath it, tension in his muscles defined their long line and strength. She sighed satisfied as he began to move within her again, committing these seconds to memory in order for her to recall when she was no longer with him.

In seconds it seemed as if there was no lull in their urgent lovemaking. They were both struck with the identical pressing hunger as before. They did not so much as share the same breath as stole it from each other. By turns selfish and demanding, responsive and giving, they acted out despair and joy in equal measure. Rough play that made them gasp with pleasure so intense that it was almost an agony also brought them back to moments of profound quiet where the passion simmered deep and raw unwilling to let it come to its conclusion.

Gray suckled her breast into his mouth. Her pink tipped aureoles puckered under his teeth and tongue. She arched beneath him, flesh ripening. Her lips parted. She made tiny mewling noises at the back of her throat. He pushed into her, rocking against his calves then the backs of his thighs. She held him, moved with him then against him.

Above them candlelight flickered. The fire in the hearth snapped. The light fragrances from the brandy he sipped earlier in the evening mingled with the heavier scents of sweat and sex. They inhaled deeply, raggedly, sometimes through their mouths as though they might taste the air then each other.

Ria's small body undulated with the power of her pleasure. Her breath caught. When it was released it carried the sweet sound of his name. His climax came a moment later, his own satisfaction as powerfully realized as hers but with a hoarse cry that was wholly unintelligible.

Surprised she had the strength to laugh, she nevertheless found herself doing just that. Gray did the same though his chuckle seemed to come deep from his belly. Gray eased himself carefully onto his side then his back, bringing Ria to lie fully on top of him. "Do with me what you want. My body is all yours," he murmured, his voice hoarse with ragged emotions.

Ria found the strength to arch an eyebrow but not her head. "You cannot be serious. I've no ability to do anything at the moment with your huge body save lie here on top of you or beneath you whichever you might prefer, soaking up the heat of your manly frame."

"Imagine my amazement then," he said, gruffly, "to find I like both positions equally well."

She sunk her teeth lightly into the skin of his neck. Instead of squirming under her as she thought he would, he brought the flat of his palm against her bottom. "Ow!" That small cry caused her to release him.

Gray soothed her indignation by laying his hand over the offended portion of her anatomy and massaging it. "Better?"

"For whom?"

"I take your point." He roused himself to kiss the crown of her hair. "Can you reach my shirt?"

She stretched, snagged the sleeve with her toes and dragged it across the floor until he caught it with his fingertips. Gray bunched the fabric in his fist then pushed it under his head to use as a pillow.

"We don't have to stay on the floor. The bed is just over there." She nodded her head in that direction.

"Can you see that it looms as a veritable mountain before us?" His question did nothing to surprise her.

Grinning contentedly, very nearly purring, Ria could see that it did. Beneath her breast she could feel the beat of Gray's heart, perfectly in tune to the beat of her own. "Two into one," she murmured, amazed at the notion. "Can you feel it?"

"Indeed, it proves my point, I think. A triumph of scientific inquiry, that two people can actually share a heartbeat."

"Romantic twaddle. But it's nice of you to puff the notion up."

Feeling not the slightest pressure to stir or speak, Ria lay quietly for a long time, soaking in all that was special about this man. Gray's fingertips traced an erotically sensuous trail from the curve of her bottom all the way up her spine and back again. It was how she knew he had not fallen asleep. "I don't want to leave you. You know that don't you?" She hesitated then said. "Gray, talk to me."

"I understand." His voice was terse with emotions and anger, the frustration very evident in his tone.

"I believe it is the most difficult decision I've ever made or even thought of doing. This was not easy."

It was as she well knew absolutely imperative to save his life.

"I understand that too."

"Did you also mean that you would come after me?"

"I meant it, Ria. I meant everything. If you leave, it will not be for long. As far as I see it, there is no reason for you to waste the energy."

Ria did not doubt anything Gray told her. The quiet resolve was deep in his voice. He cared for her and from the extent of what he told her about Blue and Evan, he would also kill for her. She didn't want him to do that, kill. "Isn't there anything I can do that would cause you to rethink your position?"

Gray's hand dipped in the curve at the small of her back and rested there a second, the intimacy leaving pleasant thoughts. "About the way I feel about you? No. Never that."

"The other?"

"No, my mind is made up even though I thoroughly understand you will make your choices as I will make mine."

Ria's cheek still rested against his chest. Her heart beat more quickly now while his maintained the same steady rhythm. Nothing they talked about ruffled him. "Have you ever called a man out?"

"Not in my short lifetime. Dastardly way to settle a difference, in my opinion."

"Never been called out?"

"Never."

"You've never met a man at twenty paces." She was groping for more information, searching for a way to convince him as to just how dangerous the earl was.

"That's right."

"He has. Twice that I know about. I'm sure there have been more times. He is an excellent shot. Both men were grievously injured. One died only a short time after he was carried from the field. I heard the other left the country as soon as he was able to travel. I'm afraid when he finds me with you, he will kill you. Call you out so you have no choice but to face him."

"Based on everything you've told me, I'm afraid there is an equal chance he will not kill me."

Her heart caught in her throat. Fear for Gray heavy in her heart she rose, moving away from him. She picked up her shift and slipped it on then stepped over Gray on her way to the dressing room. She remained there washing and collecting her thoughts until she judged enough time passed. While she understood she could not leave this evening, she did make plans to do so.

She would have to find a way.

When she stepped into the bedroom, however, she saw she had been too generous with the allotted time. Gray was comfortably situated on his bed looking for all the world as if nothing had been said between them that would anger or frustrate him. She noticed he had even picked up after himself, setting his garments neatly over the chair.

"I had hoped you would leave. Perhaps the other men have not retired for the evening. You could chat or you could check on Blue and Evan. I'm sure they've every reason to attempt escape. I thought you would have something to do."

"Did you? Odd, that. I am perfectly comfortable here, in my bed. There is nothing pressing for me to accomplish this evening." He patted the space beside him. "Come, Ria. Have done with your thoughts of my demise at the hands of the earl. It is the earl who should worry if he does anything to harm you." He paused in thought, his brow rising up to give her reason she might not like the next words coming from his lips. "Or perhaps did you think to slink out the back door when I'm not looking? The other men are with their wives doing what we were doing a few minutes ago, so there is no one to chat with except you."

"No, of course not. I don't slink. You convinced me it would not be prudent of me to treat my life in such a careless manner."

She sighed softly then regarded him closely. It seemed he was doing the same to her. She was not suitable for him to wed. She didn't think she could remain his mistress for the rest of her life. Sometime she would have to leave him.

"You may think to ask Donal or even the duke for safe passage to Glasgow. Without my express permission, neither man will concede to your wishes even if their wives begged, which they won't." He was still patting the bed beside him, smiling, the handsome grin too much to resist.

The problem was as she approached the bed, she thought desperately, Gray didn't have any idea how immoral and ruthless the earl was and that he would stop at nothing to have what he wanted including killing anyone who managed somehow to get in his way. She knew Gray would do just that, get in his way. If that happened, living with herself would be impossible.

"You would keep me here against my will," she sighed heavily, sitting down beside him, allowing him to take her into his arms.

With his touch her body shuddered in instant and sweet response, needing him more than she ever thought possible. He was naked, the sheets pulled to just below his waist and god help her she wanted him again.

"Does it appear you are staying in my bed in protest? You know you are free to come and go as you please."

He chuckled softly as she rested her head against his chest her hand on his belly, tracing lazily circles that she knew would arouse him.

"You will always bring me back," she murmured thoughtfully wondering if that meant always even when they grew old.

"Yes, this is true. Perhaps instead of worrying about me and if I've ever participated in a duel, you should ask me if I've ever killed a man." He stroked her arm, sliding his long slender fingers down then up seeming pleased with his words.

"Have you?" She propped herself up so she could see into his eyes, the silver blue glinting in the meager light.

"You forget that I lived in a place that is not exactly as civilized as the cities in Scotland. For God's sake I lived with the Cherokee for over a year. I learned their ways very efficiently, went on raiding parties with them. Saw and did things I never want to encounter again in my life. If you don't believe me, tomorrow morning take a look at Blue and Evan. I could flay every inch of skin from their bodies and their hearts would still beat." His voice turned angry and frustrated, too, as he sought to convince her he could take care of her that she didn't have to keep running. "Yet, I also don't want you to see the violence that so easily can come from my hands."

"I suppose I do forget. You hide it well; rarely speak of those times. It seems you want to forget them. You are such a gentle soul."

She inhaled a long savage breath, wishing for a life that she couldn't have until the earl's ended. Even then she could not stay with this man. She was nothing, just a child who'd lost her parents at an early age and been placed in an abbey because no one wanted her.

"Only around you," he said, his voice turning soft a warm caress against her face. She ran her hand along his chest, enjoying the feel of his hair against the palm of her hand. "People who know me understand a far different side of me than you do. Daryl was right. I've changed over the last five years. Life has changed me. There is a hard ruthless edge to everything I do and see. Yet somehow you have given me a new perspective on my life and how I wish to live."

"Sometime you must talk about this existence you had in America."

Her curiosity drove her to ask questions she knew he didn't want to answer. Holding it inside her was driving her mad.

"Not tonight."

"Why?"

He bent to kiss her. Her lips were parted. She wanted the kiss but she needed answers more. She would not leave him tonight or tomorrow night she decided as once more his lips ravaged hers. His hunger was obvious in the slant of his mouth against hers combined with the harsh demands he made. She needed to forget the one major and obvious reason why she could never stay with him. She loved him. He deserved a woman who could give him everything she could not.

"Because we have better things to do than talk about a time I don't want to remember."

His mouth slanted across her soft open lips, his tongue finding hers in an urgent and sweet exploration.

She melted into his embrace, her body responding as tendrils of fire shot through her. For this one moment, although she knew it wouldn't last, she was his and he was hers. His hard body next to hers was an aphrodisiac calling to her. The enchantment he created too real to ignore. She could no more resist him than stop breathing.

The tenderness melted her heart. Perhaps that was why she didn't think he could ever best that horrible man. He would hesitate and that very second, he would lose. Even though he told her he had killed, she almost didn't believe him except for the fact he had no reason to lie to her. She had no idea what he spoke of as well as what transpired during his life the previous five years. Yet his words began to take shape in her mind. Perhaps it was more what he didn't say.

Ria moved against him as his hand found certain erotically sensitive spots, encouraging her to forget all the probing questions in her head. Ultimately, she understood he would not speak of anything he didn't want to talk about despite her curiosity. She could only hope that someday he would give in to her probing questions.

Perchance for the time being she should let him protect her and damn the consequences. From everything he told her, he would endure most anything to keep her in his bed. Conceivably tonight had been just about her whims. She needed him and needed for him to tell her how he felt.

What was almost too much to deal with was the fact she loved him with all her heart. She never meant to fall in love, never meant to put his life in danger, never meant to reduce his life to this fragile existence that seemed to exist only one second at a time. When she hid in this house months ago, she'd only sought a few moments of shelter from the demons following her. Fate kept her. Fate sent her a man who she could love.

When she looked at Daryl and Lacie, she saw women deserving of kind hearted and tender men even though she'd been told both men possessed a hard dangerous edge. She saw women who would make the man they married proud of them. Because of her sordid past, she could be nothing of the sort for Gray. He deserved more.

This time the loving was slow and gentle, none of the frantic eagerness that existed between them earlier. All urgency vanished. He moved gently and slowly her passion grew. One large hand tenderly cupped her breast while his teeth and tongue played with her mouth, danced inside. She arched her back as one hand slipped downward across her belly to invade more intimate territory. His fingers sliding between her thighs, a deep throaty purr caressed the back of her throat. He took the soft sound into his mouth.

Her fingers splayed across his back, nails running along his spine down to rest on the hard tense muscles of his buttocks. She moved languidly against him as his hands settled beneath her, lifting her higher.

"I cannot wait any longer," he whispered against her ear even as his teeth bit tenderly, worrying it then sipping the skin along her neck, grazing tender flesh with his teeth, soothing with his hot tongue. He kissed her again, his mouth molding across her, hard now and more demanding.

He aroused and enticed every part of her as she slowly felt the beginnings of her release. Driving inside he continued working magic with his fingers and lips. She arched up, the result of his efforts left her spinning out of control, her body searching for his, uncontrolled tremors raking over her body. She cried out his name as he sucked the words into his mouth.

She felt his release, as he drove deeper into her. He cried her name with a husky growl before settling down on her. His weight above her enchanted her. That alone gave her strong feelings of protection she craved even knowing by itself it wasn't enough.

She closed her eyes. She must have slept deeply. When she woke, a soft golden light pulsed inside the window with the curtains moving gently. He was gone from the bed. He would have risen early to see the men in the stables and if they were still alive. Perhaps he was enjoying a cup of tea with his brother as well as the duke.

Indecision was all that she accomplished the night before speaking honestly to Gray. While she still feared for his life and felt an urgent need to put him out of danger, it didn't seem there was anything she could do about his determination to keep her close.

The inadequacies of her situation haunted her. She understood how his relationship with her was detrimental for him. Her own reputation could be tarnished no more than it already had been.

"Good morning."

The object of her thoughts strode into the room, a broad smile on his strikingly handsome features. With a heartwarming and very lazy grin, he asked, "Are you going to lie about all day in bed?"

She snorted with a hasty comment on her lips. "You did wear me out last night. Perhaps I just don't have the stamina you have."

She sat up stretching while trying to keep the coverings up to her neck, understanding full well if she didn't, they would make love before anything else happened this morning.

"Well, it is only natural. A man always has more strength than a woman." He set the tray he carried on a table before pouring her a cup of tea and handing it to her.

Ria gave up then letting the coverings pool around her waist. She held the saucer in one hand and the cup in the other. "Thank you," she said. "You should probably leave so I can get dressed."

He regarded her closely, his gaze sweeping the length of her and back up, a thin smile on his face. She saw the passion grow in the depth of his deep green eyes. Her own body heated in response to his slow perusal as she thought about the ways his hands and mouth explored her, ignited her into flames she could never ignore.

She set the saucer and cup on the table beside the bed before pulling the cover to wrap around under her arms. "What do you have planned today?"

His broad shoulders lifted for a moment, his smile lazy. "Not much. I intend to spend the day with you making you happy. Tomorrow we will pack and make our way to Edinburgh the next day and hopefully the end of all your problems. We will beard the lion in his den so to speak."

She could only hope but what he thought would be the end, it would only be the beginning of a new set of issues. Ria didn't want to dwell on things that could never be, but she needed to impress those things on Gray so he would let her go. He'd tried to tell her what her life was like before had nothing to with now. He was wrong. Dead wrong.

"You can believe that. I don't." She rose, striding across the room to find a robe. Wrapping it around her, she ordered a bath. "Should I join you downstairs in an hour or so?"

"I will see you in the library."

He turned, leaving as quickly and as easily as he entered a short while ago.

She sighed heavily, sitting down, her head resting in her hands. Ria didn't know what to do or how to fight this man who stole her heart.

~ * ~

Later that afternoon the Duke of Southcliff sifted through papers that had been delivered to him earlier, frown lines creasing his face. When he received the information, he excused himself finding a quiet place where he could read the entire contents without interruption. What he read answered many questions but also created more.

At this moment, he stared out the long window in the library watching as the rain clouds cleared while a few cascading rays of sunshine warmed the earth. Vacillating thoughts swept through him. He didn't know how Gray would react to the knowledge he discovered. He wasn't sure if he was ready to tell him until the other problems whirling around Ria were solved.

Yet Leslie understood Gray deserved to hear all the truth.

As Gray and Ria believed, she was not a nobody. If his

information was correct, foul play killed her parents. The odorous scent of premeditated murder burned his nostrils scorching the delicate lining of his lungs as he read farther and uncovered more damning evidence. That same vulgar set of circumstances sent her to the abbey where William could find her when he wanted her. It also cemented the fact she would have nowhere to go when she came of age.

The earl sought revenge against her family feeling used by them or perhaps deprived of what he believed was his. Ria. Her given name was Maria McKenzie. Upon further reading, he discovered that the earl actually pledged his troth to Aila, Ria's mother, but she refused him.

Donal entered the room, surprising him from his mordant uncovering of facts. Leslie cast his gaze back to the pages on the desk then to his friend. He asked Donal to meet him here today to help him with just how much information he should give Gray. At the moment, Leslie wasn't at all sure Gray would deal with anything he could reveal with a calm head.

Leslie understood those feeling all too well having experienced something similar with his wife Lacie and the man who nearly managed to convince her through his vile actions to annul her marriage to him. It had taken him too long to persuade her not all men were despicable creatures willing to take from women things they did not wish to give. He returned from his last assignment to find Lacie hiding from him and denying him the sweet intimacies of her body that a husband expected.

Leslie sat behind the imposing desk, a snifter of brandy in front of him. Negligently leaning back and stretching his legs out in front of him, he smiled grimly. "Don't know what we can tell your brother. This is all such a tangled mess of deceit and lies."

For a few poignant seconds, Donal sipped his brandy then stared at the amber liquid in his glass slowly swirling it as if that action would give him much needed actions. "He's in love with her and she doesn't believe she is good enough for a man of his position. What a conundrum."

Leslie's laugh was harshly deliberate. "Ach, his little Maria McKenzie is more than good enough. One might argue her pedigree would preclude her from marrying beneath her station. Wedding a second son would hardly have been her mother's and father's wishes."

"Where is my brother? We should probably make sure he is not privy to what we discuss here until we know what we think he can handle. By the way, what is her pedigree?"

Tapping the tips of his fingers on the desk, vague thoughts flitting through his head. "It seems her father, Birk McKenzie was a duke, the Duke of Southmoor. Her mother was Aila. The earl coveted Aila. When he couldn't have her..." Leslie shrugged nonchalantly. "That's when things took a new and malevolent turn."

"He decided no one could have her?" Donal asked seeming to see the drift of the conversation. "Something must have gone terribly awry since Aila also perished."

"I'm not sure that was the case. By then I'm pretty sure that William understood he would never have Aila McKenzie. When Ria's parents died, Edinburgh was ripe with seeming speculation that it was not an accident but nothing could be proven. Ria was left alone and with no one, no other close relatives to claim the young child, her fate was in question."

"Someone should have been found to take care of her a guardian, a long-lost aunt or uncle."

"There was, but said relative lived in North Carolina. By the time he was contacted and reached Edinburgh there was no trace of the little girl."

Leslie now sat on the edge of the desk, one leg propping him in a half sitting half standing position, the other leg hanging over the desk. Pensively he sipped his brandy.

"Can I assume there has been no trace of who she was until now? That you've discovered exactly who she is? You have proof of her real identity?"

Leslie nodded, his body tense, fingers tightening around the crystal in his hand "The sisters in the abbey were given her name and birth certificate when Ria arrived. William knew that in order to claim what he wanted, he would have to have said proof when the time was right. I was able to gain the papers. Although it wasn't easy. The originals are no longer at the abbey but in Gray's safe just waiting for the pending reveal."

"So, I'm assuming the earl meant to marry her when she came of age? That must have happened several years ago. Why didn't he do just that? All would be done now." Donal appeared puzzled by that news.

"He would of course have need of her permission. I doubt if he wanted to wed her. I believe he just wanted to beget a son. The commitment was not something he desired."

"A son would have inherited the title as well as the money from the estate. He would have been made the boy's guardian," Donal finished for him. Then, "Even if the boy was a bastard?"

"Yes, but Ria didn't have any children that we know of, boy or girl. She has told Gray she is infertile, yet the truth of the matter is probably closer to the fact the earl is barren." Leslie continued the conversation as well as more of the much-needed information.

"Bloody eyes but what will Ria think when she learns the truth? This would be overwhelming for anyone," Donal said. "She is no longer a poor commoner but an heiress and rich as Midas."

"So, Maria McKenzie is a very wealthy woman as soon as she can be confirmed at the rightful heir. Her son, if she has one, will become the new Duke of Southmoor. This is all very interesting. I'm sure Gray will be more than concerned now that she needs an entirely different kind of protection."

"I think the earl plotted to gain the wealth. Everything he did by keeping Ria prisoner in his home pointed in that direction," Leslie said. "He must have been furious when she managed to find a way out of his grasp.

Chapter Seven

As it turned out, Leslie and Donal decided to give all the new information he found about Maria McKenzie to Gray. It was decided he should not be blindsided by the knowledge but would be better served by knowing all that he was up against as well as the reasons for the earl hanging on so tenaciously to a woman previous thought to be a commoner.

Two days after Donal and Leslie's conversation in the library and a day after the news was imparted to Gray the three couples left for Edinburgh with the intention of residing at the Duke of Southcliff's home in the city. The entourage included three carriages, ten of the duke's most trusted men as well as several servants. The children remained at home with Millie, Harry and Charles.

When they pulled up in front of the townhouse, the skies opened up, rain sluicing to the ground and creating rivulets of water running down the streets. The furious downpour came on them too quickly to avoid it. They all made a mad dash to the door and laughing as if children when they finally found their way inside the home. Their cloaks dripped on the floor and rugs, tiny puddles forming around their sodden feet.

Gray smiled lazily at Ria, bending to kiss her forehead briefly. Water beaded on her face and eyelashes. The mad dash gave her cheeks a radiant glow. He wasn't at all sure what they were going to do about the earl or how they were going to go about doing it. Proving anything would nearly be impossible after all these years. They could confront the man with the proof of Ria's true identity then she could claim her inheritance. The rest was her story versus his.

The day before Donal and Leslie had apprised him of the

situation. While they hashed over all the possibilities, none of their plans proved to be satisfactory, finding various loopholes in every scenario. Before they showed their hand, they needed to be sure what they were planning would not put Ria in further jeopardy.

For now, they would continue to search out more evidence while they tried to figure out a way to explain things to Ria. The knowledge would be difficult for her. Gray understood she might reject him as well as his attentions now that her lot in life changed so dramatically. She of course could not stay with him as his lover or mistress depending on which term one wanted to use to describe their relationship. He certainly didn't care about her wealth or her possible title. He was a wealthy man in his own right. As for him, his time in America convinced him that titles were a bit antiquated. The possibility of her having a child with him was slim to not at all. Most times he'd taken precautions against that very thing.

Leslie's in-house servants had been given notification the day before about their pending arrival. Now they bustled around the foyer, taking coats and ushering the chatting couples into the drawing room at the front of the house.

Leslie stood at the fireplace, an unintelligible expression crossing his grim features. "Brandy? Wine? Tea?" To break the ensuing silence, "I assume my lovely wife would prefer a glass of wine." He turned to grace her with a knowing smile.

She grinned shamelessly cocking her head to one side and batting her lashes flirtatiously at her husband. "Actually, I'd prefer the brandy if you don't mind. I've a feeling I'm going to be in need of something stronger by the time we finish here today."

He held a snifter up in a grand gesture then proceeded to pour her a generous amount. "As you wish," he told her his voice smooth.

Gray was sure he had intimate plans with her for as soon as they were finished with this first introduction to his home and the hour or so before dinner.

"Daryl? What would you like?" Leslie stared at her with an approving smile that was between Donal and his wife.

"Believe I'll choose what my sister is having also. Brandy for me too," she said as Donal's hand rested possessively on her shoulders, his fingers tightening slightly.

"It must have been a long arduous ride today," Leslie laughed as he turned his attention to Ria. "Brandy for you also?"

"Tea please. I think I've had, well... I'll wait until this evening to have my glass of wine with Gray. Then we can talk more thoroughly about our visit here since I was unwilling to accompany him in the first place."

"Ah, some delicacies to hold us over until dinner." Leslie looked up as one of the servants arrived with a tray of food. "What is this, a strawberry concoction of some sort?" he asked, picking up a small tart and popping it in his mouth. "Delicious. Cook has outdone herself this time. So, we have sweet treats. I see sliced ham and roast beef, some cheeses and breads as well. Thank you, this will certainly tide us over until dinner."

They chatted amiably about very little of importance while Gray thought over the things he would have to tell Ria tonight after dinner. He supposed the tale could be told over their usual glass of wine before bed would be the best time. It was something he was looking forward to. He wondered just how she would take the news.

Dinner passed uneventfully; afterward the men retired to the library to smoke and drink. The women ended up in the drawing room with a glass of sherry each, chatting about their impending trip tomorrow to the dressmaker.

"When are you going to tell Ria," Leslie asked seeming impatient to set their so far nonexistent plans into action. Well, they did have a dinner planned two nights from now with the earl along with a few other respectable and important lords to be in attendance for her unveiling. It was at that time he would introduce the long-lost Maria McKenzie heir to the McKenzie fortune linked with the news her first born son would become the Duke of Southmoor.

"Tonight. Don't see how I can put this strange story off any longer. It's so twisted in deceit and lies, I'm not sure where I should begin."

Gray would delay hurting her forever if he could, but the real problem was how she would react to the news. For some reason he couldn't fathom, he didn't believe Ria would care about any of it, a title for a son she didn't have or the wealth. He was deathly afraid that with the new found groats she would leave him. That was all she wanted to do was leave for Glasgow or America. He would still go after her. This time her leaving however would be as she once told him for his good. Now it would be with her best interests at heart.

"Who are you inviting to dinner?" Donal asked curiously. "Besides the earl."

Leslie rattled off a list of names, few of which Gray remembered from his family's infrequent visits to this side of Scotland. The only one of great importance was the earl. His reaction to seeing Ria could be damning. Gray had a strong suspicion the earl was used to surprises and would manage to stoically hide his shock.

With the hour drawing late, they all made their excuses before retiring to their individual bedchambers. The duke gave Ria her own bedroom but Gray expected her to be sitting in his when he arrived ready to explain the entire sordid story from beginning to end. He would be disappointed if she wasn't there. If so, he would have to seek her out because during their nightly chats was the best time to give her the information that would effectively change her life forever.

When he stepped inside the room, he wasn't disappointed. Ria was curled up on a sofa, sipping her first glass of wine. The pink satin robe she wore hugged her curves. At the beautiful sight before him, he was more inclined to take her to bed than to spend the next hour or so in conversation. He suspected they would finish the bottle before the night ended.

For several more seconds he watched her as he propped himself against the doorframe arms crossed in front of him. Even though she'd not been raised among the gentry, she had an unmistakable regal bearing about her. When she noticed him, she turned, her deep blue eyes focused intently on him. She smiled softly, her lips parted and moist as if she hoped for a kiss. He'd be more than willing to oblige her but only after the little talk they needed to have. If he kissed her before they spoke, they would be in bed together and nothing would be accomplished.

Before the evening drew to a close, he hoped she still felt that way. He drew in a ragged breath, pushing himself away from the doorframe. Striding quickly to her side he sat down then poured himself a glass of wine. For a timeless second, he closed his eyes, drawing in much needed courage as if he could find it in the air he was breathing.

"I'm not really sure why you insisted we come here with the duke and your brother. Being in the city bothers me more than I want to admit. I constantly find myself looking over my shoulder to see if Blue is there." Hesitantly, she reached out to touch his arm.

"The duke is an indomitable force when it comes to ferreting out sordid information of any sort. In your case he has learned a great deal about your past. The men he travels with are operatives of his. They research everything thoroughly. All of which you should be apprised of."

His gaze fell on the slender white column of her neck, the steady pulse of her heart at the base.

"That doesn't answer my question or my concerns. Perhaps we could leave for home tomorrow now that I've done my duty. Truly, I'd like to leave this city and everything it reminds me of behind."

She flashed him a brilliant smile, one that usually melted his heart. If they were to see this end in a manner they wished, he could not allow her to deter him. He looked away when her lashes gently fluttered against her beautiful high cheekbones.

Her not so subtle attempts to seduce told Gray she had not a heard a word of what he'd said or she didn't acknowledge the truths he was setting in front of her. This was obviously a tender subject needing to be handled with a delicate finesse he wasn't feeling at the moment.

He cleared his throat, wishing like the devil the dinner in two days' time would be over and done with simply because that would mean she would know everything that needed to be known. Hopefully, the earl would be in jail or on his way to Botany Bay.

"You need to have an open mind and remember everything I'm going to tell you is true and can be proven."

Regarding her closely, seeing the frown lines mar her small face, he groaned inwardly. At least now she was listening.

"Very well." She sipped her wine, paying little heed to him at the moment, seeming to concentrate on the darkness outside the window. Sensuously leaning back, once again she closed her eyes, dark lashes fanning across white skin. This time it wasn't to coax a response from him. "Go on."

"I suppose I should start at the very beginning. Unfortunately, I'm not really sure what that is." Nervously, he was drumming his fingers on his thigh. This was not an emotion he was used to nor did he like it.

"Beginning is always good," she said, her voice soft, uncaring once more. "You understand there is little you can say that will change my opinion."

His chuckle left him wondering about his own feelings. "Is that what you think I'm doing. I don't want to change your opinion of anything."

"What do you want to do?" she questioned.

"My only purpose is to impart some major facts about you and where you came from."

"You do want to change my mind."

"Not that." With a grimace of discontent, he ran his hands through his dark red hair. "Don't know what it is I want. Don't think I want anything except for you to be happy."

"Take me home."

The beginning, he reminded himself then sighing heavily, "Leslie discovered your name, which is Maria McKenzie, but you probably already knew that."

That seemed to catch her attention as her gaze quickly shifted to him. "To my knowledge only the earl and the nuns knew me as Maria. As to my last name, I think I forgot it years ago. Now that you say it, it seems familiar. I suppose it could be true."

"When you got away from the earl you decided to go by Ria. Was that a way to keep him from finding you?"

Thinking about her courage, all she went through just to survive, gave Gray a new understanding of this woman. If she didn't want to stay here, she shouldn't have to, shouldn't be forced. Yet if she didn't see this through to the end, she would never feel safe. He could take her to America. Dear God, that was the last place he wanted to go. There were just too many sordid memories there.

She drew in a long-ragged breath of air then shaking her head she went on to say, "No, Midget always left out the first part of my name. Ria stuck. It was easier for the children. Not that Maria is such a terribly difficult name to say but when he called me by my name, seems the first part of always got left out."

Her words created a tentative smile in his heart, tentative simply because the rest of the information he was about to impart would create the opposite emotion. Slanting one eyebrow upward, he began again.

"Leslie has your birth records recorded in the abbey which proves you are Maria McKenzie." He spoke softly knowing the information might not mean anything to her.

This seemed to spark a bit more interest. "What are my parents' names? I can't recall but then it was so long ago."

"Birk and Aila."

She was shaking her head now, "I think I only knew them as Mama and Papa."

Gray was besieged with the need to wrap her in his arms, hold and shield her from the demons tagging along with her life. Perhaps none of this needed to be said. He could take her to Maryland to the plantation there. They wouldn't have to worry about the earl again.

"The earl murdered your parents. Of that there is no sound proof. It's just a theory Leslie has pieced together from some of his more knowledgeable sources." He heard the tiny gasp of surprise but decided to continue before he lost the nerve. "He placed you in the abbey without telling anyone of your whereabouts. He wanted you even then and was willing to bide his time until you were old enough to bear a child for him."

"Why? None of this is making any sense, no sense at all. Have his child?" she queried, her eyes widening.

"No, I don't suppose it makes much sense."

He did pull her into his arms then branding her with a long heated kiss. Inside her mouth was warm and sweet. He searched, explored the tender sensitive flesh until she responded in kind. She molded her sweetly pliant body against his while it seemed to Gray, they both wanted to forget this conversation at least for the moment.

Appearing to want to learn more, she pushed away from him and he allowed the conversation to continue. "So, perhaps you will say something that does make sense. The earl wanted me to have his child?"

Gently he touched her cheek, ran a finger along her chin. "You are not who you think you are."

"Of course I am." Her hands rested on his chest, fingers spread wide as if she meant to push him away. "I know exactly who I am."

"No, you don't."

"Then...?"

"Your father was the Duke of Southmoor and your mother the duchess. According to the men and women Leslie's operatives questioned, they were very much in love and adored their beautiful daughter, you."

He went on to explain what the rumors were about the earl and her mother, the way he coveted her, which eventually precipitated in their violent deaths at his hands.

Clearly, she was shaken, the news of her birthright as well as her parents' death coming as a great surprise. "Murdered?"

"That is what was suspected. The only way we will know for sure is if someone could drag a confession from the earl."

"Which would be highly unlikely," she said.

"Were you the only person at his mercy?" he asked, suddenly wondering if he had held her parents in the same place he kept Ria.

For a moment she looked out the window then almost begrudgingly turned her head toward him again. "When I was first in his home, I believed I was alone with him, although I knew he didn't stay there all the time. I did, however, have the suspicion there had been someone else before me. He held clothing that was my size. Seemed unusual because I don't think he purchased the garments, at least not at first. I eventually out grew the gowns he provided."

"When you made your escape, you weren't the only person held."

"No, there were others who saw other men. The men paid him to use the women. We were just whores to the males who visited. Unless we were being punished for some reason, none of us saw or spoke to each other. He rarely allowed me to see the other women, at least not in the beginning. As I grew older, he sent me to some new man almost every night."

"You never conceived?" His curiosity spinning out of control, he understood his need to discover the truth, yet her pale face and wide eyes were rapidly changing his thoughts.

She inhaled a long deep breath of air, looking at him, tears pooling in her eyes. "I did once. A few weeks later I miscarried. He punished me as if it was my fault, keeping me alone in a room for over a week with only water to drink. He withheld food for several more days."

Gray held himself in check, keeping his thoughts to himself. The urge to kill the earl was front and foremost in his mind. His fists clenching, he tried to speak with a calmness he didn't feel. "Why do you think you are infertile? If you conceived once?" he asked his legitimate question, remembering the one time he'd been so immersed in their pleasure he forgot to withdraw from her. His gut tightened thinking they might have created a child that time two months or so in the past.

"That was the only time, nothing before or after. It seemed I was with him or someone else almost every night. If I wasn't barren, don't you think I should have conceived?" Her voice sounded tight and thready, barely discernible in the darkening room.

"Yes, but not if the earl was unable to create a child. He wanted an heir, a son from you and was desperate. When he wasn't successful, he gave you to others in hopes that you would. Sometimes stress or lack of food or if a woman is too thin plays a part in a woman's ability to conceive. That fact was well noted in the tribe."

"Why? Why did he want a child so badly and with me?"

They finally came to the reasons of her kidnapping linked to the harsh way in which he treated her, "He wanted to become a duke, at least pretend he was. He coveted the title. While he couldn't legitimately be the Duke of Southmoor, his son by you would. He would also become the trustee of your estate and your legal guardian until you came of age."

"I don't understand any of this," she murmured softly, looking at him with wide questioning eyes.

"If you had his son, he would come into another fortune. As it seems his was or is dwindling at a rapid pace."

"I don't have money." She seemed startled by his comment.

"Of course not, at least not that you know of, but in a few days, you will have more groats than you will know what to do with."

He was actually pleased for her. She would be able to do anything she wanted. She would also come to realize the daughter of a duke could not be the mistress of a second son or anyone for that matter, at least not without creating untold scandal. His remaining time with her would be short.

Silence enclosed the two of them for several minutes while each was immersed in their own thoughts. It seemed to Gray she was going over everything he told her and perhaps creating more unanswered questions in her head. She leaned against him while he wrapped an arm around her slender shoulders, enjoying the moment even though it was bittersweet.

Decisions would have to be made and soon.

"I still don't want anything to do with that dinner. The earl is going to be there, isn't he?" Clearly, he felt the shuddering of her slim body against him, finding himself seized with thoughts of murder.

"He's been invited. I would be shocked if he didn't come. Curiosity will bring him. I'm sure he understands that something is afoot. I'm also sure that someone has told him the duke has been looking into his past. His tentacles invade the city. A man with his proclivities must know what is happening in every facet of law enforcement."

Standing for a moment, she walked to the window peering down on the street and the traffic below. "I think if I was in the same room with that man, I would be physically sick. I can't do it, Gray." She whirled then. Her tiny hands fisted at her sides her face flushed with passion as well as determination. "Truly, I cannot bear to face him."

"You have to," he said simply. "There is no other choice for any of us. We have begun this revealing of Maria McKenzie. The task cannot and will not be abandoned. You must face this man with the courage I ken you possess."

"No."

"Seeing you, dressed lavishly in a new silk gown will make him do something foolish. He will want to control you again. At least that is our hope. If so, we can then proceed with the next part of our plan."

"I don't have a silk gown." Her voice was harsh yet shaky. He understood some of her fears, but he realized not all of them. He could try to empathize yet he would never comprehend what happened in the privacy of the earl's home.

"The ladies will take you to a dressmaker tomorrow. While there is not enough time to have something made expressly for you, a silk gown can be fitted to your body. I'm sure between Lacie and Daryl you will have something exquisite. In that case, you will not only look the part but you will be beyond beautiful."

"I don't have any groats." It seemed she meant to persist in this aspect of her newfound status.

He didn't heed any of her protests. "Of course you do. All you need to do is explain who you are then sign your name. Leslie has seen to the transfer of your inherited fortune into an account with your name on it. You are a very wealthy young woman. Once you have made your debut, you should have countless young men vying for your hand."

"So, I sign Maria McKenzie? I feel as if I would be forging someone else's name. And..." she paused, touching his chin. "I don't want countless men vying for my hand. Don't want to marry."

"It is your name," he said realizing how close he was to losing her.

Every moment sent their lives spinning in opposite directions. He would lose her without every telling her how much he loved her. He would tell her now but the timing was not right.

"I've never been to a dressmaker." Her voice was whisper thin.

It seemed to Gray she might very well resort to her usual behavior and run.

He couldn't let her run.

At the moment she had nowhere to run to. If she tried, she could find herself in even more of a precarious spot. He rose, pacing the room and wondering about what the future might hold for either of them. Second thoughts about the dinner in a couple of nights assailed him, sending shivers of cold into his bones.

Mayhap it would put her at risk.

"I will keep you by my side the entire evening. The earl will not get close to you. I give you my solemn vow. If you are worried, you have no need as you are no longer alone."

His breathing had grown just as ragged as his voice. A sudden tremor of apprehension and foreboding passed through him swirling to land solidly in his gut as if he just swallowed a stone.

"I appreciate the gesture, however you and I know how impossible that might be even though I will hold you to your word." Her thin smile told him she was more worried than he was.

"What else do you want to know?" he asked willing to continue the conversation with her yet needing at the same time to hold her in his arms and reassure.

She looked down at her folded hands. "I want to know how they died and if my mother had been the first person, he held captive. Do you think he tried to sire a boy with my mother first? Then," she paused looking at him with moisture filled eyes, "I want you to flay all his skin from him then let me spit in his face."

~ * ~

If Ria appeared the picture of a woman perfectly relaxed and in her element the next day, she wasn't. While Lacie and Daryl chatted nonstop on the way to the dressmaker Ria sat back, closing her eyes and listening intently to the wheels of carriage rattle on the cobblestone pavement. There, of course, had never been an opportunity to have clothes made expressly for her. Now the thought that she could actually purchase anything she wanted overwhelmed and terrified her at the moment.

Sitting up, she regarded the two women across from her. With a huge breath of air, "What happens at the dressmakers? What will she, they do?"

Daryl laughed, grinning at her sister's look of despair because she was sure Lacie knew what she was going to say before the words actually exploded from her lips, "She will take one look at Lacie's huge bosom and claim she does not own enough fabric to cover her."

Lacie tossed her reticule at Daryl. "You don't have to be mean just because you are jealous."

"Of course I'm jealous. What woman wouldn't be? Do you suppose this is the same dressmaker Leslie used his hands to tell her what size you were before you were even married? The same one that when our brother found out about, very nearly called Leslie out?" Daryl leaned forward, patting Ria on the hand. "You will be just fine. It will be fun. Just wait and see."

"The dressmaker will take you into one of the backrooms in order to complete your measurements for all the other times when you might want to purchase something that is not ready made. After that, we will try to find something for you that can be adjusted to your size today so we can pick the gown up tomorrow in time for the dinner."

"If you like, we can look through the fashion plates and samples of the material then order you some new things. You have the coin to buy anything you might want."

When they stepped inside the store, Daryl announced, "We need to dress this beautiful lady from toes to head. She has, literally, nothing to wear."

Ria stood straight in an attempt to defend herself. "I have two dresses as well as underthings."

Ignoring Ria's spontaneous comment, "We need all the fripperies and frothy underthings a lady would want," Lacie went on to say, her voice soft as she smiled at Ria, "and we need to find a suitable gown for a special dinner party tomorrow night. Do you have anything she can try on?"

"Let me take her back to the fitting room first. I'm Cora by the way," she said as she walked to the back, Ria obediently following.

Feeling totally overwhelmed as the lady had her undress, clucking as she removed each item, "I don't need or want all those things the ladies told you."

"Of course you do," Cora clucked some more, wielding her tape measure with a proficient air. "Now I've several gowns that might suit you for your dinner engagement. One is a lavender rose with blond lace outlining the corsage. It will fall gracefully from your waist. The lady who ordered it changed her mind and settled on a different gown. I also have one of a deep rich blue that will make your eyes sparkle, bringing out the beautiful shade of blue. I'm sure your husband will appreciate either one."

Ria was, for a moment, mortified, unwilling to explain to the lady she didn't have a husband, was in fact his mistress or lover instead. As the reality of who she was as well as what happened to her began to set in, she was bombarded with the horrible feeling she would never fit into any world. This new one she was finding herself in was not of her liking.

"Now you just stay here. Don't you go anywhere. I'll bring you some dresses to try on and see if you like them. The ladies said you needed everything. I've a few day dresses you can look at also." Her skirts whirling, she was out the door before Ria could say anything.

Wrapping her arms around her shoulders, she sat on a little bench in the cubicle, wishing she was home and playing with the children. Thoughts once more of the dinner party in just over twenty-four hours left her breathless with fear. She would come face to face with the earl for the first time since the night she escaped him over two years ago.

A ragged breath caught in her throat.

She mulled over the pieces of information Gray told her. Had the earl really thought to sire a child in that awful repulsive way? He had to be insane to think she would have ever allowed him guardianship of any child of hers. She began to wonder if she was indeed barren. Perhaps Gray was right. It had been the earl all along who could not make her pregnant.

"Here you go," Cora stepped into the room with an armload of gowns. "The ladies you are with want to see you in every one and it seems a gentleman arrived to add his opinions to theirs. I assume it is your husband."

Ria looked up, startled. "Who?"

"Why it must be your lovely husband, Graham Chamberlin, the rapscallion. Knew he would wed one of the most beautiful ladies I've ever seen. Not that the other two ladies sitting out there aren't beautiful, but you my dear," she fluffed out her hair, regarding her thoughtfully for a few seconds. "Put almost every other lady to shame. You are newlyweds, yes?"

She caught the gasp of surprise in the back of her throat. "You know Gray?"

"I do. He and Donal used to come in here from time to time with their mother, lovely lady she was. He was always bored to tears though and always getting into things he shouldn't. He was such a dear and incorrigible child but always getting disciplined."

To Ria her laugh sounded more like a cackle, but seeing the broad grin on her face was the first time Ria felt comfortable since walking in the door and hearing the tiny bell announce their presence.

"Mr. Chamberlin is picking out all kinds of things for you. He told me you would probably refuse the purchases if left to your own devices, but I'm to insist. He also told me that if you don't buy them, he will." She clucked again fiddling with the dress Ria put on, making adjustments in various places. "Now you go out there so you can show everyone just how gorgeous you look."

Ria nodded and holding her breath stepped into the room. The lazy smile on Gray's face nearly stole what little was left of the air from her lungs. Lord, but he was handsome dressed in his dark blue frock coat, tailored perfectly to his broad shoulders, his buff pantaloons showing off his heavy-muscled long legs, his dark green eyes gleaming with appreciation as his gaze roamed the length of her.

"That's perfect for you. You must get that one." Lacie clapped her hands delightedly. "Let's see the other one now."

The afternoon continued pretty much as it started. When they left the store, Ria had an abundance of orders including satin slippers, gloves and hats as well. One day dress fit her to perfection so Graham insisted she wear it home telling Cora to toss the other one into the rag bin.

Cora agreed to bring the gown she was to wear at the dinner party by in the afternoon and the other items would be delivered as they were finished. Once more Ria found herself totally overwhelmed by the changes that were coming about through no attempt of her own.

Lacie and Daryl also purchased numerous items just enjoying the fun of shopping, an entertainment Ria was far from familiar with. Yet now, wearing the new dress while sitting next to Gray in the carriage, she felt a new sense of accomplishment and pride. She had no idea what was expected of her in this new role, but she felt confident Gray would help her with all the details.

"I thought you would put up more of a fight," Gray said, leaning back to peruse her more thoroughly, his hand on her arm. "You now look the part, the daughter of the duke and duchess of Southmoor."

"Thought I would too." She spoke softly wondering what on earth was getting into her.

He shot her a mocking glance, his smile telling a wealth of information. With a finger under her chin, he turned her to look at him. "You won't mind having so much money then?"

"No, maybe not. I thought for a moment you were going to pay for everything. I couldn't allow that."

She supposed that but had been terribly relieved when he didn't even make a gesture toward paying for her purchases even though Cora made sure they both knew she didn't approve of Ria spending her own money on the acquisitions.

When they arrived home, both Leslie and Donal were gone leaving a message they would hopefully return before dinner but not to wait for them. One of the servants brought them refreshments. They retired to the drawing room chatting and avidly discussing the day's events. The ladies had tall glasses of lemonade. Gray sipped a brandy seeming to watch her every move.

She ached to talk with him privately, to tell him some of the new revelations that crossed her mind thinking on her changed circumstances. Telling him how she felt about their relationship seemed imperative except for the fact she wasn't sure exactly how she did feel. Ria wanted to continue as they were even though she understood Gray would refuse that idea. He would tell her they could not be lovers. It wasn't appropriate, yet that was what she wanted, the status quo to remain exactly as it was now.

He seemed overly patient with her. His presence at the dressmakers encouraged her to make decisions and it seemed he understood that while Lacie and Daryl's attendance was nice, she barely knew them. Her insecurities were getting the best of her when Cora explained about the gentleman waiting to see her new gowns. Despite her earlier efforts, she had been more than relieved when Gray showed up to help.

An hour later and right before dinner, Donal and Leslie sauntered into the drawing room smug expressions on their handsome faces seeming ready to explain something of importance. It appeared the time spent had not been wasted.

"What is it?" Gray immediately rose, slanting her a quick glance his smile giving her confidence.

Ria didn't understand but just looking at these men with the set single-minded expression on their handsome faces sent a dark shiver down her spine, tingling all the way to her toes. She sipped at the tea as she waited for something to happen, good or bad.

"We should talk privately," Leslie said to Gray indicating he wanted to go to the library.

"I believe we are beyond private in this matter. Everyone here knows the story, at least I assume Lacie and Daryl understand all the implications that have been revealed these last several days. You did tell them about Ria and her past, didn't you," Gray said harshly.

She was surprised at the intensity of his voice and the way he spoke up for her, realizing she should be privy to all that was decided or even what they learned. He slanted her a broad smile along with a nod of his head as if he understood her feelings.

"Very well," Leslie said almost reluctantly. "Over this day as well as last night, I've had two of my best men following William. He's been a very busy man. Just as we suspected he realizes his affairs are not what he assumed and is trying desperately to tie up any loose ends he can find. Unfortunately for him, we have left him none."

"We imagine he's feeling some pressure here but doesn't know what it entails. He visited several men of importance, one being a judge, another a magistrate. We believe these men are in his pocket." Daryl poured a snifter of brandy for her husband as he looked over the room. "Thank you," he smiled thoughtfully at her his attention then going back to the matter at hand.

Leslie cleared his throat, turning his consideration once again in Ria's direction. "Early this morning he went to see Blue. When he left the hovel Blue lives in, the earl seemed more than agitated, beyond angry as well. I'm sure Blue apprised him of his situation and that he wasn't going to lend him any support. I'm also sure Blue told him his little Ria was no longer sporting black hair and that she was the Maria he'd been looking for these past two years. With one hint of the unusual color of your hair, the earl is sure to comprehend that you've been living with Gray. Your disguise worked very well, fooling the man you were hiding from. I'm sure he had numerous tentacles out in search of the white-blond young woman. Since your hair color is rare you would not have been difficult to spot."

"Then he will have some idea that the dinner is about me and probably why he was invited. I'm sure he will have some plan in motion to snatch me away. What do you think he knows?" Ria asked, considering all the aspects of this and the monumental implications.

"That's just it. He can't have any idea except what you tell us." Leslie paused at the window, ceasing his pacing. "He must surmise by now that you were in Blue's little group of thugs and that Blue thought you to be a young boy, until he discovered you weren't."

"Which is not very much knowledge," Ria whispered, her voice husky, feeling as if they assumed too much. In the process were not going about her reinstatement into society in a timely manner. "It is only because of you linked with the intelligence you've received that we know who I am, who I don't want to be." She paused, looking at Gray while wondering about his thoughts, seeing inside his mind would be terribly nice. Would he want her inheritance just as the earl did? Was he a fortune hunter? "When this is all over, is there any reason that I cannot go back to being just Ria?"

"When this is over, you will have responsibilities you cannot deny, one being the management of the McKenzie estate for a probable heir," Gray told her, his voice gentle. "You will never again be just Ria. Try to find a way to put that thought from your mind."

Shrugging off his words, she decided then and there he was wrong. "Even if I have responsibilities, I've no idea what to do, what

feel alive and in control, at least for a tiny moment in her life. When Leslie began to speak again, she was wrenched back to the chilling seconds she was soon to encounter once more and reminded of tomorrow night's dinner and the horrifying meeting.

Her gaze drifting to Gray, "I would like to retire for the evening if you don't mind. I think I'm in need of a solid night's sleep."

"You prefer to skip dinner?" Gray asked.

"This conversation has taken away any appetite I might have had," she said. "Please stay."

One eyebrow rose in a fine arch, a mocking look on his full lips. "A solid night's sleep?" he queried, his eyes simmered with desire. "Do believe I will come with you. These refreshments have done quite well to assuage my appetites, all but one in any case."

After a moment between them, she nodded, rising to find her way to her room. A deep breath later and half way up the steps, she felt Gray's strong masculine presence behind her. It was truly disconcerting while he knew she was once more trying to flee, run from him, from her very real terrifying fears for her life. It seemed as if she'd been frightened for her entre short life. Even in the abbey, she remembered the debilitating fear. At the time, she didn't know where or why but after the earl kidnapped her, she realized he'd been watching her, always hovering nearby.

The nuns seemed to also be afraid of him. Now she knew why and with a little more thought she wondered if they had known about his plans for her from the very beginning.

Gray caught up to her then, his hand resting lightly but with a hint of possessiveness on her shoulder. "I don't think you should be alone with your thoughts right now. It cannot be good for you to dwell on the darkest part of your life or even what your future might hold."

Of course he was right but she couldn't bear to look at him and wonder what was going to happen in two days, couldn't bear to lie in bed with him, knowing this might well be the last time yet she couldn't bear not to. He made it perfectly clear to her that he would not stand in the way of her duties. Whatever those were.

"If you hold me in your arms tonight, I'm afraid I'll never stop crying."

Her breath whispered out the last few words, moisture rising in her eyes. One moment turned into two then more as he wrapped an arm around her before sweeping her up and into his arms. She was cradled next to his hard chest, her head resting on his shoulder, his heartbeat throbbing close to hers.

Gently he settled her on his bed, coming down on top of her, his mouth taking hers in a long demanding kiss. He kissed the corners of her mouth, nibbled across her lips. Her tongue joined his, searching out the sweetness and warmth inside. Even while they kissed, she knew these memories would have to last her a lifetime.

Unless there was some way...

Why did she have to have those particular parents? For almost all of her life she believed she was a worthless orphan, the concept tangled in her memory with other ones all created by the nuns.

She moaned softly, needing him, craving everything about Gray. His hand cupped her breast, the thumb gently grazing across her nipple, her clothing and unwanted barrier between them.

"You have too many clothes on," he chuckled, a deep throaty sound, as he trailed a hot line of kisses down her neck then across the top of her bodice. He pulled her to a sitting position, quickly undoing the buttons and sweeping the new garment over her head. The gown landed on the floor in a soft swish of fabric and lace.

"So do you."

She felt temped to laugh at the intense look on his face as seething hot desire filled his vivid, green eyes. She had not left the drawing room tonight with reflections of Gray, having been so immersed in her thoughts for her future life.

Low in his throat he made a gruff strangled sound as he finished removing everything she had been wearing then moved to his clothing. Naked, he stood over her for a few timeless seconds before he came down on top of her.

"I want you, Ria. I will always want you. If you leave me, I will always find you." His tongue curled around one taut nipple while his fingers roamed the length of her leg, settling on her belly for a moment before searching higher until he tenderly cupped her other breast in his hot hands. To Ria it seemed he'd never been as gentle or as caring as he was at this moment.

Heated rapid kisses, placed strategically down to her belly left her writhing against his mouth. His fingers touched the intimate softness between her thighs as he roused more passionate response from her. She closed her eyes as her fingernails scored the length of his back. Her body arched against his as he deepened the pressure.

His mouth returned to her then just as she parted her lips for him when he came between her legs, she parted them for him also. If this was her last plunge into paradise with the man she loved, she meant to make the most of what little time she had with him.

His fingers explored intimately, searched and enticed primal longings while his tongue did the same. When her fingers tightened around his buttocks, a masculine groan rumbled from his chest. As their hands mouths and fingers found all the erotic sensuous spots they'd learned about each other, Ria's pleasure spiraled ever higher and hotter. A magical inferno of passion burned inside her as her body reached for his, craved the enchantment only he could create. Tiny sounds centered in the back of her throat ached for release just as the rest of her body begged for the same. It seemed he tried to prolong the climax of their love making for as long as possible.

When she reached out to touch him, he stopped her. "No, not this time my little one."

He slowly entered her, her body quivering with need, tightening around his hard length as he became part of her. "Please, please, Gray."

For several seconds he held still, rising above to look at her as he smoothed a few tangled strands of hair from her face. "This is not the last time. I promise you that. We will find a way to be together."

Oh, how she wanted to believe his words, yet she couldn't, not after all the things they'd spoken of. Then he was moving again. Her body accepted all of him as she reached for that final pinnacle that would give her even more pleasure. The tremors in her body began slowly then as he moved more rapidly inside her they seemed to explode within her as she writhed against him, crying out his name.

For several seconds he lay on top of her, his weight pressed against her gave feeling of contentment. He moved to the side, running a finger along her arm and across her collarbone.

I love you.

He smiled at her as if he understood what she said. Softly, he kissed the tip of each breast, watching them harden once more. She would love him for the rest of her life.

~ * ~

If Gray and Ria were having a wonderful evening in each other's arms while forgetting their problems, the earl was having the opposite type of night. He'd spent the day discovering most if not all his secrets and plans were revealed and unraveling before his very eyes. As the day passed, he was beginning to realize there was little he could do about it. Tempted to run, his arrogance and conceit led him to believe he would get away with his crimes to rise another day.

Then to receive an invitation to the Duke of Southcliff's residence for a late dinner the next evening, left him shouting vulgar swear words at the servants, giving them good reason to run in the opposite direction. This wasn't supposed to happen even though he feared as much the night Maria escaped him.

The little slut, how dare she do this to me?

What to do now, he wondered as he ran his hands through his hair, his body quivering desperately as he thought about her sweet pliant body beneath Chamberlin. He didn't doubt she shared herself with him. No, he didn't doubt it at all. She was always more than willing with him, at least after he disciplined her several times. He realized even while he didn't want to admit to the fact that he was unable to sire a child. It wasn't Maria's problem at all, which was why he brought in other men to do the duty for him.

He didn't like to share her though as the thought of raising another man's brat sent another bevy of swearing. Now, he might not get the chance to raise the Duke of Southmoor, the heir apparent. He would have to plan wisely while he found a way to get the girl back in his control.

She would do anything for Ollie, as Blue told him just yesterday when he went to see him about capturing Ria. He smiled, a plan beginning to take shape in his head.

Ah, but to learn the little spitfire posing as a boy was his Maria. She had been within his reach for nearly two years yet he let her slip through his fingers. It wouldn't happen again. He was now headed to the manor house to check on the two girls that were still residing with him as well as prepare Maria's rooms for her residence. If he had any say in the matter, she'd occupy them soon. Gray and his cronies were fools. All he would have to do is wait until they let her out of their sight. All it would take would be a few nebulous seconds.

His only misgivings were that she might remember how she got out so easily the last time she was here. After that fiasco, he checked all the locks and fixed the single one that had not worked as well as the alarm that would sound if she made it that far.

Perhaps he should give up on the game. Gleefully, he rubbed his hands together thinking of having her tender sweet body beneath his again. As much as he disliked the notion of another man claiming her, he would have to give her to others if he thought to breed her.

The trip to his house seemed interminable, the hour passing by at a snail's pace as he rode through pot-holed back roads. Now that he was here though, he strode up the steps to the second-floor bedroom he always kept ready for her. Stepping inside, he saw that his servants followed his orders to the letter. Everything was in place including the shackles if she proved to be reluctant or if she needed discipline. He smiled feeling the warmth pool in his loins at the image of her naked against the wall, her arms held fast above her head.

This was perfect.

Next, he strode to his own suite of room. Everything had been refurbished. New silk wallpaper hung on the walls. A rich new carpet was on the floor. The bed had also been replaced with dark blue curtains falling around the massive bed.

His sex toys hung on the far wall as a reminder to any of the women he asked for that they should obey his every command. Even when they did, he sometimes used the harsh forms of sex enjoying their soft pleas for mercy as well as their screams of pain. The images empowered him. His breath came in a rapid pant as his heart raced in anticipation.

He would never cave into a woman's please. Mercy? Women didn't deserve clemency.

He sat down on a blue brocaded chair facing the fireplace. A bottle of brandy had been left on the nearby table. Pouring a snifter and swirling the contents, he thought of the pleasures to be had in two days if all his plans came to fruition.

Yes, if that was the case, he would have Maria McKenzie in his possession once more.

Chapter Eight

Sun filtered in through his window as Gray blinked a few times to clear his head. Sleep for him had been elusive, waking often with images of Ria with the earl. He inhaled a deep draught of the fresh spring air, hoping to erase the nightmares. Ria was sprawled across him in a tangle of arms and legs, her soft warm breasts pushing against his chest reminding him of last evening's pleasures. They spent most of the night in each other arms almost as if this evening was going to be their last.

It wasn't.

If anything, he meant to create new memories with her. He'd spoken with Leslie the day before. The duke agreed to look into her estate along with the managing of the money as well as the land. He bent over, tenderly kissing Ria's forehead, her closed eyelids, her nose. Peering at her sweetly parted lips then brushing a soft kiss across them he said, "Wake up, sweetheart. It's the big day and we've a lot to do, many things to discover about your new life."

She groaned as he laughed, delighted with her and her sleepy-eyed look. She ran her small pink tongue across her lips unconsciously tempting him. During the night he decided on a plan of action, unwilling to give her up now that he found the woman he needed no, craved to spend the rest of his life with. True, she had responsibilities beyond her control now. There was no seemly reason why she couldn't share his bed and his life if they married. After the dinner he meant to set about arranging that very thing. The banns could be called the next Sunday.

He told himself many times he would never venture down that path again, yet deep in his heart he knew Ria wasn't anything like his first wife. She would never betray him or run off with the first man who came along. Watching his brother with his wife as well as Leslie with his, he realized not all women were lying jaded sluts. He felt sure he could trust Ria with his heart.

Languidly, she stretched, arching her back, her white breast tipped with tight pink buds pushing provocatively in the air. One would think he would have tasted them enough last night. Still, the sight stirred him even more profoundly than he would have thought.

She faced him and with a ragged breath said, "I still don't want to attend this dinner tonight. It's not good of you to make me do it," she told him peevishly. "I would be perfectly happy to remain here in this room until all the shenanigans are accomplished. Seeing the earl again terrifies me."

"Without you, there are no shenanigans. We cannot think to have the dinner when the woman playing the leading role is not there."

The light tap on the door sent her scurrying beneath the covers, only her eyes peaking above the sheets as one of Leslie's servant brought in a tray with tea and scones for their enjoyment. He rose from the bed, stark naked, strolling toward the servant.

The man placed it on the table ignoring Gray's state of undress then ever so somberly said, "Will there be anything else, sir?"

"Two baths, one here as well as one in the lady's room, please." Gray watched, as the man looked at him, a disapproving expression on his face. Well, it wasn't a servant's position to like or dislike anything he did nor did he care over much, except when he considered Ria's reputation linked with the possible gossip among the servants.

"Very well," the man said then with a quick well-practiced pivot he strode from the room, the door closing quietly behind him.

Gray strode to his dressing room, finding one of his robes and handing it to Ria to put on. He did the same with a second one only for himself. "Are you hungry? You should be since you barely ate anything last night. I watched you picking at a few things then we both missed dinner for more pleasurable pursuits."

"Much more so than last night."

She sat on the bed with the covers pulled around her.

"Good then." He handed her the robe, wondering at her sudden bout of shyness. "Come, let's eat by the fire."

For a few minutes, they ate their breakfast keeping thoughts to themselves. She seemed far away from him. He wondered what exactly she was thinking and if she would even tell him. His thoughts all centered around Ria as well as what they would do tomorrow, where they would be. If he gained his wish, they would be headed back to his house to discuss their future and see the children. Before he left them at home, he never realized how much he would miss them.

"What are you going to do today?" she asked between bites of scone smothered in melted butter and strawberry preserves.

"I'm not sure. I think we need to make sure tonight goes as planned then pray there are no surprises. Leslie must have something in mind. I will speak with him later on."

"Can we stay here for a while? I will have to get ready soon enough but with nothing to do, I'm sure I'll be ready to jump out of my skin by the time this all comes to pass. I know I will not be able to put anything from my mind."

"Another hour or so."

Her half smile was endearing. He placed her hand in his, felt the fine trembling.

"I see."

He was sure she did not. "I've a few errands to run, none that will take much time. Perhaps you should dress casually then come downstairs whenever you want. It will give you something to do. Will also help you pass the time." He knew she still didn't feel entirely comfortable with Daryl and Lacie. He hoped the feeling was short lived and by the time the couples returned to Glasgow, she would be over her wariness.

She lifted her small white shoulders slightly, a sad look in her eyes. "I've never had friends let alone women friends. I've not the faintest notion what to say to them."

"Just be yourself," he told her before he saw her look of chagrin caught by her wide eyes.

"And what would that be, the earl's whore or Blue's common house thief and pickpocket? It was good thing Dodge and Ollie both had very nimble fingers or Blue would have discovered my ruse sooner."

He grimaced realizing the truth of what she told him then ignoring her statement about the thievery. "You speak well enough around me. I'm sure the ladies would not find you lacking."

She wrapped her hands in the robe's fabric, looking up, moisture in her eyes, "There is a third role I've been playing. Gray's mistress or lover, I'm not sure which one it is." She waved a hand in the air, "Whatever term applies the best. I wouldn't know."

A slap in the face couldn't have been more telling. His gut tightened hoping to rectify that problem sooner than later, "Have I forced you in any way?"

"No," she told him, shooting him a hard critical glance, "but it doesn't change the truth, does it? I have nothing to say to any lady who is respectable. Both Lacie and Daryl are well-thought-of, so unlike myself."

He had no more answers, nothing else to say that would change her mind. He rose then, popping the last piece of scone into his mouth before washing the tasty morsel down with a drink of tea. "I believe I'll take my bath before the water grows to chilly to be enjoyable. Will I see you downstairs in an hour or so?"

"Yes, if you think it is for the best. You are right about one thing. I do need to keep my mind occupied." Slowly she walked from the room.

He watched the gentle sway of her hips as she left him. She would weather this storm. After his bath he dressed casually for the rest of his day before descending to the first floor.

No one else seemed to be up and about. He supposed it was because he'd retired early with Ria last night. Gray sat on a velvet sofa, picking up a copy of the *Edinburgh Evening Courant.* He began to glance through the paper. Immersed in some interesting tidbits, he didn't hear Leslie walk into the room an hour or so later.

"You're up early. Is Ria up also?" Leslie asked as he poured himself a cup of hot tea that had just been brought into the room. His glance was a probing one as Gray studied Leslie's hard features, features that only softened when the duke looked at his wife.

"She is but I've got to tell you Ria is a bit of a wild card where tonight is involved. The dinner is the last place she wants to be. The earl is the last person she wants to see. I've no idea how she is going to get through the affair." Gray folded the paper, setting it on his lap while he watched the Duke of Southcliff's stoic unchanging expression.

What the man was thinking, God would only know.

"Of course, Ria doesn't have to attend the dinner but the effect her presence has on the earl is vital to our mission as well as the plans that will be put in motion tonight. If he doesn't see her, his hand will not be forced. If that is the case, we will have to wait longer. What is it that has her quailing in her shoes if I might ask? It seems to me you should be able to pat down most if not all of her fears."

Gray let out a short bark of laughter, thinking Leslie had no idea. "You've not been listening very well."

Perhaps he had been listening. It didn't seem now that he thought about the ensuing conversations, that either one of them told Leslie what she'd gone through at the hands of that man. It was unconscionable. Any woman would tremble if put in front of him.

"Perhaps someone has not been forthcoming on that particular matter." Leslie's voice was not only gruff but also condemning to a certain degree. "There are certain salient issues that Ria doesn't want to speak of, and I'm sure she should not have to divulge what went on behind the closed chamber door in the earl's household." A dark eyebrow arched sardonically.

"I don't think she particularly cares other than the fact it is painful to recall, excruciating to speak of. She would like nothing more than to forget every horrible image. It will take some time for that to be accomplished. The earl's presence in her life again is going to make it damn hard to forget."

For the next few minutes, silence hung heavy in the room, each man with thoughts of his own. Gray tottered on the verge of telling the entire sordid tale before reversing his thoughts only to change his mind again. Why he vacillated, he wasn't at all sure.

"I don't see why it's important for you to know the contemptible details," Gray murmured, searching his mind for a reason to speak plainly. He didn't have to investigate very far, having remembered the first night Ria came to him, wanting to give him pleasure.

Leslie cleared his throat, rocking back on his heels for a moment as he seemed to regard him closely. "Perhaps not and yet..." he paused as if thinking. "Is it just too hard for her to talk about?"

"I believe I'm the only one who knows even half of what happened to her while I'm also sure even I don't know everything," Gray said, looking to the stairway as if he was about to see Ria descending or one of the other ladies, anything for a diversion. "She didn't exactly tell me."

Leslie shot him a curious glance, a half-smile forming. "I don't think I'll ask how you found out. Suffice it to say, your word is good enough."

Gray waved a hand in the air, having made up his mind. "Come with me." They left the drawing room going into the library before locking the door behind them. "I don't want anyone else to overhear what I'm going to say. Don't want Ria to hear me tell you of the ordeal that lasted several years. I'm sure she wouldn't want the wives to know. Thank God she was not beaten down. A woman of lesser courage would have experienced just that."

In Gray's mind Ria's bravery grew exponentially as more and more came to light. His only hope now was that Leslie would say nothing more of the secrets he revealed. Sequestered in the library, Gray began the grisly tale of Ria's life after she turned fifteen. The many nights she spent in terror waiting for the earl to call her to his bed. The pain and degradation she experienced at his hands. No woman should endure anything such as what she had, but she never quit fighting, never stopped looking for a way to freedom. When all this started, she was a young innocent young woman. Strangely enough, she might be a bit jaded but she was still innocent, naïve in the ways of sexual encounters.

When Gray finished his story, Leslie said nothing for several moments, his grim features set in single-minded lines of determination. "Then we must make sure no one ever suffers at his hands again, don't you think?"

Gray nodded, understanding what those sentiments were from almost the first moment he met Ria but he'd also know he couldn't achieve that outcome if left to his own devices. Before this exchange

Leslie had no idea of the extent of the earl's perfidies. Now he did. "I believe even this story may not paint the complete picture clearly. There is no doubt in my mind she has not told the entire story. Much of it I gleaned from what she didn't say but how she acted."

"He would love nothing better than to turn the tables on all of us and somehow capture all the ladies for his use," Leslie said.

"You're right I'm sure."

At that thought, Gray felt bile rise to his throat.

"You have forewarned me. I have every confidence in Lacie and Daryl if they are also made aware that this is more serious than even I thought before. Forewarned is forearmed," he murmured thoughtfully.

"Of course."

Gray had the express notion Leslie was speaking of something else, his countenance seeming vague for a second, even a lifetime away.

He turned then, lifting the glass of brandy to his lips and drinking. "Our ladies are very capable of taking care of themselves in an emergency. They are also very well versed in the use of pistols. If I speak to them of the ever-present dangers, they will not go anywhere unless they are armed. It is not something I wish for them, but under the circumstances essential."

"Ria is not so fortunate. Charles and Harry meant to teach her but there has really been no time. She does not like to leave the house." Gray felt a shiver of apprehension sneak down his spine. Women and pistols? Not always a good combination.

He understood on the frontier as well as in times of war, many females became just as competent with weapons as the men in their lives. Glasgow and Edinburgh were hardly on a frontier nor was anyone at war.

"Flynt MacTavish, their older brother, didn't pay much attention to the girl's growing up as I'm sure you are well aware of that fact. They did as they pleased. One of the things that pleased them was learning how to shoot and ride as if they were men. Quite frankly, Lacie's accuracy frightens me. I've thought many times that I don't want to leave her angry." At that notion, he chuckled as if remembering something private.

"What are you going to tell them?"

"That they should strap a pistol to their leg and keep one in their reticule too. Before, when they were forced to take matters into their own hands, there were five. Now there are only two. Don't want them to take undo chances but do want them prepared if and when need be."

Gray choked on his drink, a bit of brandy slipping from behind his lips. "What do you mean?"

"Doesn't hurt for a female to be prepared for any emergency." He grinned knowingly. "Much better than not having the means to fight a man if necessary. Did you hear about the time they made the two men who tried to kill Flynt strip? They marched that pair naked to the docks then with a Turkish prince we all know, put them on board before sending them on their way to Turkey to become slaves."

Gray had no idea what he could say to something like that. At the moment, he wasn't even sure he believed the duke. The tapping on the door effectively ended the conversation between them. Seeing the hour was growing later, Gray made an excuse to leave. He wanted to see Ria, tell her what transpired here in the library between Leslie and himself. She, he decided yesterday, should and deserved to know everything even if it might hurt her.

He had no illusions that she was immune to anything.

Leslie's voice stopped him again, "If Ria is willing, I'd like to speak with her about the estate she inherited along with a few other monetary things that will concern her. If you wish to join us, you of course are also welcome."

"I will see what she has to say."

Myriads of things sweeping through his head, Gray strode up the steps looking in Ria's room to find her sitting by the window a cup of tea in her hand.

When she heard him, she turned, smiling. "I trust you had a good conversation just now?"

He nodded approaching her, "I've come to see if you would meet with Leslie downstairs. It's about the estate you've inherited. Probably best to make some plans since it's been left idle for all these years."

Not that it really mattered to him, he was wealthy in his own right yet he did wonder at the extent of her properties.

"My estate, inheritance." She exhaled a little puff of air before making a face of distaste. "Is it necessary? Can't it just be handled now by..." She was shaking her head, crease lines marring her lovely face. "I suppose not."

"You are smart. Do you really want to leave those things in the hands of someone else? Don't you believe you should at least have the information in hand to make some decisions?" His voice had been rather curt. He couldn't help but grimace at the change in her expression.

"You think I should see what my parents left me."

"Yes."

"Very well then." She stood and accepted his arm as they walked from the room and downstairs.

In the library, Gray once again locked the door behind them. Ria pulled a chair in front of the desk. Gray sat on a velvet sofa not too far away. He smiled at the prim regal bearing that was not foreign to Ria. It was almost as if she never spent a day on the streets of Edinburgh or the rooms the earl designed especially for his entertainment.

"Gray tells me you wish to see me." Her hands were folded in front of her, her back stiff. She possessed an air of regal apathy.

"Relax, Ria, this will not be at all painful," Leslie said, a half smile on his face, his eyes alight with some unmentioned humor. "Anything you decide today you can always reconsider tomorrow or the next."

Gray didn't see anything humorous in this meeting. If what he said would serve to ease some of Ria's all too real fears, he would admit defeat at the hands of the older man.

It seemed to Gray she did try to relax somewhat as she settled into the chair.

"I'll try," she said, a weak smile gracing her features. "Perhaps you should get on with this."

"You are not going to your execution, Ria." He cleared his throat before speaking, "Very well, I will proceed. First, you should be apprised you have funds in the bank of Scotland. As they did at your parents' deaths, they still have your name on them."

She lifted her shoulders in a hesitant shrug. "I don't know what to do with them, the money, how to handle them. It's all foreign to me.

Nothing in my education at the abbey could have prepared me for this future."

"Really, there is nothing you need do. Your parent's solicitor has managed them quite expertly all these years. I sent a message to the man. He has been informed and given proof of your identity that you do indeed exist."

"And..."

"With his skillful management and of course with very little being spent except for the upkeep of the McKenzie properties, they have nearly tripled in size since your parents' death and you went missing."

"I see."

With an impatient wave of his hand in the air, Leslie went on to say, "Of course you don't understand. Now you have the responsibility of making the decisions. I would advise you to continue employing this man who is honest, trustworthy and loyal to the McKenzie clan. He has served your family's interest well over the years. It is my earnest opinion that you cannot do wrong by him."

"Alright," she paused in thought, gazing at her hands for a moment. "I do trust you and since I've nothing else to go on but your advice..." once more she hesitated before speaking then looked to Gray. "I will trust the man you speak so highly of. If I'm in need of funds, what do I do?"

Leslie smiled, "a good question. If you like, you can have a weekly or monthly allowance for your personal use. I strongly suggest that is what you do. It will be sent to you on a regular basis. That way you do not have to make trips into town if you are still living with Gray or if you choose to live at one of your residences. "

Once again, she looked at Gray as if he would make the decision for her. All he could do was give her a reassuring smile coupled with a masculine lift to his shoulders. "It's up to you."

Leslie was not quite so neutral as he continued expounding his advice. "An allowance would be the easiest and probably the most suitable for your needs. If it is not enough, you can always leave word that you need more and on the other hand if you find you don't have need for as much as is given to you, change it."

"It's that easy?" she asked, surprised by the ease at which everything seemed to be rolling out in front of her.

"Indeed."

"So, why don't you tell me how much I might need?"

They spoke for a while. This time Gray joined the conversation. After a few suggestions and counter suggestion an amount was agreed upon. Gray was sure it was more money than she would ever use, but Leslie shrugged and said we would obviously see in a month or two. She didn't need to pinch pennies.

"Now," Leslie went on to say with an even broader smile on his handsome face, "the McKenzies owned several properties. Over the years they have been kept up although the furniture has remained covered since no one has been in residence. They kept a townhouse here in the city. They have a large manor house north of Edinburgh, a home in London as well. Ria, they were very wealthy. You might want to visit the homes, although London will not be quite so easily accomplished. A trip would have to be planned."

"All that," she murmured softly, her breath seeming to vanish. Looking to Gray, "I could not possibly go alone and living in the city is abhorrent to me."

"All of that. We might have time to visit the townhouse today." He pulled out his pocket watch. "No, I suppose not. It is too late. Tomorrow maybe or perhaps the next might be more suitable. Gray's home is not that far from the McKenzie place. All exploring can be done at your leisure." With that said, he handed over the keys to all the properties.

If Gray thought Ria had been overwhelmed before, the incredulous feeling of powerlessness she felt now would not even come close. Her body trembled uncontrollably at the notion of what she was facing.

~ * ~

Ria blinked a few times as she began to accept the truth that was now her life. Each time she believed she conquered her fears and was beginning to cope, something new popped up. She was appreciative but wary of it all. Despite everyone's encouraging words, she had the strong feeling something would leer its evil head before taking it all away. Not that it mattered too much, she was used to living with nothing. Truly, she knew she could do it again.

The thought she now owned three homes sent a tickle of laughter to her belly. In all her life, she would have never believed anything like this would ever come to pass. Even in her dreams, she never dared to aspire so extravagantly. Admitting then to herself her imaginings had been of living safely with food in her stomach. Then, "It is getting late as you said. I suppose however distasteful I find it, I should get ready for the evening."

"As we all should," Leslie said as he stood.

Gray rose also, waiting for Ria a smile on his face. She walked to him, a strange hope filling her with confidence. "Will you come to my room with me?"

He nodded, a grim expression on his visage. She wondered too what he was thinking about all this. She was perhaps wealthier than he was. What little she comprehended about men was that they liked to be in control. Would he want nothing to do with her now? She cringed at the thought.

Holding onto his arm, they walked. She felt his solid frame against hers, enjoying the play of muscles against her. When they reached her room, stepping inside, she turned in his arms, wishing she could tell him she loved him. Instead she pulled his head to hers then standing on the tips of her toes, kissed him.

He responded by sweetly parting her lips, his tongue searching inside her mouth. Gray swept her into his arms, striding quickly to the sofa he sat down with her on his lap. Pulling away from her, "What was that all about? Although a sweet kiss initiated by you in the afternoon is very pleasant. I'm not complaining, mind you."

"I wanted a taste of normalcy." She touched a finger to his lips, a soft sigh parting hers. "Every morning when I wake up, I'm thankful for you finding me and giving me shelter."

"As I am for you," he admitted, his voice husky with desire. "You will find a new routine soon. In time, you will understand what is to be expected. From everything Leslie told us, you are a extremely wealthy woman, an adult in control of her funds as well as her life. You can have whatever your heart desires."

What she desired more than anything was Gray Chamberlin, his arms around her at night, a life with him. She wanted his children too. Money wouldn't buy that. "Can I even have you?" she said, her voice soft before she looked away. "No, I'm sorry that was not fair of me."

"You can have me whenever you want me," he told her, "Except for now. Now you have to get ready for the upcoming dinner. Look, there are packages on the bed. Do you want to see what is there?"

"I'd rather that you make love to me." Her voice was wistful. The simmering darkness in his eyes told her he wanted her as much as she did him.

"After dinner if you still feel the same way, I promise. We will spend the night doing whatever you want." He stood, setting her on the floor before striding to the mound of packages lying on a large table in the room. With a smile on his face, he said softly, "Look at all this. You bought all of this with your money. You didn't even begin to put a dent in your funds."

Holding back for a moment before unwrapping the first of the many parcels, she looked at him for affirmation. "I suppose this is what Christmas might feel like." Although she remembered Christmas just a few months ago with Gray, which had been the first Christmas she could really remember. Other than vague images of a lifetime past, she'd had nothing resembling this. While there had been packages for her and the children, she stifled a little shudder thinking again, something she decided she probably shouldn't do.

"Perhaps it will be what Christmas in your future will look like," He bent, kissing her forehead briefly before he sat down to watch. "Open them." It seemed to her he was more eager than she was to see what was waiting for her.

She did, pulling out all kinds of frothy underclothes trimmed with lace, satin slippers and gloves. There were a few hats but when she got to the last and largest package, she hesitated. Looking at Gray, "This must be the gown meant for tonight."

He nodded, "I want to see it on you again. The gown brings out the color of your eyes, highlighting the unusual color of your hair. Although the blue gown did the same, would you like me to leave while you put it on?"

She shot him a sardonic glance. Then smiling softly, "Why would I want you to do that? Besides the fact we were naked in each other arms only a few hours ago, I need a lady's maid. I'm afraid you have just been hired."

A burst of laughter surprised her then he said in all truthfulness, "Truly, I do a much better job removing clothing."

Petulantly, she countered, "If you want to see the gown on me..." Purposefully, she let the sentence hang, wanting him to finish the words for himself.

Several tense minutes later, all the frothy lacy underclothing that went with the dress as well as the gown itself was on her slight frame. She looked at herself, realizing all the years of constant strain had made her too thin. Recalling all the nights she'd gone to bed hungry was not difficult. Those days had been a constant in her short life, representing the difficulties presented to her. She blinked back the moisture rising in her eyes.

He stepped back, his gaze travelling the length of her, eyes deepening in color. "When your hair is fixed you will look every aspect of a woman in your position. If your parents had not met an untimely end, who knows what title you would hold now or who you would have wed. You might have become a duchess in your own right."

"What position is that? A duchess? I doubt that."

She smiled demurely at him, knowing he would be thinking of his hard body possessing hers. She didn't want to think about anything but the present, didn't intend to dwell on the past and what might have happened if her mother and father had lived. She tilted her head slightly to one side, watching as his eyes darkened even more. "There isn't time for what you are thinking. So, behave yourself while you try to figure out if you can fix my hair."

"An impossible task for these poor fingers. You would not be pleased with the results. Again, I do much better releasing a woman's hair of its pins and combs than putting the locks into a respectable place."

Lacie waltzed into the room just then, a grin on her lovely features, "You've no need to even try. I've brought my maid. She will do an amazing job with Ria's hair. Now, out with you." She made a shooing motion with her hands. "You need to dress, also, or have you forgotten the occasion as well as its importance?"

"No, I have not. Will you come for me when Ria is ready? I would like to escort her downstairs."

"Absolutely," Lacie smiled prettily, continuing to try to shoo him from the lady's domain, her hands resting on his arm as she walked him to the door. "She will want to feel as if you have her back."

Ria watched him leave the room, intent for several moments on the empty doorway, wishing he would return sooner than she knew he would. The slight trembling of her hands since she woke up this morning knowing what she would have to face tonight had not left her. She looked to Lacie who smiled back with an encouraging grin. At Lacie's suggestion, she sat down at the dressing table.

"What are you going to do?" she asked, frowning into the mirror. "There really isn't very much to work with. It's so short." Her hair had grown a few inches since she'd been living with Gray and perhaps someone skilled could successfully make something out of it.

"Just you don't worry," the maid said as she began to arrange the thick locks on top of her head.

Artfully, she brought some curled tendrils down to frame her face. A few ribbons the color of her gown were wound into her hair.

The process took little time. Before she knew what was happening, Lacie was showing her how to apply a tint to her lips as well as her eyelids. Ria's face was powdered and lashes darkened. The woman sitting in front of the mirror was no longer Ria. She didn't recognize her.

Her thoughts a day or so ago as to why she couldn't be just Ria came to mind as a shudder of apprehension swept through her. Perhaps the earl would fail to recognize her.

"Leslie thought you might like this. When I explained to him the unusual color of the gown, he made a trip to the bank and looked through the safe deposit box your parents owned. There he found an array of jewels. He thought this necklace combined with the matching earrings would go nicely with your dress. What do you think?" she asked, setting the box on the table before opening it.

Ria gasped when she saw the sparkling amethyst stones surrounded by diamonds. Reverently, she touched each stone in the necklace before glancing to stare at Lacie's face then Gray's.

"These are mine now?" The whispered words could barely be heard.

She felt giddy, childlike as she realized the truth.

"These and many more. It's all part of your inheritance. Now let me put this necklace around your neck."

"I will," Gray entered the room then. "I couldn't help but overhear. I knew she was ready."

Lacie handed him the necklace. He placed it around her neck fastening it then holding her hand in his he pulled her to her feet. "You are the most beautiful woman I've ever seen."

Ria felt the heat rise to her cheeks, having never heard him speak so reverently honest before. Had never thought she would hear the words Gray spoke from any man. "Thank you."

"It is not just because of the dress and trappings that go with it. I see a sparkle in your eyes that has just not been there before as well as a becoming blush to your cheeks that has nothing to do with the tiny amount of makeup you wear. Come, I hear the earl has arrived. Leslie is entertaining him in the drawing room. Daryl and Donal are there also. Lacie, would you like to take my other arm?" he asked as Ria held on to one for seemingly dear life.

As they descended the stairs and even as Gray squeezed Ria's hand reassuringly, she felt what little confidence she possessed slipping away. Her throat dry, her knees weak, she struggled to tug a breath of air inside her lungs. Lord, but she felt this way already? What would she feel when she actually saw the man she dreaded? Would it be so terrible for her to turn and run to her room?

"Everything will be fine, Ria. You don't have to worry about anything nor do you have to say anything. I will remain by your side. I'm sure Leslie will do most of the talking. This is the type of subterfuge he is known for."

She hoped Lacie was not taking his words in the wrong way. The very idea that anyone would enjoy this form of confrontation boggled her mind. Suddenly, they stood in the doorway. Gray paused a moment, allowing Lacie to waltz beautifully into the room then stand by her husband. The smile on Leslie's face as well as the glint in his eyes at the sight of his wife was very similar to Gray's when he first saw Ria this evening. He had felt the same way at Ria's appearance.

The conversation stopped, all eyes turned to her and Gray. When the earl saw her, the brandy he'd been drinking spewed from his lips, his eyes hardening with anger and displeasure. Leslie tossed him a sardonic smile, knowing he'd managed to surprise the man.

Slowly, Gray strode into the tense room, Ria still holding tightly to his arm. Surely the earl must have guessed by now that she had been closer than he thought. Yet seemingly tonight he was surprised. They walked until they were closer, Gray stopping more than several arm lengths away.

"Do you know Ria McKenzie?" Gray asked mockingly, knowing well and truly that the earl did indeed know her, had terrorized her for years using her for his own nefarious purposes.

The earl chocked back his words of contempt Gray was sure lingered distastefully on the tip of his tongue. "Delightfully, she has been found."

"I didn't know Maria was lost," the earl said, seeming to gain back a bit of his composure. "Nice to meet you. I knew your mother and father quite well."

She stiffened, conscious of the fact he murdered them to get to her mother then her when his first efforts failed to materialize. "What can you tell me of them? It seems I don't remember much. I was thrust into an abbey at an early age, no one telling me anything."

"You're the very picture of your mother. Come, let's not linger on the dead. Don't we have more enjoyable things to talk about?" He lifted his glass to the group, his eyes riveted on her.

They chatted for another hour or so before dinner was finally served. The meal seemed to go on forever as Ria continued to cast her longing gaze to the stairway and a quick escape. The earl was quite unable or unwilling to offer much to the conversation buzzing around his ears.

The men retired to the library for a round of brandy and cigars while the women left to their own devices sat in the drawing room. Ria wanted to hear what was going on in the library yet understood she should not invade the male dominated territory. Both Daryl and Lacie kept her from creating a scene by keeping her from barreling unannounced into the male domain.

"Come now, what was your impression of the earl?" Lacie asked, smiling around the room, seeming to wait for confirmation of her feelings. "Did he seem as nasty to you as he did to me?"

"He's a pig," Daryl said as she poured them all a glass of sherry. "His jowls bounce when he talks. I would be willing to bet his soft white belly does as well. What a deplorable man."

Ria nearly lost the sip of wine she just drank, a smile growing as Daryl spoke so honestly about the earl. She had awful memories of the man's soft white belly as well as his protruding member. A shudder wracked her body, once more wishing those memories from her mind understanding even with time they might not vanish.

"I believe you've summed it up quite nicely," Lacie agreed with her sister. "Can you imagine having to go to bed with that lily white pig? I would literally find a way every night to keep away from him."

"No, not at all, we are very fortunate in our choice of men. They are commanding and try to be controlling, but they generally give in to us."

If the two girls knew what had happened between her and the earl they would probably not be speaking so plainly. As it was Ria held a deep-seated appreciation of their honesty.

"You are both right. It is nice that he does not hold a place in anyone's heart. He is an ogre of a man and unpleasant."

The girls stared at her a bit open mouthed. "I knew you and the earl had a history of sorts. I'm guessing there is much more no one has told us," Lacie said, her smile changing to a frown at the topic.

"Anything you wish to share?" Daryl asked, one elegantly sculpted eyebrow arched. "We are both good listeners. We've sisters and Hope, our sister-in-law who is the best listener of all of us. You can tell us anything and we promise not to judge."

Ria did want to tell them everything. She was terribly afraid they would be so shocked they would faint. She didn't think there was any way they wouldn't judge. They were gently bred women and deserved to kept that way.

"Well, what I do know is that because of the earl and his evil propensities, my husband wants us to carry two weapons when we run our errands tomorrow. He must be a very dangerous man for sure."

Ria felt the blood drain from her face at Lacie's words. The earl was dangerous but these two ladies would most likely hurt themselves if they showed weapons against the man.

Daryl seemed to sense her distress and coming to realize something needed to be said, "We are really quite proficient with firearms. We've used them in our defense before, even used them to capture a ruthless criminal, a man who tried to murder our brother."

Shocked she looked from one lady to the other, realizing that these two women were indeed ladies and they also possessed unusual capabilities for the weaker of the species.

Lacie seeming to assimilate what Ria was thinking, straightened and shaking a finger at her, "Women are just as smart and capable as any man. Don't ever forget it. You survived on the streets as well as whatever the earl did to you. You are skilled at many things first and foremost at survival. For a woman, that is probably the most valuable skill of all."

"Now, we would like to understand you better. We can do that if you explain what happened to you."

"You don't have to if you don't want to but really, Ria, don't you think it would help us in our quest to stay out of his grasp?"

Ria was nodding her head in agreement despite her reasons for keeping the truth from anyone and everyone who didn't need to know. Finally, after several strained seconds with the women staring expectantly at her, she gave in to their curiosity.

Running her tongue across her lips and inhaling a deep breath for courage she began with her installment at the abbey.

"I was too young to remember much," she told them, closing her eyes for a few seconds as she tried to reveal the most important facts. "Thinking back, I've vague recollections of my mother and my father. There were images of laughter, which have all but faded. Only these past few days have a few of the pictures returned to me. At times, I thought I was foolish to be thinking about parents I wasn't even sure existed."

"How awful, we also lost our mother and father, but we had our older brother to take care of us and see to our needs," Lacie said with a grimace and a look at Daryl. "You say you were six?"

"I think so. Even now I can't completely remember. I wasn't mistreated there, just ignored except by one man who came occasionally to visit. At the time, I didn't realize he was coming to see me. Didn't realize it until he took me away and introduced me to a life of sin and sexual depravity."

"The earl?"

"Yes."

Ria felt the shudder that always swept through her at the mention of the man she most abhorred in her life. When she closed her eyes, she saw the chains as well as the whips along with some of the other things he used to subdue her, train her as he often told her. They were used to discipline her so she would learn to act as a proper lady would. She later came to realize he wanted her to act as a proper whore.

"What happened after you left the abbey?"

Ria went on to tell them of the years she spent with the earl and the things he expected of her, leaving nothing out. She figured if she was going to tell the story she might as well say everything. She told them of her escape as well as how she discovered the children. Dodge suggested the disguise, finding her clothing and the boot blacking for her hair.

"When Blue learned I wasn't a boy, my life changed for the better even though I nearly died from the merciless beating he administered. He never believed we would be able to escape. If we hadn't, both Ollie and I would be in a whorehouse now. Thanks to Dodge we made it out of the city and to Gray's manor."

Ria spoke of the way Blue beat her and how Gray found her

hiding in his attic barely able to move she was hurt so badly. "He saved my life. If he'd arrived even one day later, I might have died."

She found a quiet sort of relief in telling her story. Even though both women appeared alarmed, it seemed they weren't too surprised by her revelations.

"Men can be horrible monsters," Lacie said as she seemed to be thinking about something, her eyes taking on a distant look of despair. "I almost had my marriage annulled because of a horrible man. I lost all trust in the male species. Thank God, Leslie never gave up on me while he relentlessly pursued what was in both our best interests."

"I was nearly drowned because of a woman. She said she loved the man who loved me, Donal. I suppose she thought that if she couldn't have Donal, no one could. Hands tied behind my back, she pushed me into the ocean. Donal saved me."

By the time Ria finished her story, tears were sliding down her cheeks, a soft sob catching in the back of her throat. It was then, when all were crying, the men walked into the room.

"What happened?" Leslie's gentle voice caught her attention as he pulled Lacie into his arms, Donal and Gray doing the same.

Ria turned in Gray's arms, her breath shaky. "I told them my story. Truly, I hope I did not do something wrong. It was distasteful but speaking of it eased my mind some."

"We drug it out of her before we told her some of our truths as well. I for one am glad that we all shared," Lacie said, leaning into her husband, his strong arm wrapped protectively around her.

"It was something you all should know. It will prepare you for the next few days. I believe with no uncertainty the earl will make a bid for Ria and perhaps Lacie and Daryl as well. He would be a fool to risk it. I believe he's not thinking straight right now," Leslie said, his arms tightening even more around Lacie before placing a gentle kiss on her forehead.

"The earl was very nearly apoplectic trying to keep his emotions shuttered throughout the evening. He will go home and plot," Gray said, watching Ria, his gaze resting on her eyes.

"None of you are to go anywhere alone. My men will always be at hand. If you recall, tonight was meant to enrage the man. We were successful in our endeavor. Now, he will do something so we must all be vigilant. Ria being the bait."

~ * ~

Leslie wasn't far off track with his wise evaluation of the earl's mood along with his reaction of that evening. The earl stormed from Leslie's townhouse, thoughts of revenge simmering in his mind. Ria even wore the amethyst necklace he remembered so well. He craved to tear the necklace from her neck and toss it in her face. Aila wore the necklace and earrings one evening at a ball. It was there he fell in love with a woman he couldn't have. It was also when he began to form his plans.

Only a few years ago, he believed he would eventually have what he sought so diligently, what he prayed for every day Ria was in his custody, brat in her belly. The little bitch lost the child then got away from him. When he finally got her back in his hands, she would pay more dearly than even she could imagine. He would find a way to get her with child if he had to find multiple men to take her every night.

He didn't yet know exactly how he was going to accomplish the feat but he was going to get her back. The carriage stopped at his mistress' home. Stomping up the steps, angry with Ria, incensed with the Duke of Southcliff and everyone else who got in the way of his plans, he slammed into her room. His eyes blazing with fury and desperation, he growled at the woman he kept in comfort as well as at his disposal.

"Whatever has you so riled?" she purred as she moved sensuously on the bed, her back arching catlike, her breasts thrusting upward, enticing him with their hardened tips. The sheer fabric of her peignoir showing every curve, every erotic place on her body, she smoothed it against her skin, tantalizing him even further. "What a pleasant surprise. I didn't expect to see you this evening."

"Didn't expect to be here." He ripped at his clothing as he strode to the bed, his cravat falling to the floor as he began to unbutton his shirt. Tearing it from his shoulders and arms, he tossed the cloth to the ground. "Take off the damn peignoir. I want to see all of you. Lord knows I pay enough for the privilege."

Her eyes wide, she blinked a few times. Didn't move to do his bidding. She moistened her parted lips as his hands ripped the fabric away, leaving the garment in tattered shreds.

"Are you in that much of a hurry?" she asked, still making no move to touch him then her hands ran the length of his chest to rest on his belly. She bent close, kissed him there then sat against the headboard, a smirk on her lush full lips, her eyes darkening with desire.

"You little slut," he growled as he struggled to rid himself of his boots along with the rest of his clothing. "I want you now."

"But of course, darling." She opened her arms as well as her thighs for him. "I'm here just for you."

Chapter Nine

The next morning Gray sat with a cup of tea, eating the marvelous breakfast cook delivered to the drawing room while he waited for Ria to come downstairs. The day was redolent with the scent of spring flowers. The sun was shining for now. In Scotland there was always a promise of rain. For the first time in the last couple of weeks, he was filled with optimism for Ria's future, yet the specter of the earl still loomed over them.

Ria was planning a trip to the dressmakers to purchase a few items for the children, especially Olivia. As much as he wanted to go with her, he was relegated to visiting his own estate manager in order to deal with the transfer of some funds from his bank in Glasgow to the one here in Edinburgh. Olivia needed dresses and things a young girl should have.

When he thought of last evening, he was worried, having bleak thoughts about the day joined with what could happen if the earl found her alone. Leslie assured him she was well guarded. Nothing would happen even if he did manage to kidnap her. Gray was sure that was Leslie's intention all along. That fact infuriated him even though he recognized the reasons. His heart in his throat, he was deeply afraid he could not live like this much longer. The need to force the earl to end his reign of terror had never been as great as it was this day.

Leslie smiled at him as if he knew his thoughts, which he most likely did comprehend. "Rest easy, nothing untoward will happen to the ladies, nothing that we cannot counter. In any case, the ladies are armed and ready to defend themselves if need be, and I've assigned several men to go along with them on this expedition."

"Your confidence does nothing to reassure me. You've no way of knowing what he will try. If he can get Ria alone, there is no guarantee of her safety. I know that is a prevalent thought of his. He might have surveillance on this home. If he does, he'll ken where they will be."

"He is out manned as well as out maneuvered. I've reliable people in place. My operatives are the best. Even if he does find Ria or either of the other ladies alone for a moment, a moment is all it will be. But when he does, if he does, we need to let it play out. There would be no other way to catch him if we don't give him a bit of leeway so he can hang himself."

Obviously Gray was not pleased with this scenario. He didn't like Ria becoming the bait for the earl. If it could be done in any other way, he assumed Leslie would have thought of it. That wasn't the case however. He had the horrifying suspicion Leslie expected as well as planned that Ria would be caught by the earl.

Ria chose that minute to show herself, a hesitant smile on her beautiful face. She was dressed in one of her new purchases, her hair done artfully again by Lacie's maid, he assumed. She was a vision in the yellow muslin day dressed trimmed in exquisite Belgium lace, her matching satin shoes peeking out beneath the hem. He rose when she walked into the room, looking every bit the role of a lady, the daughter of a duchess.

Her lips were slightly parted, her deep blue eyes wide as she looked at him. He thought she was indeed looking him over from head to toe. If she'd done that before, he couldn't recall. Her confidence seemed to grow more each day.

"What are your plans?" he asked, even though he knew they were planning another trip to the dressmaker.

He hoped that was all she had scheduled as he held his breath waiting for her answer.

"I wanted to buy some new things for the children, especially Ollie. She needs to feel like a girl, not the boy she's pretended to be for so many years. And you?"

"It would help if you called her Olivia. That is a girl's name. She needs to be reminded of the fact." His words sounded harsh as he watched Ria grimace at his statement.

"Perhaps you are right. Did you have plans for today?" she asked again as if hoping to change the subject.

He wanted to stay by her side, but that was not possible so he took solace in the fact the duke's men would guard them throughout all of their errands. "I would like to go along with you, join you at the dressmakers. Alas, I don't think it's possible. Perhaps later in the day if all goes according to plan."

"I've ordered three new gowns for Olivia," she said, grinning impishly at him. "Is that better? I'm afraid the name change will be a most difficult habit to break."

"I, well..." he ran his hands through his dark red hair. "I was going to say I don't care. I would be lying though. If we want her to feel like a girl, we need to treat her as one, including calling her by her name."

"You're right, of course. She does want to wear dresses. She will get used to her real name now that her very existence doesn't revolve around the fact she is supposed to pretend she is a boy. I don't think Olivia ever wanted to be a boy."

"You asked me earlier about my plans. I mean to see my estate manager. Since we are here in town, I suppose business should be my main concern. I cannot help worrying about you."

He was planning on meeting with the man but now changing his mind he intended to play guard with Leslie and Donal. The sooner this all reached its final conclusion the better.

Daryl and Lacie waltzed into the room, chatting nonsensically. "Are you ready?"

Ria nodded then turned, placing a chaste kiss on Gray's cheek. His hands behind his back he rocked on his heels as he watched them leave. Shivers of fear washed through him and he was sure something was going to happen today. Reaffirming the notion to follow the ladies he decided again to put his plans off for another day. He strode to the front of the house, watching the carriage trundle away and telling himself despite the strange sensation of foreboding, nothing was going to happen.

Walking to the stable behind the house, he saddled his horse. His path took him in the direction of the carriage, staying far enough behind that he hoped no one would notice his presence. The idea that he didn't trust anyone else to guard Ria was a fact he didn't want to think too much about.

The ladies stopped at more than one dressmaker's shop as the carriage slowly moved through the city. The day seemed to drag on for him. He would have abandoned them if not for the eerie feelings niggling in the back of his head.

The earl showed every sign of a desperate man last evening at dinner even though he tried to hide behind a stoic mask of indifference. It was apparent to all who were there that he was fuming inside, the rage barely tamped down. Gray was afraid he would take that fury out on Ria if he did get his hands on her.

At the third stop Gray dismounted. Tethering his horse at a hitching post, he found a bench and sat down. Keeping his eyes on the door he watched as the ladies once again disappeared inside. They were there for so long he finally decided he might have to give up on this strange endeavor when he was joined by Donal and Leslie.

"Didn't want to leave anything up to chance?" Leslie laughed as he leaned against the wall of the tavern where Gray had stopped. "Neither did we." Leslie said confirming his very real fears.

"They might be in the little shop for a while. Why don't we go inside and get a pint?" Donal said eyeing the dark interior.

"I'll tell one of the guards to get us when they leave," Leslie said as he approached a man standing near the carriage.

Inside the establishment they ordered a few things to eat and drink then leaning back in his chair, Gray studied the two men. "How do you do this?"

"Do what?" They seemed to answer together even though the question was directed at the duke.

"Act so nonchalantly almost as if you do this every day." Gray sipped the ale he ordered casting his gaze in the direction of the door. He didn't feel at ease, yet the other two men appeared as if nothing was going on, as if it was an absolutely normal day.

"Suppose we're used to watching out for our ladies, expecting them to act foolishly even though they've always seemed to have the upper hand. They've a nasty habit of finding trouble where one would least expect it. This time of course is different."

"Do you and Ria have any plans once we've rid Scotland of the earl?" Donal was leaning back in his chair, tipped precariously on two legs, his expression vague.

"I want to marry her," Gray said, "If she'll have me. We've still a lot of things to figure out but..."

"You love her. Kind of thought so by the way your gaze follows her around the room every time you're together and how your voice gentles when you speak about her. It's not just that it's the way you look at her as if you want to devour her."

Donal's eyes narrowed for a few seconds and Gray was sure his brother was thinking of the woman who abandoned him that time long ago, taking his child with her.

It was the beginning of his despair. For so long he cared about nothing, not even his own life. "I love her," he acknowledged again, realizing a weight seemed to have been lifted from his shoulders. Slowly, Ria was healing him.

"Have you told her?" Donal asked. "It would probably be appreciated if you did. Now, everyone told me I should say those words to Daryl but pride and fear of a rejection caused me to hold back until it was almost too late. While I knew I desired her and wasn't going to let anyone else have her, I was terrified of the love word." Donal had this faraway look in his eyes as if he was remembering another time and place.

Gray realized he knew very little about his brother. Neither sibling had been very good at correspondence except where business was concerned, always hiding their feelings.

"They are on the move," one of the guards interrupted.

A lump caught in his throat. "Everything alright?"

"Seems to be," the man said, but I only saw two women get into the carriage."

"Only two?"

"They could all be there but..."

When they stepped outside the door of the tavern, Lacie was just climbing inside and another guard headed in their direction.

Seconds passed so slowly Gray wanted to yell. Then the man stood in front of them. Gray's breath caught in the back of his throat.

"Seems he has her. The coachman saw him with Miss McKenzie's arm, striding toward another vehicle. She was struggling against him, looking over her shoulder at us as if she wanted to be rescued. At first, I wasn't sure it was Miss McKenzie but when she didn't get inside the carriage right away, the duchess took a look and turned to me, her mouth set in determined lines. Told the coachman to follow and me to get to you as quickly as possible."

"Good, you did the right thing, now go back to the carriage and make sure no harm comes to the ladies," Leslie said grimly. "Keep your distance."

"You aren't going to send them home?" Gray asked.

"Wouldn't want to deprive them of their fun," Leslie murmured, yet the look in his ever-darkening eyes told a different story.

"Fun," Gray nearly choked on the word, in this instance refusing to believe the duke could possibly go along with the wishes of his wife. "What the hell kind of statement is that?"

"Well," Leslie said slowly, "one born of a couple of years of the MacTavish sisters trying to fight their own battles as well as those of their husbands. There is nothing to be done about it nor is there any way to stop them. If I sent them back, they would only find another way to help rescue Ria. In my mind it's better off knowing exactly where they are and how far in front of me, she is." Leslie last words were gritted out, his fists tightly clenched. "Once more, she will receive a long lecture, but she will not take heed. Never does."

Gray tried to make sense of what Leslie said but wondered at the fact that Lacie and Daryl would risk their lives to help Ria. Then he realized Ria would most likely do the same if the other two ladies were concerned. If he wasn't so damn terrified, he'd be proud of the women.

They quickly mounted. It didn't take very long to find the carriage and follow at a discreet distance. Gray wanted to rush ahead and find the earl's vehicle. Needed to reach Ria before anything else happened to her. This was the part of the scheme he didn't like, using Ria as the attraction.

Ria did not deserve to become the enticement in this plan. She would be terrified by now, yet she should also know that this time someone would rescue her. She would not have to live with the earl or play his games.

At Leslie's command, Daryl turned down a street set to retrieve a magistrate. Apparently, Leslie had been there a few days before explaining the plan and telling them a trap was set. Also, that they would come for him when the time was right.

"I ken what you're feeling, Gray, but you have to be patient," Leslie said from somewhere behind him.

"Easy for you to say," Gray muttered.

"No, it's not because I intend to allow Lacie and Daryl to rush ahead of us into the earl's house. I already told her I won't interfere unless interference is necessary."

"You did what?" Gray asked astonished any husband of sound mind would do such a thing.

Leslie shrugged staring ahead of him as if he didn't want to take his gaze away from the coach that held his wife. "It's easier to live with her if I give into some of her whims. While the earl is a dangerous man, it's only because of the subterfuge and lies he encircles himself with. She has her weapons as does Daryl. I would not be surprised that by the time we reach them they have the earl on his knees and at their mercy."

Gray wanted to laugh at the sheer ridiculousness of Leslie's words. This was a man, well known as being part of an intelligence agency that was one of the best in the world. Why on earth would he put his wife at risk?

What to do?

He was sweating inordinately, his hands shaking while this man seemed to have a cool and way too calm veneer for his way of thinking.

"You cannot be serious," he murmured still aghast at what Leslie had been telling him.

"We," and he pointed to him, "will be close by. No harm will come to any of the women. By the time tonight ends, we will have the earl exactly where we want him, on his way to Botany Bay."

"How can you be so sure?"

While Gray heard about this man from his brother, he'd had little contact since he left for America over five years ago. He could not imagine a man of the duke's stature ever allowing his wife such liberties. Good God, she was putting herself, her life, in danger.

"I have to be. If I'm not, I'd be reduced to a puddle of insecurities. Lacie and Daryl will make decisions for themselves. They will defy their husbands if they think we are wrong. The only way to deal with my little and very charming spitfire of a wife is to let her have her way in as many things as possible. I've done everything in my power to make sure nothing happens to her. As she has so often and very succinctly told me, she could get hit crossing the street and die."

Strangely enough, Gray caught himself holding his breath during Leslie's little speech. Now, he let it all out at once. He found himself unable to stop shaking his head at the lunacy he just heard, was unable to believe his brother went along with the duke in this convoluted philosophy.

"I for one do not find favor with your line of thinking," Gray grit out, his voice heavy with disdain, fear for Ria taking on a more decided direction after this conversation. Leslie couldn't possibly expect Lacie and Daryl to have the wherewithal to rescue Ria.

"It's not at all what you are thinking, Gray. We will be only one step behind them. They both know my highly skilled operatives will be only a half-step behind them. There really is nothing to worry about. The earl is not a dangerous man, at least not in the way you are thinking. He is not violent."

"I rather believe rape is violent. Ria is not the only woman or young girl he has forced himself on."

Anger was turning to fury as Gray continued to doubt the validity of Leslie's decisions. He spurred his horse to a faster pace, unwilling to leave this to chance. Truly, he didn't care if he intercepted the coach carrying Ria and pulled her from it and into his arms.

"Do not be so sure. If he is not caught in the act and if he doesn't confess, he cannot be prosecuted," Leslie said, raising his voice. "Even though he has kidnapped Ria that act is among the least of his crimes. With his money and influence he would merely receive a tap on the wrist."

His words were finally coming to mean something in Gray's fragile yet tense frame of mind where Ria's safety was concerned. He slowed his horse. He needed for Ria to find peace and Leslie's way was most likely the only way at present. Ria spent so much time cowering in fear it was time for it all to end.

"Very well," Gray muttered, feeling the world closing in around him.

He would wait, at least for the moment.

The sun was beginning to set now as the men headed from the city. A slight breeze blew from the east, cooling the land more quickly than Gray would have liked. Tension invaded him, his hands shaking as they tightened on the reins, making his horse skittish. With a curse he relaxed his hold.

As they turned down a rutted lane, trees and brushes along the side seemingly overgrown, he understood why this location was so perfect for the earl. A few seconds later, Donal and a magistrate joined them.

Along the length of the road they traveled in silence, seconds turning into minutes. Gray's thoughts were never far from Ria as well as the fear she must be feeling. His gut tightened as he watched and waited, searching the road in front of him, wishing he could stop what had been put in motion. He didn't enjoy waiting as he remembered the journey through the Maryland forest in search of his wife and his child. Through two long days of riding, he hoped to find them alive, believed that perhaps they would survive.

His hopes and prayers were dashed when he finally found them. The Cherokee left no doubt how they felt about the white man's invasion of their land. All three, his wife, the man she ran away with as well as his son were killed and tortured.

His breath came in quick and sharp when the road took a decided bend. They pulled up, seeing two carriages stopped in front of a looming old manor house. The first instinct that came to mind was to run inside.

"The guards are at the door, I see," Leslie said, his voice so calm it left a void in the eerie silence following. Gray thought the man's nerves must be made of ice. "We need to stay out here for a few minutes, let everyone do their job. Since the house seems to be encased in stillness, I'm assuming nothing noteworthy has happened as of yet."

"Or he has subdued all concerned and now they are doing his bidding." Gray gritted out, his hands clenching tightly wondering at the abilities of the duke's men.

"According to everything you recounted to me, he likes to prepare the women. Ria has been away for some time. I'm sure he has something special in mind for her. What he plans for her will not happen in the next few minutes."

Leslie's voice was too unruffled as well as too calculating for Gray. "That is exactly what I'm afraid of. He knows she cannot give him what he wants. Why not kill her?"

"Ah, but we both know she still can give him that child, the next Duke of Southmoor. He will not give up trying. It's what he's wanted for too long now. He's like a man possessed," Leslie's voice was cold and calculating as it seemed he had his prey cornered.

His words didn't make Gray feel any better as he watched and waited for a signal of some sort. He expected Leslie was waiting along the same lines. Time seemed to stand still as he became aware of every sound emanating from the forest, every tiny rustle of a leaf, a hoot of an owl or the swish of the wind through the bushes.

When Leslie finally nodded his head for them to dismount, Gray felt as if an eternity had passed in just those few slender moments of time. Time, in his mind, that had been wasted. Truly, it had not been that long but to Gray it had been among the longest minutes of his life.

Silently, they made their way to the looming manor house. Darkness hid their movements, their shadows dancing with the slender light of the moon sparking off surrounding trees. When they reached the door, it slowly creaked open. One of the duke's guards stood by the entrance, nodding toward the stairs leading to the second and third floors.

The three men crept slowly up the steps, ever watchful, listening for any sounds that might indicate a struggle, nothing but the soft restless noise of their boots on the steps. Gray wished for his knee-high moccasins. At the top of the stairs a miniscule light caught his attention.

The loud report of a gun nearly had Gray running up the steps.

Only Leslie's hand on his arm stopped him, yet all three men moved more quickly, tense and ready for what they might discover.

"Now, we want you just as naked as the women you bring here."

It was Lacie's voice they heard through the closed door. Leslie motioned them forward but with caution. Another shot rang out.

Now it was Daryl's voice they heard. He was only catching bits and pieces. "Take your clothes off. That was just a warning shot. I wonder if you would like to be able to walk the last years of your life or perhaps you would rather crawl. The next shot you make me take will shatter all the bones in your foot," There was a long drawn-out pause along with more conversation he didn't understand. "No, perhaps the next shot should be to your groin."

Gray grimaced looking to his brother who nodded with a slight lift to his shoulders, "Yes, I suppose she can be a bit vicious when it comes to someone she loves."

Poised at the door, they waited longer before entering. Gray felt as if all his nerves tangled together in a congealed mess.

"Ria, get the key and put him in the irons. Perhaps the other ladies here would like a full-frontal view of this pig," Lacie said her voice clear and resolute through the door. Then she laughed softly.

Leslie nodded before he pushed the door open.

~ * ~

Ria left the carriage waiting to take them home, having forgotten the blue ribbon she meant to purchase for Olivia. "I'll be back in just a second," she told Daryl. Once more inside the small shop, she looked to the back of the store where the laces and ribbons were located. Quickly she made her way, turning sideways a few times so as not to knock a bolt of cloth from a table.

After picking out the perfect shade of blue, she turned and was assailed by hot sweaty lips next to her ear. Her breath caught in the back of her throat as she pinched her lips together. She would know that acrid scent anywhere. *The earl.*

"Come along now. You knew it was just a matter of time before

I found you and brought you home where you belong." The words slithered down her spine as she took in what he was saying.

Before she could cry out, his beefy hand was pressed over her mouth, his other arm around her neck began to cut off her air. "Won't do you any good to scream now because no one will come to your rescue. They are all outside waiting believing you safe and sound. Oh, you thought you were being so verra clever but no, you can't out smart me, Maria. I will always find you no matter where you hide."

He headed out the back door, dragging her along beside him as she struggled to loosen his arm from around her throat. Wrapping her fingers round his wrist she tried desperately to scratch him, give him some reason to cry out and draw attention to himself. All her attempts to dislodge his arm were useless.

The alley was bare, no one to plead to for help. She was quickly losing consciousness as the seemingly endless seconds flew by. They reached the street. She saw the carriage he was headed to, saw the duke's vehicle down the street. Reaching out to the men standing around she renewed her struggles, hoping some would see and come to her rescue.

Suddenly she was thrown inside the waiting coach then found herself tossed to the floor. She heard the earl give brusque directions then he was inside and before she could inhale, the vehicle was moving along at a steady clip. She struggled to sit, thoughts of flinging herself from the door uppermost in her head. His booted foot on her back, stopped her, kept her from moving.

"You will not try to escape. If you do, I'll render you unconscious. The trip will be more pleasant if you stay right where you are. I always did enjoy talking with you. You were always so very amusing with your defiance. After that so much fun to discipline when it got out of hand."

She closed her eyes now, praying someone saw her distress and would send people after her. Thoughts of Gray now prevalent, his warm sultry kisses in the middle of the night, the way even a simple touch never failed to inflame her senses. A soft sob of despair she'd been trying to hold back left her breathless and weak. She was indeed his bait. So, she prayed this would not all be in vain.

"Ah, a sob for what you are losing for Gray. Are you already with child? Perhaps you will gain a son. I never did tell you why I wanted you so desperately. Suppose you know all about that now." He laughed and the sound sent another shudder whirling through her.

"I know." She tried desperately to show a modicum of courage and defiance even though she understood she would be punished for it. "You will never have that son. As you well know, I'm barren."

"Ah, but it is not you who is infertile. As much as I never wanted to admit to the fact it was me who could not sire a child. I can, however, rend you pregnant with another man's seed. I will have them lined up by night to take you. Indeed, the beauty of it is that you will never comprehend who sired your child."

She needed to think about more pleasant things. It would do her no good to worry about what might happen to her. "Can you let me sit, please?" It was still her intent to find some means of escape. She could not do that lying on the floor beneath his foot.

"I'm not stupid," he sneered, once again his laughter sounding diabolic as well as insane.

"You're mad," she whispered, wishing she had not said the words, hoping he'd not heard them.

"No, just insanely pleased to have you at my beck and call again. I will use you, don't think I won't just because it will be necessary to lend you to the other suitable men I find in order to get you with child. They will all be men of good breeding. I might even allow them to remove that gown from you. It is quite suitable. Its exquisiteness gives you a regal heir. Even as I explain how I found you in the gutter then under my tutorial taught you the fine way of acting you now possess."

"Where are you taking me?" she asked, hoping to garner some type of direction. If she ever escaped him again, she needed some idea as to where she could go to find help.

"Why, to your home. I would say new but I'm sure you will find it familiar in so many ways."

Remembering the shackles on the wall, the whip he teased his victims with as well as the pain each time she was forced, she fell silent then unwilling to share verbal exchanges with the man. He babbled for timeless minutes as the carriage rolled on unheeded. She felt the change from the city streets to the country road as they made their way from the city.

When the carriage finally ground to a halt, she didn't know if she should feel relieved or more terrified. Yet when his boot was removed from her back and she could inhale something besides a ragged breath of air, a sense of relief did fill her. She could fight now.

"We are home, my dear," he said, his voice taking on a hard edge as his hand wrapped around her wrist before tugging her from the floor, nearly wrenching her arm from its socket. "Tell me you are mine."

She shook her head refusing to say such disgusting words. "No."

He twisted her arm behind her back as she cried out. He went on to say, "Oh, I think you will."

The pain he inflicted was agonizing yet still she refused to say what he wanted to hear. She was still shaking her head, tears sliding down her cheeks, "No..." the single word died away.

"Say you are mine and I will take the pain away. Say that you are mine."

She could continue to refuse even though she knew he would continue on this vein until he had his way. "I'm yours."

"Good, now tell me that you will never leave me."

Those were just meaningless words. "I will never leave you."

He didn't release her arm but he no longer kept it twisted behind her back. "We shall do well together. You are not nearly so defiant as you used to be."

She let out a tiny moan of despair. His laughter once again haunted her. She would have to remember the more pain the man inflicted the happier he was. Showing him her emotions was not wise. She learned that a long time ago. The trick now was to remember that fact. The road behind her leading to his home was empty.

"No one is coming," he told her with a haughty arrogance, "why should anyone come after a little slut? Someone who gives her body to most any man who wants her? That is what you are, my dear, and you will never be anything else no matter how hard you try or how many new gowns you buy with money that should be mine."

"You really believe that?"

She felt shocked to hear those words. Horrified to realize how truly crazy he was.

He tugged on her arm, striding toward the house. She was suddenly afraid if she ended up inside, she would never see the light of day again. Trying to resist, it seemed he lost all patience. He swung her over his shoulder then strode to the house.

The door must have been unlocked as well as open because he stopped only long enough to kick the door open. When he headed up the stairs, she knew where he was going and what he meant to do. She shivered unable to deny or hide her terror even as she continued to struggle, her arms and legs flailing against him. He would shackle her naked to the wall in his bedroom then leave her there until she told him what he wanted to hear.

Last time he slowly cut her clothes off, one small article at a time, leaving her defenseless and terrified so very vulnerable she almost cried out at the horrific memory. Climbing up the steps she resisted, tugging against him, even managing to make him lose his balance. He stumbled, cursing but never released her even while he was sprawled on the stairs. She fell, toppling on top of him, his arms wrapping around her.

"No!" she cried out thinking he meant to start the torture here but he only laughed.

"I've waited too long to take you on the steps. In my bed or up against the wall would be preferable where you will learn subservience again. It is too bad I have to start from the beginning. A woman should have no power." His words were a loathsome sneer just as his gaze bore into her seemed to undress her.

"I will spit on you." She understood the folly of the words before his hand struck her hard on the face sending her to her hands and knees. Moisture brimming in her eyes, she fought the hot threatening tears. They would do her no good, would not keep him from his vile inclinations.

It had been so long since she retreated into the world of her imagination, resorting to loosing herself in a magical nonexistent land. She did that now, stumbling as he pulled her once more to her feet, her mind filled with hazy images of happier times.

Yet she could not erase visions of Gray, the way he held her close, his gentle caring nature, the fire his touch inflamed. She would hold on to those things when someone forced her, while she was tortured in the very room the earl meant to rape her.

She would rely on her memories to get her through the nightmare enclosing her with a powerful realism she could not deny no matter how she tried. Quickly, she inhaled a long life giving breath of air, stealing the courage from thoughts of the children as well as Gray. This would have to do for the moment, would have to last her until Gray came for her.

They promised she would be safe, promised no harm would come to her.

Yet she also heard words like trap and bait. She was to be the lure that would bring the earl to his downfall. She possessed no confidence in any of that happening. He held all the power here, inside his home. They would never be able to find a way inside.

By the time anyone found her it would be too late. She thought if he touched her again, she would find a way to kill herself. Gray would no longer want her even as a lover. To think only a few hours ago she harbored thoughts of becoming his wife, perhaps have a child with him, one who would inherit the title as well as the wealth. A babe who could indeed continue the legacy of the McKenzie clan.

Inside his bedroom, he shut the door then tossed her to the floor. For several intense seconds she watched him, her thoughts wary. He pulled off his waistcoat, setting it on a table before he strode to a cabinet and poured himself a glass of whiskey. Sitting down on a chair, he sipped slowly, his gaze running over her. She shuddered, convulsions overwhelming her.

"I think you've grown more beautiful over the last year or so we've been apart. There is a ripe fullness to your body that wasn't there when you left me. I believe your breasts have gown. I will wait a little to sample them."

Having a healthy supply of food since Gray found her probably helped that. She had been rail thin but that fact helped her disguise herself as a boy while she was in Blue's hands. Since finding Gray, she'd been pampered and adored. *Love*, she thought, even though he never told her he loved her, she felt it.

"I would like you to let your hair down now." He watched her over the rim of his glass, his beautiful green eyes darkening. "It is such a beautiful and unusual color. Is that why you colored it with boot blacking? To conceal your identity? I supposed it worked rather well."

She wanted to defy him, to tell him he could go to hell, but all the lessons she learned at his fist were still present in her head. Slowly, she brought her hands upward, finding the combs that kept the short silver white locks secured to the top of her head. Strand by strand her hair fell, winding and curling at the tops of her shoulders, curling in front of her until all was loose.

"You don't have anything to say?" he sneered, "Cat got your tongue?"

He stood. She was sure he would walk to her, slap her again but he sat back down. "Ah, I'm in too great a hurry I'm afraid. I must discipline myself so this will take longer."

She knew what would come next, just didn't know when. Shocked to her core she watched him set his drink on the table before he left the room. He returned a few minutes later with a tray of food, slices of cheese and ham, berries of different varieties as well as a bottle of wine.

"You hungry?"

Her eyes widened, afraid if she ate anything, she would lose the contents of her stomach. She was shaking her head even while he poured her a glass of wine. "No."

"Perhaps this will help your childish nerves. Come sit across from me so we can discuss your upcoming discipline."

This was nothing she'd expected. Hesitant and wary she stood then walked to the chair, accepting the wine.

"What? No thank you? I thought I was being very pleasant. After all I have only our best interests at heart, a son and a dukedom."

She drank the wine. The liquid seemed to gurgle and roll in her stomach, reminding her of the evening conversations she had with Gray.

Unable to help herself and her unraveling nerves she suddenly blurted. "Would you get this over with?"

His smile was the devil's own. When he spoke, he leaned toward her, "You are in a hurry for the pain? I would think you would want to prolong this for as many minutes as possible."

Her face drained of color the resulting chill left her frozen to the bone. "No, but..."

"Very well," He set his glass on the table, doing the same with Ria's. "If you are in such a great hurry, you will go to the wall."

Ria had not meant to blurt out her feelings. The longer he took in this cruelty the better for her. Yet she gave away her fears.

He nodded his head toward her then the wall as if he was a patient man. He wasn't. She swallowed the stone of terror in her throat before she slowly walked to the chains. When she stood before them, he rose and walked to her picking up the lash as he made his way to her. He slapped it against his hand a few times.

"Put the slave collar on," he told her, his smile widening as he watched her bend to his will.

Her hands would not move even though she willed them to do so.

"What? You defy me already?" He ran the lashes across her, terrorizing as he did so. "I suppose I don't really mind. Always did enjoy a bit of defiance, resistance that could be disciplined."

"No." Frantically, she was shaking her head, hair falling swirling around her. "No, no I'm not," she couldn't help but stammer as slowly she raised her hands and locked the collar around her neck. The frigid clamp of steel sent the cold penetrating all the way to her soul. Tears ran down her cheeks, soaking her gown. She tried to bring herself once more to that world where nothing would harm her but she could no longer conjure the image. Today she saw everything clearly, too clearly.

He held one hand in his, kissing the palm, trailing kisses up her arm seeming to delight in the terror filled shudder wracking her body as she pressed herself against the wall. Locking the first iron around her wrist, he reached for the second.

The door suddenly burst open. Ria once again was shocked by the appearance of her saviors, Lacie and Daryl, yet she feared they would meet the same end, secured to this damn wall, having noticed two more sets of shackles that had not been there before. She wanted to cry out to them, tell them they should run while they still had the chance, but the words eluded her.

"I wondered when the two of you would get here?" the earl said, a smile on his face. It didn't seem he noticed the pistols pointing in his direction. If he did, it didn't seem to bother him.

"Unlock the shackles," Lacie said, her gun pointed at the earl.

"Or what?" he asked, still grinning as if he didn't believe he was in any danger.

He must realize if the ladies were here, Donal and Leslie, perhaps even Gray would not be far behind. His life was in jeopardy. He must be so madly insane he didn't realize that as a possibility. Her hopes were suddenly much better than a few seconds ago.

Lacie shot, the bullet grazing his scalp, blood dripping down his face. He laughed, "You are not a very good shot. Mayhap you should give me the gun, lest you hurt yourself."

"I was not meaning to kill you. What I shoot at I don't miss. That was my or what," Lacie said smoothly. "Since I don't want to hang for murder, I mean to only shoot where it will do the most damage without killing you."

The earl belligerently crossed his arm in front of him, seeming not to believe her. "You will give me the weapons. I will only discipline you a little. Not as much as Maria because she has been gone for so long. She should have understood her fate when she left my home."

"Do you like to walk? If you do not unlock Ria, I will shoot you in the foot," Daryl said a half smile on her face and I'm a much better shot than my younger sister. I've had more than a year longer to practice."

"I do believe we should shoot him in the groin," Lacie said a wicked smile on her tiny face. "Don't you think what would fit the punishment much better? We could render it impossible for him to force another woman."

The earl backed up a step, his hands covering his manly parts as if he finally was coming to believe what the sisters were saying as the truth. "No, I don't believe you. You would not do such a thing. You are gently born ladies."

"Do you want to test me?" Lacie asked one elegantly formed eyebrow arching skyward. "Unlock her."

He did then, taking the key from a pocket. She was free and rubbing her neck and wrists where the metal scraped. Never in her wildest dreams would she believe anything like this could happen.

"Now, we want you just as naked as the women you bring here."

"William, that is your name," Daryl said, taking one step closer. "Take your clothes off. That was just a warning shot." "I wonder if you would like to be able to walk the last years of your life or perhaps you would rather crawl. The next shot you make me take will shatter all the bones in your foot,"

Frown lines creased his brows. "You want me to do what?" His voice trembled his eyes were huge and terrified.

"No, perhaps the next shot should be to your groin," Lacie said again.

"You heard me. Remove each and every article you are wearing, or I shoot. Still haven't decided where though." At her words she pointed directly at his groin.

He followed the line of her gaze. His hands shaking, he began with his boots, hopping on one foot then the other, after several minutes he was stark naked his belly shaking with his fear.

"Now Ria, since you are not holding a gun, I would like you to chain him to the wall. Make sure you stay a bit off to the side so you won't get in the way of my shot if I need to take one." Then to the earl, "don't try anything I really am an excellent markswoman."

It was only a minute later. The earl stood in the spot he intended for Ria his neck in a slave collar, his arms stretched above his head. The door swung open.

The three husbands as well as numerous men of the duke's guards stood open mouthed at the doorway. It seemed even the duke and Donal were shocked by what they saw while broad grins slowly formed across their faces.

"As usual you arrived too late," Lacie said a huge smirk on her face. "I'm thankful you let us dish up the punishment. I think there are some ladies in the house somewhere who might like to see this, maybe even use the lash on him. It is such a splendid idea. I'm glad I thought about it."

Leslie nodded to his guards who went in search of the other occupants of the house.

Ria could barely stand as she was helped with the aid of Gray to her feet. She leaned into him, wishing to put this place as far away from her as possible. Her breaths were ragged, her heart pounding, she closed her eyes, reveling in Gray's strong hands holding her so close. She survived. Now all she wanted was to move on with her life.

Gray looked to Leslie. "We are leaving. I've had our things moved to my townhouse so we will not be staying this evening with you. I think Ria has been through enough and will be happy to have more privacy."

He scooped her into his arms then striding down the steps, he reached the front of the house and his horse in record time. After mounting, he pulled her up in front of him, cradling her in his arms. For many timeless minutes, they rode in silence. Ria set her face against Gray's chest, enjoying the strong comfort his presence gave her. She felt the play of his muscles as he kept the horse at a steady clip

She closed her eyes, exhausted by all that happened since she left the house this morning. She'd known for some time the earl would come for her. She'd also understood it would be a harrowing experience. Now all she wanted was to soak in the comfort of Gray's strength and understanding.

Gray seemed to be fine with her silence, realizing after the trauma she just went through she was not yet ready to talk. She would in time. Gray would listen as he always did.

Suddenly, she couldn't help herself. Pushing slightly away from him, "Am I really safe now?"

His voice rumbled against her, "Yes, even from Blue. The magistrate was at the earl's home when all this transpired. Leslie arranged a speedy trial for him. There is a ship leaving in the morning for Botany Bay. He will live out the rest of his life laboring for the crown in an inescapable prison."

"Good. He still sought a child, was willing to do anything to get one from me. I shudder to think what would have happened if he succeeded."

For a while she stared blankly at the road passing in front of them, the many vehicles in the streets of Edinburgh, the people. It was just beginning to sink in that she was free of the man. In truth now, she no longer had to look over shoulder.

"You can be yourself, Ria, whoever that is. The future is yours to make of it what you please," Gray told her, a huskiness to his voice she didn't recognize. "It is time for you to figure out what you want and seek it out."

He stopped then, setting her on the ground before dismounting himself. Leaving the horse at the hitching post in front of what Ria assumed was his home, he picked her up again. When he reached the door, it seemed to open by itself. Millie stood at the entrance. Gray set her on her feet. It was then she saw the children as they rushed to hug her. Charles and Harry stood a little way back, looking uncomfortable as they shifted from one foot to the other.

"Dodge, Ollie, Midget." Her arms open, she hugged them all as they surrounded her.

She looked at Gray, "Thank you. This is what I needed."

"Your dinner is waiting for you, hot water has been brought to your rooms," Millie said as she watched them, hands folded in front of her a wide smile on her face.

The next several hours passed sweetly with Gray and the children. She felt as if this was who she was meant to be. This person surrounded by these loving people was Ria. She didn't think she needed to look for herself any longer. Yet when she thought of her other life linked with the responsibilities, she had doubts.

~ * ~

The earl watched the four young women as they walked into his bedroom, their eyes no longer wide with fright. He was naked and vulnerable. The position he was in now didn't sit well with him.

Somehow, he managed to lose all control. This wasn't right.

The magistrate Leslie brought before him was not one he had in his pocket. He suddenly felt a great deal of apprehension at this scenario, his life seeming to pass in front of him as all the repercussions of this day coming down to haunt him. He even confessed to Maria how he killed her father, how he held Aila here trying to impregnate her. As the magistrate cast the sentence without benefit of a trial, he knew he was doomed.

"No, ye cannae do that. I demand a trial," he cried out incensed. "Ye cannae just send me away to some fate worse than death."

"We can and we will," Leslie said. "It is far better a fate than rotting in a Newgate prison where you will never feel fresh air on your face. At least you will not rot in darkness surrounded by rats."

"Who knows, you might like it there," Donal added with a smirk.

The earl felt all the blood drain from his face. He swallowed hard as he watched the women he mistreated for so long. Leslie gave him to them, to do with as they pleased short of killing him.

Shaking his head, he watched the gleam in their eyes. "No, no, no," His voice died into nothingness as the whip lashed across his legs, then his stomach and chest.

"Do you like this?" one of the women asked.

"Surely you must enjoy this as much as you assumed I did," another spoke up as she took her turn with the lash, brandishing the whip enough to make him grimace while sweat dripped from him.

And so, it went, the magistrate turning his back on him, allowing whatever the women wanted to carry out.

"Ye cannae allow them..." His voice trailed off as the lashing grew in intensity. He moaned as a welt was drawn in his skin just above his groin.

After nearly an hour, "Time to end this as much fun as it seems you are having." The magistrate held out his hand for the whip before giving it to one of the operatives Leslie left behind to make sure the earl would not be able to make an escape.

He unlocked the shackles, watching closely. "Get dressed." He stood back, a smirk on his face as he watched him fumble with the clothing, his fingers shaking so hard he could barely fasten his buff-colored pantaloons or slip his arms through the well-tailored jacket.

The ladies and their men left him in the hands of the magistrate and several other men he assumed were constables. After the women had time to torment him, he was allowed to finish dressing before he was carted off in chains to the ship waiting at the docks.

Sent below into the bowls of the ship he joined other prisoners. The hold was dark and stunk of unwashed bodies. One man glared at him as he pushed back against the wall.

He didn't dare say anything, didn't dare do anything except close his eyes and pray.

Epilogue

Gray stretched his long legs out on the bed above the bakery in Glasgow, waiting for Ria to come to her room after work and find him. He smiled to himself, hoping she would be as happy to see him as he was to see her. He'd missed her in too many ways to count.

They returned home from the ordeal but Ria wasn't quite the same. She was brooding and quiet. Her mood was so solemn he feared for her. When she disappeared about the same time Leslie and Donal left for Glasgow, he didn't have any doubts that she went to the western city with them. Even though she had the funds to purchase a home there, he guessed she would take up residence above the bakery. It was her way of finding some small measure of independence from his as well as her newly found responsibilities.

He told Ria many times if she ever left, he would follow her and bring her back home. She was testing him, at least he hoped that was part of what this move was all about. He loved her and wanted to marry her, but she'd always had too many self-doubts.

Now he would find out if she wanted to spend her life with him. He meant to ask her to marry him as soon as the time was right. Donal lent him Justine his cook for the evening. The wonderful French lady fixed a fine French meal including a few bottles of Champagne for the two of them, having sworn her to secrecy.

Lord, but it had been nearly three months since he'd seen her. He missed her desperately. The children told him not to come home unless Ria was his wife. He stifled a small laugh at their ultimatum thinking it might be easier to talk about than to accomplish. He meant to be persistent though.

His heart thrummed beneath his chest as he heard light footsteps. A few moments later, the door to the bedroom opened and Ria's small gasp of surprise caused him to smile. Everyone, all of Daryl's employees, had kept the secret.

"I hope that is a good gasp and that you're happy to see me. If you recall, I told you I would come get you then bring you home if and when you ever left."

He watched her closely, noticed the slight flutter of her hands as she lifted them to rest beneath her chin. Her eyes were wide, lips moist and slightly parted. The need to kiss her swept through him as if a summer storm settled in his veins.

She wasn't smiling yet his stomach lurched as he thought she might not be happy to see him."

"I recall." Her words were softly spoken.

Untying her apron, she opened the lid of the dish set on the counter in the room, looked at the meal before replacing the lid. She picked up one of the bottles of champagne then tilting her head a bit sideways, she turned her attention to him.

"Justine's work, I see. What did you have to offer her to do this?" Her voice held a whimsical hint of amusement.

"Nothing. She was more than happy to help play matchmaker. She is a romantic at heart, at least that is what I've been told by Donal." He moved to the side of the bed, nodding his head to the spot beside him.

"Matchmaker? I dinna ken." She stood as if frozen in time her expression puzzled by what he said. "Why do either of us have need of a matchmaker?"

"She wants to see you happily married. Me too. Do I have to explain everything?" he asked, patting the bed beside him since she didn't take him up on the first gesture. "Come sit and I'll answer a few questions as long as you answer some of mine. That would be a fair trade, don't you think?"

Cautiously and with obvious reservation, which had Gray sweating, she slowly stepped toward him. "I'm not feeling as if I should trust you overmuch."

"What is there not to trust? I've always been straightforward with you."

He smiled at her still patting the bed and trying valiantly to look sincere. Well, he was sincere. This moment, he just wasn't sure what her feelings were. "Why don't you bring the champagne and glasses? I'll open the bottle. In time, maybe you will relax a wee bit after you've had something to drink.

Ria looked to the door then back to him, still hesitating. With a huge draw of air into her lungs coupled with a dramatic whoosh of the same air, she did as he suggested. Climbing awkwardly onto the bed, she sat beside him. He accepted the bottle of champagne from her. After popping the cork and leaning against the pillows he propped behind them, he poured the sparkling wine. Watching the bubbles, he sipped.

He held his glass up, "Here is to us and I hope our future." Over the rims of the crystal glasses, they gazed at each other, Gray with all the hope he could muster that tonight she would agree to marry him. "Now do you have any questions for me? Ask away then it will be my turn."

For several unending seconds that seemed to stretch into eternity she finally asked, "Why did you come here?"

He set his head against the backboard, his long legs stretched out in front of him, trying to relax and make sense of the complicated emotions surging inside. Opening his eyes and looking into her crystal-clear ones, "One of the reasons is because I told you if you ran from me, I would always find you and bring you home."

"That is not a verra good reason, Graham Chamberlin, at least not one that sets well with me. It doesn't speak of emotions or feelings."

"Seems that's why you ran. To see if I meant what I told you. Now you know."

Her eyes darkened, the hand holding her wine trembled slightly as she tried to sip. "I do and I suppose that means you're a man of your word. But I already knew that." She looked away for a moment. When she looked back, moisture shined in her eyes. "We should eat before the meal gets cold."

"You are running again, even running from the questions you want to ask me. Very well, you are right. I wouldn't want to waste the food. Would you like me to serve? When we're finished, we can get on to more important topics."

Her lips were parted and moist. Her tongue swept across the full bottom one. He yearned to pull her into his arms. Kiss her until she told him what he wanted to hear from her. His heart sped as he watched her.

She nodded for a few seconds seeming to think, "If you don't mind. That would be nice."

"I hope you are hungry," he murmured, knowing he was starving but not for the elegant dishes sitting here but for Ria.

He missed her as did the children. She was such an integral part of his life. He didn't know if he could live without her.

He dished up two plates before returning to his seat on the bed. They ate in silence for several minutes, Ria continuing to look at him from beneath her long sooty lashes. Finally, he put his plate aside, watching her move the remnants of her food around on her plate.

"Are you finished?"

At her nod he took her plate, setting the tray of food and dishes in the main room of the small upstairs apartment. Slowly, he walked back to the bedroom, thinking there was so much to say to each other and he didn't know exactly where he should start.

"So, you asked a question, now it's my turn I suppose." He continued without giving Ria a chance to agree or disagree. "Why did you leave?"

She smiled and with a tiny very feminine lift to her shoulders, she said, "I needed time to think."

What the devil did that mean? Time to think? "What did you be needin' time to think about?" His voice was curt and he didn't mean to pressure her.

As they sat on the bed together, a lot of things were becoming abundantly clear. One huge thing that would rise between them if she didn't address it.

"You don't need to get testy," she told him, starting to move from the bed and put distance between them he didn't want.

With a long-drawn breath, "My apologies, Ria. These last months have been trying for me. I couldn't come right away. There was business then Olivia was sick.

"Sick? Why didn't you say so? You could have sent a message." Her eyes were huge and moisture pooled in their dark blue depths.

"She is fine now. I didn't send a message because I was not positive where you were off to besides avoiding me and the conversations we needed to have. I didn't ken if you still cared for the children or if it was just me you were running away from." He was almost angry now, deciding she had a lot of explaining to do. Her departure had been so sudden it even took him by surprise.

She started to get off the bed, but he stopped her, holding her hands. "I wasn't running away from anyone, especially not the children. What was wrong with Olivia?"

"You were running from me, weren't you?" His voice held a calculated calmness yet he was seething deep inside.

"No." She turned back to him, here hands on his chest. "Yes."

"Why?"

She turned from him for a few seconds, her breaths uneven, ragged. He understood she was in some turmoil. He had a pretty good idea what that was but she needed to tell him the truth. She would not be able to deny him much longer. He meant to stay here in Glasgow until she had no choice but to face her new life as well as the possibilities of one with him.

Her soft pink lips parted as she ran her tongue across them. "I told you before when all the facts about my life were unveiled, I didn't know who I was. That's all. I felt pushed from one place to another, from one person to the next. I was told of all my responsibilities that I knew nothing about dealing with." She bent her head for a moment. "I was terrified."

"All good reasons but I don't think that was all. You knew all along I would help you overcome any obstacle you didn't understand. I meant to always stand by your side."

When he bent closer to kiss her, she stopped him with a tiny delicate fingertip on his lips. "I don't think you should do that."

Kiss her? He planned on making love to her tonight after all was hashed out between them.

"Why?"

"I love you, Graham Chamberlin," she told him her voice trembling. "I want more than anything to be your wife, but you always said you would never marry again. If you kiss me, I'll not be able to think a coherent thought."

"Ria..."

"Wait. You don't have to say anything, I understand completely. Until," she swept her tongue across her lips. "Until just before I left, I thought the same thing. I didn't think I could have children, wasn't sure if I wanted one of my own."

"I've been a fool, Ria. I love you too. I came here to ask you to marry me. Together we are better than when we are separated. We need to put aside what other people might think as well as the expectations that you are marrying beneath your station. If you can do that, I'll make sure the rest of your life is uneventful."

"If I had not met you, I would have never known who I really was. For that as well as putting my fears aside, I owe you so much."

"Nay, you owe me nothing. 'Tis you who taught me how to love again. Will you marry me, Ria?"

She closed her eyes. He was so afraid she was going to tell him no. She placed a finger on his lips.

"I will wed you if you want to be the father of the next Duke of Southmoor."

His stomach rolled as he put together what she was saying. A fierce joy swept through him. "You're pregnant?"

She nodded, her lashes lowering once more. "Of course, we don't know if the babe is a boy or a girl. Will it matter?"

Lord, but he'd never thought to have another child of his own. The three children Ria brought with her he thought to be enough for a lifetime. He got down on one knee, her hand in his, "As long as you are with me for the rest of my life, nothing else will matter. I'll cherish a boy or a girl, more if we are blessed." He kissed the top of her hand as smiled up at her.

She did smile back then. "It was your wicked kiss, you know, that made me fall in love with you."

He laughed then, "Should we put it to the test?"

"Aye, Graham's wicked kiss."

Coming Soon by the Author
at
Rogue Phoenix Press

Feeling Etienne's Love

Chapter One

Paris 1824

Elisa Moreau stepped inside the brothel in Paris with her delivery in hand. She turned at the doorway, shaking out her rain stopper, water sluicing into the alley even as the wind gusted around the corner sending the door banging behind her. The hard fast drops pounded on the roof above. It was truly a nasty day outside. She hoped inside her reception would prove to be a bit warmer than the weather.

She inhaled deeply enjoying the smell of freshly baked bread linked with other delicious, tempting aromas filling the kitchen. The cook, Francois, was a particular friend of hers, so he tolerated her presence in his kitchen like no other. She supposed it was so because she'd known him from birth, played with the pots and pans along with the measuring cups in his kitchen. Vividly, she recalled his thinly veiled curses when he couldn't find a utensil he needed.

Once a year she handed over the books for the madam in this Paris brothel as well as those for her mother in her brothel in the city of Bordeaux. Her mother saw to her education even while she protested the need for such a thing. Now she appreciated her particular skills, realizing she was a very lucky woman.

Elisa always entered Margaux's establishment through the

servant's entrance behind the building before making her way through the kitchen. Angelique, her mother, insisted that no one see her entering or leaving the brothel to protect her reputation. Anyone who knew her, everyone she cared about understood she was the daughter of a notorious and wealthy Madame. What difference did it make whether she entered through the back or the front door? Still, she never argued with her mother or her mother's best friend.

The two women had known each other for years, Margaux beginning her career with Angelique in the bordello in Paris until Angelique moved her business to Bordeaux leaving the brothel in Paris to Margaux. Both women spent the years keeping Elisa from seeing the seamier side of their business all the while failing miserably in their attempts. It was just too difficult to keep a precocious child from exploring and seeing things she shouldn't. Despite the lectures coupled with dire warnings until Elisa was sent away to the small cottage in the Bordeaux region of France, she continued to do and go as she pleased within the building owned by both her mother and Margaux. In the country her behavior changed little. However, she had fewer opportunities to find trouble. Her bodyguards kept a constant watch over her, steering her away from her curiosity, turning her life into one of avid boredom.

She stopped in the kitchen, sampling some of the delicacies that would be served later this evening when the business was at its prime hours. Madam Margaux prided herself in her kitchen as well as the food along with the very expensive wines she served her clientele. At the moment, except for the ladies chatting about the evening to come, the house was very nearly empty. A small game of chance was going on in a backroom. Other than that, only the people who lived in the brothel were about.

"*Bonne journee*, mademoiselle Elisa. How is your day? It's not so beautiful out there but at least you did not get a soaking. That rain stopper of yours must be doing a good job." Francois greeted her with a broad grin holding his arms out for a hug.

"I like the rain," Elisa said with a smile and a wink, searching the platters already heaped high with mountains of food. "What have you got here that warrants a taste before I bring these documents to Margaux?"

"Ah, I see you've been keeping yourself busy with your work. Seems as if a lady as beautiful as you with such sparkling and unusual blue-violet eyes would have a man by now. You spend too much time burying your nose in your books and not spending time with your friends."

Her heart had been with one man since she was six-years-old when he kissed her on the lips, twirling her in a grand circle while she told him she loved him. Remembering that hot summer day, as well as his sudden appearance near her small cottage with his friend Gil. His smile was a quirky half-smile with a dimple showing on the other side of his mouth. Whenever she thought about that gorgeous dimple, she wanted to kiss him there.

The two young men had been riding bareback, wild and free, shouting and yelling their pleasure as they wove their way through the vineyards of the Bordeaux countryside. Neither wore a shirt. Their skin was bronzed from the sun, sweat sliding down their well-muscled chests. She didn't know why she recalled that so vividly but nonetheless she did.

"What are you grinning at, *mon amie*?" Francois asked. "A special young man who will whisk you away from all this boring everyday drudgery? Oui, I hope it is so."

A wave of heat rose to Elisa's cheeks. She waved her hand in the air not really wanting to divulge her secret desires to Francois who would most likely tease her incessantly. "Nothing." She popped a small delicacy into her mouth rolling her eyes at the incredible taste. "*Tres bon.* I'd ask you for the recipe but I know you'll refuse."

"Ah, oui, you change the subject quite handily for a young woman. Your verbal skills perhaps are too sharp for a sensible man. You must change your ways. Stop intimidating the masculine species." Francois laughed as he pulled a tray of tiny lavender cakes from the oven, the icing sitting nearby waiting to decorate the morsels. "But I will not pursue the question. It seems you keep secrets from me. I suppose you share those secrets with Margaux. Should I be jealous?"

"Some," she reluctantly admitted, knowing there was very little anyone except her mother knew about her. Margaux was a woman who would never judge. She was a sounding board for her even though mother never judged either. She always wondered what Angel, the Madame, was thinking versus Angelique her mother. When she spoke, she would always have to figure out which persona was listening to her.

She enjoyed Paris as well as her friends from school even though she was growing bored with the endless parties along with the secrets dalliances she didn't want to find herself caught up in. None of those people would stay friends with her if they knew what her mother did for a living, yet many of the young men she knew frequented this brothel as well as her friends' fathers. The ties of home linked with the small cottage where she lived tugged at her heartstrings. Perhaps it was time to leave the city and return to a place where she felt more comfortable.

"You going to see Margaux? Bring her this tray of snacks, this pot of tea also. Both of you enjoy with my blessings. Don't leave without saying goodbye. I will give you a little something to take with you to your apartment."

"I will. *Merci beaucoup.*" Elisa kissed his chubby cheek before she swept up the tray and headed for the lavish suite of rooms where Margaux lived, her heart racing. She knew Margaux would ask her questions about her love life. All her answers would be the same as the last time she was here. For many years, she tried to keep the mention of Etienne Dubois from the talks they shared. It was useless. Eventually she gave in telling the madam all about him along with that day she fell in love with the young man.

On her way upstairs, she stopped several times to chat and say hello to the women she'd befriended over the years. She understood these ladies as well as why most of them sold themselves. Her mother had been in the horrible position of having a baby coupled with having no husband when she first entered the business. At that time, Angelique had no way to support herself let alone her child other than to sell her body. When she rose to the position of madam of her own bordello, she vowed that any lady who wanted out of the business she would help them find their way.

With her foot pressed against the hardwood, Elisa tapped on the door. "Margaux, it's me, Elisa. May I come in? I cannot open the door. My hands are full."

The door swung open. A beaming Margaux with open arms awkwardly embraced her before kissing her on both cheeks. "*Bonjour,* and how are you this fine day?"

"Happy to have all your books completed. You made a fine profit this year, enough to take a vacation although you never seem to want to do that. You should find some time for yourself, even if it's just to visit Bordeaux and my mother." Elisa brought the tray to a small table in the drawing room of the suite of rooms Margaux occupied.

"I do not like vacations. They are a horrible waste of my time. Who would run this place if I wasn't here? Tell me. Francois? Bah," she paused thoughtfully seeming to realize any number of people could keep it going for a few weeks. Then with a heavy sigh, "Do you want to chat first or talk business first," Margaux asked, pouring the tea. "Sugar?"

"Non. Let's talk business then you can grill me on all my nonexistent beaus. My status has not changed since last I was here." Elisa laughed thinking suddenly her status might never vary. She'd never had a beau. Still only thought of Etienne coupled with that one chaste kiss so many years ago.

Margaux would berate her for still feeling love for this young man she never trully knew. Despite her attempts to do just that, she couldn't help the emotions sweeping through her whenever she thought of him. Every time she closed her eyes at night, she would see the wild young man and the debonair smile flashing on his handsome face as well as his dark brown eyes sparkling with some unknown joke.

Elisa picked up the box containing all her work before settling down on a comfortable chair. She quickly brought out the ledger, which she carefully designed so Margaux could easily read the results of her business this past quarter.

By the time they finished, the sun was beginning to go down. The crowds outside the madam's door had become more boisterous, the music livelier. The night was clearly going to be busy, but Margaux didn't show any signs of wishing to visit the customers.

Margaux reached forward, touching the back of her hand. "Now it is time for you to tell me about yourself as well as what you've been doing for the past months since last I saw you. I pray it has not been all work and no play."

"That's what I was afraid you'd ask. I've not really done anything you would approve of or for that matter disapprove either." Elisa looked to the window and the last dying rays of the sun which had just managed to peak out from behind dark gray clouds. No, she'd pretty much kept to herself, distancing herself from the people she'd met at school before they would find out who her mother was and in the process shun her themselves.

"So, you have not found a young man to replace your Etienne Dubois. You need to look farther than the end of your nose, young lady. Eligible men don't just fall out of trees, you know." At her look of surprise, Margaux cleared her throat. "I spoke with your mother a few weeks ago. It was a vacation of sorts as Bailey drove me to Bordeaux for a long-needed visit, a much-needed visit for both of us. Between the two of us we decided your young man must be Pruitt Dubois' son. We put together the things you told us. It was not too difficult to come to that conclusion."

"I didn't know his name at the time." She was just as surprised as she supposed the look on her face told Margaux. "I was only six when the rogue kissed me. Since then I've been in school in Paris. Mother thought it best to send me away. Now I understand why."

"She didn't want you that close to the young man who stole your heart when you were just a little girl. He was way too old for you at the time. Could have taken advantage of you," Margaux was laughing but the humor suddenly vanished.

"As you point out, he is or was too old for me then, nevertheless. He would not have found a six-year-old interesting. I don't believe for one second he would take advantage of me." Elisa thought on the lost years and wondered why she was still so enamored of someone who didn't know or care that she existed. It was with great difficulty that she tried to push thoughts of Etienne Dubois from her mind, telling herself she didn't even know what kind of man he was. He could be cruel or hateful. He could be a womanizer.

"Until now."

"I suppose, until now. Don't know how old he was then so I certainly don't know his age in the present."

Margaux leaned back in her chair, her hands clasped together beneath her chin. The pose was one of her favorites. "He frequents my place from time to time. I heard he has been to several other countries over the years. It seems he always returns with the law on his heels. He is not the sort you want to be acquainted with, especially not a man worthy of your love. Not the sort you would want as a husband even if he was amenable. By his actions here, in this establishment, Etienne Dubois is far from amenable. He is not for you, Elisa. Not good enough by far. You need to forget him, put him in the back of your mind. Find a man who will treat you with respect."

Elisa felt her heart sink at Margaux's words. She wanted his behavior to be heaped with praise, not liking the fact that now she was discovering Etienne was a bounder and a cad of the worst sort.

"Why was the law after him?" she blurted the question she really didn't want to know the answer to.

"From what I've heard mostly fathers searching for him so he would marry their daughters. He's obviously not the marrying kind." She sat up as a knock on the door caught their attention. "Come in."

It was Francois personally delivering dinner. "Your assistant, Gabriella, is not feeling well today. She asked if I could bring this to the both of you and not to have any worries. When the new girl arrives, she would personally see to her and make sure she is comfortable. A room is waiting for her along with a list of possible clients."

"I had wondered where Gabriella was but I was so lost in conversation this afternoon with Elisa, I didn't think to ask. I can see to the new girl when she arrives."

"No," he laughed, "she made me promise to insist you visit to your heart's content. You see Elisa so seldom. In any case, your bodyguard will be at the front door. He will let Gabriella know when the new girl arrives."

When the cook left, "Would you like me to pour the wine?" Elisa rose, examining the bottle and the writing on the label. "This bottle comes from the Dubois vineyards. So, you do business with the older man, with Etienne's father?"

"I do and when Etienne is in town for his usual short visits, he handles the sales personally. After the deliveries are seen to, he partakes of a night of pleasure, on the house. Otherwise, his friend Gil takes charge of the shipments of wine. I suppose it must have been Gil with him that day Etienne made such an impression on you."

Waving her hand in the air before sipping the wine she'd poured, "It must have been. I've heard that except for his travels they were always inseparable. Do you know why he is always travelling?" Elisa couldn't stem the curiosity she still felt for this man. It was something she could not vanquish from her heart.

"Gil would have made a much better man to lose your heart to. I don't suppose he kissed you too?"

"Unfortunately, he did not dismount before sweeping me into his arms for a quick kiss along with a lasting impression."

"How is your mother?" Margaux asked seeming to think it necessary to change the subject. "Last I heard she was doing better than ever. Thriving actually."

Elisa let out a long-drawn out sigh, unsure of how exactly to answer the question posed to her. Her father showed up last year, demanding a part of the business, a business he had nothing to do with over the years. Angelique's lawyers were the best and kept the unwilling partnership from happening, but he'd shown up several more times at the brothel, drunk and demanding free service.

"Mother is feeling her age. At least that is what she would tell you. Father has visited the bordello several times expecting full use of any woman he finds attractive. Each time the girl he was with was severely beaten. Mother's guards have orders to throw him out if he ever comes again, however his presence has been a painful reminder of her past. A place she does not wish to visit or recall."

"No, I suppose she doesn't. Vividly, I recall her story. With you just a wee babe, she ran from him in the middle of the night. If not for the kindly madam she met, the two of you would have starved. That single moment changed her life for the better, although I realize many condescending people would not see the circumstance in that light."

Leaning on her elbows with her chin resting in the palms of her hands. "Tell me about Gil. Does he also visit here? Perhaps he would be a better more responsible choice for my heart. I could always try to meet him. See if there was something for me." Elisa laughed then, wishing for what she wasn't at all sure. "But I wouldn't know how to go about meeting him."

"Gil is more responsible," Margaux paused for a moment still smiling, "He is still a rake. Not someone for an innocent like yourself. Neither Gil nor Etienne are anywhere close to settling down. It has been suggested that when the right woman comes along, the man will change. From all the circulating stories I've heard, I doubt if Etienne will ever differ from the path he's on. Some men just don't have it in them to be satisfied with only one woman. Even if that woman is as lovely and precious as you are." Margaux stood then, walking to the window and staring out at the city. From her vantage point Elisa knew she could see some of the landmarks that people visited Paris to attend. The view from her window was quite picturesque.

"How are you doing besides monetarily? Have you ever wished that you could leave this work and find an honest man to keep you in the lap of luxury surrounded by children?" Elisa asked, half grinning half knowing the answer.

"So, you change the subject from you to me. You do that quite handily." She stayed at the window. "The lap of luxury. I think this is the best it gets. I've got everything I've ever wanted coupled with more money than I can ever spend. Why would I want a man to beat me down? To command and order me?"

"They are not all like that." Elisa was determined to see the best in men. She had to or she would give up on her dreams of a home and family. Children were part of her dreams.

"Name one who is not," Margaux challenged.

Elisa sipped her wine, the silence echoing in the small room while she tried to think of someone. She could not.

"I didn't think so," Margaux said sarcasm coating her voice.

"There must be some. As you well comprehend, I don't know many men. Actually, only a few boys from school who have tried to steal kisses a time or two. I've told them no. They are not interested in me as a person, just what they can glean from me."

"Good for you. We both know and I'm sure your mother has told you more than once, kisses lead to other things. Things we don't want to deal with. If you ever get into trouble, I want you to come to me if you don't feel your mother will understand."

"Since there is no one I'm interested in, I'm sure that will not happen. No kisses... I could only hope for one more from..."

"Do not dream of that man any longer. He is not worth your time." Margaux shook a finger at her. "He is incorrigible. Where women are concerned, Etienne has only one thing on his wicked man's brain."

"Wicked man's brain?" Elisa laughed understanding the drama of the moment. "Whatever does that mean?"

Margaux poured them both another glass of wine. "You should clear your mind of that man and..."

"And what?" Elisa challenged, wishing for more information. "I don't know anyone in the city. Heaven knows you cannot introduce me to any of your customers. They would think the wrong thing. How am I to meet a man who will take my heart away from Etienne? Tell me that."

"We have many of the best in the city who come here. There are dukes and earls many wealthy bankers along with lawyers." Margaux turned from her view, "I would have to figure out some way for them to meet you outside this building. I'm afraid I don't have any idea how to go about that. Perhaps Bailey can figure something out."

"No, I don't suppose there is any way for that and I'm actually grateful. I'm not in a hurry to marry or meet a duke. That could prove to be very boring. Duke's tend to be stuffy, don't you think? There are plenty of years ahead of me."

"What are you planning?" Margaux asked appearing suddenly wary.

"I'm going back to the country. Mother has promised security for me. I miss the home I grew up in the countryside with it rolling hills. I like to walk down the rows of grapes as well as watch the sun set behind the hills. The moon is bigger there, the stars brighter, so bright sometimes it seems one can reach out, touch them with my hand. When there is a storm, one can feel the excitement to their very bones." She held up her hands a chuckle following. "I'm not giving up on finding a husband. Maybe a nice vineyard owner would take my mind off the elusive and roguish Etienne Dubois."

"Perhaps one would. Now, I'm not trying to get rid of you but would you like an escort home tonight? The hour does grow late. I would make sure you get through this part of Paris safely. At night it can be dangerous for a woman alone."

"I'll hire a cab right in front of your door. I promise to keep my hood over my head so no one will recognize me. Should we finish the wine then call it a night?" she asked feeling a sense of relief now that the conversation about her love life appeared to be over.

"Of course, a cab would be perfect. I deposited the money you earned in your bank account. Do you have enough money with you for the fare?"

"Just enough and not a penny more. Mother taught me not to carry a lot of coin with me while I'm in the city."

Elisa closed her eyes and drank small sips of the wine, feeling the effects of the alcohol as it seemed to warm her while making everything a bit hazy. How many glasses did she drink? Perhaps she should see if there was an empty room so she could stay the night. It wouldn't be the first time she spent the evening in a brothel. It most likely would not be the last.

Her mother used to let her stay at the one in Bordeaux during the week when she was younger. She had seen things young women should not. Still, she was fairly innocent in the ways of men and sex. The lectures from both Angelique and Margaux had been numerous as to what she shouldn't do, but they'd never told her what to expect if she wanted to have sex with a man. From what she'd seen in the brothels along with what the two women told her, the knowledge was all a jumble in her mind.

"What has you grinning?" Margaux asked setting her glass on the table. "You have this strange look in your eyes."

"I was thinking about what I do know coupled with what I don't know about sex. What I've seen and what you and mother have told me. None of it makes senses. It's all a confusing tangled mess in my head."

"And it's best we keep it that way until you are betrothed. When that happens, I will be more than delighted to explain everything as I'm sure your mother will also. At that time, not a moment sooner, will either one of us enlighten you as to the ways of a man and woman in love. It is much different than what goes on beneath this roof."

She sighed softly, a small whisper in the evening air. "I've changed my mind and thought I might ask if I can stay the night. If there is an empty room that is. I'm tired and it seems the wine has crept up on me. I'm a bit dizzy headed."

"Yes, of course. I'll call Bailey. He can escort you to one of our vacant rooms upstairs." Margaux rose from her chair, a small groan as she kneaded her back. "Just as with your mother, age might be getting the best of me. Sometimes it hurts just to stand up if I've been sitting too long."

"I can find my way. Is it the room on the third floor? The one I stayed in a few months ago?" She placed a kiss on Margaux's cheek.

"No, at present the only empty one is on the second floor, first door on the right. Do have a nice rest."

"Thank you. I'll see you in the morning then." Elisa felt a strange exhilaration. It was a feeling she couldn't put a word too. She didn't understand the sensation as she felt as if something momentous might be about to happen, something that would sway the course of her life.

"Perhaps. I don't get up so early any more. If you are up and need to be on your way, then go don't wait for me to rise."

"I won't. I'm awfully tired. I'm not sure how early I will be up. I know I've got until the afternoon." Thought of lazing the morning in bed appealed to her vanity. She'd not thought to do anything of that sort in ages. Mayhap she was the one who needed a vacation.

Elisa walked from the room then into the main hall. Looking around, the scene in front of her was much different from when she arrived. Music played loudly. Men along with scantily clad women were scattered around, sitting on couches, kissing and doing other less platonic things. Over the years, she'd become used to this panorama as she visited Angelique as well as Margaux. She grinned despite her mother's best efforts to keep her away from this. She felt at home.

Second and third thoughts assailed her as she thought of the pros and cons of staying the night. At the front door, she stopped for a moment before realizing she left her cloak in the kitchen when she came in through the back. Perhaps she should leave that way too. She didn't want to walk in the dark alley though. Most of all didn't want to wait for Bailey to escort her. No, she would go to the room Margaux spoke of.

Second floor, first door on the right.

She didn't make it very far before a large hand, settled around her arm roughly stopping her. "There you are. Been looking all over for you. Where do you think you're going?"

"I don't know what you mean. You need to let me go." She was surprised as she felt a moment of discomfort but was sure this could be easily explained.

"You the new girl. I've got to get you settled then find some work for you. A possible client list for your inspection is at the front door," he replied.

She tried to brush the hand away, which seemed to have tightened over the last second. Panic set in, "Let me go." She wasn't the new girl. She wasn't going to peruse a client list.

"You having second thoughts about this job? Can't do that. You signed a contract for a month. Have to fulfill it."

"I don't know what you're talking about." She summoned as much force as she could. For Elisa this was a shattering scene, something she'd not expected. The man coupled with his arrogance along with the wine left her with a loss for explanatory words. The Neanderthal probably wouldn't believe her anyway. Where was Bailey? "Let me go. If Margaux knew I was having second thoughts, she wouldn't force me."

He turned her, shaking her slightly. "Can't do that. The madam would have my hide if she found out I let the new girl leave without fulfilling her contract. While it's no matter to me, why did you sign something you weren't willing to fulfill?"

Elisa understood arguing with this man wasn't going to get her anywhere. After all, his point was well taken. The man didn't know her, would of course assume she was something she wasn't. She just needed to find a familiar face. "I want to see Margaux."

"New girls don't get favors. You need to learn to call her Madam Margaux. Now I'm going to take your cloak. Do you have a valise? Then you are going to behave yourself. Do as you're told. Everything will be fine if you do."

He let her go then. Momentarily, she thought to dart into the kitchen. Francois would defend her. Tell this man she was hardly the new girl, however when she turned, her gaze rested on the stairway, her breath catching in her throat. The sight was something she dreamed of almost every night since their first kiss.

"Etienne..." she whispered softly, staring at the man wide-eyed who stopped and was now looking over his shoulder straight at her.

Inside her chest, her heart thundered, beating so rapidly she thought she might swoon. She couldn't be sure this was Etienne. Still, he looked as she imagined him. He was taller, his shoulders broader than she recalled. His dark hair was disheveled, a thick strand hanging across his forehead in that charming way the six-year-old girl remembered. She wanted to get close enough so she could see the sparkle in his deep brown eyes as well as the quirky, dimpled smile she remembered.

He pointed at her. "I want that girl."

~ * ~

Earlier that afternoon, Etienne wiped the sweat and blood from his face. Gil landed a few good punches to his face. His friend was an established boxer and he'd spent the night before drinking and gambling. He touched his nose, grimacing a moment while at the same time, hoping it wasn't broken again. The women in his life would of course, appreciate the slight flaw fawning over him to get his attention. He grinned

"You're getting old," Gil said with a chuckle as he wiped sweat from his body then dipping his towel into a basin of water he repeated the process. "I didn't used to be able to best you so soundly or so quickly."

"Just as old as you." Etienne shot back without hesitation, thinking he needed to spend more time with this type of physical activity rather than those with the ladies. "Just a bit rusty on my boxing skills. With a little time, I'll be back to my old pace."

"It's your lifestyle. You should think about settling down with a good woman."

"Don't suppose you know any? I certainly don't," Etienne laughed, looking in a mirror and dabbing at the blood over his eye. Where women were concerned, he was more than slightly jaded. No one would believe him but his heart had been broken several times during his younger years. Besides, his life at the moment didn't lend itself to serious dalliances. Working for the French government took all his concentration. Distraction was not an asset to his work. Now, he vowed to never lay his heart on the line again. He poured water into a basin before splashing the liquid on his face, feeling the cooling droplets slide across his body. "Need a bath before tonight. Want to come with me?"

"For a bath, no. You seeing a lady or are you going to the bordello?" Gil asked, grinning at him as he also cooled his body with the water.

"No, gave up on good ladies. Present me with a naughty one anytime. Get into too much trouble with the good ones. Seems they expect certain favors I'm not willing to offer. Going to Margaux's. Might do a little gambling beforehand. See how my luck is running." Etienne thought on the last girl he bedded. When her father discovered him in her bed, he had to go out the second story window without his boots to escape a marriage. That was the last time he would put his life in jeopardy, especially when he knew of a respectable brothel, a place where he could have a night of pleasure without being worried about his life and limbs. He walked away from that night with a turned ankle and he was just glad nothing had been broken.

"Guess I'll join you. Don't have anything better to do. Madam Margaux's establishment is usually quite the thing?" Gil asked grinning.

"Heard there was a new girl coming tonight. Perhaps I'll give her a try." Etienne was toweling his hair knowing he needed something new in his life even if it was a whore. Perhaps she was new to the business, not just to Margaux's establishment. A virgin, non, he didn't want to dally with an untried lady while having to worry about hurting her.

"Heard she's a virgin. Personally don't want anything to do with virgins," Gil said as he towel dried his golden hair.

Two hours later the two men entered Margaux's establishment. Etienne grinned, planning his night. He had profits from the delivery of wine this morning. Now he was going to relax and enjoy the games as well as the spirits. If things went his way tonight, he would enjoy more than the gambling. A night spent in a willing woman's arms was just what he needed before he left on his next mission.

Bailey led them through the rooms to one in the back with a cluster of small tables. Brandy as well as wine flowed freely. The stakes were high. They sat with some other gentlemen. A few minutes later the cards were dealt. He leaned back in the chair a cheroot in his hand, smiling. When his funds were plenty, he rarely lost. It was only when he was desperate for money that he would come out of the game with less than when he entered into it.

Tonight, he was restless though. Gil had presented new ideas, ones he needed to consider. His father was after him to settle down and provide grandchildren, an heir to the Dubois vineyards. He didn't know where to find a good woman, one who his father would approve of. Certainly, he wouldn't find that type of respectable woman in this house of ill repute.

Possibly he was tired of playing the games of love. Maybe he was looking in all the wrong places. If he found someone, he would settle down and become a decent human and father he hoped. Problem was he seemed to gravitate toward women who, well, women who were less than ladies. They either wanted him for the sex or for what he could give them. He decided the next country he visited, he would lie about who he was then maybe, just maybe, he could find a suitable woman.

"You in or are you just going to stare at your cards?" one of the players asked with a smirk, apparently sure of his hand.

"In," he said, fingering his cards, still acting distracted yet he was fully alert and sizing up the expressions on every man's face. Perhaps this was as good a hand as any he was going to get tonight.

The games continued for a few more hours until Etienne tired of the sport. He'd won a sizable amount. Luck was with him. Most of his winnings he planned to lavish on the prostitute he was going to spend the evening with. He smiled to himself thinking of the night to come; of soft breasts, a sweetly curing hip, the sweet velvet between the woman's legs.

"I'm done," he said, stretching his gaze to Gil with a silent question. "You coming or staying?"

"Tired of cards. So..." Gil stood seeming a bit confused, running his hands through his hair, his expression one that told Etienne he wasn't sure what he wanted. "Not really in the mood for a woman. Think I'll go to the apartment. See you tomorrow afternoon for another boxing lesson."

Etienne let out a long chortle wondering what was Gil truly up to. "I will be giving you the instructions, *mon ami*."

"You can hope."

They spent some time in the foyer, chatting and watching the women as they showed themselves to the two men. "Change your mind?"

Etienne asked as he saw the slow smile of appreciation cross his friend's face when a certain woman with huge breasts and swaying hips approached them.

"Perhaps the little red head is appealing tonight. Seems she has all the necessary assets." Gil stared at her while she stepped closer, her hand on his shoulder her breasts pushing against his chest, her silver-blue eyes twinkling. "Guess I'll stay."

Etienne watched his friend leave with the woman. Searching the room, he didn't find anyone especially tempting. He leaned against the wall, his arms crossed in front of his chest. Perhaps he should just leave. Maybe what he sought couldn't be found here tonight.

"You need a woman?" A blond with sparkling brown eyes pressed against him, running her hand along his chest, pushing her ripe full breasts against him.

Her lips were too red, her face too made up, but, "What the hell?"

"I can ease your stress," she murmured softly taking his hand. "Along with whatever else ails you. Don't ask questions. Don't judge."

He realized she must have seen the money he won. Once again, the lady wanted what he could give her not him. The fact didn't help his jaded heart even when he reminded himself he was in a bordello. Lord but he wanted someone who wanted him. "You could give it a try," he told her, thinking once more what the hell. She was a warm willing body to relive his baser needs. That was all he needed tonight.

Warm and willing.

Scotland called to him. He was going to be sent there on a secret mission. His operatives were on their way. He'd yet to receive the details. Next week, after seeing his father and saying his goodbyes, he would head to Glasgow. He'd never been to the land of kilts and bagpipes. Perhaps that country would give him a new interest, some lady he could call his own. Yes, he would go to Glasgow. Tonight however, he meant to have sex with the woman standing next to him.

"I will do more than try," she murmured as his hand slipped around her waist before moving higher to rest just below her breast. He felt the small shiver of passion as her pliant woman's curves molded against his. She tossed her head sending a wave of blond curls around his arm.

"Where is your room?" He started forward, matching her small steps as they headed up the stairs while he explored more interesting spots with his hands.

A whisper in the noisy room caught his attention. Halfway up the steps he stopped, turning to search the room. His heart caught in his throat as his gaze rested on a woman near the door. Her back was stiff as were her shoulders. There was something intriguing about the provocative face, the soft lips as well as the tilt of her regal chin. She met his gaze, moistening her lips with the tip of her tongue then slowly closing and opening her eyes. For a moment, his heart forgot to beat.

He had never seen a woman as beautiful or one that had him lusting after her with just one look. The darkening of her eyes spoke of passion. Her sensuality seemed to take over every part of her, calling his name as no other woman could. What the devil was she doing in a bordello when she could have any man she wanted? His actions now might impact the rest of his life, but damnation he couldn't resist.

"I want that girl." He didn't know if she was the new girl but the talk around the table tonight had revolved around a new woman coming to the brothel. He'd never seen her here before. He understood the price would be higher. As he also knew the madam would indulge him in this, simply because it seemed Margaux had a soft spot for him, spoiling him when others scorned his ways.

"Mais non," the blond said.

"Sorry, sweetheart. You can find someone else." His full attention turned to the young woman.

The manager standing beside her placed his hand on her waist before whispering something he couldn't hear. She nodded as if accepting his request. Slowly, they made their way up the steps and toward him. Her lips were parted invitingly even as he saw the flush paint her cheeks along with the slight trembling of her petite frame. She was everything he could ever hope for.

He met her halfway, taking her hand in his. Before bending over, he caught her gaze with his, *"Enchante mademoiselle."* He kissed the back, felt the shiver pass from her into him, and knew he'd remember this night forever.

"Bonsoir," she spoke softly, her words whisper thin as he sensed

the potent surge of energy sweeping between them. He felt the soft flutter of air as she let out the breath she'd been holding. Then she looked upward, their gazes meeting his in a haze of powerful desire he could read clearly in her eyes.

She wanted him.

He watched as she seemed to try to inhale a large dose of air, her bottom lip finding purchase beneath her small white teeth. He thought of tasting that full lip, putting his teeth where hers touched. Beside him her body trembled. "You have nothing to be afraid of." His voice was soft and throaty from the rapid rise of passion. "Come, we can talk first if you'd like. Don't have to rush anything tonight."

His hand was on her tiny waist. He was guiding her upward to her room, but he wasn't sure where to go. She seemed to sense his hesitation then she looked at him with wide vividly unique blue-violet eyes. "Where are we going?" Then she paused again for what seemed an eternity as she looked around.

"To your room. You have been assigned a room, haven't you? Or is it too soon?" He didn't want to wait or go downstairs until something could be arranged.

"Oh." She sounded surprised, her eyes widening with sudden comprehension. "My room, I thought. Second floor, first door on the right."

"Good, now that was not so hard." He felt a small chuckle rise from his belly as they turned down the hallway to stop at the first door. It swung open. He waited for her to walk inside before he closed and locked it behind them, leaving the key in the door. Clearly, she was nervous. He wanted her to relax.

She stood in front of him, her hands clasped tightly in front of her, nearly white, blond hair falling in soft very touchable curls around her face while the rest was piled neatly on top of her head. Her uniqueness stole his breath. Did she have any idea how beautiful she was?

"What do we do now?" She looked to the floor then back to him, her blue-violet eyes shimmering with some emotion he craved to discover. For a moment, her hand fluttered upward and toward him before she drew it back.

"Take all our clothes off." He watched the expressions flit across her face then thought better of his statement. While that was his intention and hers to be sure before the night's end, perhaps this was too soon. If she were the new girl this would all be uncertain for her.

"Do we have too?" She looked up startled wide eyes staring at him.

He kept his laughter behind his teeth. "Non, but it would be more fun if we did."

Now she looked down, plucking at her skirts before he could say anything more, she touched his chest with her small hand. "If you say so."

Perhaps something else to speak of would be prudent at this time, "Do you have a name?" He spoke gently in a fervent attempt to ease the way for her.

"Do you?" She sounded defensive. He wasn't too sure why. He only asked for a name.

Perhaps she wasn't as nervous as he thought. He would have to proceed with caution before he could see just what was going to transpire next. He bowed low, "Etienne Dubois at your service."

Turning her head away for a moment then looking at him and with a few blinks of her eyes, "Elisa."

"A pretty name for a pretty lady. Do you have a last name?"

"Just Elisa."

Realizing she would give up only so much, he granted her the omission for now. In the scope of things her last name was hardly important. After tonight, he didn't plan on seeing her again.

"Just Elisa are you the new girl?" he asked, suddenly wondering just how new she was to all this. If she was still a virgin, Madame Margaux would charge him double. He realized he didn't care. All his previous notions coupled with his reservations about bedding a virgin vanished.

She was shaking her head then, seeming to deny the fact but everything about her actions described a novice. "No, well, yes, I suppose I am new to all this. Don't understand what is expected of me though. Never been with a..." Her moist tongue swept across her lips leaving them wet, enticing very pink. She invited him with such delicate gestures.

The knock at the door surprised him, averting his attention from Elisa. When he opened the door, a man was standing in front with a tray of food along with a bottle of wine.

"This is for you and your lady friend. Enjoy," he said, handing the gift to him before backing away a step then holding out a parcel wrapped in tissue paper. "This is also for the lady so she is more comfortable this evening."

"Thank you," he said as he backed into the room turning to Elisa. Surprised, "Do you know what that was all about?" Etienne asked as he set the platter on the table before handing the package to her. He returned to lock the door again. It was unusual for food to be served to the guests unless they paid for it in advance, also unusual for packages of any sort to be delivered.

This time she was nodding her head in what seemed to be a continuous motion, "Madam always sends food and wine to my room when I stay the night. Since my remaining here is usually spontaneous, she sends me a peignoir to wear. Comfortable yes."

Those were puzzling words ones to think about at a later date. Right now, he didn't really care. The night was looking better with each passing second. He hadn't eaten since breakfast that morning. He was hungry for food as well as the so very beguiling young woman standing before him. He didn't plan on taking her strange words at face value.

"You must be special," he said, studying her closely for some clue as to what was rattling around inside her head.

She shrugged her shoulders slightly, giving him a wobbly smile before she spoke. She opened the gift, pulling out a dark blue negligée and robe. "I suppose I am."

"The madam doesn't do this for her other girls. Do you wish to change now or later?" Etienne wanted her to change now wishing to see her in the confection.

"Later. I wouldn't know," she sighed softly stepping forward as she seemed to watch him from the corner of her eye. "I'm not really hungry but you go ahead and eat. I'll pour the wine."

He rummaged around on the tray heaping two plates with food then accepted the wine from her shaking hand. Evidently the arrival of food did not make her any less nervous.

She ate sparingly while he used the time to satisfy his belly before moving on to the second part of the evening, which would inevitably satisfy other parts of his needy body. He did have the entire night with her having paid for it beforehand while making sure the extra money he gave would go directly to her.

Now, Elisa peered at him over the rim of her glass. Seemed to be staring at his mouth. He adjusted his position in a feeble attempt to calm his eager man parts, the lust for this beguiling lady beginning to take over his body along with his mind. Well hell, he never responded to a silent invitation such as she was sending so quickly or so intensely.

"Is there anything you'd like to tell me about yourself?" he asked pleasantly, hoping she wouldn't turn into a chatterbox but it would be nice if she said something, anything.

She lifted her tiny shoulders in a hesitant shrug. "Not really."

That was what he thought. He set the plate down and with a pleasant voice, he asked, "Should we get to it then?"

"To what?" She moistened her lips before following suit, her eyes crossing. Setting the glass down, her gaze roamed the length of his to settle on his rapidly hardening crotch.

What the devil did she think she was doing? Those were the actions of a practiced courtesan.

Blood rushed to his groin. "I'm sure you know as to what I'm referring. Why don't you change into that lovely confection that was sent up to you?" He couldn't help the slight tinge of frustration he was sure she heard. Being blunt was not his usual way, nor had he ever needed that aspect.

"I still don't know what you expect. But what I do understand is that you mean to have sex with me. Just not really sure what all that entails. Madame Margaux did tell me when the time..." She stopped just when he was getting interested, a becoming rise of color to her cheeks following.

"When the time?" Lifting an eyebrow, he queried hoping to pursue this line of conversation more thoroughly, his mind spinning with too many fascinating scenarios to settle on one.

"It doesn't matter." She waved a hand in the air, some of the wine in her glass spilling out. "Oh, my..." She looked at him, growing even redder then set the glass on the stand taking a cloth and wiping away the red drops, her hands pushing against her breasts as she cleaned her gown.

He took her hands in his, "You don't have to be nervous. I'm not going to hurt you. Never hurt a woman in my life." But he'd never had a virgin. He was becoming increasingly sure Elisa had never had sex before even though her previous statements confused him countering that very thought. He'd never seen anyone so skittish and unsure of herself before the sex act, one she'd agreed to.

What to do?

He certainly wasn't going to walk away.

"I didn't think you would." She paused. "Hurt me. I've wanted this with you for so long."

"Go, change into the negligée. We can proceed from there." He inhaled long and hard. What the devil was she talking about? To his recollection he'd never seen this woman before.

"Fine," she rose, striding into a dressing room. He heard a small curse. She was back, turning away from him. "I need help."

He chuckled softly as he brushed the long silken curls away from the fasteners. Deftly he undid the dress then her corset. The gown as well as the other garment fell to the floor.

"I will be right back."

He sat, waiting for her return, thinking on all that had been said between them, still puzzled. When she appeared in the room her hands clasped in front of her, his breath caught in the back of his throat. She looked so tiny and frightened. He needed to erase that look of fear from her eyes.

"What do we do now?"

"Perhaps a kiss would relax you. We can take this slow and easy one small step at a time. After all we have all night. Promise to tell me what you like and don't like."

"I'm sure I'll like your kisses as much as your smile and the little dimple." She touched the side of his mouth with a fingertip. "Right here."

Etienne couldn't help but groan. He held her hand in his, the protruding finger now resting on his lips. Nibbling then sucking it into his mouth, he smiled anew at the surprised gasp that followed.

"Did you like that?" His question in any other case would sound insincere but now and with the pleased expression on her face he was glad he took the time to ask.

She nodded several times before a veiled sigh escaped her soft pink lips, "Oh, yes. It makes me feel things in places I've never thought of before. There are butterflies flitting about in my stomach."

"Good, I'm glad." He slowly began removing the pins from her hair, watching as the silken tendrils fell around her shoulders, lightly touching her ear, the column of her neck then following with tiny little nips of her flesh. "Your hair," he paused thinking and remembering another time very long ago, "is unusual. I've only seen its color one other time. I'm trying to remember."

"Wh-where," she stammered, her eyes wide an emotion he didn't know how to interpret.

He brought one of the loosened pieces to his cheek, letting the softness caress him. "It is nothing." He remembered Angelique's white-blond hair. That thought gave him a pause in his memories. There was another time. He searched his mind. It seemed the image would not resurface.

"No, tell me," she whispered, reaching out a hand to rest on his chest.

"Then you tell me something about you?" he asked. "It seems only fair."

"Alright then. You're right of course. If you share then so should I." She played with the lace around the neckline of the robe she wore inadvertently lowering the bodice slightly.

He wanted to take her hands in his, slow the nervousness but he didn't think anything would help at this point. "I saw your hair color on a madam in Bordeaux. I believe her name was Angel. Now it's your turn. While I'd like to learn your last name," he wasn't sure why he had a change of thought on this, "tell me anything you like, something you feel comfortable sharing."

She stiffened seeming to think better of a reply that he knew almost blurted from her lips. For a few seconds she ran her tongue across them.

The silence seemed to echo in the room while she appeared to be thinking about what to tell him. "While I've never been in a room alone with a man, I've spent time in a brothel."

Those words shocked him. By her actions, he would have never guessed such a thing. Yet her innocent shyness delighted him. Deciding it was time to end the conversations, determined though to take them up later, he placed a gentle kiss on her neck then higher, taking her earlobe between his teeth and tugging gently, one hand cupping the back of her head. Tiny sounds rippled from her throat. At that moment he knew everything would work out.

Shivering beneath his touch, she turned in his arms then leaned into him, her back against his chest while he continued with lips teeth and tongue to trace the line of her neck and along her collarbone.

With a wistful sigh, "Do you do this often? You seem to know what you're about?"

A low belly laugh rumbled from his throat. She turned toward him again, a puzzled expression on her face, lips slightly parted in question. "Probably more than I should. I'd like to know what you're thinking but I'd rather kiss you so I can show you there is only pleasure to be had in what we are about to do here this evening. Do you trust me?"

"You told me earlier to take my clothes off but I don't want to, not... Do you mind? Don't believe I can make my fingers work to do something like that. Are you going to remove your clothes too? I'd like to see your chest. I saw it once a long time ago." Her fingers rose before softly caressing his cheek. The wistful expression as well as the revealing words left him in a state of stunned shock. A long time ago, perhaps that was when he saw her. If only he could remember.

He groaned at her simple words when they registered in his mind. Pursuing this line of conversation was not something he could do right now, not when she was softening under his tutelage, relaxing beneath each gentle kiss. He knew in minutes he would have her naked beneath him, He would be deep inside her velvet warmth.

Velvet fire.

Long enough to remove his shirt he stopped kissing her. He began again, her hands resting on his shoulders. They were soft, touching him. Her nails were well trimmed, not overly long. He tugged on her bottom lip then soothed it with his tongue, pressing inside and meeting the sultry warmth of hers while her hands rose to the back of his neck, tugging him closer.

"I'm going to take your robe off now," he said as he pulled away, his brows drawing tightly together.

"Do you have to?"

"We spoke of fairness earlier. If my shirt is off then..." He intentionally left the words unsaid and hoped she would fill in the blanks.

"...my robe should be off. Still, I can't do it." Her words were so quiet he had to lean forward to hear her. "My fingers..." she sighed as she held up her shaking hands for him to see.

"Not a problem." He wanted to undress her slowly. The undoing of each tiny bow down the front was followed by a soft kiss along her collarbone. Tenderly he pushed the fabric from her shoulders. Again kisses, gentle kisses, nipping kisses followed the semi-unveiling of her white flesh.

Her soft sigh of pleasure gave him reason to grin, yet his patience was slowly coming to an end. When he entered the room with her, he'd thought to have her beneath him in a matter of minutes. At least an hour had already passed. Even now, this slow seduction was making progress. He guessed by the time he was inside her, she would be hot and exciting, wild and passionate.

She sat in front of him now, her thin negligée all that stood between their lovemaking. Her tight puckered nipples pushed beguiling against the silken fabric, enticing and tempting ever part of him. He set her against the headboard before coming between her slightly parted legs.

He sat back, looking at her kiss-swollen lips loving the tangle he'd made of her hair. Her eyes were wide with what he hoped was desire coupled with raw dangerous passion, hunger that could make a man hard with the ecstasy. While he undressed her, she'd said very little. Now, her breaths drew in and out in short wisps of air. When he tenderly sipped at a pulse point, he felt the rapid beating of her heart. He had no doubts she would be ready for him.

"I'm going to remove the rest of your gown now." He stopped staring at her, his gaze slowly raking the length of her, intrigued by the darkening of her eyes. "All but your stockings. Now, help me out and lean forward."

She did as requested. He slowly undid the tiny bows at the top of each shoulder as he watched the silken fabric slide the length of her to pool around her hips. Her scent was lavender mixed with vanilla.

Her legs were spread for him, the dusky rose tips of her breasts responding to his gaze, tightening without even being touched. To his jaded heart she was a vision of desire and passion. He believed for the first time in his life she might want him, not just what he could give her.

That remained to be seen though.

He wanted to laugh. It was all she could do not to try to cover herself, but she didn't know where to put her hands.

"What about you?" she asked.

"You thinking of what's fair along with what is not?" He sat on his bed, pulling off his boots then stood. His wide grin seemed to give her a reason to return the sentiment. He found the fastening on his pants and slipped them off. He stood in front of her naked.

Her gasp of surprise coupled with the widening of her eyes startled him. "I never thought..."

"Thought what, sweetheart?" He was still grinning pleased with her innocence.

"Don't laugh at me."

"Never, thought what?"

She caught her bottom lip beneath her teeth. Then she whispered, "That you would be so large."

While he expected those words at her startled look, he had no idea what to say in response. In all his life, he'd never bedded someone who was so unknowing in the ways of the flesh. It was truly a shame; she was destined now to spend most of her life in a brothel. He was almost tempted to whisk her away from this place. He didn't. As he well knew the madam would have his hide if he attempted such a foolish thing. This lady would prove to be a gold mine for Margaux. Either that or he would have to pay a small fortune for the privilege to make her his mistress.

He came down on top of her, kissing and caressing every tender erotic spot he knew of. He left no part of her untouched, reveling when her hips began to rise to meet him, her back arching imploring him for something more. Her breasts, the hard tips, her navel he left nothing unattended. Higher and hotter, he felt the same enchantment. Kisses, nibbling caressing, tasted the sweet essence that was Elisa.

"Etienne..." her softly uttered words touched his soul. "Please."

He understood all too well what she was saying to him but she didn't. Another moment of remorse or hesitancy snaked through him. He'd never been a man to wallow in remorse or guilt. Someone would have her first. Why not him? She had not said *non*.

"Elisa," he whispered, his voice hoarse with need. She was an unknowing enchantress. This exquisite joining that hadn't even happened yet was magic. Sweat beaded on his forehead. A soft sheen of moisture covered her body. His lips seduced the satin hard tips of her breasts while his fingers found the swollen velvet knot of ecstasy that would bring her more gratification than she'd ever felt before. Sending her to a place of sweet satisfying delight was his only thought.

He didn't know what to expect when he came inside her tight sheathe. Slipping a finger inside, he moved slowly. He touched her maidenhead. Sucked in his draught of air. Once more, he almost stopped, not wishing to cause her pain.

She's a whore. It makes no difference that she has never done this before. Someone has to be her first. This is what her life will be from now on.

Truly he didn't know if he should take this slowly or just get it over with.

Well hell.

With a long deep breath in his lungs, he pushed inside, drove into her then stopped at the constricting of her muscles linked to the small cry of pain. Her nails bit into his shoulder. She beat at him with her tiny fists, pushing at him even while he understood she wanted him to leave her be. He wasn't going to do that.

Couldn't.

Minutes ticked by so slowly he thought he'd rip the clock from the wall. For too many seconds to count, he held his breath, waited for her pain to subside. Held it until finally her nails biting into his shoulders relaxed. He found that her hips were rising to meet him once more.

"You said you wouldn't hurt me," she said accusingly, a lone tear slipping down her cheek.

"I didn't think I would. Didn't know you were a virgin. This pain only happens once. Is that what Margaux was going to tell you my sweetheart?" Slowly, he was moving, the velvet softness within, her fire compelling him, taking him deeper and deeper into her wet velvet core.

"Etienne..." the one word slid out slowly.

His name on her lips was heaven. "What?" He smiled at her as she reached out to him, gently touching the side of his face.

"Open your eyes. I'm going to make up for the pain inflicted. Going to help you forget everything but the honeyed joy." His lips closed over hers while his fingers danced evocatively in all the places that would give her the greatest pleasure.

"I love your half-smile and the dimple," she murmured softly.

He pushed her words aside thrusting into her, needing release himself but waiting for her to feel the tremors sweep through her, the mindless blast of ecstasy that would last only seconds in the process changing her life forever. Finally the spasms seemed to envelop her as she cried out his name, reaching for him as he drove deeper and harder into her. He didn't stop until she began to calm and her body seemed to slow.

"Did that hurt?" he queried, hoping her answer would be what he needed to hear.

"No, but it was somewhere between pain and pleasure, something I've never thought could exist."

He pulled her to him, caressed her back, letting his hand rest on her derrière, thinking the next time might be even more pleasant.

~ * ~

Pruitt Dubois sat in the lush apartment where Angelique Moreau resided in Bordeaux. The cold January temperatures had changed to warmer spring like weather. It was March. The daffodils were poking their heads from the grounds while the trees were blossoming with leaves and flowers. Angelique thought for a moment this was her favorite time of year.

"Etienne quit looking for Elisa?" he asked, one white eyebrow arching upward.

"When he couldn't find her in Paris, he came here, but you

already know that," Angelique said, her voice soft with the pain she felt. "It's for the best. The way in which he lives now, he would not make a suitable husband for my daughter. In any case, I'm sure he does not wish to be a husband. It appears to me, he is much enamored of bachelorhood."

"Is it for the best?" Pruitt waved his hand in the air in disagreement. "I have judged Etienne in the past but to imply he cannot change, does not sit well with me. He deserves to know the truth of the matter. It is not right to keep the truth from him."

Angel knew that look well. She also understood how much he wanted his son home, hoping for a grandchild and an heir to his vineyard. This time when Etienne showed up here Pruitt thought it was for good only to discover he left for Glasgow as soon as he understood Elisa was not planning on speaking with him.

"I believe so and so does my daughter. She is not ready to take on a husband of such experience. She is still very young. I believe she made a grave mistake by giving herself to Etienne as does she." Angelique did not want to hand Etienne the news, but he would discover the truth soon enough. What mattered is what he would do with the information. In truth, she acknowledged begrudgingly he deserved the truth. Just before Pruitt stopped by three months ago, she received a message from Margaux, explaining what happened on that now infamous evening. Now, three months had passed by. Elisa knew the truth. Etienne did not.

"Why is that? There is something you are not telling me. I don't believe Etienne has asked for her hand or for anyone else." His voice grew harsh and agitated as he asked the question, his gaze riveted on her.

Angel squirmed a bit under his intense scrutiny. She didn't know what to tell Etienne's father. "We both hoped for something more between our children, however, it won't happen anytime soon. He's gone. She's somewhere between Paris and here. When she comes out of the self-imposed hiding, I'm sure she will go to the country home. We both know how much Etienne detests the country and the tiny villages. Perhaps if Elisa had stayed in Paris, there would be hope for them."

"There is something you aren't telling me." He leaned forward picking up her hand in his. Focused on her, Angelique did not want to meet his gaze but she understood she would have to do just that.

"True but tonight is not the time. I need to speak with my daughter first." She withdrew the hand then walking to the window, she stared out at the city, enjoying the twinkling lights. "It is getting late. You will want to stay the night. I'm sure the ride home would not be wise in the dark. There are bandits, you know."

"Perhaps with dinner I can discover what you have been keeping from me all this time. It is not too difficult to make assumptions. Secrets are hard to keep, Angel. You have never been good at hiding your thoughts from me. Never."

"This secret is not mine to tell." She wondered at her daughter and her actions. The note from Margaux said very little. She would need patience. Coming to conclusions now would just not do for either Elisa or herself.

Pruitt stood beside her now, a hand on her shoulder, gently massaging her tight muscles. "You need to relax, *mon ange*."

His angel. She was really no one's angel. Under the circumstances Angelique was afraid relaxing was impossible. It was just like her intrepid daughter to get herself into trouble of this sort, trouble with a man she'd wanted since she was six. Angelique was sure this was the first and only time Elisa had sex. There had been no men in her life. For some reason, she thought herself in love with a man she knew from a single encounter years ago. It was just like Etienne to take advantage of an innocent.

She turned, stepping back at the same time to put a meager amount of distance between them, a bit of anger rising inside at Pruitt's words. "You know very well I'm not an angel."

"Just because you were forced into this business by necessities you had no control over does not make you a fallen woman or change your nature. Look at yourself. You made the best of a horrible situation managing to thrive in the process." Pruitt walked to the sideboard to pour himself a whiskey before sitting down. He crossed his legs, watching her. "You need to share whatever it is you are hiding from me as well as the rest of the world. Now I understand the world should not know but I've been your friend when you've needed one. It will make all things better for you. Someone to share the burden with."

"Perhaps you are right." She let out a deep breath of air, treating herself to a glass before sitting down across from Pruitt. Second and third thoughts assailed her as the seconds passed slowly. She tried to form the words in her mind.

"Well." His eyes brightened when she gave him hope that she would relate her secret.

She inhaled several breaths of air, listening to the clock along with the soft patter of spring rain on the window. Closing her eyes, she thought about holding a baby again, running a finger along its soft cheek. She would be a grandmother sooner than she expected. By that title, she shouldn't have to change too many diapers, but she would. She waved a hand in front of her face as if she'd spoken the words. *Don't get ahead of yourself and don't surmise what might have happened after one encounter. It was, after all, only one encounter. I must have patience and wait for news or confirmation. Elisa still has refused to say anything.*

What to do? Did she truly believe she had the right to tell Pruitt the truth about his changing life? The facts were all that she could relate despite the feeling deep in her belly that her daughter was with child even as the soon to be doting grandparents discussed their children's sex lives.

"Well?" he prompted again, seeming to begin to lose any semblance of patience. His grin changed to a frown.

Angelique smiled at him, understanding she would have to swear him to secrecy. He could not under any circumstances divulge a word of this to anyone until Elisa told him herself or until she left the telling of the truth so long it could not be avoided.

Once again, she was getting ahead of herself. She needed to speak with Elisa She prayed her daughter was on her way here and didn't plan to remain in seclusion. Margaux had not spoken to that bit of information so perhaps she didn't know. She wondered if Elisa even new or thought she might be with child. It had only been a few months.

"You must swear that you will remain silent. Nothing I say here can leave this room." She cleared her throat, knowing he would say the necessary words to gain her confidence. If anything, Pruitt Dubois was a man of his word.

"Very well. I swear that whatever you divulge here today will remain here and that I will not say a word to anyone."

"Even Etienne?"

"Yes, even my son."

Slowly she sipped the whiskey she poured herself almost an hour ago, watching the leaves on the tree outside her window rustle with the breeze. His tapping fingers on the crystal brought her back to the present and the fact he was making another attempt at patience, something that didn't suit him.

"I am only guessing. I have no proof. It is just a feeling in the pit of my stomach. September sometime, you will be a *grand-pere*." A rush of guilt swept inside at the revelation she should have avoided at all cost. This was not her story to tell.

When she looked up, however, it was amusing to her how his eyes began to light up as the words registered in his head. "I assume that night they spent at Margaux's is the cause. It couldn't be anyone else?"

"It was and before you ask, I've never been more positive even though it happened only a couple of months ago." She felt a flame of anger spark inside. How dare he question the morality of her daughter when his son... She swallowed hard. When his son tossed skirts at whim.

"You're angry. I should have never even thought it, but I'm excited to finally know that another Dubois could be on the way as we speak."

"You cannot say anything. Unless Etienne comes home and marries my daughter the *bebe* will be a Moreau. Not a Dubois."

Other Books by Christine Young
Available at Rogue Phoenix Press

My Sweet Broc
Bad Boys Book One

He's a bad bad boy...

Broc Wallace is a fun-loving rake who never thought any beautiful woman could melt his heart. He lives life in the present enjoying the camaraderie of his friends and the pleasures of his mistress. When Bliss races into his life, he is ill prepared to deal with her secrets or give up the tenor of his life. When the truth is revealed, he finds himself unable to forgive and forget the betrayal.

... but she's sweet for him

Bliss MacTavish knows she's playing with fire when she refuses to tell this bad boy her name. He tempts her with sweet whispers of seduction knowing her innocent nature will be unable to refuse all he yearns to give her. Deciding to follow her heart, she finds the repercussions more than she bargains for when she gives herself to this bad boy.

Crazy for Cam
Bad Boys Book Two

He's a bad bad boy...

Lord Cam MacEwen, Viscount of Rosehill, tries his best to be proper and court the lady of his dreams in the acceptable way. The feat proves impossible when the lady in question uses every means at her disposal to tempt him. He fights his jealousy for another man as well as the need to make her his own, finally giving in to her irresistible passion.

... but she's crazy for him.

Chelsea MacTavish wants the bad boy she fell in love with and kissed just before her eighteenth birthday. With feminine wiles and irresistible allure, the sensuous lady plans to best Cam at his game of hearts and make him forget his need to court her properly.

Falling for Flynt
Bad Boys Book Three

He's a bad, bad boy...

Fascinated by Hope's loss of memory yet haunted by her sultry beauty, Flynt is irresistibly drawn to the stoic miss—and into her troubles with the sultan who wants her for himself. When he discovers she is the sister of his best friend, his pride keeps him from pursuing her and making her his.

... but she's falling for him.

Raised in a harem but now penniless, alone and without her memory, Hope must discover a way to remember all that she has lost. She finds a way to continue with her life as a servant in Flynt's home. The first sight of Flynt steals Hope's breath as well as her heart. Can she overcome her fears and give herself to the man she fell in love with.

Dancing With Donal
Bad Boys Book Four

He's a bad bad boy...

Once a bad boy always a bad boy, Donal Chamberlin's carefree ways come crashing down around him when he meets the ravishingly beautiful Daryl MacTavish, the innocent little sister of one of his best friends. He is determined to win her heart as he sets his sights on marriage and an heir. His past gets in the way of his quest when a woman he once loved threatens Daryl's life.

... but she's dancing with him.

Daryl has seen the control her sister's husbands hold over them. She yearns for a life where she makes decisions for herself. No man will have power over her. But no man kisses her the way Donal does. No man can make her forget all her goals leaving her helpless to give up her dreams. Yet Donal is determined to dance through all the barriers she thrust in front of him, pursuing her until she says yes.

Loving Leslie
Bad Boys Book Five

He's a bad bad boy...

Leslie Stewart, Duke of Southcliff is stoic, set in his ways, a spy who is used to having his life well ordered. He expects life to continue on in this perfectly conventional fashion. He assumes his bad boy status while keeping mamas and debutantes at arm's length. An heir is needed but Leslie has every intention of finding a woman who doesn't covet his wealth and tittle. He is irresistibly drawn to the headstrong young lady who becomes more beautiful as she develops into a woman.

...but she is loving him.

When Leslie kisses Lacie MacTavish, she knows even at the tender age of fifteen this is the man of her dreams. Forced to wait until she comes of age, Lacie withdraws into herself. Now she is eighteen and Leslie has returned from a mission for the British Government ready to claim her as his bride. She refuses him and he must find a way to seduce her and in the process create a burning passion within her, which she cannot deny.

Pleasing Arie
Bad Boys Book Six

He's a bad bad boy...

Arie Demir has never been denied anything in his life. He takes what he wants. What he undeniably yearns for is the beautiful redheaded spitfire he sees in a restaurant in Glasgow. At every turn, she confuses him by disputing his power over her. Alison refuses to accept the fact he owns her. While Arie tries desperately with patience and tenderness to drive her wild with new sensations, his scorching kisses ignite the fires of her very soul to make her understand he is all she will ever want.

...but is she pleasing him?

Alison Fletcher never expected to find herself kidnapped and sold to a whorehouse then bought by a Turkish sultan to become his slave. She vows to never surrender to the arrogant man who believes he owns her. She is stunned by the magnificently handsome man who awaits her compliance. Unexpectedly, she finds Arie the lesser of all the evils. The hidden depths of his mesmerizing dark brown eyes hold her into their power; his muscular embrace makes her weak with desire. She is his to do with as he wishes.

Foolish for Piper

The pickpocket...
Piper has spent her life surviving the streets of St. Giles Parish in London, a den of iniquity and crime. Masquerading as a boy she escapes the whorehouses the young girls are sent to as they come of age. The day she encounters Brett MacLachlan begins the same as every other one. When she picks his pocket, she has no idea her life is going to change irreversibly.
... and the mark
Handsome aristocrat Brett MacLachlan has come to London for his amusement only to find his world turned upside down by a thief and her dog. From the moment he spots her, Brett knows there is something intrinsically wrong. In his arms, Piper discovers passion and joy. Yet secrets of her past haunt her, and a scar will tell the true tale as well as

her identity.

Taylor's Destiny

She traveled to another time and place to change destiny...

Enjoying a day of sailing, Taylor Maxwell never expected after a suffering a concussion she would wake up in another century. A resilient independent woman in the twenty-first century, the blond beauty is ill prepared for life in the 1800s. Her first sight of the naval captain who rescues her makes her heart stop, giving her hope for her future.

His life is transformed by a woman who appears from nowhere...

Born to a life of ease, Reid Stewart defies the dictates of those born to aristocracy and chooses a life of adventure in the navy and as a spy for the crown. When he discovers a nearly naked woman on the bow of small sailing ship, his heart warms. His love for Taylor and his need to protect her from a man who pursues her might cost him his life as well as hers.

Caitlin's Duke

She played a fiddle in an Irish pub...

Caitlin O'Shea Is the most beautiful woman Roc Leighton has ever seen. With her blue violet eyes and long black hair she captivates him. In turn he mesmerizes Caitlin. Caught in the power of his gaze as he watches her, she is wise enough to know he desires her but will never give his heart to her. Caitlin has vowed to never be any man's mistress.

And fell in love with an English Lord...

Roc knows the first time he watches her play the fiddle and dance around the pub, she will be his next mistress. Despite her protest, he will find a way to convince her that her place is with him. While Caitlin's determination to keep her vows, fate takes a cruel turn and she is forced to seek refuge with Roc.

Catching Meara
Book One in the McKenna Clan Series

Meara Thorton was a feisty, world-class computer hacker—cornered by the FBI and shockingly given the chance to be their newly acquired technical analyst. Brilliant and intuitive, yet aching with the loss of everyone she has cared about, her restless heart led her to discover a love she fought and a world she didn't know could possibly exist.

Sweet Sexy Sadie
Book Two in the McKenna Clan Series

From the first time Sadie's eyes met those of Brody McKenna in the hot Sierra Madre Mountains, theirs was a potent attraction—not gentle, slow, and easy, but hot, hard, and all-consuming. The daughter of a dysfunctional family, Sadie had dreams no man could wrench from her with hot sex and an all-consuming passion. She'd challenge this alpha male with all the strength she possessed. But her red hair, fiery temperament, and indomitable spirit obsessed Brody... and he knew he had to find a way to show her he was more than he appeared and convince her to make a life with him.

Sweet Misbehavin'
Book Three in the McKenna Clan Series

Cast adrift after fleeing the home of Jokul, the ice demon, Atantsi, a firestarter, grew to womanhood as she moved through time to keep the demon from finding her. Though stubborn and courageous, she was ill prepared to use powers she had not been taught. Her first sight of the intoxicating Carr McKenna left her breathless, and her second encounter gave her hope for a future she never thought she had.

A playboy, a second son and a shifter, a man who thought his life would be carefree, Carr McKenna was shocked to discover the woman he'd paid as an escort is a firestarter who is running for her life. He is the leader of all the McKennas around the world and that he has multiple powers. His passion for Margo and the need to defend her might cost him his life as well as hers.

Sweet Talkin' Sugar
Book Four in the McKenna Clan Series

Lyonesse McKenna, was dreaming or was she? From the instant Lyn saw Deacon McClain across a black jack table in a crowed Las Vegas casino the unmistakable attraction sent Lyn's senses flying into overdrive. Her family of shapeshifters believed in soul mates. She'd always been skeptical yet she couldn't help but question the way her heart sped when he looked at her.

When Deacon appeared in Las Vegas he knew his first job was to save Lyn from a Sea Demon, but the next order of business was to convince her he would someday mean more to her than she'd ever expected. But her stubborn nature and unbendable spirit consumed Deacon... and he had to chase away all the demons real and imagined in order to win her heart.

Sweet Surrender
Book Five in the McKenna Clan Series

Ripped from her family at the top of Infinity Cliff, Kimi McKenna finds herself thrust somewhere into the future. Dark elements threaten to destroy the earth unless Kimi can work together with the white witch to stop the destruction. Confused by her mate's role in the conspiracy, she refuses to acknowledge the connection. But amidst raging fire and attacks on the people she is coming to hold dear, she allows Maska O'keefe into her heart.

Maska O'keefe has loved the beautiful shapeshifter for years. Unable to save her life years ago, he vows to watch over her as he is given a second chance to convince her that even though he is a witch and not a shifter, they are indeed soul mates. Kimi's divided loyalties between her family and the cause she is now a part of will determine their relationship. Only the part she plays as the messiah can bring this to a conclusion in the final battle.

Dakota's Bride
The first book in the Lakota/Pinkerton Series

When Emma St. John received her brother's letter imploring her to escape her stepfather's vengeful scheme and to trust Dakota Barringer with her life, she was willing to chance it. But the handsome, brooding riverboat owner Emma found in Natchez a danger of another kind. For Emma soon found herself surrendering to an unrelenting desire.

Raised by the Sioux when his parents were killed, Dakota had been betrayed once before by a white woman. He wasn't about to trust another, especially one claiming that her stepfather, a powerful U.S. senator, had framed her as a murderess. But he couldn't let Emma's intoxicating effect on him. Now Dakota would risk his very life to protect the innocent beauty who had seduced him with her tender love.

My Angel
The second book in the Lakota/Pinkerton Series

A BEAUTY IN BUCKSKINS
When her father decided to send her to a finishing school back East, Angela Chamberlain refused to be confined to stuffy drawing rooms. Instead, the daring spitfire who could shoot like a man and ride like the wind longed for a life of adventure and romance—and she knew exactly who could give it to her. Devil Blackmoor was a hired gun with a dangerous reputation. But Angela was willing to go to the ends of the earth to capture the handsome devil's heart.

A DEVIL IN DISGUISE
He'd come to America looking for excitement, but Devil Blackmoor got more than he bargained for when he encountered a

beautiful rebel who answered his kisses with a wild innocence that touched his very soul. Yet standing between them were more obstacles than either ever dreamed. For Devil had strapped on a gun for the wrong man. And that made Angela his enemy. Now he'll have to choose between his duty and the woman he loves more than life.

The Locket
The third book in the Lakota/Pinkerton Series

The year is 1894. Seeking revenge for crimes against his family, Misha Petrovich follows a path that leads straight to Ariel Cameron's boarding house in Mist Harbor, Oregon. A family heirloom in Ariel's possession leads Misha to believe she is guilty. The locket has been handed down to the oldest girl in the Petrovich family for generations. Ariel is innocent of wrong doing, but her father is not. Misha is torn by his feelings for Ariel and his need for restitution against her father. Knowing that the relationship between them is fragile, Misha does everything in his power to protect Ariel's father. His efforts are to no avail when her father is shot. Ariel comes to realize Misha's steadfast courage and determination to protect her and her father despite what has happened to his family. Ariel's love and devotion heals Misha's heart.

The Talisman
The fourth book in the Lakota/Pinkerton Series

Running from a marriage that lasted one night, Dr. Moriah McKeown discovers the land she has settled on is coveted by determined and lawless men. Yet the proud young woman who once vowed never to abandon her home has second thoughts when her adopted children are threatened. Her only recourse is to enlist the aid of a dark, dangerous gun for hire.

Haunted by the past and a betrayal he will never forgive, Ian Civanovich uses his fast gun and his reckless courage to forget the faithlessness of a woman in his past. He will trust no female—nor will he rest until the threat hovering over Moriah McKeown is put to rest.

Forever His
The fifth book in the Lakota/Pinkerton Series

Struggling to come to terms with the part she played in Jacob St. John's death, Etta Barringer resigns from Pinkerton Agency and seeks peace and solace in a Rocky Mountain Cabin.

Jacob has vowed to discover the reason Etta has betrayed him, sold him out to his enemy and left him for dead.

Isolated in their cabin, they discover their love for each other and learn to trust. But the trust is shattered when Jacob learns she is married to his sworn enemy; the man who left him in the desert to die.

Allura's Secret
Twelve Dancing Princesses Book One

Allura McClellan is horrified by her father's decision to take out an ad in the Times awarding her to the man strong enough and smart enough to win her hand and uncover her secrets. She's an intelligent young woman who takes great delight in the freedom allotted to her by her father. She's well aware that marriage would effectively curtail the adventures she's shared with her sisters and cousins.

Hunter Gray is nothing like the other men who've arrived to vie for Allura's hand in marriage and everything that goes along with it. However, he is the first to refuse to concede defeat and pursue her despite her attempts to disguise her true appearance. It's her temperament that is of more concern to him than her looks. Hunter has worked all his life with the hope of someday owning his own land. Now that it looks like there's a very real possibility that everything he's ever wanted is within reach nothing is going to deter him – including Miss Allura's disagreeable disposition.

Amorica's Wager
Twelve Dancing Princesses Book Two

Amorica Hepburn was sent to London to find a husband. Finding a man was the last item on her agenda. With her two cousins, Amorica wagers she can dissuade her suitor before the others. Despite her efforts she discovers a chemistry that cannot be denied. Suddenly she is the arrogant man's wife, pledged to a marriage neither desire. But swept off to his ancestral home above the Dover cliffs and into his strong embrace, Amorica is soon possessed by a raging passion for the husband she had vowed to despise...

Damian Andrews couldn't afford to trust the emerald-eyed spitfire who happened upon his secret. Amorica's hatred of all men of his kind only inflames the war that rages between them. Still, he can not control the intense desire his stubborn bride inspires, or make her surrender to his will until he has conquered the headstrong beauty on the battlefield of love...

Ravyn's Marriage of Inconvenience
Twelve Dancing Princesses Book Three

A REGAL BEAUTY

When the duchess decides to wed her to a wastrel and a fop, Ravyn Grahm takes matters into her own hands and declares her engagement to another man. Instead of fessing up and telling her great aunt what she has done, she goes through with the pretense. Ariec Lakeland is the bastard son of an earl and has a dangerous reputation. But Ravyn is willing to do most anything to keep the duchess from discovering the lie.

A DEVIL-MAY-CARE SMUGGLER

He'd bought land in America, looking to put down roots and end his life of adventure, but Ariec Lakeland got more than he bargained for when he encountered a beautiful heiress who made a promise she didn't want to keep. But the promise could not be undone and standing between them were more obstacles than either ever dreamed. Ariec had made plans to spend the rest of his life in America and that was at odds with Ravyn's plan of living in England and running her father's estate. Now, he'll have to choose between his dreams and the woman he loves more than life.

Christel's Sunrise
Twelve Dancing Princesses Book Four

He Made Her An Offer...

Life has thrown Christel McClellan some experiences that could have devastated a less determined woman. Beautiful, self-assured and fiercely independent, she is trying to forget the loss of her stillborn child. But is the child alive?

She Couldn't Deny...

Life is carefree for Ryder MacLaren who loves to see what is on the other side of the sunrise. Laird of Clan MacLaren, he is wealthy, handsome and happily unencumbered... until stunning Christel McClellan enters his life. When he hears her story, he believes the child she thought dead has been sold to a wealthy buyer.

Storm's Passion
Twelve Dancing Princesses Book Five

SHE MADE A PROPOSAL...

Life strikes Storm Graham a shattering blow when she learns her father has bartered her to a man she detests. Storm is beautiful, self–assured and fiercely independent, and refuses to be a pawn in her father's schemes, yet she can find no way out of this bargain made in hell. Going on the offensive she asks the wealthiest man on the eastern coast of England to marry her, never believing she might fall in love.

HE TRIED TO REFUSE...

For Hadden Johnston life has provided everything he ever wanted, including a sanctuary for homeless children. He is wealthy, handsome and happily unencumbered... until stunning Storm Graham marches into his life and proposes a marriage of convenience. Yet this type of marriage to a woman who inflames his senses is far from acceptable. If he's going to be tied down, he will move heaven and earth to have this woman warming his bed.

Gotta Have Fayth
Twelve Dancing Princesses Book Six

A regal beauty with raven hair and piercing blue eyes, Fayth Graham is unwilling to parade herself in front of the wealthy Lords of England during the season. Seeking a means to dissuade any man wishing to wed her, she seeks a way to ruin herself for marriage. When she unexpectedly meets a man with sparkling gray eyes and an infectious grin, she decides this is the man who will keep her from agreeing to obey.

He returned from six months at sea, looking for a few nights of pleasure with a willing lass, but Jarret Kinsley got more than he bargained for when he met a beautiful debutant who responded to his kisses with a wild innocence that touched his heart. Yet the obstacles looming between them might rip them apart. Both had vowed never to marry, so when consequences of their dalliances got in the way, Jarret would have to choose between the life he's always desired and the woman he loves more than life.

Ella's Pleasure
Twelve Dancing Princesses Book Seven

A WHISPER OF PLEASURE
Ella Hepburn was an auburn haired debutant from the harsh Scottish coastline—a wild innocent to be seduced and tamed. A spirited beauty, she captivated Drake Montgomerie's jaded heart—while succumbing to the smoldering desire she felt for her unyielding suitor.

A WHISPER OF DANGER

In Drake Montgomerie's glittering world of money and privilege, young Ella discovered passion and desire could overcome everything she'd been taught to resist—entangling Drake, the heir apparent, in a lethal coil of aristocratic family intrigue. But grave peril would only nurse the sparks of a love that knew no limits and a magnificent ecstasy that would not be denied.

Eveleen's Seduction
Twelve Dancing Princesses Book Eight

A WHISPER OF SEDUCTION

A brutal attack on Eveleen Hepburn's cherished island off the Scottish coastline leaves her shattered and bewildered. Learning a man she once trusted can kill as easily as he can breathe even though the deed saves her life, creates questions that need answers. An innocent beauty, she enchants Logan Maxwell's cynical heart—giving in to the raging passion she feels for her mysterious suitor.

A WHISPER OF INTRIGUE

In Logan's Maxwell's world of espionage and privilege, young Eveleen discovers truths about herself she never expected, and a need for passion and love can overcome all her fears if she learns to accept certain truths. She finds herself entangled in a lethal battle for land that was once owned by French nobility, taken from them during the revolution and sold to Maxwell. But grave peril would unleash the flames of love that simmers, creating a magical union that cannot be refuted.

Tavia's Deception
Twelve Dancing Princesses Book Nine

WHISPERS OF DECEPTION

When her father decides to send her to London for her season,

Tavia Hepburn resolves to see the world instead. The raven haired beauty decides to disguise herself as a lad and find employment on a ship bound for Barcelona as a cabin boy. But she never bargains on finding passion and love to a red haired sea captain who rescues her from certain death.

WHISPERS OF MURDER

For James Macmurra, the world is black and white until he meets a young debutante, who turns his world upside down. He's unable to deny Tavia's intoxicating effect on him. In a match tense with obstacles, unwillingness to divulge secrets, and unforeseen peril, irresistible desire and passion grows into undeniable love. James would risk his life to shelter and protect the innocent debutante who seduces him with her sweet love.

Larena's Fascination
Twelve Dancing Princesses Book Ten

WHISPERS OF FASCINATION

Fiery, free spirited Larena Graham never wanted to marry a duke. She is thrilled to be in love with the fourth son of an aristocrat, Gavin Broon. But when it seems Gavin ignores her, she set her sights on politics and bettering human life. Unsuspecting intrigue and a plot against her, she continues her dangerous plans despite Gavin's wishes.

WHISPERS OF TRUST

Gavin has every intention of properly courting the beautiful Larena until he must leave the city in order to put his affairs in order. Returning to London, he finds the woman he means to make his own is embroiled in political protests that could lead to a prison ship. Larena must learn to trust the handsome Scotsman whose most pressing mission is to protect her and keep her from harm.

Tira's Education
Twelve Dancing Princesses Book Eleven

WHISPERS OF EDUCATION

Learning how to build ships is Tira Hepburn's only dream until she meets Jamie Lundin and her world is turned upside down. With her raven black hair and vivid green eyes, she tempts Jamie and pushes him to defy his vows. She never bargains on finding an irrevocable love and a passion to a man who cannot fulfill her dreams despite his burning desire for her.

WHISPERS OF A BARGAIN

Arrogant and self-assured Jamie is brought up short when Tira captures his heart. All his carefully made plans are put to the test when he decides to teach her the art of ship building if she will spend a week with him alone on his ship. He is unable to deny Tira's intoxicating effect on him. When Tira leaves him behind unwilling to live with him without the benefit of marriage, he races after her. Jamie will risk everything to shelter and protect the innocent debutante who seduces him with her sweet love.

Aidan's Love
Twelve Dancing Princesses Book Twelve

Whispers of Love

Aidan McLellan has loved since she first set eyes on him as a young girl. Spontaneous, wild and eager to grow up, Aidan haunts his waking thoughts day and night, insinuating herself into his life. With her fiery red hair and sparkling sapphire eyes, she seizes Blade's heart even while he tries to resist the innocent child until she becomes a woman.

Whispers of Courage

Blade has waited what seems a lifetime to claim the woman who captures his heart as a little girl. Claiming his inheritance before his younger brother takes what is rightfully his, Blade must convince Aidan of his sincerity after years of avoidance and wed her before his father dies so he can return home, securing his rightful place. Everything is put to the test when his life as well as Aidan's is threatened by the man who once called him brother.

Twelve Days to Love

When Archer Steele shows up at Calanthe Durand's failing plantation with an alligator over his shoulder, Cali thinks she's never seen a more handsome man. During the war she had to defend herself and her servants from both union and confederate soldiers. Independent and self-sufficient, she vows to never marry.

But Archer Steele has different ideas. The first time Archer sees Cali in town, he feels an instant attraction. He decides he will do everything and anything to convince the beautiful Miss Durand he is worthy of her love. During the weeks leading up to Christmas, he gives her twelve gifts in hopes she will fall in love with him. Yet they are faced with challenges they must overcome before Cali can commit to a marriage.

Door to Heaven

Jessica Lawrence is the stepdaughter of a woman born in the twentieth century transported back in time to the year 1868. An acclaimed suffragette, she raises Jessica to believe in the equality of women. Jess Law believes everything she was taught, and when the time is right she becomes a private investigator. Courageous and impetuous, Jess finds danger in her quest to save all women from white slavery. Her passionate mission results in a wedding to Roc Newman, a man she knows can steal her heart...

Roc can't trust the sapphire-eyed spitfire who invades his home in search of secret papers and knocks him flat with her karate moves. Jessica's refusal to obey his wishes serves to inflame the war between them. Still, he cannot control the intense desire his reluctant bride inspires, or make her surrender her independence, until he has conquered the headstrong beauty on the battlefield of love...

Rebel Heart

HER REBEL SPIRIT DEFIED HIS OUTSIDERS SOUL...
She was velvet and silk, eyes the color of a summer storm and amber hair. Victoria DeMontville, because of a promise and a codicil to her father's will, was forced to marry one man to protect her from another. She hated Cameron Savage with a fierce passion. But to hold on to her genetic research and find a cure for the deadly Signe virus, she must pretend to love the enemy at her door, come with weapons of fire to melt her icy heart...

HIS OUTSIDERS TOUCH IGNITED RAGING PASSIONS...
He wore a mask, disguised as the Phantom, a true legend come to life. Even as war and debate over new genetic research engulfed them all, he would find his greatest adversary in the beauty who'd branded him an outsider and barbarian, the woman he was born to possess, his soul mate.

Safari Moon

Solo St. John, a wildlife photographer, is preparing for a trip to Alaska. Suddenly, Solo finds women of all sorts invading his privacy, his home and his office, all cooing nonsense words and blatantly throwing themselves at him. Solo doesn't know why, and he has no idea how to rid himself of the persistent women. He finally decides to beg a favor of his best buddy Nyssa Harrington.

In love with Solo for the past ten years and knowing he doesn't return her feelings Nyssa doesn't want to talk to Solo. She knows if she accepts his phone call, she will not be able to resist the temptation to hope again.

Straight to Heaven

Running from demons, Alexandra McMurdie stumbles into Forbidden Ground where up is down and elements of nature are contested. Though a strong independent woman in the twenty-first century' she is unprepared for life in the 1800s. Her first site of the formidable James Lawrence makes her heart skip a beat, giving her cause to reconsider her desperate need to find a way home.

Born with a silver spoon, James' life was torn apart during the War Between the States. Moving west he vows to put the life he once knew in the past. When he discovers a half-frozen woman near Gold Hill, his heart begins to thaw. His love for Alexandra and his need to keep her from a man who has pursued her through time might cost him his life as well as hers.

A Valentine's Anthology

The Lending Library-a fantasy by Christie L. Kraemer
Faeries try to fit into the human world when the forest where they make their home is destroyed by a mysterious enemy.

Chasing Rainbows-a contemporary romance by Genene Valleau
An eccentric aunt, an inventive uncle, a mother who wears poodle skirts, and a brother who wears pearls provide a hilarious backdrop for the courtship of a young woman who yearns for a "normal" family.

The Gift-an historical romance by Christine Young
A man and a woman on opposite sides of the Civil War get a second chance at love after one final battle returns soldiers to their war-torn homes to rebuild their lives.

A St. Patrick's Day Tale
Christine Young, C. L. Kraemer, Genene Valleau

Tumble through time…
…to Ireland in 1817, when tensions are high between Protestants and Catholics and fae people guide the fate of villagers. A lovely Catholic lass stumbles upon the weakly ritual fisticuffing between Irish lads. She

falls into the lap of a handsome young Protestant. Family ties, grudges, and two conniving faeries threaten their budding love. But the faeries outsmart themselves when they hijack a time machine that has mysteriously appeared in their forest and are whisked to…

…Eugene, Oregon in the 20th century, amid a property feud between the local faeries and night elves. The conniving faeries from Olde Ireland try to stir up more mischief. However, a warrior gnome convinces the magic folk to control their own destiny, and forces the intruding faeries to take refuge in the time machine again, spinning their way toward…

…A modern day castle in western Oregon. An eccentric inventor is determined to reclaim his wayward time machine and save his beloved wife from her latest misadventure. If only they can travel safely past the black hole…

a May Day Anthology
Christine Young, C. L. Kraemer, Rosemary Indra, Genene Valleau

Highland Miracle — Christine Young
HURTLED THROUGH TIME, Sean Michael Sterling, landed in the midst of a May Day celebration he didn't understand, assuming the role of Laird Sterling.

ILLIGITAMATE CHILD OF NOBILITY, Reagan Douglas searches for a way out of her half brother's house.

Defying the Odds — C.L. Kraemer
The night elves on the hill aren't happy without their magic. They concoct a plan to punish those who were involved in the act that rendered them almost human. Meanwhile, Uther, the rogue night elf, has returned to woo the Librarian to be his eternal mate.

Love in Bloom — Rosemary Indra
When childhood friends reunite it takes two fairies and a matchmaking daughter to help them admit their true love for each other.

No More Poodle Skirts — Genie Gabriel

After drifting for years in the innocent age of the 1950s, a woman struggles to join today's world by finding a career and a new love, with some help from her zany family.

Once Upon a Christmas Moon
Christine Young, C. L. Kraemer, Genene Valleau

TWELVE DAYS TO LOVE

When Archer Steele shows up at Calanthe Durand's failing plantation with an alligator over his shoulder, Cali thinks she's never seen a more handsome man. During the war she had to defend herself and her servants from both union and confederate soldiers. Independent and self-sufficient, she vows to never marry. But Archer Steele has different ideas. The first time Archer sees Cali in town, he feels an instant attraction. He decides he will do everything and anything to convince the beautiful Miss Durand he is worthy of her love. During the weeks leading up to Christmas, he gives her twelve gifts in hopes she will fall in love with him.

BOOTS AND BLADES

An ancient evil from the old country has arrived in the high desert of Oregon. Gnome children are vanishing then re-appearing, showing various stages of traumatization. Tiamoon, warrior gnome, will put her skills to use alongside Killian, a handsome warrior, also in need of a cause.

CHRISTMAS PAWSIBILITIES

With their world destroyed and their space ship malfunctioning, the dogizens of Planet Canid have little choice but to crash land on Earth. They face tortuous experiments at the hands of the Geeks in Green... or they can trust an eccentric inventor and his zany family to deliver the Canine Queen's puppies and help them celebrate new lives.

VISIT OUR WEBSITE
FOR THE FULL INVENTORY
OF QUALITY BOOKS:
http://www.roguephoenixpress.com

Rogue Phoenix Press

Representing Excellence in Publishing

Quality trade paperbacks and downloads
in multiple formats,
in genres ranging from historical to contemporary romance,
mystery and science fiction.
Visit the website then bookmark it.
We add new titles each month!

www.ingramcontent.com/pod-product-compliance
Lightning Source LLC
Chambersburg PA
CBHW061938170626
46813CB00006B/2455